Motive for
Murder

OTHER BOOKS AND AUDIO BOOKS
BY MARLENE BATEMAN

Light on Fire Island

a novel

Motive for Murder

An Erica Coleman Mystery

MARLENE BATEMAN

Covenant Communications, Inc.

Cover image: *Women's Eyes Spying Through a Hole* © Korionov. Courtesy of istockphoto.com

Cover design copyright © 2013 by Covenant Communications, Inc.

Published by Covenant Communications, Inc.
American Fork, Utah

Printed in the United States of America
First Printing: June 2013

19 18 17 16 15 14 13   10 9 8 7 6 5 4 3 2 1

ISBN: 978-1-60861-241-3

To Amanda

ACKNOWLEDGMENTS

I OWE A DEBT OF gratitude to the readers who spent time going over the manuscript. Many thanks to Holly Horton, Barbara Roberts, Howard Roberts, Kelly Sullivan, and Annetta Cochran. I want to thank fellow writers Rachael Anderson, Rebecca Talley, Braden Bell, Connie Sokol, and Don Carey for their insightful comments and helpful suggestions.

A special thank you to my terrific editor at Covenant, Stacey Owen, and also to Samantha Millburn, for all her help.

I also want to thank the great cooks that tested the recipes: Monica Miles, Dawnelle Stanger, Chaleh Reed, Melanie St. Onge, Kimmi Abbott, Kylie Fitts, and Esther Heaps.

PROLOGUE

It was impossible to relax. Groaning, he swung his legs over the side of the bed before checking his watch for the third time in twenty minutes. He still had a few minutes. Perhaps he ought to call his wife. No, she was too perceptive. Might start asking questions. He'd call later—when it was over.

He paced the floor. Grabbing the remote, he idly flipped through the channels then went through them again—and again. Another check of his watch, and it was time to go. The blinds were already closed, but he turned a table lamp on. It was dusk and he hated coming back to a dark motel room. Digging into a pocket, his fingers touched a cool, hard surface. He fingered the switchblade to reassure himself then pulled out his wallet, making sure his key and the paper he'd tucked in earlier were still there.

Avoiding the front desk clerk, he went out the back way. It felt good to get the stale air out of his lungs. He hated cheap motels. Perhaps after tonight, he wouldn't have to deal with them anymore. *If* everything went as planned, that is.

He zipped his jacket against the rain that had begun to fall. He could have taken a cab, but doing so might lead to problems. No, walking was the way to go. He'd chosen a motel that was close by so he set off briskly on foot. Although his hopes were high, his brow was furrowed.

If anyone had been paying attention, they would have seen an older man of medium height with a face not unlike that of a rat. His nose was pointed and his eyes were dark and beady. The heels on his shoes were worn down and his pants faded, the hems frayed.

Having memorized the directions he'd been given, he turned the corner at a preschool. Traffic was light, but he averted his face when anyone drove by. He was getting close. Turning right on Carroll Street, he went down the west sidewalk until he reached 2612. That was it all right. Unkempt shrubbery, tall trees, and a sparse lawn surrounded a dilapidated house with a bright blue door. Swallowing hard, he took a deep breath. It was important not to show that he was anxious or tense. Surely everything would turn out as planned.

He glanced up and down the rain-dampened street. There were a number of cars parked, but there was no one in sight. He crossed the road and was momentarily thrown off when he saw a sign directing him to the side door. He headed in that direction and ten yards away felt an odd sensation—an impact—like someone had poked him hard in the back with a broom handle. Knocked off balance, he tried to turn to see what had hit him but found himself falling forward. Putting out his arms to break his fall, he was aware of pain that was quickly swallowed up by a profound blackness.

CHAPTER 1

THE ATMOSPHERE WAS TENSE AS the audience collectively held its breath, waiting, waiting, waiting. Although the water was still, everyone knew big things were going on below the surface. Something riveting was about to happen. The wait seemed to last forever. Then the water suddenly split, and a huge, shining, black and white creature exploded into the air.

Shamu.

Hundreds of cameras clicked, and applause erupted throughout the stadium.

As gravity asserted itself, the whale fell back into the water.

For Erica Coleman, it was one of the high points of the show at SeaWorld. Yet those moments of anxious waiting—knowing that big things were happening unseen below the surface—were disturbingly similar to impressions she'd gotten lately from Wendy, her longtime best friend who sat beside her snapping pictures.

Erica pushed the troubling feelings aside and clapped along with Wendy's eight-year-old son, Brandon. His baptism tomorrow was one of the reasons Erica had flown across the country, arriving in Florida yesterday. His face was a study in rapture, his attention riveted on the big screen, which showed the jaunty trainer waving at the audience. There was no doubt that if Brandon had been asked what he wanted to be when he grew up, a trainer at SeaWorld would top the list.

Erica's green eyes sparkled as she nudged Wendy to look at Brandon. Smiling at the rapt expression on her son's face momentarily eased the strain that the past few years and the painful divorce had etched on Wendy's face. Still, with attractive hazel eyes in a pert face, Wendy was just as pretty as when she and Erica had gone to college together at the University of Utah.

After gathering up hotdog wrappers, napkins, and water bottles, Erica, Wendy, and Brandon threaded their way through the crowd. Outside the stadium, Brandon clambered aboard a statue of Shamu and posed for a picture. Erica gently pushed her friend forward and took pictures of Wendy with her arm around her son's shoulders. Brandon and his mother were alike in many ways; both of them were good-natured and friendly, and each had light brown hair and open, interested expressions.

Brandon insisted on taking a few pictures. Erica swept her long, auburn hair behind her shoulders then put her arm around Wendy's waist. They struck several poses, giggling as though they were teenagers instead of two women in their thirties.

As they crowded together to review the pictures, Wendy frowned at Erica. "How come you look like you could be in a magazine and I look like I've just run a 5K?"

Erica laughed. "Oh stop it; you look great!"

Brandon examined the pictures. "Erica's taller than you are, Mom."

"I'm also two years younger, but we won't talk about that," Erica said, grinning. She then snapped a picture of Wendy, who had her mouth open in outrage. Wendy grabbed the camera and deleted the photo as they started off.

"I wish Megan could have been here," Wendy said.

It was a generous statement, Erica thought, having been present when Wendy had asked her moody eighteen-year-old daughter to go to SeaWorld with them. Megan had groaned, making it clear that answering was a pain. With a roll of heavily lined eyes and a toss of long hair that had been dyed coal black, Megan had snapped that she'd already said no a hundred times.

At the walrus show, Wendy, Erica, and Brandon were in time to watch the antics of the mime who was mingling with people as they took their seats. He found plenty to mimic, including a scrawny twenty-something young man whose wide-legged pants were nearly falling off. The mime pulled his own pants down past his hips and swaggered behind the man in an affected punk walk, causing the audience to howl with laughter. Once again, Erica wished that her husband and three kids could have come with her.

They stayed at SeaWorld until closing time then drove home in the gathering darkness. Wendy parked on the road in front of her house, which was partially hidden by overgrown red cedars. The flower bed was full of weeds, and on their way to the front door, the trio passed tangled coral-bean shrubs and palmettos with their saw-toothed edges. The house was also in a tumble-down condition, with gutters that hung limply from the roof. The only sign of any recent attention was the freshly painted front door, but the bright blue only made the untidy appearance of the rest of the house more noticeable.

It didn't take long to put Brandon to bed; then Wendy and Erica went to the front room. They were still talking when Megan walked in the front door. Her look of surprise quickly turned fierce.

"What are you doing?" she asked, glaring at her mother. "Waiting up to check on me? You were probably hoping I'd be late so you could ground me." There was no chance for Wendy to reply as Megan stormed on. "You know, I'm an adult now. I shouldn't even have a curfew!" Without waiting for a response, she stomped down the hallway.

Erica looked at Wendy. "And you were worried she might not come home in a good mood." They dissolved into giggles, and Wendy grabbed a pillow to stifle her laughter.

* * *

A makeshift bedroom in the basement had been arranged for Erica, and she slept soundly on the fold-out couch. When she came upstairs the next morning, Wendy had already left for Friendly's Restaurant and Ice Cream Parlour, where she worked as a waitress. Brandon was rummaging through the cereal boxes but stopped when Erica volunteered to make French toast.

"Today's the big day, isn't it?" Erica said as she beat the eggs. "You get to be baptized."

"Yep." Brandon's eyes were shining.

"I guess your mother has talked to you about the covenants you'll be making."

He nodded. "The bishop did too. I'm going to be washed clean. I'm supposed to remember Jesus and obey His commandments." Brandon's voice was eager. "And I'm going to be confirmed and get the Holy Ghost."

"That's right," Erica said. "I'm so glad you decided to follow Jesus and be baptized." Brandon gave her a wide, happy smile.

Since Megan was still in bed, Erica left a plate for her in the microwave before starting to clean the house. Wendy had invited a few neighbors and friends over that night to celebrate. Brandon helped by putting things away, moving chairs while she swept, and taking out the garbage. When Wendy returned that afternoon, Erica could tell she was stressed at having to work later than planned.

"Everything's under control," Erica reassured her. "When you called to say you'd be late, I went ahead and made the éclair shells. All you have to do is get ready."

Looking around the house and sighing with gratitude, Wendy murmured, "You're a miracle worker."

* * *

Forty-five minutes later, the doorbell rang. Wendy poked her head, full of hot curlers, out of the bathroom. "Hey, Erica, would you get that? I'm sure it's Stephen."

Finally, Erica was going to meet Stephen Watkins, the man she'd heard so much about. After Wendy's divorce three years ago, she'd been slow to date, fearful even. Erica had hoped she could find someone who was a member of the Church, but eighteen months ago Wendy had met Stephen, a widower, and they had hit it off. A few weeks ago, Wendy had confided that her mild-mannered boyfriend seemed to be getting serious about the *M* word.

Erica opened the door to a pleasant-looking man in his early forties. After introducing herself, she said, "Come in and sit down. Wendy will be ready in a few minutes."

Stephen radiated such a feeling of prosperity—with his smartly tailored suit, matching handkerchief and tie, and highly polished shoes— that Erica almost brushed off the sofa before he sat down.

"It's good of you to come so far. Utah, isn't it?" Stephen sounded impressed. "Wendy told me the city, but I've forgotten."

"I live in Farmington. It's a little city about sixteen miles north of Salt Lake City. My husband, David, works on the police force there. Luckily, I've got a brother, Chris, who works for United Airlines. He's able to get me companion passes so I can fly standby," Erica said candidly. "I couldn't afford it otherwise."

"It's expensive to fly all right," Stephen said, his dark eyes sympathetic.

Megan came down the hallway, wearing black from her turtleneck sweater down to her knee-high boots. She was a big girl and, although not overweight, took after her father, who was a large man. Megan stopped dead when she saw Stephen.

Stephen looked at her with his rather long but kindly looking face. "Hello, Megan," he greeted her pleasantly. "Good to see you."

"Yeah, right."

Stephen took no notice of the sarcasm—or of Erica's look of consternation. Wendy had already warned her about Megan's aversion to Stephen. Megan went to the far corner, perching awkwardly on a chair, and Erica began bombarding Stephen with questions to cover Megan's silence.

Then Wendy came dashing down the hall. She was calling over her shoulder, "Come on Brandon. Time to go!" She turned to greet her guest. "Hello, Stephen!" Her movements were restless and jerky as she straightened her collar, smoothed her hair, and bent over to adjust her heel strap.

"Now, where did I put that stuff? Oh, there it is!" She scooped up a plastic bag and began ticking off her list: "Towel, comb, underwear, baptismal outfit." When Brandon came in, she hugged him to her. "Don't you look nice!" Then she smiled at Stephen. "I think we're all set!"

As they went through the door, Megan told her mother, "I'm going to drive over."

Wendy turned in dismay. "But we're all going with Stephen. Don't you remember he's taking us out to dinner afterwards?"

"I can follow you," Megan said, with some exasperation.

Wendy gave in. "Oh, all right."

* * *

Stephen pulled behind the cream-brick church building and parked in the shade of a glossy-leafed magnolia tree. A number of people were already in the Primary room. Wendy led the way to an open row near the front, but they were one seat short.

"No problem," Stephen said. "I'll get a chair." Erica, Brandon, and Wendy filed in and took their seats. Stephen put a chair beside him for Megan, but she ignored it and sat in the back. Studiously, she disregarded her mother's discreet hand signals to come sit with them.

Giving up, Wendy glanced toward the door, where a tall man in a navy suit stood perusing the crowd. When Wendy half rose and beckoned to him, he came over. His brown hair was marked by a little gray at each temple. Wendy gave him a quick hug.

"Thank you for coming," she said, smiling as she began introductions. "You've already met Stephen Watkins." The two men shook hands firmly.

"And this is my good friend, Erica Coleman. Erica, this is Lee Grover; he manages the restaurant where I work."

Lee was nice looking with straight, good features and a firm mouth, but when he smiled, his face was transformed and he became positively handsome.

"Nice to meet you, Erica," he said, his blue eyes friendly and warm. "I've heard nothing but wonderful things about you." His voice was deep and interested, and she noted with a smile that his tie was straight.

Wendy added, "Lee's the Cubmaster in our ward."

Brandon spoke up excitedly. "I'm going in to Cub Scouts!"

"You're going to have a lot of fun," Lee promised.

After a short program, it was time for the baptisms. Children from the audience clustered in front to watch as an eight-year-old girl was baptized. Then, with Wendy smiling like she couldn't stop, the bishop led Brandon into the water and baptized him.

As the pianist played a medley of Primary songs while the children changed, Erica's thoughts drifted to her family. Initially, they had planned on coming along, but David's police chief had been unable to accommodate his request for time off, so they had all stayed home.

To Erica, it was vital to attend Brandon's baptism and support Wendy, who had recently started attending church again. After all, Erica had been the one to introduce her to the gospel when they had been in college. One semester, Wendy had had a hole in her schedule, and Erica invited her to go to institute. Wendy enjoyed it so much she began taking a class each semester and eventually started taking the missionary discussions. Then Wendy fell in love with Dennis Kemp, who hated organized religion and persuaded her not to join the Church. It wasn't until after Megan was born that Wendy decided to be baptized anyway. Wendy had remained active until shortly before she and Dennis divorced, three years ago. After two years of inactivity, Wendy began attending again last year, although Erica still didn't know why she had pulled away from the Church.

Life had settled down for Wendy until the past few months when her e-mails and text messages to Erica had become strangely tense and terse. Although Erica had only been in Florida one day, she could already detect an underlying tension in Wendy's manner.

The piano music stopped, and Erica came back to the present when the two, newly baptized children came out. *Two.* Such a nice and even number, Erica thought. After a short talk, it was time for the confirmations. Brandon sat on a chair, surrounded by Lee and others who held the Melchizedek Priesthood. As the bishop performed the ordinance, confirming Brandon a member of The Church of Jesus Christ of Latter-day Saints, Erica felt the warm, swelling presence of the Spirit.

Later, Wendy corralled everyone in the hall to take a few pictures. She whispered something to Brandon, who then asked Megan to have her picture taken with him.

Handing the camera to Erica, Wendy explained with a wink, "I knew Brandon could talk her into a picture." Then she slipped in to stand beside Brandon and Megan. Right after the flash, Megan muttered that she would wait out in the car.

Wendy hugged Erica. "I'm so glad you were here. It means so much to me!"

"Don't thank me; thank Chris!" Erica said, making Wendy laugh. She knew Erica's younger brother from their college days when she had been a frequent visitor at their home.

The sunny morning had given way to a late afternoon that was gray with lowering clouds. Rain looked likely as they drove to Charley's Steakhouse. Megan had little to say at the restaurant, but Erica, Stephen, Wendy, and Brandon chatted easily and had a great time.

Since her house was small, Wendy had cleared the large room in the basement to provide a gathering place for her guests. Erica moved her luggage into a closet and went upstairs into the small, cozy kitchen to help. Wendy was a plant lover and had several philodendrons and a fleshy jade in colorful pots on the floor. On the windowsill, below a white scalloped valance, were two African violets, which Erica had spaced an even distance from each other the moment she arrived. There had been a third one, but Erica's compulsive tendencies caused her to cringe at uneven numbers, and it had been relegated to Wendy's bedroom for the duration of her visit.

Lee, dressed casually in tan slacks and a sport shirt, came early to see if he could help.

"That is so nice of you!" Wendy said gratefully. "I borrowed some folding chairs and tables. Could you take them downstairs and set them up?"

"Sure thing."

While Erica cut the tops off the éclair shells,[1] Wendy made a small sound of impatience. "Look at this!" She pointed to the pudding box. "I

---

1   See appendix at the end of the book for this recipe.

meant to get instant, but this is the kind you have to cook! I wish we'd made something simpler, even if they are Brandon's favorite." Measuring out the milk, she spilled some in her hurry.

"Where's Megan?" Wendy cried, yanking off a paper towel. "She ought to be helping!" She shouted for her daughter just as there was a knock at the back door. Rolling her eyes, Wendy whispered, "Great! I bet they heard me." Her cheeks were flushed as she went to the door and directed the early birds downstairs.

Erica had put on disposable plastic gloves and was lining up the éclairs in neat rows when Wendy returned. "For goodness sake, Erica, haven't you been tested for OCD yet?"

Erica looked up in mild surprise. "It's not being obsessive *or* compulsive to have things nice and straight. And if you mean the gloves, you ought to thank me for being so sanitary while handling food."

"I could argue with you, but I'll save it for another time. Hey, would you mind stirring the pudding while I clear a place in the freezer for it?" A moment later, she gasped, "Oh no!"

"What's the matter?"

"I forgot to freeze ice cubes. And we've *got* to have ice for the punch!" Wendy's voice was high pitched, and there were spots of color on her cheeks.

Rats. This was a glitch Wendy didn't need, Erica thought—not when she was so anxious.

"Don't worry," Erica said. "I'll run to the store and get a bag. It won't take long."

"Oh, would you? That would be great! My keys are on the dresser in my bedroom."

It had started to rain lightly. Droplets sparkled among the leaves in the bushes and trees and spangled the grass in the front yard. As Erica backed out in the gathering dusk, a couple walked up. Seeing the small sign Wendy had put up directing people to the side door—so they didn't have to track through the house to get to the basement—they went around the house.

After pulling onto John Young Parkway, Erica turned on the road that ran alongside the church. The lines were long at the grocery store, and she hoped Wendy wasn't stressing about how long it was taking. As she drove back, the headlights rushed ahead of her on the road, cleaving the darkness and the rain, which was falling harder now. Erica had to park across the street from Wendy's house and was nearly to the door when she stopped suddenly, catching herself as she nearly fell over something.

It was the still figure of a man lying facedown on the driveway. He was strangely unmoving. The light from the porch illuminated a puddle alongside him, which was growing bigger by the second. A chill shivered down Erica's spine as she noticed that the puddle was streaked by dark red threads that ran and merged with rivulets of rain.

CHAPTER 2

WHY WAS THE MAN so still? If he'd only tripped, surely he would have been trying to rise. Perhaps he had hit his head and knocked himself out. Erica knelt and touched the man's arm. Nothing. She shook his arm in an effort to rouse him—gently at first, then more roughly. There was only a cold rigidity.

It couldn't be.

Reaching for his neck, Erica felt for a pulse. Nothing. Then she noticed a hole in the back of his jacket—small and round. Rising abruptly, she stumbled into the house and dialed 911, giving the address with a shaky voice. She hung up, knowing she ought to tell Wendy but unable to make a move toward the basement. Erica couldn't go down there—not with the look of distress she knew had to be stamped on her face. Everyone would want to know what was wrong.

Because of her police training and experience as a private eye, Erica was usually equal to anything—remaining poised and unruffled no matter what—but finding a body in the driveway of your best friend's house was not something anyone could take lightly. Erica felt a deep trembling reaction inside and began to pace. At a mirror in the hall, she paused long enough to see a pale face, long, tangled auburn hair, and green eyes that were dark with shock. Erica went back to the kitchen on rubbery legs. Should she go back outside? Even though he was dead, it seemed dreadful to leave him alone on the ground.

Her hand was reaching for the doorknob when Stephen came up from the basement. Seeing Erica's face, he moved toward her quickly. "What's the matter?"

"There's a man outside. On the driveway. He's been shot."

Looking stunned, Stephen started for the door. "I'd better see what I can do."

Erica laid a hand on his arm. "No, it's too late. I've already called the police."

"But surely I ought to—"

There was the sound of footsteps on the stairs, and Lee Grover appeared. "What's going on?" he asked. "Where's Wendy?"

Thinking quickly, Erica turned to Stephen, "Go downstairs and make sure everyone stays there." When he hesitated, she encouraged, "Go ahead. I'll wait for the police."

With an agonized glance back, Stephen went to the stairs. A moment later, Erica heard him speaking gently but firmly, apparently ushering someone back downstairs.

"Why are the police coming?" Lee asked. As Erica explained, the wail of a distant siren drew nearer. Erica was peering between the blinds when she heard a sound and turned to see Wendy and Megan coming from the front room. Megan was breathing hard, as if she had been running. As Wendy looked from Erica to Lee, her face became taut.

"What's wrong?" she asked in a strained voice. "Did something happen to Brandon?"

"Brandon's okay," Lee said in a gentle voice. "But you ought to sit down." Wendy practically fell into a chair. Megan came in too, tripping as she did but catching herself.

"There's a man outside in the driveway," Erica said in a low voice. "He's been shot, and I think he's dead. I called the police."

There were a few moments of dumbfounded silence. Then Wendy cried out, "Shot? But how? And who is it?"

"I don't know. He was lying there when I came back. He can't have been there very long." Flashing lights shot through the blinds, and the sirens stopped. Wendy stared through the window as if hypnotized by the lights.

"I'm going to go and talk with them," Erica said. As she glanced at Megan, their eyes met for a brief instant. There was an odd look in the girl's eyes, but there was no time to analyze it before Megan looked away.

Paramedics arrived shortly after the police, but there was no need. The man was dead. Police swarmed around, stretching yellow and black tape to keep curious onlookers back. A young officer with short-cropped hair came in the kitchen and began writing down the names, addresses, and phone numbers of those downstairs, while a husky, older policeman went downstairs. Stephen and Wendy sat at the table and were joined by Lee, Megan, and Erica. A sense of unreality permeated the room, and by looking at the others, Erica could tell she wasn't the only one feeling strangely separated, but not isolated, from the turbulence going on outside.

* * *

When a knock came at the back door, Lee opened it to a big man in his fifties with thinning brown hair. "Good evening. I'm Detective Sergeant Patrick Lund of the Kissimmee Police Department." His voice had a tangible air of authority as he looked at them with penetrating blue eyes. "Detective Miller and Detective Carlson are assisting me. They'll be working outside while I talk with you folks." He shrugged off his rain-spattered jacket and listened intently as Erica and the others gave their names. He held out a beefy hand to shake theirs one by one.

Detective Lund's handclasp was firm and warm, and his voice—strong and deep, suiting his large frame—was steady and full of empathy. Erica felt reassured by Detective Lund's manner and appearance. He was clearly in command of the situation and looked to be both shrewd and sensible.

"I'm sorry, Mrs. Kemp, I know this must be very traumatic for you." He glanced at Wendy's trembling mouth and the way she was holding Erica's hand. "Which one of you discovered the man?"

"I did," Erica spoke up.

His manner was quiet and unhurried. "Do you mind if we go into the other room? I'd like to ask you a few questions."

Erica started to rise, but Wendy clung to her hand.

"We won't be long," the detective assured Wendy with an intuitive grasp of the situation. Letting go, Wendy folded her arms. Stephen slid his chair closer and put a protective arm around her.

Detective Lund and Erica went through the arched doorway into the small front room, which had comfortable, though somewhat shabby, furnishings. On the wall were nondescript pictures in plastic frames and as Erica went past, she straightened one that had tilted. She went to the armchair in the corner and smoothed the thin beige slipcover before she sat down.

Laying his coat aside, the detective sat on the couch, which sank under his bulk. There was barely room for his knees and with a brief apologetic look, he pushed the coffee table out a few inches. "I know this is very upsetting," he began, "but as clearly as possible, tell me how you found the victim." He watched, puzzled, as Erica straightened the table.

"We can relax now that it's straight," she said with a pleasant smile then, with succinct efficiency, answered the detective's question. Detective Lund reached into one of his cavernous pockets and gingerly extracted a small plastic bag that held a driver's license. He held it towards her.

"Please don't touch this. Do you recognize this man?"

The picture showed a man with gray hair, a narrow, pinched, rodent-like face, and hopeful-looking eyes. The name on the license was Gregory Tyson.

"No, but I've only been in Kissimmee three days."

He put the bag on the coffee table and pulled out a notepad. "Where are you from?"

"Farmington, Utah."

"You're here on vacation?"

"I came to visit my friend, Wendy Kemp," she said.

"You said earlier that you went to the store. Did you go out the front door or the back?"

"The back door."

"Did you see anyone or notice anything unusual?"

Erica thought. "No."

"What time did you get back?"

"I'm not sure. I think I left about ten to eight, and it took longer than I thought, so it was probably between 8:15 and 8:30."

"Right." He scribbled on his pad. "Before you discovered the victim, did you see or hear anything out of the ordinary?"

Erica shook her head.

"To your knowledge, had any of the guests left before you got back to the house?"

She thought about Wendy and Megan coming into the kitchen from the front room. But they must have been in one of the bedrooms.

"Not that I'm aware." Her voice was a touch hesitant, and Detective Lund noted it with a telling glance. Erica had a question of her own. "That man, Gregory Tyson, he was shot, wasn't he?" When the detective nodded, she added, "You'll perform an autopsy, though, to make sure the gunshot was the cause of death?"

He looked at her with a guarded expression. "That's right. You seem very informed."

"I used to be a police officer. My husband still is. Now I work part-time as a private investigator."

"Ah, that explains it," he said, looking less wary. "You've been so calm and collected; I was beginning to wonder." Detective Patrick Lund gave a slight smile.

"Do you think it was a robbery gone bad? I wouldn't think so since the man still had his wallet."

"How do you know he still had his wallet?"

"If you found his driver's license, he must have had his wallet."

"Ah, right." He looked at her again. "It's too soon to know the motive, but I'm inclined to agree with you that it probably wasn't a robbery." The detective asked a few more questions then asked her to send Wendy in. When Erica delivered her message, Wendy's fingers were twisting and clutching each other. She rose shakily.

"It'll be all right," Stephen assured her. "He'll want to talk to all of us, I'm sure."

With no door between the kitchen and front room, Erica couldn't help overhearing. In a voice that quavered at times, Wendy answered his questions. No, she hadn't heard any shot, but then, she'd gone to the basement and there was a lot of conversation going on. Yes, she had been in the house all evening. To her knowledge, no one except Erica had left the house.

When she returned, Wendy was walking as if she feared the floor might move suddenly if she wasn't careful. Then Wendy's foot hit the table leg and she stumbled. Lee and Stephen both jumped to catch her, but Stephen was closer and steadied Wendy while Lee stood solicitously nearby, his brown eyes worried.

While Detective Lund questioned Stephen, another detective came in and asked Wendy for permission to search the house since the murder weapon had not been located outside.

Brandon came up and sat by his mother while Megan talked with Detective Lund. She came back wearing a slight, inscrutable smile. Brandon looked somewhat anxious when Lee returned from his interview and kept looking at the man's face as if searching for answers. Ruffling the boy's hair, Lee said the detective wanted to talk to him next.

"He wants to see me?" Brandon sounded excited.

"Just wants to ask you a few questions," Lee said.

It was a relief to see Brandon come out looking relaxed and comfortable. "He wants to see you again, Erica," Brandon said.

"I was wondering if you could help me," Detective Lund said. "I know this is Wendy Kemp's home, but she, ah . . . seems to have reached her limits, so to speak, and you seem to have a level head on your shoulders—mostly." He glanced at the coffee table.

Erica smiled modestly. "It always pays to be neat and tidy. Now, how can I help?"

"I need to talk with everyone in the basement. If you could send the guests up one at a time, it would be a great help."

In her brisk, capable way, Erica took charge. Besides bringing people up, she made sure there were fresh snacks put out and videos for the children to watch. Although Erica encouraged Brandon to stay with his friends in the basement, he seemed to be aware of his mother's distress and came up often to search her face anxiously. He relaxed only when Wendy hugged him and smiled. Brandon didn't seem to notice how tenuous that smile was.

Megan was also affected, with emotion showing in her watchful eyes. She always had an intensity about her that demanded attention, but tonight it was more marked than normal. Her awkwardness was also more pronounced. Once, she spilled a plate of cookies when going downstairs and another time dropped a plastic tumbler, which made everyone jump when it hit the kitchen floor.

Through the open doorway came the muted tones of those being interviewed—shallow waves of conversation rising, breaking, and subsiding in uneven shifts. Several times, other police officers or detectives went in to confer with Detective Lund.

When the last of the guests had been allowed to leave, Detective Lund thanked Wendy, Erica, and the others, saying he would stay in touch, then he left with the last uniformed officer.

"Okay, Brandon," Wendy said. "You've been up long enough. Time for bed." Surprisingly, he accepted her decree. No one else, however, showed any inclination to leave. Instead, they moved to the front room, all of them talking quietly except for Wendy who kept wiping at her eyes. The tears came faster until suddenly, jumping up as though she had springs in her heels, Wendy ran down the hall to her bedroom. Erica followed and, sitting on the edge of the bed to hug her friend, felt hot tears drop onto her shoulder. After a few minutes, Erica got a box of tissues for her friend and waited until the storm of tears subsided.

"I can't believe a man was actually murdered right here!" Wendy balled up her hands, her fingernails pressing crescents into her palms. It had to hurt, but Wendy was oblivious.

"Why don't we say a prayer?" Erica suggested.

Wendy wiped her eyes. "All right. Just give me a minute."

Thank goodness Wendy had the gospel back in her life, Erica thought as she waited. After Megan was born and Wendy had been baptized, Dennis started drinking heavily. Years passed, and their marriage began floundering. From time to time Wendy mentioned that she and Dennis were going to the bishop for counseling. Then, abruptly, she filed for divorce. Erica assumed there had been a major fight, but for the first time since they'd known each other, Wendy did not confide the whys and wherefores.

Wendy squeezed her hand then slipped to her knees. Erica knelt and said a heartfelt prayer.

"It's going to be all right now. Don't worry," Erica assured her. Wendy nodded. Although her eyes were bright, they held a childlike trust. Wendy had always trusted her implicitly—sometimes too much. Sometimes Erica wondered if Wendy would have been a stronger person if she hadn't always been so willing to step in.

"Erica, would you stay a little longer? You're always so calm and know what to do. I don't think I can get through this without you." She sounded lost. It would be different, Erica thought, if Wendy had family that lived closer, but Dennis's company had transferred him to Florida.

Erica hesitated only a few moments. "I'll talk with my boss at Pinnacle Investigations, but I'm sure it'll be fine. I completed my cases before I left, and since I only work part-time, Doug lets me be really flexible with my schedule. But Wendy, you need to try and keep it together for your children."

Mentioning them did the trick. Wendy straightened as though stiffening her spine. She might struggle occasionally with her emotions, but Erica knew Wendy always tried her best for her children.

"Now, let's go back to the others," Erica said. "I'm sure they're worried about you."

* * *

"Are you all right?" Stephen asked, full of concern, as Wendy sat next to him on the couch.

"Yes. It's just so awful about that poor man."

"He must have been shot right before I drove up," Erica said. She turned to Wendy. "Had all your guests arrived before I got back?"

"I think so."

"One of them could have shot him while you were gone, Erica," Megan pointed out. "That's what the police think. Why else would they search the house for the gun?" There was a brightness in her eyes that Erica found disturbing.

"Did anyone come who wasn't invited?" Erica asked.

Wendy hesitated. "I don't think so, but to tell the truth I can't even remember who was here and who wasn't." Her voice sounded tortured. "I can't believe someone was killed right outside my door."

"There are a lot of crazy people in the world," Lee stated.

"Maybe he was a spy and someone was following him," Megan piped up again. "He ran to our house to get help but was shot before he could get inside."

Everyone stared.

"What?" Megan said defensively. "Does anyone have any better ideas?"

"It was probably a robbery." Lee's face was tight.

"That's possible," Erica acknowledged, "but robberies aren't all that common in the suburbs, and besides, the shooter didn't take the man's wallet." Lee, Stephen, and Megan looked at her with surprise.

"Erica's been a private investigator for years," Wendy explained. "She's really good too." The others nodded as comprehension dawned.

"Maybe it had something to do with gangs or drugs," Lee said.

"Since the victim was older," Erica said, "it's unlikely he was a gang member."

"Then he was probably a drug dealer!" Megan said.

It was a sobering thought but one entirely in line with the neighborhood, Erica knew. "The police will look into that, and they'll also do an autopsy and check for drugs." She looked at Wendy. "Do you know if there any drug houses close by?"

"I'm not sure, but I've wondered about a couple of places," Wendy admitted.

"If he was a drug dealer, he could have been shot because he was carrying a lot of money," Megan said.

"He wasn't a dealer," Stephen said quietly. He sounded so sure that everyone turned to look.

Lee asked, "How do you know?"

"Because I knew him." Stephen's voice sounded as if he were in a dream. "Gregory Tyson and I were friends."

CHAPTER 3

Everyone looked at Stephen, stunned.

"I knew Gregory Tyson from when we worked together in Chicago." His words were clipped. "My brother Richard, Greg, and I all worked for the same company, Cicero—different departments, though. I quit after Richard passed away."

"So Greg moved here to Kissimmee too?" Lee asked.

"No. He stayed on, but he was laid off a few months later. I thought Greg said he was going to move to Memphis, but I could be wrong."

"Did he call and let you know he was in town?" Erica asked.

"No." Stephen looked perplexed. "I'm surprised he didn't. But then I've only talked with Greg a couple of times since I moved here."

"When was the last time?"

"About a year ago."

Wendy said, "He must have come to see you."

"But why wouldn't he call?" Stephen appeared troubled.

Megan had been listening intently. "So the man *wasn't* a stranger," she said, looking triumphant as she eyed Stephen. "He was coming to see you! Since you knew him, I guess that makes you the prime suspect."

"Don't be silly," Wendy replied in an irritated voice. Then she turned to Erica. "That's not true, is it?"

It certainly was going to make the police take a good look at Stephen, but she didn't want to say so—not with Stephen wearing a worried crease between his eyes as he studied Wendy, who was nervously twisting her hands. "The police will do a thorough investigation and find out why Tyson was in Kissimmee."

"That's obvious," Megan burst out, seeming intent on fueling her mother's angst. "Since he showed up at our house, he *had* to be coming to see Stephen. And since Stephen's the only one who knew him, the police will probably arrest him!"

"Megan, that's enough," Erica said. "What you're saying is simply not true."

"The police aren't going to arrest anyone without evidence," Stephen added. "And since I'm innocent, there's nothing to worry about."

"But innocent people get arrested all the time," Wendy said, her face going pale. "A while back I read about some man who was just released after being in prison for *twenty years*. He was innocent, but it wasn't until they ran some DNA tests that he was cleared."

"You're getting carried away," Erica reminded her. "The police haven't named Stephen a suspect or even a person of interest, and you've already got him in jail?"

Lee agreed. "Wendy, it's been a terrible ordeal tonight and you're exhausted. The police will investigate and find the killer. It was probably some punk in the neighborhood."

There was a small snort from Megan, who got up and left. Shortly after, Stephen and Lee said good night.

After locking the door, Wendy leaned against it. "I can't believe Stephen actually *knew* that man! Megan may be a drama queen, but she has a point: it seems like Stephen knowing the guy would make the police suspicious." Wendy stepped over to Erica and put a hand on her arm. "I know it's a lot to ask Erica, but could you investigate while you're here?" There were amber flecks of light in Wendy's eyes—an amber that seemed to appear whenever she was moved to intensity. "Please? You're such a great private investigator. Maybe you can find out who killed that poor man. Then the police won't suspect Stephen."

"You don't need to worry about him," Erica began but stopped when she saw Wendy's lip tremble.

"Oh, all right. Since I'm going to be here, I guess I could check around a little."

"Thank you, Erica. I knew I could count on you!" Wendy threw her arms around Erica. Then she pulled back. "But what about David and your kids? Will they be all right without you for a little while?"

"Are you kidding?" Erica smiled. "My parents live only two doors away. They jump at any chance they have to drive the kids to piano lessons, go to soccer games, or help with homework. Two of my married brothers also live nearby. I have great sisters-in-law too. They're always helping me at home whenever I have to work unusual hours."

In the basement, Erica pulled out her foldaway bed then checked her cell phone. David had left a message, but she'd call in the morning because she was too tired. Then, after clicking the light off, then on, then off again, she lay down, and despite a great, smothering fatigue, Erica found herself staring into the darkness and listening to the intermittent creaks of the old house for a long time before sleep finally came.

* * *

When Erica woke, her head ached dully and her bones were as sore and troubled as if she'd been in an accident. Remembering the events of last night gave her the odd feeling of being in a vivid, palpable dream. After pulling on blue jeans and a layered top, Erica called her husband.

"Hi, beautiful. How was the baptism?" David asked. "I called last night, but you must have been busy."

"You have no idea."

Erica told him everything. A seasoned police officer, David was able to retain his composure.

"Did they catch the guy who did it?" he asked.

"No, and as far as I know, there were no witnesses."

"And the dead guy was a friend of Stephen's?"

"Yeah, and the odd thing is Stephen didn't even know his friend was in town. Wendy about flipped when Megan said Stephen would be the number-one suspect."

"That girl is just a little ray of sunshine, isn't she?"

"Now Wendy's scared the police might suspect Stephen."

"I bet she's scared. It's hard to get married when one of you is in the clink."

"David!"

"Just kidding. Hasn't Stephen popped the question yet?"

"No. I'm starting to wonder if Megan is the reason he's holding back. Stephen's very nice to her, but Megan acts like he's Attila the Hun in a suit."

"Maybe she doesn't like the idea of having a stepfather."

"Could be, but Stephen really is good to her."

"How is Wendy doing today?"

"I haven't been upstairs yet, but last night she was having a hard time. She told everyone about how an innocent man had been jailed for years—"

David interrupted. "And she thinks that's going to happen to Stephen."

"Exactly. And . . . uh, one more thing. Last night, Wendy asked me if I could stay a little longer. She wants me to look into things."

"What? I thought you were coming home tomorrow!"

"I was, but . . . she's really upset, David." This was met by silence, and Erica went on. "Honey, she really needs me right now. I hope you don't mind, but I've already told her I'd stay. All she wants is for me to do a little investigating."

"I've never known you to do a *little* of anything," her husband said with an edge to his voice. "And it's more than a little premature for her to think Stephen might be arrested."

"I know, but Megan scared her. If you could have seen her face—"

"It's not *her* face I want to see."

"Don't pout."

"I'm not pouting," he countered in his classic pouting voice.

"Wendy's my best friend, and she needs my help."

David sighed audibly. "I understand. She's lucky to have you. 'Friendships multiply joys and divide griefs,'" he quoted. "Thomas Fuller."

Erica smiled to herself. She and David liked to exchange quotes—ever since college when they'd taken an English literature class together. "I'm glad you understand. And Wendy does have a lot to deal with right now."

"She always does," David grumbled. "But you've always been the rock Wendy depends on. I just hope you can get to the bottom of this as soon as possible."

"I will. There's only one thing—I've never worked on a murder case before."

"Investigating is investigating. And you've always had a knack for finding out what you need to know, which is why you've been able to solve every single case you've worked on."

It was true. Even when faced with puzzling cases, Erica had an amazing memory and an ability to see little details that others overlooked, along with unexpected flashes of intuition that later proved to be true. However, despite what she'd told Wendy, Erica still worried about being away from her children.

"Will you guys be okay for a little while? Can you can handle being Mr. Mom?"

"That's one thing I don't have to worry about," David laughed. "Your mom stepped in the day you left. You know how she loves to take charge. It's her antidote to the empty nest syndrome. Plus, Amanda and Jocelyn have been making sure we're well fed. The fridge is stuffed."

David often teased Erica about her family being a tightly knit bunch, but just as often he was grateful for their help. Erica's parents, Barbara and Howard Taylor, owned a large farm in Farmington and when their children married, they gave each couple a large building lot as a wedding present. Erica's oldest brother, Konner, his wife, Jocelyn, and their daughter lived a few houses away, as did her younger brother, Chris, and his wife, Amanda, with their three children.

"I'll give Mom a call and let her know I'll be staying a little longer," Erica said.

"By tonight, she'll have a schedule worked up for piano lessons, soccer practices, and homework. She's almost as organized as you are, if such a thing is possible. So don't worry. Tell Wendy you'll stay, and make sure her future husband doesn't get sent to the slammer." His voice turned serious. "Just make sure you don't step on any toes. You ought to talk with that detective before you get too involved."

"I'll do that. I know how you policemen hate civilians poking their noses into your business."

"That's true," David said with a grave tone to his voice. "Of course, you're not quite on the same level as a civilian. You said that one detective last night seemed to trust you. What was his name?"

"Patrick Lund. I liked him," Erica said. "He's the kind of person who listens more than he talks, but when he does speak, people pay attention. He seems very capable. Besides that, he's about the size of a moose. He's not someone you'd want to get into an argument with."

"Hopefully he'll be open to outside help."

"He seemed like a good guy. Anyway, even if Detective Lund objects, he can hardly stop me from investigating on my own. Hopefully I'll be able to help Wendy."

David's voice softened. "Yeah, she's had it pretty rough. She doesn't need any more."

"That's for sure," Erica replied. "Now, tell me how things are going there. How are the kids?" Erica felt a wave of longing to see her children; Abigail, who preferred to be called Aby, was fifteen, Ryan was twelve, and McKenzie, or Kenzie for short, was ten.

"Oh, they're great. They wanted to talk to you last night. I'll get them in a minute."

"I miss them and you so much it hurts. I've got my laptop so we can use Skype to talk online and see each other."

"That's a great idea." He then asked, "So, what are you going to do today?"

"We'll go to church if Wendy is up to it."

There was some background noise and scuffling on the phone and the sound of children's excited voices. Apparently, her husband was being overrun. "I'm surrounded by a pack of wild, man-eating beasts." David sounded breathless. There were giggles in the background. "They're frothing at the mouth and threatening dire consequences if I don't give up the phone. Farewell, my love!"

* * *

When Erica went upstairs, it was easy to see from the dark circles under Wendy's eyes that her friend had slept little. Since Wendy didn't feel up to church, Erica offered to go with Brandon. Megan was going to a friend's ward.

Wendy was asleep when she and Brandon returned, so Erica whipped up one of her specialties, Twice Baked Potatoes[2]—with chopped ham, whole kernel corn, and grated cheese melted on top.

"Would you go get your mom and Brandon?" she asked Megan.

When they had all gathered, Erica put the potatoes in the middle of the table.

With an evil grin, Megan asked, "Did you wash your hands with that special soap of yours—the one with the rocks in it?"

"Of course, and the rocks are pumice. Lava has other cleaning agents too."

Erica put the potato she'd marked with a toothpick on Megan's plate.

After prayer, Megan took a careful bite then looked up with a pleased expression. "Hey, these are great!" Megan said. "And thanks for leaving the ham out of mine."

"She always makes the most wonderful dishes." Wendy smiled. "Erica's quite the gourmet chef."

"I'm hardly that!" Erica said with a laugh. "I'm too busy to spend hours in the kitchen although I do like to cook. Cooking is a very

---

2   See appendix at the end of the book for this recipe.

precise activity. I think the greatest recipes are easy and taste great, so I'm always on the lookout for recipes that are delicious yet easy to fix."

Later that afternoon, Erica called Detective Lund.

"Yes, of course I remember you," he replied in his strong, distinctive voice. "Don't apologize for calling on Sunday; I asked you to. So, how is your friend Wendy? She was pretty shook up last night."

"She's doing better today."

"Glad to hear it. Say, aren't you supposed to fly home to Utah tomorrow?" At first, Erica was surprised he remembered, but then detectives were trained to remember details.

"Yes, but Wendy asked me to stay. Someone told her that Stephen would be considered a suspect because he's the only one that knew the victim, and that got her worried. You see, she and Stephen are nearly engaged."

"Being acquainted with the victim is hardly an indictment," the detective said, amusement in his voice.

"I told her that, but Wendy was upset. She asked me if I could look into things a little. I'd like to help if I can."

"That's, er, kind of you to offer, but we've got everything under control." Detective Lund's friendly tone had cooled off considerably.

It was to be expected. Erica chose her next words with care. It was important that he know that regardless of his stance, she planned to investigate. "I'm sure you do. I also know that well-meaning but misguided civilians can be troublesome. However, as I told you, I used to be a police officer, so I know enough not to make your job harder. I just wanted to let you know that I'm going to be investigating, and if there's anything I can do, I'd be glad to help."

"I appreciate the offer, but our detectives are trained and experienced." Although his tone was courteous, it was also painfully wary.

"I'm sure they are," Erica said calmly. "I am too. I've been a private investigator for ten years. I just thought that since I'm living where the crime took place and that my best friend's boyfriend has a direct connection with the victim, I might be able to provide some assistance."

It was obvious she'd hit a nerve when Detective Lund hesitated. Then he went on, "Over the years, we've found it best not to involve civilians. It rarely works out."

"I might be of help when interviewing." Erica kept her tone pleasant. "I've found that people who won't talk to the police will often open up to me."

Detective Lund mulled that over. "That may be, but a murder investigation is a matter for the police." He paused. "However, if you do come up with anything useful, I'd appreciate you calling me immediately."

Erica smiled to herself. *Advantage—Erica Coleman.* She replied, "Do you have any leads?"

"Not yet, but we did find the murder weapon: a .357 Magnum. It was thrown in some bushes across the street."

It came as a bit of a surprise that he would be so forthright. Apparently Detective Lund's bark was worse than his bite. "I don't suppose there were any prints."

"Wiped clean."

"I see. I still think it's doubtful Gregory Tyson's murder was a botched robbery since he had his wallet," Erica said. "Especially since he was shot in the back. Usually, when robbery victims *are* shot, they're shot in the front."

"That's right," said the detective, sounding a touch surprised himself.

"It could have been a random shooting," Erica mused, "but drive-bys are usually committed by gangs and occur at houses where a gang member lives or at a drug house, and Wendy's home is neither."

"We're checking on that."

I bet you are. Erica knew they would also check all the homes in the area. "Since Stephen knew Tyson, there's got to be some sort of connection there," she stated. "It's too much of a coincidence for Stephen's friend to be shot outside a house where he's attending a party."

"I thought the same thing," Lund said grudgingly. "We're looking into that. Detectives are contacting Tyson's wife, family, and friends."

"Was Gregory Tyson from Memphis?" When the detective replied affirmatively, Erica asked, "Do you know how long he'd been in Kissimmee?"

There was some hesitation, then Erica heard the riffling of papers. "Tyson checked into the Starlight Motel on the evening of April 30—two days before he was shot."

Now Erica understood his hesitation. Although Detective Lund was reluctant to give out information, he didn't mind sharing things Erica could easily find out on her own.

"It's odd, though, that Tyson didn't call Stephen when he arrived in town. I wonder why."

"Maybe Tyson didn't want to alert Stephen."

Erica processed that quickly. "You think Tyson was after Stephen? What makes you think that?"

Again he hesitated, as though tempted to say something. Then he sidestepped the question. "We don't know much at this point."

Brick wall.

"I'll talk to Stephen again," Erica said. "You know, if Tyson didn't call Stephen, that brings up a very important question."

"Which is?"

"How did Tyson know where Stephen was going to be last night?"

* * *

Monday morning, Wendy was flipping pancakes on the griddle when Erica came upstairs. Last night, Stephen had dropped by with a newly released DVD, which served to distract them all.

"Sorry about the pancakes, Erica," Wendy said.

"Why, what's wrong with them?" Erica asked.

Wendy had a devilish grin. "They're round." She turned to her daughter. "Erica likes all things square, even pancakes."

"How can you make pancakes square?" Megan asked.

"With a wonderful little tool known as a knife," Erica said.

As Wendy put a plate of pancakes in the microwave, she asked Megan to set the table.

"Wow, what happened here?" Megan gazed in wonder at the open cupboard where glasses, saucers, and bowls were neatly lined up and arranged according to size.

Leaning over to see, Wendy shook her head ruefully. "You've done it again, Erica. The only thing that surprises me is that you waited this long. Usually you're a little faster."

"She's done this before?" Megan asked.

"Don't you remember her last visit?" Wendy said, pouring out pancake batter. When Megan shook her head, her mother said, "It's just as well. You might have been scarred for life."

Megan opened another cupboard where cans of peas, beans, and corn were stacked precisely next to cake mixes, macaroni and cheese boxes, and cereal, all in descending height.

"You can see everything!" Megan said in amazement. "And all the labels are facing out!" Erica smiled, resisting the impulse to blow on her nails and shine them on her imaginary lapels.

After a quick prayer, Brandon started eating while Megan opened the cupboards under the sink. Plastic and metal scrubbies were in a plastic bowl, cutting boards were on the left, and the dish soap was on the right. Going to the next cupboard, Megan asked, "When did you do all of this?"

"I woke up about two and couldn't get back to sleep."

"Let me guess," Wendy said. "You couldn't stop thinking about how the cereal boxes and canned goods were so disorganized."

"I'm surprised you can sleep at night," Erica replied in a serious voice.

Megan looked at Erica as if she were an alien. "Do you keep your own house like this?"

Erica smiled. "Of course. Doesn't it feel good to have everything so organized?"

"Doesn't it freak out your kids?"

"Au contraire! They *love* being able to find things," Erica said cheerfully. "I could give you some pointers if you'd like."

"No thanks," Megan said, taking another pancake. "My friends think I'm weird enough."

As Wendy poured the last of the batter, she said, "You know, Erica, you ought to have your own TV show—like *The Nanny*—where you go into homes and teach people how to organize everything. There's only one problem: you'd do all the organizing yourself."

"Mock me if you will," Erica said, drawing her tattered dignity around her. "But you'll thank me the next time you need chocolate pudding *and you can actually find it.*"

As Wendy brought over a stack of pancakes balanced on her spatula, she was startled by a sudden honking of a car, and the pancakes tumbled to the floor.

"Chill *out*, Mom," Megan said, putting her plate in the sink. "It's just Kimberly. She's giving me a ride today."

"I thought Stephen was going to take you to school."

Megan groaned. "Please don't mention him. I just ate."

"Did you call and let him know you didn't need a ride?"

"What do you think?" Megan snapped, grabbing her backpack. In a flash, she was gone.

"I don't know what Megan has against Stephen," Wendy muttered. "That's why she wouldn't go to SeaWorld with us—because I'd invited him." She handed Erica more pancakes. "Megan was furious when she found out he'd canceled at the last minute."

Erica took a bite. "Her loss. We had a great time, didn't we, Brandon?"

The boy's face lit up. "It was great! When can we go again?"

"Not for a long time," Wendy replied. "Those tickets were expensive. We're going to be eating macaroni and cheese forever."

"Yeah!" Brandon cried with delight.

Wendy looked at him then shrugged. "One man's poison—" Then she mumbled, "I wish I knew why Megan doesn't like Stephen."

"Don't worry about it, Mom," Brandon said in an effort to console his mother. "Megan hates everyone." Then he added with a knowing look, "It's just a phase."

* * *

When the doorbell rang ten minutes later, Wendy said, "That'll be Stephen." Erica heard him ask if Megan was ready.

"A friend stopped and picked her up," Wendy explained, looking regretful. "I meant to tell you that I'd be able to take her to school today, but I forgot. I'm sorry she didn't call you. I really appreciate you taking her to school last week so I could work those extra shifts."

"No problem. It wasn't any trouble—Osceola is close to the office, and I was glad to help." Stephen saw Erica in the kitchen and called, "Hi, Erica! How are you today?"

"I'm doing good, and you?"

"Fine, just fine."

Erica walked into the front room; she noted that Stephen was dressed in a stylish suit—a different one than he'd worn at the baptism. He had a handsome red silk tie and a pair of shoes that looked just as expensive as the ones he'd worn on Saturday.

His tie was a little crooked, and Erica reached out and straightened it. When Stephen leaned back and blinked in surprise, she explained, "I knew you'd want it straight."

Wendy shook her head. "Sorry about that, Stephen. Erica's got a mania about ties—and everything else—having to be straight." She peered through the open door at Stephen's silver Lexus parked out front. "Who's that with you?"

"That's Jaime. She just started working in the office. I told you about her." He beckoned to Jaime, and when she opened the door, he called, "Come here and let me introduce you."

Slim and long legged, Jaime Russell strolled to the door. She was in her late twenties, and as introductions were made, Erica noticed the perfection of her smooth, olive-tinted skin. Jaime had a rather prominent nose, but it gave her face a distinctive look.

"It's so nice to meet you," Jaime gushed, shaking Wendy's hand with her well-manicured one. "Stephen never stops talking about you."

Erica noticed how Wendy was looking at Jaime's form-fitting, chocolate-brown suit, which was made of some thin material suitable for Florida's temperatures. Then Wendy smoothed her hair and tugged at her blouse. "Ah, Stephen's told me about you too."

"Good things, I hope," Jaime replied with a calm smile, seeming assured that would be the case. "I was so lucky to meet Stephen when I moved into Lake Tivoli Gardens. The apartments are beautiful, and everyone's been so friendly and helpful. That means a lot when you're new in town." As she spoke, Jaime's beautiful eyes—which were so dark they appeared black—were never long absent from Stephen's face. "I was job hunting when Stephen told me that his office was looking for an administrative assistant. That's what I was doing before I moved here. It was fate!" She beamed at him.

"It certainly was perfect timing," Stephen agreed. "Our receptionist has been doing double duty but wasn't able to keep up with everything."

Jaime glanced at her watch. "It's good to meet you, but we'd better be off."

Erica and Wendy waved good-bye, then Erica shut the door, opened it slightly, then shut it again.

Wendy frowned. "Do you have to do that? It's driving me crazy how you open and shut the door twice."

"Au contraire," Erica said. "I shut the door first *then* opened it once before shutting it again. I just wanted to make sure it was really closed. Anyway, how long has Jaime been in town?"

"Long enough to get her claws into Stephen," Wendy said tartly. In the kitchen, she barked at Brandon. "Look at the time! You're going to have to run now to make the bus!" Her son flashed her a look of surprise before rushing out. It was the first time Erica had heard Wendy speak so sharply. Erica knew Wendy's impatience had nothing at all to do with Brandon and everything to do with that pretty young thing who was riding off to work with Stephen Watkins.

* * *

That afternoon, the elementary school got out early so teachers could prepare for parent conferences. Erica was putting peanut butter on celery sticks when Brandon came home. Dropping his backpack, he scampered across the kitchen, and she showed him how to put raisins on top of the peanut butter to make "ants on a log."

"My mom used to make these for me, and now I make them for my kids," Erica said. They sat at the table, munching away happily as Brandon told her about a DVD his teacher had shown about outer space.

"My favorite planet is Jupiter, but I like Mercury too," he declared. His easy companionship was a change from Megan, who barely said hello before grabbing a snack and taking it to her room.

Gulping down the last of his milk, Brandon asked, "Do you want to go play catch?"

"Sure, that would be great!"

The backyard was small but charming. An untidy, sprawling rock garden spread unevenly in a corner where flowers preened in the afternoon sun—candytuft, dwarf iris, rose mallow, and English daisy. Florida holly crept up the sagging back fence, and midway up the small rectangle of lawn was a huge, rounded beech tree.

Tilting his head and wearing a slight frown, Brandon looked around at the lawn and flowers. "It looks funny. Different," he said, appearing puzzled.

Erica cleared up the mystery. "That's because the weeds are gone. I thought it would be a nice surprise for your mother if I did some weeding and pruning to make things tidier."

"But the bushes are square now." Brandon pointed at several.

"Don't they look great? Now, are we going to play ball or what? Go on back."

Brandon's light brown hair, which was usually in his eyes, flew out as he ran. He was solid but moved quickly—a tightly wrapped package of coiled energy. When she threw the ball, Brandon reached for it too soon, tipping it away so he had to search for it in a yaupon bush, whose jagged-edged leaves looked like they had been gnawed by insects. They continued tossing the ball back and forth until it became apparent Brandon could go on until the middle of next week. Begging off, Erica went to sit in a swinging bench that was shaded by the neighbor's magnolia tree.

Brandon continued on, throwing the ball high in the air and trying to catch it—missing more than he caught. Finally, Brandon came to sit beside her on the swing, tossing the ball a foot or two in the air. Once, Erica stopped the swing suddenly with her feet just as he threw the ball.

As it rolled away, she teased, "That was an easy one. How come you missed it?"

"You stopped the swing," he complained, running after the ball, but his smile showed that he held no grudge.

"I'm glad you came for my baptism," Brandon said, sitting beside her again.

"Me too! That was a very special day. How does it feel to be baptized?" When there was no immediate answer, Erica looked at him, surprised to see him looking troubled. "What's wrong?"

His eyes remained focused on the ball in his lap. Erica gave him a few moments then slid closer and put her arm around his shoulders, which were tense. She gave him a reassuring squeeze. "It's okay if you don't want to tell me. But if you do, I might be able to help."

He appeared to be debating with himself, glancing up at her several times. Finally, in a halting voice, he said, "I want to follow Jesus."

"Of course you do. When you were baptized, you promised that you would try your very best." Then, thinking she knew what Brandon was getting at, Erica added, "But it's okay to make mistakes. Everyone does. We just have to repent, and then we can be forgiven."

There was a pause then a small voice, "I don't like lying."

"I don't either. It's always best to tell the truth. But even if you told a lie, you can always go back and tell the truth."

"I need to choose the right. Because I'm baptized now." His voice was very serious.

"That's right." She gave him an encouraging look.

"Why do people lie?"

The question was so all encompassing that Erica was hard put to answer. Maybe this wasn't about a lie Brandon had told. "I suppose there are a lot of different reasons."

Looking at her, Brandon asked tentatively, "Is it okay to tell you?" A worry line appeared between his eyes. "I don't want to be a tattler. Megan says I'm a tattler."

So it *was* about someone else. Erica squeezed his shoulder. "It's okay to tell me."

Some of the anxiety left his eyes. "The night I was baptized, Lee told me he'd made the éclairs. But when the police came, he said my mom made them."

Erica felt a great sense of relief. Was that all? It was too bad Brandon had been disturbed by such a small thing. Then again, why *had* Lee said he'd made the éclairs? When Erica had gone for ice, Wendy had been working on them.

"When did Lee tell you he'd made them?"

"When he brought them downstairs. They had sprinkles on them," he said, his voice full of disapproval. "My mom never does that. Lee said he wanted to surprise my mom so he finished them. He didn't know you don't put sprinkles on éclairs." He wanted to make sure Erica understood that important fact.

"Why didn't your mom finish them?"

"I don't know. Lee said she was gone."

"Gone?"

Brandon wanted to get back to his point. "Lee told the policeman my mom made the éclairs. He shouldn't lie."

"You're right. People shouldn't lie, but we can't *make* other people tell the truth—they have to decide that on their own. What's important is that we always tell the truth ourselves. And we shouldn't judge other people if they make mistakes. We need to treat them nice because everyone makes mistakes."

Brandon nodded, looking relieved. Obviously, he'd been very troubled about this.

"I'm glad you told me," Erica said. "But you won't tell anyone else because it wouldn't be right to talk about other people's mistakes, right?"

"Right." Brandon's eyes had drifted to the fence where a cat was squeezing through a hole. Brandon jumped up, letting his glove and ball fall to the ground as he ran to the cat.

Erica followed. "Is this your neighbor's cat?"

"Yeah. Her name's Zoey." The cat butted its head against Brandon, who laughed.

"I have a couple of cats at home," Erica said, pulling a pair of plastic gloves out of her pocket and putting them on before sitting on the grass and petting the cat. "Oh, you're a pretty thing, aren't you?" she cooed.

"You carry gloves in your pocket?" Brandon asked as the cat curled itself around the boy and began a rusty, rumbling purr.

"Saves a lot of time. This way I don't have to go back to the house or stop at a store."

Brandon scratched the cat behind the ears. "But why do you wear gloves?"

"Germs. Who knows where this cat has been." She paused. "You want a pair? I have extras."

He shook his head and turned his full attention to the cat. Erica's mind began to churn as disagreeable thoughts popped up like sharp, small pebbles on a smooth stretch of sand. Why would Lee lie to the police over such a small thing? But what bothered her more was Lee telling Brandon he didn't know where Wendy was.

Erica remembered how Wendy had come into the kitchen from the front room. At the time, she figured Wendy had been in one of the bedrooms, but she could just as easily have come in the front door. *Had* Wendy left the house? And if so, why? And why had Lee felt it necessary to cover up for her? Those questions led to other, more unsettling ones. If Wendy had indeed left the house, where had she gone and what had she been doing? And more importantly, why hadn't she told Erica or the police?

CHAPTER 4

TALKING WITH LEE SHOULD CLEAR up some of the questions that came from talking with Brandon. Erica would go see him the next morning. She also wanted to ask Wendy a few questions, but when Wendy got home, she was late and in a hurry to get ready for an early date with Stephen.

"Of course you can borrow my car!" Wendy was delighted. Every time Erica borrowed her car, the first time she drove she ran it through a car wash and vacuumed it. She also wiped the seats, steering wheel, and dashboard with the moist towelettes she kept in her purse. After the first time, Erica usually settled for just cleaning the seats and steering wheel.

When Erica had finished cleaning, she set out for the motel where Gregory Tyson had stayed. Erica knew the police were done questioning motel employees or else Detective Lund wouldn't have given her the name of the motel.

The Starlight Motel could have used a fresh coat of paint. Erica opened the door, closed it, then opened it again before walking through the foyer where a flowered maroon couch and striped chairs rested on well-worn carpet. The old-fashioned, heavy curtains at the windows gave off a slightly musty air. The woman at the front desk, whose name tag read "Daisha Pepin," was in her thirties, with high cheekbones, and cornrowed hair. She spoke in a clear, brisk manner and agreed to answer questions when Erica explained she was a private investigator. Unfortunately, Daisha had little to tell her. She'd been off the night Tyson had checked in and hadn't had any contact with him during his stay.

When Erica asked if she could talk with members of the staff, Daisha looked a little dubious. "I suppose so, as long as you don't take too much of their time."

"It'll only take a few minutes," Erica assured her. "Can you tell me who was on duty that day?" Daisha looked put out but in a few moments produced the schedule while grumbling that the police already had the list. Erica jotted down the names. All but three were working at the Starlight Motel that day. Daisha paged those employees one by one to the front lobby, where they sat on the couch, looking slightly alarmed. They were all willing to talk but kept one eye on the efficient Daisha, who was watching them as well.

It was a small motel, but Tyson had kept a low profile, and the first three people she talked to did not remember him. Apparently, Tyson was not the type of man who stood out.

"We see so many people," one of the maids explained. "There's no way to remember them all."

The next girl, a petite, dark-eyed girl named Sho, did recall seeing Gregory Tyson. She seemed a little nervous as she peered at the picture Erica had clipped out of the newspaper.

"Yes, I remember him." Sho shot a quick glance at Daisha. "I already talked to the police."

"I'm a private investigator," Erica explained again. "Did Tyson act different in any way or do anything odd?"

"No." Sho seemed bored and shifted in her chair.

"Did he seem happy, sad, or angry?"

Sho shrugged. "He asked me where the ice machine was. I showed him. That's all."

After talking with the last employee, Erica returned to Daisha. "When will the three employees that weren't here today be on duty again?"

Daisha checked the list against the schedule. "Miguel works on the grounds. He'll be here on Friday. So will Jenny, but she works in the office and doesn't usually have any contact with customers. Matt Watters is on vacation. He left Sunday."

The day after the murder—might there be something to that? "When will he be back?"

"In a couple of weeks. He went to Colorado to hike and camp."

"Did he leave a number where he can be reached?"

Daisha looked at her stoically. "I can't give out private information."

"I understand, but could you call Matt and ask him to call me?" She received a cool stare and a shake of her head. "All right," Erica conceded. "How about if I leave Matt a message. Would you give it to him when he gets back?"

"That I can do."

* * *

Under a fair morning sky that was robin egg blue, Erica dropped Wendy and Brandon off at parent-teacher conference—promising to return in thirty minutes to pick them up. Erica then drove to Friendly's Restaurant, a large dusty-pink building where Lee worked as a manager. The neat flower beds in front added bright splashes of color. When she opened the door, closed it, then opened it and walked in, she saw Lee standing by the front counter, his head tilted slightly, as if puzzled. With his hair hanging over his forehead a bit, Lee looked boyish and rather solemn—until he smiled. Then there was an amazing transformation, and he looked like a different man—one that would make any woman's heart beat faster. How strange, Erica thought, that Wendy had fallen for Stephen rather than this man.

"I don't want to bother you at work," Erica said apologetically, "but if you have a few minutes, I'd like to talk to you. Or would it be better if I saw you after work?"

"This is a good time. We always have a bit of a lull after breakfast." Lee led the way past well-spaced tables that had vases of fresh daisies and were set with lemon-yellow tablecloths and napkins. The floor to ceiling windows let in the light and gave the rooms an open feeling. They took a booth in a far corner.

"Wendy asked me to investigate, and I wanted to ask you a couple of questions," Erica began. "I hope you don't mind."

"Of course not." Lee's blue eyes looked interested.

"On the night of the murder, you told Brandon that you had made the éclairs. Later, you told the police Wendy had made them. I was with Wendy when she started making them but had to run to the store. *Did* you finish the éclairs?" Ever since her talk with Brandon, Erica had puzzled over this. She hoped Lee had a good reason for not telling the truth because, for some indiscernible reason, she liked this handsome, good-natured man.

He compressed his lips momentarily and, without dissembling, said, "Yes, I finished them."

"Brandon said you made them because Wendy was gone. Do you know where she went?"

Lee Grover grimaced slightly then admitted he didn't. "When I came up, Wendy was working on them. A bunch of people came, and she asked me if I'd take them downstairs and mingle. But after a few minutes,

I came back up to see if Wendy needed any help and I couldn't find her. I even checked the bathroom and bedrooms. She'd filled the éclairs but not frosted them. There was a can of frosting on the counter, so I put the frosting on. Later, I heard Wendy tell that detective she'd been in the house, so I figured I must have missed her somehow."

He sounded sincere. And it was nice of him to finish the pastries, but—"Why did you tell the police Wendy had made them?"

Lee was looking off to the side when he replied, "Well, she'd done most of it. It didn't seem important who had frosted them."

Erica studied the man with the deep, arresting voice who was busy looking left, right, and down but not at her. Since they had met yesterday, Lee had always looked into her eyes as they talked. The fact that he wasn't now spoke volumes. She had the feeling Lee didn't believe Wendy had been in the house the entire evening. Yet he hadn't come out and said so. Why was that? Could he be trying to protect her? Odd bits and pieces began to fall into place—the way Lee's rather sober face came to life whenever Wendy was around. How he always seemed to go out of his way to be near her.

Suddenly, Erica felt like smacking her forehead as she had a flash of the blindingly obvious. *Lee liked Wendy.* He liked her so much that, in his own way, he was trying to protect her.

That's why he'd told the police Wendy had made the éclairs—he didn't want them suspecting her. There is a human tendency to believe people that you care about, and that's what had to be at play here, she decided. Wendy had said she was in the house, and Lee believed her. Yet there was a bit of doubt, too, mixed in with some other anxieties she didn't quite understand. Quite possibly, Lee was wondering the same thing as Erica: where had Wendy disappeared to that night?

He spoke up. "I suppose I ought to tell the police that I finished the éclairs because I couldn't find Wendy?" Lee appeared very hesitant about linking those two facts together.

"As soon as possible." Erica was definite. "Did you ever ask Wendy where she went?"

When Lee shook his head, Erica picked up her purse. "I'd better let you get back to work. Thanks for talking with me."

"Before you go, would you like a piece of pie? On the house?"

She was about to say no, but Lee called to a passing waitress. "Carmen, bring this young lady a piece of our signature pecan pie."

Erica smiled. "I never could say no to pecan pie. It's one of my favorites. Thanks."

As she ate, Erica thought back. Where could Wendy have been when Erica had made her horrifying discovery? And what about Megan? They'd both come into the kitchen together. She'd thought at the time they had come from one of the bedrooms, but Lee had checked them. The only other possibility was that they had come in the front door. But why would Wendy leave when she had company? And why use the front door when she always used the side door?

And after the murder, Wendy had been very emotional, her nerves stretched thin and close to the breaking point. Did that mean anything? Probably not. Everyone had been emotional that night, especially Megan. What was going on with her? She'd been acting strange lately. But then, so had her mother. Next on Erica's agenda would be to talk to Wendy. She needed to find out two things. Where had Wendy gone that night, and why had she lied about it to the police?

When Erica was done, she pushed her empty saucer away. On the way to the exit, she glanced at a table and stopped. The salt and pepper shakers had been left in the middle of the table, so Erica quickly moved them back where they belonged, one on each side of the chrome napkin holder. Satisfied, she started off, but at the next table the shakers were also out of place, to the right. Erica leaned over and put them in their proper positions.

When she straightened up, an older couple, both of them using canes, approached her. "Could we have a table, please?"

"Oh, well, actually I don't work here."

They looked at each other then at the table Erica had just arranged. The man was bewildered. "But you were straightening the tables—"

"Yes, well—the shakers weren't lined up." Looking at the table, Erica said brightly, "It looks much better now, don't you think?" The hostess finally noticed them and hurried over. "Here, this lady will be glad to help you." She then left as quickly as she could.

* * *

Wendy and Brandon were waiting in front of the school. Once they got home, Brandon went off to play. Inside, Wendy got a broom and started sweeping the kitchen. Erica put on rubber gloves.

"I wanted to ask you something," Erica said as she moved the dining room chairs for Wendy.

Jabbing under the table, Wendy replied, "You're using your serious voice. If it's about the murder, could you leave it for another time? The last thing I want to talk about is that horrible night."

Rats, Erica thought. Well, she did have another question. "Is there anything else bothering you? Besides the murder, I mean."

For a moment, the broom hung suspended above the floor. "Why do you ask?"

"The past month or two, you've seemed different—anxious."

Starting in again, Wendy moved the prayer plant and swept behind it. "Nothing more than the usual: raising an eight-year-old, trying to survive a teenager, working full-time to keep creditors at bay. You know; lift that barge—tote that bale." Her tone was light, but Erica detected an undercurrent.

"I'd be glad to listen if you wanted to talk about—anything."

"Oh, I'm fine," Wendy insisted as she got the dustpan. "Don't worry."

Sighing, Erica decided to drop it even though she felt dissatisfied. "Here let me take that," Erica said, taking the dustpan over to the sink.

"You don't have to rinse out the dustpan!"

Erica chuckled. "Right. Next you'll tell me you don't have to wash your garbage can every time you empty it."

"You don't have to. It's lined with a plastic bag so the can stays clean."

Erica looked surprised. "I'm glad everyone doesn't feel that way."

"I hate to break it to you, but they do." They went into the front room and when Erica sat on the couch, she fingered the afghan lying over the arm. "This sure is pretty. Where did you get it?"

Wendy's face split into a delighted grin. "I made it."

"*No way!*" Erica spread the afghan over her lap, examining it more closely. "My mom crochets a lot, and someday I'd like to learn how. This is just beautiful! And I love the colors—such pretty shades of blue! When did you learn to crochet?"

"One of the ladies in my ward taught me. We had a service auction for Relief Society enrichment night. One lady offered to teach crocheting, and I bid and won. Erlinda spent a lot of time with me. "

"Well, it's gorgeous." Erica folded it carefully. "So, do you like your ward?"

"They've been great."

"Good. I wondered because you said you'd stopped going to church." Erica stroked the afghan absentmindedly. "You never did tell me what happened. All I know is it had something to do with the bishop." She regarded Wendy with contemplative green eyes. "If you still don't want to talk about it, that's okay."

A shadow clouded Wendy's face. "Yeah, well, it was all connected to the problems Dennis and I were having. I went to see the bishop, and he was very helpful until—" Wendy gave a depreciating little shrug. "I don't like to think about it. Anyway, Dennis was doing a lot of drinking then. You know."

Erica did. Before his marriage, Dennis only drank occasionally, but when Megan was born, he started drinking more. By the time Brandon was born, Dennis was getting drunk fairly regularly.

"I remember you telling me that even though he was drinking a lot, Dennis thought you were the one with the problem."

"That's right. Almost every night after work, he'd stop by the Fox and Hound Pub and have a few drinks with his buddies. Then, he'd come home and get angry about something I or the kids had or hadn't done. *We* were the ones doing things wrong, he said."

Erica remembered one of the times Wendy had called in tears. Dennis had come home and tripped over Megan's backpack, which he then kicked without considering the heavy books inside. After a fair amount of cursing about his sore toe, Dennis had thrown the books and the backpack onto the front lawn, refusing to let a crying Megan retrieve them. She had to wait until dark to sneak out and gather them. There had been many such episodes, some more ominous than others, with grabbed arms or an occasional push.

"Sometimes I wondered why you stayed with him so long."

Wendy's amber eyes snapped a little. "What was I supposed to do? I had no money, no job skills, and two kids. If I left, I would have had to go to a homeless center."

"You could have come and stayed with me."

"I know," Wendy said in a softer voice. "But I didn't have the airfare, and I wasn't going to have you pay our way. Besides, it would have been hard—seeing you and David. I was always so jealous of you guys."

"Of us?"

"Yeah." Wendy leaned her head back against the chair. "You've got such a great marriage. David is so thoughtful and understanding—besides being so good-looking. Of course, in the beginning, Dennis was loving and thoughtful too. It was when he drank that he became impossible.

When Dennis sobered up, he felt awful about the things he'd done. He couldn't apologize enough and kept saying he was going to change. I should have listened to my mom. She always told me you can't change a man—unless he's in diapers."

The humor helped dispel some of the tension. Then Wendy added, "After we separated, the bishop recommended that Dennis and I see a marriage counselor."

"I was surprised when Dennis agreed to go."

"I was even more surprised when he also agreed to meet with me and the bishop." Wendy's voice was glum.

"You told me he stopped drinking. Did he really, or was he just hiding it?"

"I think he really stopped. I started believing we might be able to work things out. Then the bishop said that I ought to—" Wendy stopped abruptly, her eyes filling with tears. "I never should have done it—" She scrubbed at her eyes and in a furious voice cried, "I trusted him! I did what he told me to do, and—and it was the biggest mistake of my life! *That's* when I stopped going to church. And I wasn't about to go back, not as long as he was bishop."

Erica stared. "I'm so sorry. What was it he told you to do?"

Taking a deep breath, Wendy glanced at her watch. "Saved by the bell. I'll have to tell you some other time. I'm going to be late for work if I don't get going." She got to her feet and stretched as though stiff.

"Are you okay?" Erica asked.

"Yeah. Talking about it just brings back a lot of memories. All of them bad." As Wendy walked out, Erica looked after her. She still didn't know what the bishop had said or what had happened afterwards, but one thing was clear: whatever it was had struck Wendy to the core.

* * *

That night at dinner, Erica asked Brandon and Megan about their days. Brandon was eager to tell how well he had done at dodgeball and that his friend Justin had gotten sick after lunch and had to see the nurse.

"Why don't you tell us about the bus ride and what kind of pudding you had for lunch?" Megan replied sarcastically. Too young to completely understand but aware she was being disparaging, Brandon looked at his sister quizzically. Megan decided to make it perfectly clear. "Who cares about your game or someone getting sick? Get real, Brandon."

The hurt in his eyes was plain to see. "It isn't necessary to talk to your brother like that," Erica reprimanded her. "After all, I *did* ask about his day. I wanted to hear what Brandon had to say." Megan rolled her eyes and took her plate to the sink.

Trying to repair the damage, Erica said earnestly, "I'm glad you told me about your day. You know, I always liked playing dodgeball when I was in school." Brandon looked a little perkier. "Hey, I'm going to walk around the neighborhood after dishes are done. Want to go with me?"

"Sure!"

Brandon rode his scooter, following Erica as she went door to door, asking if anyone had seen anything unusual the previous Saturday night. Most of those that opened their doors were leery and said little. A few didn't answer the door, but if Erica happened to glance back, she often caught a glimpse of a face peeking out or curtains swinging back into place.

When they got back, Erica went into the backyard and called her husband, who answered promptly. "Hi, gorgeous! How was your day?"

"Long. What about yours?"

"You'll never believe what happened," David said

"What?"

"My police chief got a phone call this morning. From Detective Lund."

"*My* Detective Lund?"

"That's the one. I was standing right there when he called. Lund wanted to check up on you and get a little information about me as well."

"Goodness. I had no idea he'd do that. What did Chief Brown say?"

"He told Detective Lund not to trust you an inch, that you were sneaky and underhanded and that he didn't trust me any more than he did you. And that I'd recently been placed on probation for stealing paper clips and Doritos from his office."

"*What?*"

"Then he busted out laughing. The chief thinks he's hilarious."

Erica was well acquainted with Chief Brown's peculiar sense of humor. "The question is did Detective Lund think he was hilarious?"

"Oh, he knew it was cop humor. Then the chief praised us like crazy. You'd blush to hear what he said about you. As for me, I'm thinking about running for president now."

"You've got me curious now—what did he say?"

"Chief Brown said I was a top-notch policeman, that I'm conscientious and fulfill my duties in an exemplary manner. He actually used the word *exemplary*. The chief said he knew you very well and that you are a first-class detective, have the utmost integrity, and are highly professional as is everyone at Pinnacle Investigations. Chief Brown told him you'd helped us out on a few cases and he trusted you completely. Then he hung up and asked me what the *blank* I was standing around for and to get back to work."

Erica laughed. "I hope that gives Detective Lund a little more confidence in me." She then told him about Megan sniping at her brother during dinner. "Thank goodness she and Brandon get along most of the time. I'm trying to be friends with her, but Megan's still a little moody and suspicious."

"Isn't that a working definition of a teenager?" David asked wryly.

Changing the subject again, Erica said, "I went to the motel where Gregory Tyson stayed and talked with the employees."

"Hadn't the police done that already?"

"Of course, but Detective Lund is not all that eager to share information with me. Besides, it doesn't hurt to cover the same territory. I might come up with something new. The employees didn't seem to mind me asking questions."

"I know I'd love it if a certain beautiful, green-eyed investigator asked *me* a few questions." She giggled, and David went on. "Did you find out anything?"

"Not really. I'm going back on Friday to talk to a couple of people who weren't there today. There's a third one, but he's on vacation." Erica then told David about the conversation she'd had that morning with Lee.

"He couldn't find Wendy? That's strange. Have you asked her where she was?"

"I was going to, but we started talking about when she and Dennis separated. There was some sort of problem with the bishop—that's why she stopped going to church—but she's never told me exactly what happened."

"But she tells you everything."

"I know. It must have been something awful."

David returned to the case. "If Wendy did leave the house, it would have been right about the time Tyson was shot. Maybe she saw or heard something."

"I'll ask her about that tonight when she gets home, but I really think she would have told me if she had. Anyway, it's still possible Wendy was in the house."

"Maybe." David's voice was hesitant. "But from what you've said, it's a pretty small house. Maybe she saw something and is scared to admit it. If Wendy did leave, let's just hope she's got a good alibi."

"She doesn't *need* an alibi," Erica said vehemently. "Wendy had nothing to do with this!"

"I'm sure she didn't, but if Wendy did leave the house, why didn't she say so? The police are going to take a very dim view of someone who lied about their whereabouts when a murder was committed." David added, "Whatever happened, there are going to be fireworks when Lee tells the police he couldn't find Wendy."

"I know," Erica said dismally. Then something hit her. "Hey, you just made me realize something."

"I'm brilliant that way."

"You said Wendy will need an alibi, but she's not the only one. Lee said he came upstairs and when he couldn't find Wendy, he finished the éclairs. *But no one actually saw him do it.* That means Lee was alone and unaccounted for too. He's going to need an alibi just as much as Wendy."

* * *

That evening, Erica was in the front room when Wendy came home. Sinking into a chair, Wendy asked, "How are the kids?"

"Fine. They're in bed." Erica set down her book and held out a bag of chocolate truffles. "Have one. It'll make you forget all your woes."

"I might need more than one," Wendy said dryly. After popping it in her mouth, she closed her eyes. "Ah, that *is* good. Reminds me of that saying from *The Pickwick Papers*: 'There's nothing better than a good friend, except a good friend with chocolate.'" Then she said, "Hand me another one. I'm on a roll."

After pausing a few moments to savor, Wendy took off her shoes and began rubbing her feet. "Oh, I forgot to tell you. I invited Stephen over for dinner tomorrow night."

With a mischievous glint in her emerald eyes, Erica asked, "Shall I make myself scarce or hide in the closet and pop out if he starts putting the moves on you?"

"No need for that," Wendy replied dismally. "It's hardly going to be a romantic evening. Jaime's coming too."

Erica was dumbfounded. "Why did you ask her?"

"I didn't. Stephen asked if she could come. He said Jaime was struggling—that it was hard being new in town and not knowing anyone.

He thought it might perk Jaime up to go out rather than have to stay cooped up in her apartment."

"Gee, isn't he romantic—"

"Oh, Stephen was just being nice."

"There's such a thing as being too nice," Erica countered darkly.

"That's not all. Lee told me tonight that Brandon called and invited him to dinner." When Erica looked puzzled, Wendy frowned. "Don't ask me why. I'd already told Brandon I was having Stephen over, and for some reason, he decided to take it upon himself and invite Lee. I called Brandon to chew him out about it, but he said he'd invited Lee because we're not supposed to 'judge other people but treat them nice.'"

Ah, mystery explained. Erica tried not to smile. "Say, I wanted to ask you something about the night Gregory Tyson was killed." Before Wendy could object, Erica hurried on. "I overheard you tell Detective Lund that you were in the house all evening, but when I came in to call 911, I didn't see you. I thought you were in the basement, but you weren't in the house, were you?" The last was spoken as more of a statement than a question.

A guilty flush crept over Wendy's cheeks, and there was some emotion Erica couldn't name on her face. "No." In a quiet voice, Wendy added, "But I was only gone a few minutes."

"Where did you go?"

"My neighbor, Suzanne, had offered to lend me a pretty serving plate. I was supposed to get it that morning but forgot. I wanted to put the éclairs on it, so I ran over to get it."

"Why didn't you tell the police?"

"Because I knew what they would think," Wendy replied stiffly. "Of course they're going to suspect me if they know I left the house right about the time that man was shot. Even without telling them, did you see the way they were looking at me?" Pent-up anxiety made her voice shake slightly. "As if I had something to do with shooting that poor man!"

"The police are going to check out everyone," Erica explained. "They are *not* going to focus automatically on you, Wendy. You shouldn't have tried to hide that you left the house. It's not going to look good when they find out you didn't tell the truth. And they *are* going to find out eventually because they're going to talk to all of your neighbors." She paused. "At least there's one good thing—your friend Suzanne can provide you with an alibi."

"Well, ah, I don't think she can."

"Why not?"

"Because I didn't actually see her." Wendy looked stricken. "You see, I called Suzanne right after you left. She was just leaving but said she'd leave the tray on her porch. But, but *you* can vouch for me. You saw me come home with the tray!"

Erica's memory was phenomenal, and she remembered Wendy had been holding a glass tray when she walked in. But there was something else. "Why did you come in the front door that night? You always use the side door."

Was there a momentary hesitation before she answered? "Because Suzanne lives that way." Then, in a tight voice, Wendy asked, "Do you really think the police are going to talk with the neighbors?"

Feeling impatient, Erica grabbed another chocolate. "There was a *murder*! *Of course* they're going to talk to the neighbors! In fact, they probably already have."

There was fatigue in every line of Wendy's face. "I should have told the police, but I was so scared. Now it's going to look ten times worse."

"There's more. I talked with Lee this morning. He'd covered up the fact that he couldn't find you that night. Lee said he was going to call and tell the police. You've got to call Detective Lund yourself—and soon."

Wendy's face was deadly pale. "Would—would *you* tell the police that I went to the neighbor's to get a plate?"

It was an outrageous request. "Certainly not. That's something you need to do now—before I see Detective Lund tomorrow."

"But if you're going to see him anyway, why can't you tell him? You got along with him so well! He likes you. And you can explain things so much better than I can." Wendy's voice was thin, and her hands were nervously twining. "I just can't do it! I can't! Please! You're so much better at this type of thing than I am!"

Her pleading finally got to Erica. "Oh, all right." She frowned. "But only because I'm going to go see Detective Lund anyway. But you owe me. Big time."

"I already owe you. Big time," Wendy said humbly.

"Oh, one other thing. I've decided to go to Memphis. That's where Gregory Tyson lived. I want to talk with Gregory's wife and boss."

"You'll be flying standby, won't you?"

"Yes, I'm so glad Chris still works for an airline," Erica said. "He'd better not get laid off either because I want to fly to Europe in a year or two. I have a couple of cousins over there that I'd like to visit—one in Strasbourg, France, and one in Lausanne, Switzerland."

"Wow! Lucky you! I'd love to go to Europe. When are you going to Memphis?"

"Early next week. I want to find out more about Gregory Tyson: what kind of a man he was, what his friends were like. The more you find out about the victim, the more you can find out about the murderer."

Wendy shivered dramatically, even a little theatrically, Erica thought. But then, murder was a horrid thing to think about.

That night, Erica called her brother Chris and asked him to start watching for open flights to Memphis. Erica went to bed satisfied at having put her plans into motion.

CHAPTER 5

Tentative rays of an early morning sun were pouring through the kitchen window when Erica came up from the basement. No one was there, but sounds of activity came from the bathroom. Through the doorway, she saw Megan in the front room, peering out the window that faced the street. Megan always looked more substantial than she actually was because of the unrelenting black she wore. As Erica walked in, the silver chains draped around Megan's waist clinked softly as she closed a loose-leaf binder that had *Osceola High* printed on the front.

"*Osceola*—I've heard that name before, in an old country-western song."

"Chief Osceola was a Seminole war leader," Megan said, shoving the binder in her backpack. "He was never really a chief, but everyone calls him that. One of the counties in Florida is named after him too."

Erica sat on the end of the couch. "He must have been a very influential man, then."

"I guess so. Chief Osceola wanted to preserve the Seminoles' way of life and so to protect them, he moved the Indians deeper and deeper into Florida."

"Because the white people were encroaching on Indian ground?"

"Yeah. Osceola tried to stop them, but the whites kept coming, taking land from the Seminoles and breaking treaties."

Erica shook her head in sadness. Then she asked, "Is *Kissimmee* an Indian word?"

"It was, but the spelling changed a lot." Megan shrugged lightly. "I've forgotten what the original word was, but it wasn't anything like *Kissimmee*."

When Megan glanced out the window, Erica said, "Could I ask you something?"

"I have to go," Megan said quickly, her guard back up. "Kimberly will be here any minute."

"This will only take a second. On the night of the murder, your mom went to a neighbor's house to pick up a serving tray. Did you go with her?"

Megan's lip curled scornfully. "Right. Like *that* would take two people."

"But you came into the kitchen the same time as your Mom."

"So what?" Her brow darkened. "We both got back to the house at the same time. I went to see a friend that lives a few houses away. Any other questions, counselor?"

Erica ignored the jibe. "Why don't you like Stephen? He seems like a nice guy."

For just a moment, Megan's eyes met hers, and Erica was aware of some pent-up, inner force emanating from her. There was something powerful here that ran deep, but Erica had no idea what.

"Stephen's a moron," Megan said shortly. "I don't think he even has opposable thumbs."

Unable to help herself, Erica laughed. Then she continued, "One other thing. When you came into the kitchen that night, you seemed out of breath. Why was that?"

"I stayed and talked too long with my friend. I knew if I was late, Mom would kill me, so I ran home. Is that a crime?"

Megan's answer seemed a little too pat—even rehearsed—but before Erica could say anything else, a car horn sounded outside. Megan turned sharply, black strands of hair standing slightly apart from one another as if in muted alarm. It was a good thing Erica said good-bye quickly, for she barely got the words out before the door slammed.

* * *

The Kissimmee Police Department was housed in a solid, redbrick building—the kind of substantial building that gave off an indefinable sense of stability and authority. Erica went through security and was given directions. Detective Patrick Lund was sitting behind a desk that was every bit as big and bulky as he was. Standing up to shake her hand, Patrick offered her a chair. He had a typical police sergeant's face, unexpressive and self-contained but with shrewd eyes.

"What can I do for you?" he asked.

"A couple of things. First, you said that I should come to you if I came across any information that might be useful."

The detective's eyebrows raised slightly. "Okay. What do you have?"

"Yes, well. This is a little difficult, but I'll start by saying that Wendy wanted me to talk to you." Patrick waited patiently, and she went on. "You see, there was a bit of a misunderstanding about the night of the murder. Wendy said she was in the house the entire evening, but actually she did leave for a short time."

"That's a misunderstanding? Most people would call it a lie."

Oh boy.

However, his reaction was not unexpected, and Erica was prepared. "Most people don't come home to find a dead body in their driveway. It blew Wendy away. She wasn't thinking clearly then but feels badly about it now and wants to set the record straight."

"I see." The detective's face was like stone. "Wendy feels bad but not bad enough to come here herself."

Not one to be flustered easily, Erica remained unperturbed. "Since I'm more used to this kind of thing, she asked me to talk to you."

With short, impatient movements that betrayed his irritation, Detective Lund yanked out a notepad and grabbed a pen. "All right. Where did Wendy go and how long was she gone?"

"She went to a neighbor's house to pick up a serving tray. She says it only took her a few minutes."

"What's the neighbor's name, and can she verify what time Wendy was there?"

"Suzanne Kilpatrick. And no, she never saw Wendy—she left the tray on the porch. I timed the walk over and back. Fast walk, two minutes. Slow walk, three minutes. One way."

Patrick Lund looked up from his notepad, impressed. "You've done your homework, I see. I heard you were a first-class investigator." He suddenly cleared his throat as if he had said too much then went on. "Since Wendy was having a party, we can assume she walked fast. But there's no way to know for sure if she went straight to the neighbor's and back."

The implication hung heavy in the air. He was testing her, Erica knew, but now was not the time to proclaim Wendy's innocence. Doing so would be pointless without an alibi or eyewitness.

Patrick continued. "It's rather a spectacular coincidence, isn't it, that Wendy just happened to go to a neighbor's house at precisely the time

Tyson was shot? The whole story sounds fishy. You don't leave your guests to go pick up a plate. Maybe she was trying to provide herself with an alibi."

Erica couldn't take offense. If she had been in Patrick's shoes, she would have thought the same thing. All she could do was venture an opinion. "I've known Wendy for many years, and I'm positive she had nothing to do with Tyson's murder."

With a slight nod, Patrick acknowledged her statement. "I appreciate you letting us know about this 'misunderstanding.' Most friends would have tried to hide this kind of information. Still, with your background, you knew we would find out about it eventually." He sat back in his chair. With a slight twinkle in his eyes, he said, "I had a phone call yesterday from Lee Grover. Apparently, he was acting on advice you'd given him. I'd venture a guess that your coming here has less to do with Wendy wanting to set the record straight and more with you persuading Wendy that it was in her best interest to tell the truth."

Detective Patrick Lund was an astute man as well as a forthright one. Erica decided to be candid herself. "Wendy was afraid that telling you might mean you'd consider her a suspect."

"She was right."

His clipped words caused a feeling of anxiety to well up under Erica's ribs. "You realize, of course, that Lee doesn't have an alibi for the time Tyson was shot either."

"We're checking him out."

"Wendy doesn't even know Tyson," Erica said. "And even if she did, she would have to be stupid to murder him at her own house."

"That happens quite frequently as a matter of fact." Detective Lund opened a folder and shuffled through some papers. He examined one. "Ah yes. Wendy is a waitress, right?" Patrick looked up and, when Erica nodded, went on. "Waitresses meet a lot of people. Even though Wendy says she didn't know Gregory Tyson, perhaps he knew her. He could easily have met Wendy at the restaurant where she works." He looked at the paper. "Friendly's. Now there's a name for you. Gives you ideas. Maybe he met Wendy there and liked what he saw—perhaps a little too much? They talked, but Wendy rejected his advances. Maybe Tyson wouldn't take no for an answer and started stalking her. Wendy became frightened and decided to do something about it."

He was fishing for information. Erica stated flatly, "Wendy would have told me if someone was stalking her."

"Ah, but Wendy doesn't always tell the truth, now, does she?"

Erica looked at the detective steadfastly. "Wendy only lied because she was scared."

"She gets scared easy, doesn't she?"

"Besides, if Tyson lived in Memphis, he would hardly be a regular customer at Friendly's."

"A lot of businessmen travel a good deal."

She thought fast. "But if Tyson came to Florida a lot, surely he would have contacted Stephen. The only real clue we have is the connection between Gregory Tyson and Stephen Watkins. If we assume Tyson was going to see Stephen, the fact that he was killed *before* he saw Stephen sends up a red flag. It could be that the shooter was afraid of what Tyson was going to say to Stephen."

"A long shot, but I suppose anything's possible," Patrick acknowledged. "I'll find out if anyone connected with Tyson followed him to Florida."

"Did you find out when Tyson arrived in Orlando?"

Again, Patrick rifled the stack of papers. Finding the one he wanted, he ran a thick finger down the sheet. "He flew in on Friday, May 1, arriving at the Orlando Airport at 8:30 a.m. He rented a car and drove to a business park in Orlando, where he spent most of the day. In the late afternoon, he drove to Kissimmee and rented a room at the Starlight Motel on Highway 192. We don't know his movements after that, but we're working on it."

"Have you found out anything about his family or friends in Tennessee?" It would be interesting to see if the detective would actually tell her.

Detective Lund evaded the question. "His family and friends are being interviewed now. They might be able to tell us why Tyson was carrying a switchblade that night."

"He was carrying a switchblade?" The meek man pictured in the driver's license didn't look like someone who would carry that kind of weapon.

As if he could read her mind, Patrick said grimly, "Gregory Tyson might have come to Kissimmee with a score to settle."

"But Stephen said they were good friends."

"Most people don't carry a switchblade when they go to see good friends." Patrick looked at her. "He also had a piece of paper in his wallet with Wendy's name and address. We'll check with his wife to see if it's

Tyson's handwriting." He reflected a moment. "I've got a favor to ask—if you're willing."

"What is it?"

"You're acquainted with Stephen. Ask him if he knows why Tyson would be carrying a switchblade. He might open up to you more than he would to us."

"Sure. I'll let you know what I find out. Also, I went around Wendy's neighborhood last night, talking to people."

"That was a stupid thing to do—" Patrick's voice was incredulous. "A pretty woman like you out alone in that neighborhood at night? I thought you had better sense than that."

"It was still daylight, and I wasn't alone. Brandon, Wendy's son, was with me."

"Oh well, that's different, then," he said caustically. "As long as you had an eight-year-old bodyguard with you . . ."

"Don't worry; I have a black belt. And if a man answered the door, I made sure they knew I couldn't talk long because my husband was waiting for me at home." Erica grinned. "Unfortunately, I didn't get anything but a lot of suspicion." Detective Lund didn't look surprised. "One other thing: I've decided to go to Memphis and talk to Gregory Tyson's family and business associates."

The wary look returned. "I told you, we've got people working on that already." Patrick's voice had exasperation as well as an authoritative ring in it. Then he challenged, "Do you really think you can get more information than a trained police detective?"

Erica stood her ground. "I'm trained too. People can be guarded when talking to the police, but since I'm in a different category they can relax. A lot of people find it easier to talk to me than to a police officer. Interviewing people is an art. If you go about it the right way, not only can you get your questions answered, you can find out all sorts of useful information. I've found that when people are relaxed, they let all kinds of information slip out—some of it very useful."

Patrick was unconvinced. "Have it your way," he replied grudgingly, "but I still don't think you're going to get any more information than our detectives."

"One of the first things we need to know is if Gregory Tyson's murder was random or if someone deliberately planned to kill him. And one thing to consider is what you've already mentioned: Wendy doesn't live in a very good area."

"That's an understatement. Your friend lives in a high crime area. We get called to that section of the city at least once a week for one thing or another."

"Maybe some thug mistook Tyson for someone else."

"Could be. It happens a lot but usually in home invasions. People kick the door in only to find out they have the wrong house or that the bums they want have cleared out."

"I'll find out what I can about Tyson when I talk to his family and friends. There's a lot we need to know." Erica used *we* in a conscious effort to make herself part of the team. "Finding out more about Gregory Tyson should give us some clue about his killer. For instance, if Tyson liked to blackmail people, we could then look for someone who could be blackmailed. If Tyson is wealthy, we'll look for who stands to inherit."

When she stood up to leave, Patrick Lund's rough expression had softened considerably. "I think I had you pegged wrong," he said frankly. "I guess I've had to deal with one too many civilians who fancy themselves crime solvers. They can be real—" He described them in colorful terms.

Erica was sympathetic. "I know what you mean. My husband and I have both come across people who can make things difficult."

"But you've actually been helpful. A refreshing experience." He chuckled and shook her hand. "You tell Wendy it was a good thing you came in. You see, besides talking to Lee Grover, we've already talked with her neighbor, Suzanne Kilpatrick."

And not said anything until now.

"Call me when you get back from Memphis," Patrick said. It was as good as him giving her his blessing.

* * *

Erica had barely gotten through the door when Wendy asked how the meeting had gone with Detective Lund. Erica gave her a full account then asked if she'd ever met Tyson at Friendly's. She had not. Wendy's face lost some of its tautness when Erica assured her everything would be all right.

At the end, she gave Erica a look that was touchingly full of trust then left the subject. "I hate to say it, but my little dinner is starting to take on a life of its own," Wendy said. "Stephen called to see if it was all right if Reed Devoe, his branch manager, came. Stephen wanted to invite

him because Reed helped him land an important contract." Responding
to Erica's dark look, she smiled winningly. "This is actually a good thing
because Stephen said he'd bring dessert. Isn't that great?" She took a quick
breath. "I told him to bring plenty because Suzanne Kilpatrick and her
husband are coming too."

"Why don't you just put up a sign out front saying, 'Free Dinner—
Everyone Welcome'?"

"I know it's mushroomed, but I didn't know what else to do." Wendy
sighed. "Suzanne called this morning and wanted to have us over
for dinner—she felt really bad about missing Brandon's baptism and
wanted to make it up to us. When I said I was having a little dinner
party tonight, she kind of invited herself." At Erica's frown, Wendy said
defensively, "What was I supposed to say?"

"*No* usually works for me."

"I couldn't do that! Besides, Suzanne said she'd make her fabulous
French Bread.[3] It's to die for—you'll see. She entered it at the county fair
and won a blue ribbon."

* * *

Friday night, Stephen and Jaime arrived together. Erica opened the
door, shut it, then opened it again to startled faces. Then Wendy came
in, dressed in a cornflower-blue blouse and denim skirt. After welcoming
them, she moved closer to Stephen as if claiming her spot. Jaime Russell
was just as attractive as Erica remembered. Her nose was a little large but
was no drawback, as it gave her a patrician look. Her only flaw seemed
to be her eyes, which were darkly cool and impersonal.

Wendy's fair skin was suffused with extra color as her eyes went over
Jaime, whose burnished black hair tumbled down in glorious waves over a
tight red sweater that showed off her slender figure. There was something
dramatic and a little foreboding about that bright, bold color that suited
the younger woman.

"When Stephen told me he was bringing pies and cookies, I got some
ice cream," Jaime said, holding up a sack. "Shall I put it in the freezer?"

The doorbell rang, and Wendy waved vaguely toward the kitchen.
"Yes, please." She then opened the door to a tall man with a long, narrow
face. "Reed! So nice to see you. Please come in."

---

3   See appendix at the end of the book for this recipe.

Smiling broadly, Stephen shook Reed's hand. "Long time, no see," he joked. "You know Wendy of course, and this is her good friend Erica Coleman. Erica's visiting from Utah. Erica, this is Reed Devoe."

If she had to guess, Erica would have said Reed was in his midfifties. He reminded her of a ferret, with his dark hair brushed straight back, streaked with grey and looking a bit greasy. Unlike Stephen, who had filled out a bit with age, Reed was still lean and trim.

"Very nice to meet you," Erica said. "Stephen tells me you're the branch manager."

Reed's eyes, which were rather hard like marbles, stared at her strangely as if there might be some deep, unpleasant meaning behind her words.

"Yes, I am," he replied slowly as though waiting for further comment.

Wendy jumped in. "When Stephen moved here, Reed was so helpful in explaining how things were run and helping him get started," she told Erica glibly. Reed's face twisted slightly as if in pain, but it failed to have any impact on Wendy, who went on cheerily. "Stephen can't say enough about how helpful Reed has been."

Erica looked from her friend's kindly face to Stephen, who wore a similar benevolent expression. They both seemed blissfully unaware of Reed's disagreeable expression. Perhaps she was reading him wrong. Maybe his ferret-like exterior hid a heart of gold.

Brandon appeared and started tugging on Wendy's sleeve. "What is it, sweetie?" she asked, ruffling his hair affectionately.

"Jaime wanted to ask you something. She's in the kitchen."

Looking faintly worried, Wendy excused herself. Stephen went with her.

To Erica's surprise, Reed began asking her about the murder. She tried to sidetrack him by giving noncommittal answers, but he persisted. At one point, in an effort to draw her out, Reed commented, "That must have been a very interesting evening."

There were a great many adjectives that could have described that night, but *interesting* was not one of them. *Dreadful* or *shocking* would have been more accurate. "It was horrifying," Erica said with feeling.

"Yes, of course. That would be a natural reaction since you're Wendy's best friend."

Erica was perplexed. "What do you mean?"

"I heard Wendy wasn't in the house when the murder occurred. Since she doesn't have an alibi, the police surely must suspect her."

How did this strange man find that out? Erica couldn't keep the distaste she felt out of her voice as she said, "The police will find that Wendy had nothing to do with the murder."

Reed's dark expression didn't change, and there was something distinctly shivery about his eyes. "It does seem strange, you must admit, that a man was shot right by her door just after Wendy left the house?"

"I hope you're not implying that Wendy had anything to do with it," Erica replied frostily.

"Oh not at all!" Reed said in a revoltingly insincere manner. "I'm just looking at it from a policeman's perspective, that's all. It's going to make them wonder, isn't it?" As his lips stretched in a tight smile, Erica decided it was the most disagreeable smile she had ever come across. What possessed him to say such things?

"I know Wendy very well, and I resent your implication." Just then, some sound made her turn. She saw a flash of blue move back into the kitchen. Wendy. How long had she been listening? Surely Reed had been aware of her presence.

"I didn't mean to offend you," Reed said impassively. "I was just making conversation."

"Which is now over. If you'll excuse me—" Erica was glad to get away. She liked neither the man nor his manner.

When the doorbell rang, Wendy was still in the kitchen, so Erica answered it. It was Suzanne Kilpatrick and her husband. They hurried to the kitchen with their loaves of bread as Lee Grover came up the steps and into the house. He watched as Erica shut, opened, then shut the door again. He took it in stride, looking at her with a face that always seemed a little impassive, eyes faraway, until he smiled. Then it was like the sun breaking through the clouds. He took Erica's hand, clasping it as if seeing her was the best treat he could ask for.

"You look very pretty tonight, as always." He had a deep, affable voice.

"Flattery will get you everywhere," Erica smiled.

Lee looked around. "I hope tonight's little gathering turns out better than the last one."

"Amen," said Erica fervently, noticing how his eyes were searching the room. "If you're looking for Wendy, she's in the kitchen."

He grinned boyishly. "I'll go say hello."

A few minutes later, Wendy came out to the front room with the others and asked Lee to give a blessing on the food. Everyone moved toward the kitchen, where Erica had arranged the food buffet style. Earlier, Wendy had told her, "You go ahead and arrange the food to your quirky little heart's content. No sense in me doing it when you're just going to redo it."

Now, Erica looked over the table, pleased to see everything organized just right: plates, utensils, and napkins on the far left, a large green salad followed by slices of French bread, then the lasagna. Pitchers of ice water were on the far end with paper cups lined up in precise rows, four across and four deep.

Suzanne Kilpatrick, a frizzily permed woman in her late fifties, encouraged everyone to try her bread.

"I'm surprised she didn't bring her blue ribbon to display," Wendy whispered to Erica.

After everyone had dished up, they found places to sit, balancing plates on laps and putting their drinks on the coffee table or corner table. Again, Erica wondered if Wendy had overheard Reed's comments. Wendy looked calm, but her eyes seemed overly bright and there was certain rigidity whenever she looked toward Reed.

Why *had* Reed gone on like he had? It was almost as though he harbored some sort of rancor against Wendy, but why that would be, Erica was at a loss to understand.

The bread *was* good, and later, when Erica went in to get another slice, Stephen was cutting the pies and putting slices on saucers while Wendy added scoops of ice cream. A plate of cookies was nearby.

"This is terrific bread," Erica commented, taking a bite. "I've got to get Suzanne's recipe."

The back door opened, and Megan slid into the room. She eyed them cautiously then looked through the arched opening to the people in the front room.

"Megan!" Wendy said with delight, "I'm so glad you came."

"This is where I live, Mother." Megan's voice dripped scorn. "Where else would I be?"

"I—I just wasn't sure if you'd be here in time for dinner." Wendy stumbled over her words. "I can heat up some lasagna for you."

"I haven't had meat for years," Megan grumbled. "But you never seem to remember that."

"There's a salad," Stephen pointed out, "and some wonderful French bread."

Her eyes flicked over him insolently. "I can see that. I *do* have eyes."

"Megan!" Wendy cried. "That's no way to speak to Stephen."

"Whatever." She dished up some green salad, added several pieces of bread, and went into the front room. Erica followed, sitting next to Megan in the corner.

"You're going to love the bread," Erica assured her. "So, how are you doing?"

"Great," Megan replied in a bored voice.

Erica acted as if she believed her. "I'm glad."

Megan nodded toward Jaime Russell. "How come *she's* here?"

"Stephen thought Jaime might be lonely since she's new in town."

"How can she be lonely when she's always with Stephen?"

She had a point there.

"What's up with her, anyway?" Megan went on. "Stephen is so gross, and she acts like he's Brad Pitt. It's sickening. Maybe she thinks Stephen's rich. Ugh! He'd have to be a billionaire before anyone would be interested in *him*."

Megan was putting into words something Erica had wondered herself. All night, Jaime had been acting like Stephen's Siamese twin. It couldn't be shyness that made her stick to his side—Jaime was friendly and talkative with others. Why then *was* she so interested in Stephen? Yes, Stephen was intelligent, kind, and thoughtful in an old-fashioned way, but that was just it: he was old-fashioned for a reason—he was years older than Jaime. Adding to the mismatch were Stephen's ordinary looks and expanded waistline, while Jaime was dazzlingly attractive and slim as a reed. It was interesting too that when Stephen had asked to bring Jaime, he made it sound as if he was befriending a homely waif instead of a beautiful, confident woman.

During the evening, it was clear Wendy was aware of Jaime's interest. As if to mark her territory, she made a point of joining them as often as possible. However, Wendy's efforts fell flat because her laughter was forced and her talk a little too animated. Jaime also seemed keyed up, Erica thought, but perhaps that was normal for her.

People stayed after dinner to visit. For a time, Erica was trapped by Suzanne, Wendy's ubercurious friend. Like Reed, Suzanne seemed obsessed with the murder and her own bad luck for not being present when it occurred. Erica was gently fielding questions when Brandon walked past clutching a handful of cookies. He looked at her guiltily and appeared vastly relieved when Erica merely smiled. Grinning back, Brandon slipped outside—probably to share the bounty with his friends, Erica thought. Finally, she excused herself and went to the kitchen to see if she could help.

"Thanks for the offer, but I'm just putting the last of the food away," Wendy said. "You go visit, and I'll be out in a minute."

Stepping into the front room, Erica kept a wary eye out for Suzanne.

Stephen noticed her. "Erica, come sit with us," he called genially, beckoning her to where he was sitting with Jamie. Reed Devoe was there too, looking like he was being held hostage.

"So, how is the job going?" Erica asked Jaime.

"Great! Stephen's been such a sweetheart. He's been so wonderful to help me even with all his worries." She gave him an adoring look.

"Worries?"

"Well, you know." Jaime directed a fleeting look toward Megan and, in a low voice, added, "With Wendy and Megan."

Erica glanced across the room too, trying to gauge if Megan could hear, but she appeared to be trapped in the corner by Suzanne and her husband.

Jaime continued. "You know how Megan acts toward Stephen. It makes things so difficult."

"Nonsense," Stephen objected. "It's hard on children when their mother goes out on dates. It's a natural reaction."

"Her behavior is extreme and inexcusable," Jaime replied artlessly, no longer bothering to lower her voice. "Personally, I think Megan is mentally unstable."

When Erica looked at her sharply, Jaime added, "Wendy ought to take her to a good psychiatrist—get some help. There are a lot of good medications available now."

"Says the voice of experience?" Reed commented dryly.

Jaime was the kind of woman who could take care of herself with perfect ease, and she laughed lightly. "I deserved that of course. Stephen always excuses her behavior, but I personally think the girl needs some classes in anger management."

How high handed she was! Erica was glad when Reed drawled, "And did it help you?"

Shaking a finger at him playfully, Jaime spoke lightly. "You're trying to get a rise out of me, aren't you? But I'm not the one with the problem."

"Megan may have some issues with me, but she's going through a difficult stage of life," Stephen protested.

At least someone had compassion. "I agree with Stephen," Erica said. "Being a teenager is rough. I'd never want to go through it again." She then looked hard at Jaime. "But then, this isn't my business. It only concerns Megan, Wendy, and Stephen."

"Of course," Jaime said sweetly, her voice like chocolate sauce. "I just feel bad for Stephen when she treats him so dreadfully."

Glancing across the room, Erica saw that Megan's cheeks were flaming and she was staring furiously at Jaime. She must have heard. Even from where she sat, Erica could sense the anger in the girl. Megan rose, as if pulled to her feet by strings, and Erica was sure she was going to come over and have it out with Jaime. There was a volcanic look of rage on her face as she approached, but when Erica shook her head at her, Megan veered off and stalked into the kitchen. Shortly after, Lee went in as well.

"I think I'll go and get us something to drink," Jaime said, uncrossing her shapely legs and rising. "I'll be right back."

"Don't bring anything for me," Reed said. "I'm going to call it a night. I took some work home that I need to finish." He stood. "I'll go and tell Wendy good-bye."

"That man never stops working," Stephen commented. "Even on Saturday, he's always in the office." They chatted until Jaime returned with three cups of coffee, creamer, and spoons.

"Too bad Reed left. He was the life of the party," Jaime said mockingly.

"Thanks anyway," Erica said as Jaime set the tray on the table, "but I don't drink coffee."

Jaime gave her a strange look. "Really? Well, you're not missing much—this is instant. Wendy told me she only keeps it for guests." She frowned slightly. "Hope that's all right, Stephen."

"I know what would help," Stephen said. "Some of those chocolate chip cookies. They make anything taste good." He started to rise, but Jaime forestalled him.

"I'm already up. I'll get them."

Erica went to the bathroom and when she returned, Jaime and Stephen were talking about work. Then Suzanne and her husband came over and joined them. Erica noticed that Stephen's eyelids were drooping. And he thought *Reed* worked hard!

Jaime noticed too. Leaning over, she nudged Stephen. "I think we'd better call it a night."

"I'm sorry." Stephen blinked and looked embarrassed. "I don't know why I'm suddenly so tired." His words were a bit slow and thick.

"It's your inner clock," Suzanne said, her voice having a ring of authority. "Once you get past a certain age, your body chemistry changes and you have a hard time staying awake."

As she spoke, Stephen leaned forward, as if concentrating very hard on her words would keep him awake. Despite that, his head dipped forward slightly as he started to nod off. He caught himself and shook his head slightly to clear it.

Suzanne's husband winked at Stephen. "Don't worry. She has the same effect on me! But it is getting late. We ought to be going." The Kilpatricks said good-bye then stopped to talk with Wendy by the front door. Stephen's eyes closed again.

"Stephen, yoo-hoo!" Jaime put a hand on his arm and gently shook him. "We'd better go before you start to snore."

Stephen opened his eyes, but they seemed out of focus. His strange, introspective look worried Erica, and she leaned toward him. "Stephen, are you all right?"

"I'm not feeling very well," he admitted in a voice that was low and slurred. Stephen had the look of a deer caught in headlights as he forced himself to keep his eyes open. "Could I have some water?"

Jaime sprang up. Leaning back against the couch, Stephen had a hard time holding his head up. It lolled forward then back as though he had no control.

"Get Wendy," Stephen whispered.

Erica rushed outside to get Wendy, who had walked out with the Kilpatricks. Curious, they followed her inside as Wendy hurried over to Stephen. Lee came over to see what was going on as Stephen's arms went limp and his body sagged.

Back with the glass of water Stephen obviously could not drink, Jaime cried shrilly, "What's the matter with him?"

Thoroughly alarmed, Erica knelt, her long hair falling in her face as she took his pulse. It was far too rapid. A light sheen of sweat stood out on Stephen's forehead, and his face was gray and pinched. A faint sound came from his lips, but it was indecipherable.

Blinking, Stephen tried again, looking up out of anguished eyes. In a voice that was low and breathless, he whispered, "Please—please—"

Looking up, Erica told Wendy curtly, "Call 911."

"What is it? What's wrong with him?" Wendy's voice was high pitched and frantic.

She was going to be no help at all. Erica turned to Lee. "Call 911. *Now!*"

CHAPTER 6

IT WAS A LONG NIGHT at the hospital. After calling 911, Lee had gone outside to wave down the paramedics, who arrived within minutes. After working on Stephen, they loaded him in the ambulance. As the wail of the siren began to fade, Erica asked Megan to stay with Brandon. She then put an arm around Wendy, who was moving like someone in a dream, and led her to the car.

They were joined in the waiting room by Jaime and Lee. At long last, a doctor came out to say they were still running tests but Stephen was out of danger. The doctor seemed reluctant to say anything more than that Stephen was being monitored closely. Wendy was allowed to see Stephen briefly, and then they all drove home to get a few hours' sleep.

Wendy and Erica were back at the hospital early the next morning. Since Wendy had to go straight to work afterwards, she wore her navy and white uniform. Stephen's door was partially open and after pulling on a pair of gloves and knocking, Erica pushed it open, closed it for a second, opened it again, and found Stephen awake, lying quietly in bed with a tired and pale face. There was a shadow of beard around his jaw, and his eyes were dark and sunken under level brows.

Leaning over the bed railing, Wendy gave him a quick kiss. "Boy, some people will do anything to get out of going to work," she teased, making the corners of his mouth turn up.

Erica's bracelets clinked together softly as she rested her hands on the bed railing. Stephen glanced at the rails. "I feel like I'm in a crib."

"How are you this morning?" Wendy asked. "Did the doctors find out what was wrong?"

Stephen's eyes dropped. "The doctor hasn't been in yet this morning. I see you're ready for work. Morning shift, huh?"

"Yes." Wendy was hesitant. "But if you need me to stay, I will."

"Oh no," Stephen protested. "I'm fine, really. I'm sure they'll let me go home this morning."

There was a light knock at the door and before Stephen could answer, Jaime strode in, looking fresh and lovely in a light blue blouse and blue suede skirt. She looked slightly surprised to see Wendy and Erica.

"Now I understand why the nurses weren't too thrilled with me," she said. "It looks like you've already got plenty of company." Jaime moved closer. "I wanted to see how my favorite boss was doing before I went to work. I know you were working on the Brookside account, so I'll take care of that. If I have any questions, Reed will help me."

"Or you could ask Diana," he said with a mischievous grin.

"True. But only if I want things set back a week or two."

Stephen explained to Erica, "Diana's the receptionist. She thinks she rules the roost and isn't always helpful to newcomers like Jaime."

They talked for a while, then Wendy glanced at the clock. "That can't be right," she exclaimed, checking her watch then looking at Erica. "I was going to take you home, but I'll be late if I do."

"Take the car; I'll catch a bus home."

"But how will Stephen get home if the doctor releases him?"

"Look, I'll take you to work, Wendy," Jaime offered. "Then Erica will have the car."

Wendy bent over and kissed Stephen. "I'll call on my break to see how you're doing."

"If I don't answer, I'll be at home, doing laps in the pool."

Wendy laughed and gave a wave as she and Jaime went out the door.

Glancing at the window, Erica asked, "Does that bother you?"

"Does what bother me?" His brows came together in a furrow.

"Oh, I'll fix it for you." Erica went over and straightened one of the slats in the blinds that was tilting the wrong way. "There. Now that won't bother you all day." She pulled a chair close to the bed. "I couldn't help noticing that you didn't answer Wendy's question. *Did* the doctor find out what was wrong?"

He looked troubled. "Something I ate didn't agree with me."

"Food poisoning? But no one else got sick."

There was a flicker of something on his face. "I don't think that was it. The doctor said she'd explain more when she got all the test results back."

"Sounds serious."

"I guess it was. Last night, one of the nurses told me that if I had gotten to the hospital an hour later, I might have died."

A few minutes later, a capable-looking woman with shoulder-length brown hair and a white coat walked in. "I'm Dr. Phillips," she said pleasantly, nodding at Erica.

"Nice to meet you. I'm Erica, a friend. I'll wait outside until you're done."

There was a small alcove with chairs nearby. Erica picked up a magazine and read about recent advances on colonoscopies until the doctor walked past.

When Erica went back in, the first thing she noticed was that Stephen's face was even paler than before. "Are they going to let you go home this morning?"

"They want to keep me until this afternoon." His voice sounded different—flat.

"Did the doctor have the results of the tests?"

There was a long pause and a short answer. "Yes, she did."

It was obvious Erica would have to prompt him. "The doctor was here quite a while."

"She, ah, had a lot of questions."

"*She* had questions?"

Stephen shifted uneasily. "Yes. The tests show that I had ingested Flurazepam. I'm probably not pronouncing that correctly. It's known more commonly as Dalmane."

"What's Dalmane?"

"Poison."

* * *

Driving on automatic pilot, Erica stopped mechanically at lights and turned where needed while her mind went over Stephen's shocking news. She had to wonder if the doctor wanted to keep Stephen to make sure there were no complications or if it was an excuse to give the police time to get involved. Erica had no doubts the police would be contacted, for it seemed highly unlikely that Stephen could have ingested the poison accidentally.

On the spur of the moment, Erica decided to stop by Stephen's office and talk to Reed Devoe. Erica pulled into the parking lot and was on her way to the front door when she walked past a half-open window.

A woman's shrill voice came floating out. "You wouldn't want to go against me, would you? There are people here that wouldn't like me telling things I know, but you more than any of them, I'm sure." It didn't sound like Jaime, Erica thought.

A man's voice replied, "Is that supposed to be a threat?"

"Look at it any way you like . . ." Erica strained to hear, but the next words were undecipherable. Then the woman whined, "Why did Stephen want you to hire that woman anyway? There's something odd about her. She's always watching everything."

"You couldn't keep up with the work, remember? In fact you said you were doing the work of three people." Erica recognized the man's unpleasant, sneering voice. Reed Devoe. "So far, she's been a lot quicker to learn than you were when you first started."

"Oh, Jaime's quick all right," the woman responded derisively. "Quick to see an opportunity when it's staring her in the face."

Not staying to hear any more, Erica went around the corner and opened the glass-plated door. A few moments later, a thin, middle-aged woman with chin-length grayish hair came down the hall and stood behind the receptionist's counter. The nameplate read Diana Evans. This must be the barracuda Stephen had mentioned. Her sharp eyes looked at Erica expectantly.

"I'd like to see Mr. Devoe."

"And what is this regarding?" Diana's voice was prickly—the same one Erica had heard moments ago.

"It's private."

Diana's V-shaped eyebrows went up, and her face hardened. Picking up the phone, she jabbed at a button with more force than was necessary. There was no sign of Jaime. She was probably in Stephen's office.

"A woman is here to see you, Mr. Devoe. No, she *didn't* give her name," she said shrewishly. Diana replaced the phone. "He'll be right out," she said with a sniff.

Reed came down the hall. "Hello," he said, extending a cool, dry hand. He had thin lips and altogether looked like the sort of man who under-tipped waitresses.

"I hope I haven't caught you at a bad time," Erica said. "I wanted to talk to you."

"Come this way." He led her into an office that was heavily paneled in a dark walnut that reflected little light and gave the room a gloomy air.

A large desk with ornately carved legs occupied the majority of the room. Reed sat behind it and from a distance regarded her with a look that was far from friendly. His dark eyes were curious.

"What can I do for you?" The words were polite but cool with an implication he had been doing something important and disliked being interrupted. The dour nature he had displayed at Wendy's house was still in force. Apparently, that was his natural air.

"I wanted to talk with you if that's all right. Wendy asked me if I'd do a little investigating. She's been very upset at having someone murdered at her house," she added by way of explanation.

"And now Stephen's sick. Jaime told me he was taken to the hospital last night."

"I just came from there. Stephen was poisoned."

Reed's hard little eyes widened. "Poisoned? Jaime didn't say anything about that."

"The doctor came in after she left. Could I ask you a few questions?"

He gave Erica a cold, appraising glance. "Playing detective, are you?"

Erica's eyes narrowed. "I'm not *playing* anything—any more than Stephen is *playing* at being poisoned." The cool note in her voice was a warning.

"He really was poisoned? How extraordinary. I would have thought—" He stopped then changed tracks. "Jaime told me you were a private investigator. Are you any good?"

Erica bristled at his tone. "Actually, I am. But getting back to what I came for: did Stephen have any enemies—anyone who might want to harm him?"

"Not that I know of."

"No unhappy customers or jealous business associates?"

"Even if there was, none of them were at Wendy's house last night."

Except for you and Jaime, she thought then asked, "So, no one here has bad feelings toward Stephen?"

"We're one big happy family." He smiled—a thin, stretched smile.

"Are there any problems between you and Stephen?"

"Not at all. We get along just fine."

Yet there was something in his tone that told her otherwise. Erica had the feeling that Reed Devoe was a secretive man, one capable of behind-the-scenes scheming. He had been watching her closely and asked suddenly, "Why, has Stephen said otherwise?"

"He hasn't said anything. I just get the feeling that you don't like him very much."

"I've always been bothered by people who have a sense of entitlement—people who think they can always have everything their own way."

Erica was genuinely surprised. "Is that how Stephen feels?"

Reed looked at her warily. It seemed he regretted speaking when he said, "I suppose everyone feels that way from time to time." Clearly, he wasn't going to say anymore.

When Reed began rearranging papers on his desk, Erica stood. "You know, wire baskets are great for organizing paperwork. You can even get them in colors." When Reed stared at her, Erica went on. "Think about it. Now, if you think of anything you think might help, please let me know."

"I'll be sure to do that," he replied impassively.

On the way home, Erica stopped at Tom Addison's Gun Shop. She had always been one to play it safe and felt the time had come. The dealer informed Erica that, since she wasn't a Florida resident, any gun she bought would have to be shipped to a dealer in Utah, and she would have to take possession of it there. When Erica gave details about her situation, the dealer explained that federal restrictions prohibited her husband from mailing her Glock directly to her but that David could mail it to the gun shop, where Erica could pick it up after filling out the required paperwork.

At Wendy's, Erica did what she usually did when her mind was full and she needed to focus—bake. Rolls would be good, she decided. She scalded the milk and as it cooled mixed the yeast with warm water and sugar. Sifting the flour, Erica still found it hard to take in that someone had deliberately poisoned Stephen. At least she had a short list of suspects—those who had been at the house that evening.

At home Erica had a Bosch mixer, but she didn't mind kneading the old fashioned way. As she turned and pushed at the dough, Erica thought about her conversation with Reed. He was an unpleasant person—the kind of man who knew how to find a sore spot and walk on it. He certainly seemed to have something against Stephen. But was it enough to make Reed try to kill Stephen? She greased a bowl and had just put the dough in to rise when the phone rang. Wiping her hands, Erica answered. While not unexpected, the call was still unsettling.

A short time later, the front door opened. Lee held it open for Wendy, who was walking very slowly and carefully—as if the world had tilted and she was trying hard not to lose her balance.

"Wendy called Stephen on her break," Lee explained gravely. "She insisted on knowing what the doctor had said." He grimaced then patted Wendy gently on the shoulder as she sank onto the couch. "I hate to leave, but I have to get back."

"Thanks for bringing me home," Wendy said in a small voice. "I'm sorry to leave you shorthanded."

"Don't worry about it. I'll call when I get off."

Erica walked him to the door. Glancing back at Wendy, Lee said quietly, "She's pretty shook up. If I can do anything, let me know."

"I'll do that. I've put off my trip to Memphis so I can be here."

When Erica sat beside her, Wendy looked at her with tortured eyes. "You didn't ask what the doctor said. Did Stephen tell you?"

Erica nodded.

"*Poisoned!*" Wendy cried. "How could he have been poisoned?"

"I don't know. Look, I hate to tell you this, but the police called a little while ago. They'll be here any minute."

"What?" Her voice was like a shot.

"Stephen's doctor must have called the police when she got the results."

It took a moment to sink in. "And since Stephen got sick here—in my house—they'll think I did it!"

"They're not accusing anyone. They need to look things over, take samples, that kind of thing."

"But I'm the one they're going to suspect!" Wendy's eyes were large and frightened. The past week had taken its toll, and now there was this shocking turn of events. "Just a week ago a man was shot outside my door! Why are these things happening to me?"

"Well, not exactly to *you*," Erica pointed out.

Wendy froze, looking stricken. "What a stupid thing for me to say. Here I am, thinking only about myself when that poor man is dead and Stephen is in the hospital. He could have died! But how could he have been poisoned here? He had to have eaten something before he got here, don't you think?" Her eyes searched Erica's face, hoping for confirmation.

"I talked to Dr. Phillips about it, and she said the poisoning was probably intentional. Dalmane is a prescription drug. It's not something you'd take accidentally."

"But who could have done such a thing? Stephen is so kind to everyone."

Just then, the doorbell rang. Wendy jumped as if a gun had gone off at close range. Erica laid a hand on her arm to calm her.

"That's probably the police, but don't worry. You didn't have anything to do with it, and we need to find out who did. Let them do their work, and they'll find out what happened."

Between the chaos of last night and knowing the police would come to investigate, Erica had left the front room and kitchen virtually untouched. This made the detectives' work easier, but Wendy's fears were confirmed when a detective cautioned her not to go out of town.

"You see!" Wendy said as they drove off. "I *told* you they would think I tried to poison Stephen. But why would I try to kill my boyfriend? Are they nuts?"

Erica took hold of Wendy's hands to stop them from clutching each other. "They're not accusing you of anything. They just want you to stay close in case they have any questions."

It was as if she hadn't spoken.

"I know they suspect me, but I didn't do anything!" Wendy's words rose higher and higher. "You've got to help me! They probably even think I killed that . . . that man on the driveway!"

"Of course I'll help you," Erica said, "but you've got to understand that the police will question everyone; they're not just focusing on you."

Her friend's shoulders sagged. "But how was Stephen poisoned? It had to be in something he ate."

"Yes. Some poisons can be injected, but in Stephen's case, it had to be ingested because Dalmane is only available in liquid and powder forms."

"How did you know that?"

"I asked a nurse at the hospital."

"What I don't understand is why anyone would want to kill Stephen."

Speaking without thinking, Erica said, "The thing to worry about now is that they might try again." When Wendy's eyes became round, Erica felt like kicking herself.

"Oh Erica, do you really think so? You've got to help him! You're already investigating—and now Stephen has someone who wants to kill him. You can find out who poisoned him; I know it!" She looked at Erica pleadingly.

Nothing like a ton of pressure to ruin your day, Erica thought. Wendy had no idea how difficult this kind of investigation could be. Still, her friend needed reassurance, not reservations.

"I'll do my best," Erica said. "But you'd better start praying that Detective Lund will let me work with him. If he does, I'll be able to move a lot faster than if I investigate on my own. Unfortunately, a lot of cops don't like private investigators."

"I would think he'd be glad to have your help." Wendy's face had the naive perplexity of a child.

"In a perfect world," Erica said with a slight smile. "As a rule, police like to handle their own investigations because they have their own prescribed way of doing things. Most policemen regard a private investigator as either a pesky nuisance or an untrustworthy interloper—sometimes with good reason, as a few private eyes can be pushy and cause all sorts of problems, like contaminating evidence or tampering with witnesses, which hurts the investigation. I came across it a few times when I was on the police force."

"Oh!" Comprehension dawned. "It's like on *Murder, She Wrote!*" she breathed. "On that show, the police hardly ever wanted Jessica's help because she was only a writer. But you're a professional, and you're so good at it!"

"Detective Lund is coming around—he's actually given me a lot of information. However, he's cautious and I expect he's had a few bad experiences of his own. Still, I'm sure he knows we can get further if we work together." She paused. "In fact, I'd better call him now. I'm sure he knows about Stephen by now, but I want him to know I'm working *with* him, not against him."

* * *

After talking with Detective Lund, Erica punched down the dough, formed rolls, and covered them with a towel. Then she called home and had her children get online. There was a good deal of laughter—and pushing—since they all wanted to be on the computer at the same time. To deal with this, Erica talked with her youngest, Kenzie, first, then worked up to Ryan, and last of all Aby, who was eager to tell about the high school tryouts for concert choir. Aby asked her mother to get online later to help with an English assignment.

It was a treat to see David as they chatted since they usually just talked on their cell phones. After telling her what was new on the home front, he asked, "Have you heard anything about Stephen? I couldn't believe it when you called this morning."

"I talked to Patrick," Erica said. "He already knew about Stephen and said he'd let me know once they had the test results back from the samples they took around the house."

"That's great. And it's 'Patrick' now, is it? Sounds like the detective is coming around to your side."

"I think he is. There are a couple of things I'd like you to do for me. Would you call poison control and find out more about Dalmane? The only thing I know is that it's only available in powder or liquid. If I call, they're going to think I only want to poison someone, but if you call—a bona fide policeman—they'll tell you all about it. I could research online, but I want up-to-date information."

"Sure. Chief Brown might be able to help with that." His police chief, Ken Brown, besides having a sense of humor, was a friendly, obliging person who was always willing to help.

"So, how's it going with the kids so far?" Erica asked. "Are you having them do their daily jobs?" It was said without hope. Although each of the children had small daily chores, Erica had long ago come to grips with the fact that she was the "enforcer" because David had a laid-back attitude about chores.

"You've only been gone a few days—why worry?"

The theme song from *Jaws* started running through her head. "Because I hate being the only parent that insists they clean the bathroom, brush their teeth, or hang up their clothes." Giving a martyr-like sigh, Erica went on. "I'll do what I can to help them with their homework online if you'll help them finish."

"Sounds good. Anything else?"

Erica explained about her stop at the gun shop and asked him to send her Glock 19—or Little Suzie as she sometimes called it—to the gun shop. "I'll be able to legally take possession of it there."

"Sure, I'll send it tomorrow. I'll feel better if you've got it."

"Me too."

* * *

That afternoon, Erica and Wendy went to the hospital and took Stephen to his apartment. Wendy made a great fuss over him though Stephen kept assuring her he was perfectly well. And he did seem fine, Erica thought, except for a new anxiety she detected in his eyes. Since Stephen was tired, Wendy told him she'd bring some homemade soup over later, and they left him to sleep.

After a brief stop at the store, they arrived home. Erica put in the rolls to bake while they started making Clam Chowder.[4] Megan came in,

---

4   See appendix at the end of the book for this recipe.

swathed in a long-sleeved black T-shirt and jeans. Brandon, wearing his Cub Scout shirt, wandered in and began looking through the grocery sacks.

"I've got some rolls baking," Erica said as she rinsed off the celery. "I thought they would go good with the soup." She handed the stalks to Megan to chop while she started peeling the onions under running water.

"You really like to cook, don't you?" Megan said, sounding as bemused as if Erica had said she enjoyed scrubbing toilets.

"I do. I like the precision." That earned several curious looks, so Erica explained: "Cooking is a step-by-step procedure, a very orderly process. If you follow the directions precisely and go through all of the proper steps, everything will turn out as planned. It's very linear; you proceed from A to B to C. It's just like detective work. When you investigate, you have to follow the steps one by one, being very precise and following procedure faithfully."

Megan asked, "And if you do all that, you'll be able to solve the case?"

"Absolutely." Erica got out the rolls and put another sheet in to bake. "Brandon, will you come and butter the tops of these rolls?"

"And tell us what you did at Cub Scouts today," Wendy added.

Brandon filled them in on making beanbag throws then picked up a roll and took a bite. Erica rolled up a towel and flipped it at Brandon's bottom. He turned, grinning mischievously.

"Wait till dinner," Wendy admonished. As she diced potatoes, Wendy asked, "Erica, I know you changed your trip to Saturday, but what time do you need to be at the airport?"

"Around 7:00."

"Why are you going to Memphis?" Megan asked.

"It's part of my investigation. I'm going to see Gregory Tyson's wife, friends, and coworkers." As she spoke, Erica blinked rapidly, her eyes smarting from the onions. "Your mother also wants me to look into Stephen's poisoning."

Some strong emotion passed across Megan's face. "Mother!" she exclaimed, her voice dripping with disapproval. "You didn't really ask Erica to do that, did you?"

"Do what? Investigate?" Wendy looked up from the cutting board, blinking owlishly in surprise. "Well, yes I did. You know Erica is a private investigator."

"You're at least paying her, aren't you?" Her voice was full of censure as she filled a glass with water. "I mean, if she's got to fly to Memphis . . ."

Erica jumped in. "Your mother and I are old friends. I wouldn't dream of accepting payment from a friend. And I get to fly for next to nothing because Chris, my angel of a brother, works for an airline."

Wendy gave her a look of thanks, but Megan still looked appalled. "Erica's the best," Wendy said. "If anyone can find out who the murderer is, she can."

The glass slipped from Megan's hand and fell to the floor. Miraculously it didn't break. She grabbed a towel and began sopping up the water.

"I think I'll go to Chicago too," Erica said as she got another towel and knelt to help. "Gregory Tyson and Stephen both worked there, and I might be able to find out something helpful."

Brandon looked at her enviously. "I wish I was a private investigator. I like flying in airplanes!"

"You've never even flown in one," Megan interjected.

Erica looked at him with a faint smile. "I thought you were going to be a marine biologist."

"I'll be both," he replied confidently.

* * *

Wendy came home that night in good time. Stephen was doing well, she said, but was still tired. Megan begged off from family scripture reading and prayer that night, so it was just Wendy, Erica, and Brandon. Afterward, Erica went downstairs to exercise then came back up to shower in order to avoid the morning rush. She turned on the TV and was able to find an old movie, *Breakfast at Tiffany's*. Erica loved watching old movies, whether they were romances, comedies, dramas—practically any genre, though she usually drew the line at westerns. She curled up in a chair with a notebook and began to organize her thoughts. At the top of the page, she wrote *Wendy* and underneath *Lied about leaving the house the night Tyson was killed*. Tapping the notebook with her pen, Erica wondered. Was there anything else Wendy might have lied about?

Next, she wrote *Reed Devoe* and under that *Chip on his shoulder the size of Baltimore*. What lay behind his unpleasantness? Could there be some hidden bitterness that had driven him to murder? On the night of the party, Reed had been sitting next to Stephen. Could he have slipped something into Stephen's food or drink?

Then there was Lee. Under his name, she wrote *Interested in Wendy*. Lee seemed so nice, but Erica knew hardly anything about him. He seemed very meek and mild mannered, but did that disguise the fact that something was going on beneath the surface? She knew of cases where mild-mannered people had been so bullied, either by life or other people, that they ended up lashing out in unexpected and violent ways. Could that be the case here?

Erica wrote down *Stephen* and then *Gregory Tyson's friend*. Stephen wouldn't have poisoned himself, but there was the possibility he was involved in Tyson's murder.

It seemed wrong to even consider Megan, that unhappy girl. Surely she wasn't capable of murder, but Erica had to write *Shortly after Tyson was murdered, returned home breathless* and *Hates Stephen*. Although the girl detested Stephen, was she so against him becoming her stepfather that she would poison him? Last of all, Erica wrote *Jaime* and underneath *Adores Stephen—too much?* Although it still seemed incongruous that young, beautiful Jaime would fall for Stephen, it made even less sense that she would try to poison him. Erica set the list aside but was still puzzling over it when she fell asleep.

Around one in the morning, Erica woke from a nightmare with a breathless gasp. The pulsating horror of the dream was still upon her, and even though she'd plugged in three night-lights, she reached over and flipped on a bedside lamp. Drawing up her knees, Erica hugged them tightly as she tried to slow her breathing by telling herself it was only a dream. She'd had several nightmares since finding Gregory Tyson's lifeless body, but this one was different.

In this nightmare, as in real life, Erica had bent over a motionless body lying on the ground. But in the dream, the man had rolled over slightly as Erica touched his arm, allowing her to see his face. Instead of the thin, pinched face of Gregory Tyson, it was Stephen Watkins staring up at her. The expression on his face was a ghastly combination of horror and pleading, as if he were begging her for help. Mutely, Stephen reached out and took hold of Erica's arm as though she alone had the power to save him.

Erica sprang out of bed and began to pace—trying to dispel the fearful nightmare. But the look of terror on Stephen's face would not fade. What could it mean? Was it one of those senseless dreams that meant nothing or was there some significance—some purpose lurking just beyond her consciousness, waiting for her to grasp it?

Why had she dreamed that the man lying there was Stephen? It must have been because he had nearly died after being poisoned. Erica shut her eyes, but she could still see Stephen's ravaged face as he lay on the driveway, mutely beseeching her for help. Yet it had not been Stephen who had been attacked. Not the first time anyway.

The first time.

Those words suddenly seemed significant, and as Erica thought back to the night of the murder, a forgotten memory clicked in her mind. When she had first seen a man lying motionless on the driveway, Erica had—for a split second—thought it was Stephen. That brief memory and Stephen's being poisoned must have been the stimulus for her nightmare.

But why had she thought it was Stephen lying there that night? The answer came quickly. Because the two men were about the same build and both had receding brown hair. Tyson had been wearing a dark jacket and tan pants, Erica remembered. Then she inhaled sharply. Hadn't Stephen been wearing something similar? She seemed to remember Stephen taking off a jacket and tossing it over a chair when he'd first arrived. Her mind churned. What was that old saying? "If at first you don't succeed, try, try again?"

Was it possible the killer had mistaken Gregory Tyson for Stephen Watkins? And, having failed to kill Stephen the first time, had tried again?

CHAPTER 7

WHEN ERICA AWOKE LATER THAT morning, consciousness came with a jolt of body and heart—with the dream still clear in her mind. All along, she had been troubled by an apparent lack of motive for Tyson's murder, but if Stephen had been the intended victim, it opened up a whole new field of possibilities. She would talk with Detective Lund as soon as possible and find out what Gregory Tyson had been wearing that night. She would also need to ask Stephen about his clothes.

In the kitchen, Megan was finishing her bowl of cereal, and Brandon was wailing, "But Mom! Why can't I have a puppy?"

"Because they're expensive, that's why." Wendy's tired voice indicated they'd been over this before.

"But Tyler said his Mom would *give* us one."

"Puppies still have to have shots, food, and a license."

"He won't eat much," Brandon assured his mother as Erica sat beside him with her cereal.

"If he's anything like you, he'll eat us out of house and home," Megan said, putting her bowl in the sink and walking out.

With a sidelong glance at Megan's disappearing back, Wendy spoke to Brandon in a low voice. "We can't have a puppy if we move."

He looked puzzled. "Are we going to move?"

"We might if I get married."

Brandon's eyes widened. "Are you going to get married?"

Wendy's face colored. "I'm not sure, but *if* I do, we'll have enough to do without taking care of a dog."

This made no sense whatsoever to Brandon, who still wore a puzzled frown. He was about to start in again, but Wendy forestalled him. "End of discussion. I've got to go to work. Now give me a hug good-bye, and go brush your teeth.

After he left to brush, Wendy turned to Erica, looking shamefaced. "I hated doing that, but I didn't want to tell Brandon the real reason. I wouldn't mind getting a puppy myself, but Stephen doesn't like dogs." There was a honk out front.

"That'll be Lee," Wendy said. "He's picking me up so you can have the car. See you this afternoon, Erica." Then with a devilish grin, Wendy added, "Hey, last time you forgot to vacuum under the seats!"

"But I did clean out the glove box," Erica called as her friend hurried out.

When Brandon came back, he asked Erica, "Do you have a dog?"

"Two of them: a Westie and a mini-dachshund. Want to see?"

He did.

When she pulled out her wallet, Brandon asked, "Is that black one the dachshund?"

"Yep. She's got real pretty markings for a black and tan." She pulled out another picture. "This one is Biscuit. She's a West Highland White Terrier. She's smart, playful, and a lot of fun."

"Gee, you're lucky to have *two* dogs. Wish I could have one."

She put her wallet away. "When I was growing up, I wanted a dog *so bad*, but my dad always said no. I cut out pictures of dogs from magazines and newspapers and pasted them in a scrapbook, dreaming of the day I could have one. Then, finally, when I was about twelve, Dad said I could get one. So, don't give up hope." She chucked him under the chin to chase away his woebegone expression. "Say, would you like to go to a pet store sometime?"

His eyes lit up. "Yeah!"

"Not to buy anything," she warned. "Just to look around. I go every once in a while. I love looking at the baby animals and the birds."

"When can we go? Today?"

She thought. "Hmm. I can't today and tomorrow; I'll be in Memphis. How about Monday?"

"Yeah!"

"Now, go get your backpack. One of the sad facts of life is that the school bus is never going to be late the same day you are."

Erica finished eating and was just heading for the telephone when Megan came in and began going through some papers by the phone. "Do you mind if I make a call?" Erica asked.

"No one's stopping you," Megan replied ungraciously.

"Thanks, I need to call Stephen."

Her statement had the desired result—Megan stopped rifling through the papers and turned to leave. "Thanks for the warning."

When Brandon came in wearing his backpack, Erica was just hanging up the phone. "You look happy," he observed.

"I am. It's always nice to have one's musings confirmed."

Brandon frowned. "What's a musing?"

"A thought or an idea."

After considering that a moment, he sighed. "I need to think of a good musing so Mom will let me have a dog."

* * *

Patrick Lund's grizzled head was bowed over paperwork when Erica walked in. Looking up, he said, "Ah, here to confess?"

"I'm not going to make it that easy for you," she said lightly, plunking herself down. "Got any leads?"

"We're following up on a few things. Nothing to get excited about." Patrick sounded morose. "The few people in the neighborhood that admit to hearing a shot say they didn't see anything. The Stay Puft marshmallow man from *Ghostbusters* could have walked down the street, and nobody would admit seeing him."

Erica smiled. "Frustrating but typical. In that kind of neighborhood, it can be hazardous to your health to say you saw something."

"You sounded serious when you called. What's on your mind?"

"I had an idea that could possibly tie Tyson's murder in with Stephen Watkins's poisoning. There just has to be a connection between the two. It's too much of a coincidence to think Tyson was randomly shot at a house where his old friend was. I wanted to run my theory past you."

Leaning back in his chair and crossing his arms, Patrick made himself comfortable.

"First, was Gregory Tyson wearing a dark jacket when he was killed?"

Patrick had to leave his comfortable position to look up Tyson's file. "Yeah."

"I recall he also had on tan pants." When the detective nodded, Erica said, "I called Stephen this morning. On the night of the murder, he was also wearing a dark jacket and tan pants."

"Small world," Patrick grunted.

"How tall was Tyson?"

A flip of a page. "Five foot ten."

"Stephen is five foot nine."

"I'm beginning to see where you're going with this, but go ahead."

"Gregory Tyson and Stephen Watkins were both wearing tan pants and dark jackets," Erica said, a lively intelligence in her green eyes. "They have the same build and are around the same height. And they both have thinning brown hair. What if someone meant to kill Stephen but mistook Tyson for him? Then, when the murderer found out he'd killed the wrong man, he tries again, only this time he uses poison instead of a gun."

Patrick looked interested, and Erica continued. "That would clear up one thing that's bothered me about Tyson's murder. He lives in Memphis. Why, if someone wanted to kill him, would the murderer take the time and effort to follow him clear to Florida and then to Wendy's house when it would have been much simpler and easier to kill him in Memphis or at the motel?"

"That's true," Patrick agreed, rubbing his chin as he considered.

"Everyone knew Stephen was going to be at Wendy's house that night. There are a lot of places the killer could have hidden while waiting for Stephen to arrive. Let's say the killer is waiting in the bushes. Then, along comes a man who is the same height and build as Stephen. The killer shoots him, only to find out later that he killed the wrong man."

"His bad," Patrick said then added, "Still, Tyson was twelve years older than Stephen."

"It was dark at the time of the shooting—and raining. And Tyson was shot in the back. Most likely, the killer never got a good look at his face."

"You might have something." Patrick betrayed his inner excitement by leaning forward, putting his elbows on the desk and lacing his fingers together. "We'll look into it."

"There is another possibility," Erica added. "Maybe the killer, who I'm assuming is from Memphis, thought that killing Tyson in Kissimmee would hide his tracks."

Patrick shook his head. "That's what I love about police work: there are always a thousand possibilities." He picked up some papers. "By the way, we got the lab results back from testing Wendy's house. "There were three cups on the coffee table in the front room. All of them had lethal amounts of Dalmane."

A jolt went through Erica. "That was the coffee Jaime brought in. She had three cups—one for me, Stephen, and herself. I didn't drink mine."

"A good thing or you might not be sitting here today." He looked at the papers. "Two cups were nearly full; they must have been yours and Jaime's. The third cup was half full."

"Stephen's."

He looked directly at her. "Why didn't you drink your coffee?"

"I'm a Mormon, and we don't drink coffee."

He raised one eyebrow and scribbled in his notebook. "Seems like I heard Wendy say she was a Mormon. Is she a practicing Mormon?"

"Yes, she's very active."

"Then why does she have coffee in her house?"

"She keeps some for her non-Mormon friends. Wendy told me once that when her friends came to visit, they always asked for coffee, so she thought it would be hospitable to have some on hand."

Detective Lund looked thoughtful. "I guess that makes sense, but it still strikes me as odd that someone would have coffee on hand if drinking it was against their religion. You don't find many Jews with canned hams tucked away in their cupboard. When you see Wendy, will you ask her to give me a call?"

"Yeah, sure."

"You say Jaime brought the coffee in. Did she make it or did Wendy?"

"I'm not sure. Wendy was in the kitchen when Jaime went to get it." Erica felt like there was a stone in her stomach.

"Did you or anyone else go into the kitchen while Jaime and Wendy were there?

She paused to think. "Reed Devoe did. He wanted to say good-bye to Wendy."

It was natural to assume the person making the coffee poisoned it, but Patrick was one step ahead. "Did you, Jaime, or Stephen leave your coffee unattended?"

Erica thought back. "I don't know about Stephen, but Jaime went to get some cookies and I went to the bathroom."

"One other thing. One of my men found a small piece of folded white paper on the floor in the front room. It held traces of Dalmane. It could have been used to bring the poison into the house."

This was a bit of good news. "That means the poison was probably added to the coffee in the front room, which means Wendy couldn't have done it."

"Hold on." Patrick was cautious. "Wendy could have gone into the front room and put the poison in the coffee while you and Jaime were gone."

"Not if Stephen was right there."

"He could have been sidetracked. Maybe he turned to talk to someone—giving Wendy time to add the poison. Or, she could have added it while she was in the kitchen and dropped the paper in the front room to divert suspicion."

The detective had a point. One thing Erica never did was reject another person's opinion just because it was different from her own because it was possible both of them could be wrong. However, there was one thing she was sure of. "If Stephen really *is* the intended target, we're dealing with a dangerous killer."

"*Any* killer is dangerous."

"Yes, but this one doesn't mind killing innocent people just to get the one he wants. If the coffee was poisoned in the kitchen, there was no way to know which cup Stephen would take. The only way to be sure Stephen got it was to put Dalmane in all three cups."

They sat in chilled silence.

Then Erica went on. "One more thing. If the killer did mean to kill Stephen and shot Tyson by mistake, he must be very confident that no one suspects him of being the shooter. Only someone with an airtight alibi for the first murder would attempt a second."

Patrick looked at her with admiration and nodded. "Okay. While I'm still not sure your theory is correct, it's certainly something to look into. We'll keep trying to find out if anyone had a motive for killing Tyson, but we'll also start checking to see if anyone had a motive for killing Stephen."

"Were you able to check passenger lists and see if anyone that knew Tyson flew to Orlando the same day?"

"Takes an act of Congress to get that information after 9-11," Patrick grumbled. "So far, no one on Tyson's flight had any direct ties to him, but we're still checking other flights."

"Did you find out why Tyson came to Florida?"

"His boss sent him to Orlando on business. One more thing—Mrs. Tyson said her husband definitely planned on visiting Stephen while he was here."

"That's good to know, but I keep wondering why he didn't call first instead of just showing up at Wendy's house. That seems rather odd."

"It's only strange if Stephen is telling the truth," Patrick reminded her. "Tyson certainly had time to call. He checked into the motel the day before."

"The big question is how Tyson knew Stephen was going to be at Wendy's house that night."

"Wish I had the answer to that one," Patrick said, scratching his head. "Maybe I'll be able to find out more in Memphis."

"I've already had detectives interview Tyson's family and his business associates." Patrick sounded a little testy. Erica thought she'd gotten the detective's stamp of approval, but apparently he had not accepted her completely.

"Did they find out anything helpful?"

"I'd rather not say until I have a chance to review the entire report."

Erica looked at him. "And what if *I* pick up something interesting while I'm there?"

"I'd expect you to tell us immediately," Patrick said firmly. When she raised her eyebrows, he added forcefully, "It's *our* job to track down the killer."

It would do no good to argue. "I understand that. And I'd like to help," she replied calmly.

Her soft tone set him back. Apparently, he'd expected a fiery response. There were a few moments during which Patrick appeared to be having an internal debate. Then he said, "I don't suppose it will hurt to tell you that our guys didn't get a lot of useful information." Grudgingly he added, "Maybe you'll have better luck."

That was a lot coming from him. She'd throw him a tidbit too. "I'm also going to Chicago next week—see what turns up there."

"Watch yourself. Another possibility is that whoever poisoned the coffee was after you or Jaime. Maybe someone doesn't want you investigating."

"Gee, but that would mean someone actually thinks I might be able to help solve this case."

"Touché." The detective smiled. "Good luck in Memphis and keep me informed."

* * *

The delectable aroma of fresh-baked Pumpkin Chocolate-Chip Cookies[5] filled the kitchen, and Erica sniffed appreciatively as she walked in. "Boy, that smells wonderful! You put plenty of chocolate chips in, didn't you?"

"Of course!" Wendy said. "I didn't dare do otherwise with you around."

---

5   See appendix at the end of the book for this recipe.

"Well, you know what they say: a little too much chocolate is just about right."

Megan chuckled, watching as her brother tried to loosen a cookie from the still-hot cookie sheet.

"Ouch," Brandon yipped, backing off and sucking on a finger.

"You are such a moron," his sister said.

"Will you *please* stop calling your brother names!" Wendy said as she slid another tray in the oven. "Hey, didn't you have a test in history today?"

Looking startled, Megan replied, "Yeah. What about it?" Her tone was defensive.

"How'd you do?"

"How am I supposed to know? The teacher can hardly correct our tests the second we turn them in." Megan sounded aggrieved. "And yes, I studied—if that's what you're asking."

Wendy looked sorry she had brought it up. "I was just wondering how it went."

"Since when do you care?" Megan challenged. "You usually don't ask about my tests, so why are you now? Trying to show Erica what a loving mother you are?"

"Megan, honey, I was just trying to find out—"

"I know," Megan interrupted. "You're always trying to find out things, but I don't *want* you butting into my private life!" She spun around and left.

Brandon noticed his mother's flushed cheeks. "It's okay, Mom," he said, trying to console her. "I like you in *my* life."

"So do I!" Erica said cheerfully. "You can ask me about my history tests any time!" That did make Wendy smile. She handed Brandon another cookie. "Now, that's it until dinnertime. Go play." As the door closed, Wendy leaned against the counter, her shoulders sagging.

"I really *was* interested," Wendy whispered. "And what does she mean I don't usually ask about things? I do! But I never know how she's going to react. Sometimes Megan tells me to quit prying into her personal life, and other times she says I'm just *pretending* to be interested. And yes, there have been a few times I haven't asked just because I didn't need her attitude. *Now* Megan tells me I don't care because I didn't ask. I can't win."

"Megan's at a difficult age," Erica said soothingly. "She's trying to find herself. The best thing is to just let it go." Then she smiled. "At least Megan's behavior gives you a broader understanding of the world."

"What do you mean?"

"As the mother of a teen, you now know why some animals eat their young." She was repaid for her efforts when Wendy began laughing, not stopping until she had to wipe her eyes.

Erica filled one side of the sink with soapy water. "I'll wash these up now."

"Someday I'll be able to afford a repairman to fix that dishwasher," Wendy said with a sigh. "Things have been tight ever since Megan turned eighteen and her child support payments stopped. All I do is live from paycheck to paycheck. Every time I think I can make ends meet, they move the ends." She started putting cookies in a plastic container. "After dinner, I thought I'd take Stephen some cookies. Do you want to go?"

"Sure." Erica wiped her hands dry and took a cookie. "But why bother making dinner? Let's have these. We'll be getting our vegetables from the pumpkin and vitamin C from chocolate!"

* * *

Later, Erica held a plate of plastic-wrapped cookies as Wendy pulled out onto John Young Parkway. Wendy asked, "Did Detective Lund have anything new?"

"He'd gotten the results of the lab tests," Erica replied. "There was poison in all three of the coffee cups that Jaime brought into the front room."

Wendy veered into the right lane. The driver of a minivan honked loud and long as Wendy swerved back into her lane. Gasping, Erica looked at her friend.

"Sorry, I didn't see him," Wendy said, looking shaken. They didn't speak again until they had reached Stephen's apartment complex. Wendy apologized again then said, "Now that I've stopped and you're safe, why don't you tell me the rest?"

Erica's heart was still beating faster than usual. "All right. First of all, Detective Lund wants you to call him."

"Why?"

"He wants to ask you some questions. Did you or Jaime make the coffee that night?"

"Actually, we both did. Jaime asked if I had any coffee, and I got it out for her and put the water on to boil. I was about to go downstairs to get some plastic wrap when Jaime asked me to measure out the coffee."

"Are you serious? That's kind of weird. I mean, it's not that hard. Why didn't she do it?"

"I don't know," Wendy said distractedly. "I guess Jaime's the helpless sort. Anyway, I did it then went downstairs. When I came up, she'd taken the coffee into the front room."

That was interesting, Erica thought. Then she looked down at the plate of cookies in her lap. "We'd better go in now, before I lose all of the amazing self-control I've demonstrated up to now and start eating these myself."

When Stephen opened the door, he smiled hugely and gave Wendy a big hug and a quick kiss. He looked at the plate in delight. "Pumpkin chocolate-chip cookies! My favorite as you well know!" He turned. "Jaime, look what Wendy brought!"

Erica and Wendy looked past him to see Jaime lounging in a chair by the window, looking beautiful. "How sweet!" Jaime said, tilting her head with its mane of black hair. Wendy's mouth opened, but nothing came out. She appeared to be having problems breathing.

In an attempt to ease the tension, Erica said, "Hello, Jaime, it's nice to see you again." Their eyes met. There was amusement and something else in Jaime's eyes—was it a challenge?

"I stopped by to see how Stephen was doing, but I'll go and let you guys visit." Jaime uncrossed her long legs and stood.

"Do you have to go?" Stephen asked, putting the cookies on a table. Wendy swiveled and looked at him wide-eyed.

With a glance under long lashes at Wendy, Jaime smoothed her dark skirt over trim hips. "Yeah, I think I'd better. But I'll see you tomorrow, Stephen." There was no doubt that little shaft was meant for Wendy.

"Do you mind if I walk out with you?" Erica asked.

Jaime shrugged lightly. "Suit yourself. Bye, Wendy. See you, Stephen."

There was a tender shaving of a new moon, almost transparent, riding high above the trees as they walked down the cobbled path. Erica said, "I'd like to ask you a couple of questions."

"Not you too!" Jaime complained. "Detective Lund called and asked me to come by the police station tomorrow for a 'few questions,' as he put it."

Erica nodded toward a wood-and-wrought-iron bench set along the pathway. "Is it all right if we sit here a minute?" Jaime was about to sit down when Erica blurted out, "Wait a minute!"

"What is it?" Jaime asked, poised for flight from the unseen danger.

Erica moved the bench slightly. "There we go. The bench was crooked."

Jaime looked at her as if she had two noses. "It was crooked?"

"I don't know what they pay groundskeepers for," Erica shook her head. Then she went on to explain that poison had been found in the coffee cups.

"There was poison in *my* cup?" Jaime's eyes grew wide.

"There were lethal doses of poison in all three cups. Stephen could have been the intended victim, but then again, it could be that someone was trying to kill *you*."

"Wendy," Jaime breathed. "She hates me, you know. She's afraid I'm going to take Stephen away from her." Then, recovering from her initial shock, she added, "I'm sure the police will be interested in knowing how jealous Wendy is and how strangely she's been acting lately."

"Be sure to mention how strange it is for a young woman like yourself to be so interested in a middle-aged man."

There was hostility in the look Jaime shot at her. "Stephen is a wonderful man—interesting, attentive, and thoughtful," she countered. "There's no one my age who can match him. Besides, if Wendy winds up in prison, he'll need someone to comfort him."

It was an outrageous statement, spoken in retaliation, and Erica knew better than to take it seriously. "Wendy would never try to poison anybody, much less Stephen. Now, going back to the night Stephen was poisoned. You went to the kitchen. Did you make the coffee, or did Wendy?"

A lazy smile played around the corners of Jaime's mouth. "Wendy did, as I'm sure she's already told you."

"Why did you ask Wendy to measure out the coffee?"

"Ah, I *knew* you'd already talked to her! Well, it's very simple; I didn't know where the measuring spoons were."

"You made coffee but didn't drink any. Why was that?"

Reflected light shone in eyes that were almost black. "I was letting it cool. Is that a crime?"

"Not yet."

Jaime glowered at her. "Are you accusing me of something?"

"I don't know. Are you guilty of something?"

Her reply startled Jaime, who replied savagely, "I didn't poison Stephen, if that's what you're implying."

"Besides Wendy, did anyone else come into the kitchen while you were there?"

"Reed came in for a minute. So did Lee and Megan. Any of them could have slipped poison into the coffee." She looked at Erica speculatively. "You might even have done it when I went to get some cookies."

"You're right," Erica admitted. "I'm probably on the list of suspects because I didn't drink my coffee."

"Why didn't you?" Jaime sounded suspicious.

"I'm LDS, and I don't drink it for religious reasons."

"Drinking *coffee* is against your religion?" Jaime sounded shocked.

"Oh, it's not as weird as you think. It's a health thing."

"Wow! Glad I'm not a Mormon!"

* * *

When Erica returned, Stephen and Wendy were sitting on the brown leather couch, holding hands and looking relaxed. Apparently, Wendy had gotten over her pique at Jaime's presence. Unfortunately, Erica was about to stir up emotions again.

First, she went to the mantle where there were three candles of varying height and moved the middle candle to the right so the three were in descending height. Then she moved the chair that was in the corner so it was flush with the wall and sat down.

"Erica," Wendy protested. "This isn't your house. You shouldn't be moving things."

A slow smile spread across Stephen's face. "Wendy's told me a little about your, ah, idiosyncrasies. Do you always move things around in other people's homes?"

"I do what I can to make the world a better place," Erica said in a self-depreciating manner. "But enough about me. Do you remember the other morning when I called and asked what you were wearing the night Tyson was killed?"

"Yes. You also asked how tall I was. I wondered if you wanted to measure me for a coffin."

Erica smiled slightly. "The reason I asked is because I think it's possible Gregory Tyson's murder was a case of mistaken identity. That night, you and Tyson were both wearing dark jackets and tan pants. You're around the same height and weight, and both of you have brown hair with receding hairlines. It was night, which made it difficult to see clearly. It's possible the killer meant to kill *you*, not Gregory Tyson."

Wendy gasped, and Stephen's face drained of color.

Erica went on. "You could have been poisoned because the killer failed in his first attempt."

"*First attempt?*" Wendy cried, her hand going to her throat. "I don't understand."

"When the killer found out he'd mistakenly killed another man instead of Stephen, he, or she, tried again, only this time with poison."

Stephen's face was a mixture of confusion. "I thought Tyson was killed during a botched robbery. That's what one of the policemen told me."

Erica shook her head shortly. "That was sheer conjecture at that point. Also, the lab results are back. There was no poison in the jar of coffee, but there was poison in all three coffee cups."

"Well then, maybe someone was trying to kill you or Jaime." Stephen's brow was furrowed.

"The police are going to look into that," Erica assured him. "But in the meantime, if someone really is targeting you, we need to take precautions—before a third attempt is made."

"Do you really think whoever poisoned the coffee will try again?" Wendy's voice was fearful.

"It's hard to say, but there is certainly that chance. If it's all right, Wendy, I'd like to talk to Stephen for a few minutes—alone."

"Why don't you go in my bedroom?" Stephen suggested. "There's an easy chair, and you can turn on the TV." Wendy walked out on legs that were not quite steady. "This whole thing has been very difficult for her," Stephen said sympathetically.

"Yes, it has." Erica moved closer and sat on the couch. "That and working seventy hours a week keeps her exhausted."

"She works too hard. I wish Wendy would let me help her more, but she's very proud." Stephen grimaced slightly. "I'm glad the person who tried to poison me didn't succeed, but at least if they had, Wendy wouldn't have to worry about money anymore. But then, she knows that."

"What do you mean?"

Appearing to catch himself, Stephen blinked suddenly, looking regretful at having spoken. "Oh, it's nothing really." Quickly, he moved on. "What did you want to ask me?"

"Do you have any enemies? Anyone who might wish to harm you?"

"No, of course not." He spoke rapidly, without thought.

It was eerie that he wouldn't meet her eyes. "You don't have anyone who dislikes you?"

"I can't think of anyone I would call an enemy."

There was an odd constraint in his manner that gave Erica the feeling he was holding something back. Then again, it could be that Stephen was too good-natured to hold a grudge against anyone and couldn't imagine someone else doing it.

She tried another tack. "It might not be someone you'd call an enemy; it could just be someone who was upset with you in the past— someone you argued with, someone who was unhappy with you. Perhaps a dissatisfied customer or coworker."

Did Stephen twitch slightly?

"No. There's nobody."

Despite his denial, Erica felt he was being less than forthright. "I'm just trying to find out who might have poisoned you," she reminded him.

Stephen looked uncomfortable. "I know, it's just that you're not . . ." His voice trailed off.

So that was it. "It bothers you that I'm not a policeman."

"I feel like a jerk, but that's it. I know you mean well, but you're not officially part of the investigation."

"That's true," Erica admitted, "but I am a good investigator. The police aren't the only ones who can find out things. Besides, I'm Wendy's friend, and I don't need to tell you how worried she is about you. Besides, there's another reason I'm anxious to find out who poisoned you."

He looked at her inquiringly.

"To clear myself. Since I was there the night you were poisoned, I'm a suspect too. Plus, I don't have a firm alibi for the night Tyson was shot except for that bag of ice."

"No one could ever suspect you!" Stephen cried. "You're much too nice."

"You'd be amazed at how 'nice' some murderers are," Erica said ruefully. "Now, I need to ask some personal questions. It would be helpful to know about your assets, including life insurance. From outward appearances, you seem well enough off. You dress very nicely, live in an expensive area, drive a Lexus."

Looking ill at ease, Stephen told her what he could, starting with his sizable savings account, his 401(k), which was significant, and a hefty life insurance policy. He had a couple of expensive rings and watches, and a few valuable paintings and sculptures that had been gifts from Anthony Bronson, his previous boss at Cicero. He concluded by saying, "The Lexus was my brother's. I couldn't bear to sell it."

"All right. Now, do you have a will?"

Stephen's eyes became remote and his back stiffened. "I had one drawn up six months ago." Once again, there was something guarded in Stephen's manner. Either he hated disclosing personal information or he had something to hide.

"That's fairly recent," Erica commented. "Any particular reason?"

"When I moved to Kissimmee after my brother died, I planned to make a will but never got around to it. You see, Richard's death made me aware of my own mortality." Stephen's normally cheerful face was solemn. "I should have done it sooner—I pride myself on being responsible and organized—but I kept putting it off probably because it brought back too many memories of my brother's death."

Erica nodded understandingly, and Stephen went on. "After I met Wendy, we talked about it from time to time. She felt it was a good idea and encouraged me to go ahead, so I finally did."

"I see. And who is the beneficiary?"

That closed look came over Stephen's face again.

Clearly, she was going to have to pull it out of him. "I wouldn't ask if it wasn't important."

In a low voice, he said, "Wendy."

Inside, Erica groaned. "And who is the beneficiary of your life insurance policy?"

"Wendy."

* * *

For the first time since she'd arrived in Florida, Erica almost wished she didn't have to talk to David that night. She'd already told him about her dream, but now she had to tell him about the poisoned coffee. As she feared, David was seriously shaken at the news.

"The poison was in *your* cup too?"

"Yes, but I didn't drink it. It was decaf, and you know I can't stand the stuff."

"How can you joke about something like that? You could have died!"

"Hey, I followed the Word of Wisdom and I'm fine."

"Are the police going to look at who might have tried to poison you and Jaime?"

"They are. And for now, everyone who was there that night is a suspect—including me."

"A suspect who could have been a victim. I wish you'd drop this." David sounded worried. "What if someone's out to get you? Maybe the killer thinks you know too much."

"My bet is the killer is after Stephen."

"*The poison was in all three cups . . .*"

"I know, and that's another reason I don't want to stop now. I get grumpy when someone tries to poison me. I mean, it could have ruined my entire day."

David groaned. "I know you're trying to be funny, but you are so *not* succeeding."

"Okay. But I still don't think I was the intended victim."

"How can you be sure?"

"Because the killer is smart. And only someone stupid would have tried to knock me off by putting poison in my coffee. A killer with any intelligence would have done his homework and found out I don't drink coffee. So if someone really was trying to get me, I'd need to look for someone who acts impulsively—someone who isn't very thorough."

"Maybe the killer *is* a psycho and wanted to kill all three of you," David suggested.

"I don't think so. This case doesn't have the earmarks of someone who's trying to take out a lot of people. My bet is that Stephen is the intended victim—because of his ties to Gregory Tyson."

"You could be right," David said hesitantly, "but I'm still worried about you."

"I'll be fine. I haven't been in town long enough to annoy someone so badly that they'd want to kill me."

David response was somber. "Gregory Tyson hadn't been in town very long either."

CHAPTER 8

THE FLIGHT ATTENDANT WELCOMED ERICA aboard the plane. Finding a spot for her bag in the overhead bin, Erica heaved a sigh of relief. When you flew standby, there was never any guarantee you would get a seat. Only when everyone else was on board and the boarding agent called your name did you know for sure you'd snagged a seat.

It was impossible for Erica to relax during takeoffs, so she busied herself organizing the reading material in the pocket in front of her, with tallest in the back, then flipped through a magazine. When they leveled out, she turned her thoughts to the case. Watching the checkered landscape below and sipping her Sprite, Erica thought how ironic it was that Wendy, the person who had asked her to investigate, presently had the best motive for poisoning Stephen. And what would happen once Patrick knew Wendy was Stephen's beneficiary? They might even think she had something to do with the Tyson murder. Erica had to find out who had actually poisoned Stephen and killed Gregory Tyson; she just *had* to.

At the airport, Erica rented a car and opened her purse to find her package of moist towelettes. After wiping off the steering wheel, seat, and dashboard, she typed the address in the GPS and made her way to a tall office building on the outskirts of Memphis. When she'd called Phil Norton, Gregory Tyson's boss, to reschedule her appointment to Saturday, he was gracious about it and said they could still meet at his office.

ABS, or Amalgamated Building Supplies, took up the first three floors of a glass and cream-brick high-rise. When Erica had called last week, the secretary had been sympathetic and given her names and phone numbers of Gregory Tyson's coworkers. She'd called most of them already and gotten a picture of a friendly, older man who loved to talk, perhaps a little too much, and who had seemed anxious of late. Nobody knew exactly why; it could have been the gloomy economy, stagnant sales, or undisclosed personal reasons. Two of Tyson's coworkers recommended she talk to Phil Norton as he had been quite friendly with Gregory.

As instructed, Erica called Mr. Norton when she arrived, and he came down and opened the locked doors. Broad-shouldered and silver-haired, Phil Norton was a well-mannered, good-looking man in his fifties. He welcomed her warmly.

"I'm so sorry to bother you on a Saturday," Erica apologized.

"No problem. I often come in for a few hours." As they passed through a room of open-air cubicles, he spread out a hand to where a number of people were busily working. "As you can see, a lot of others come in as well."

Phil Norton's office was spacious. Erica nodded in approval at the even number of windows and bookshelves. Phil led her to two leather chairs that were separated by a small round table.

"This is a little friendlier than me sitting behind my desk," Mr. Norton said with a pleasant smile. He had a relaxed way of talking that made Erica feel at ease. "Now, you said you wanted to ask some questions about Greg, but I've already spoken to the police." He eyed her curiously. "I'm sorry, did you say you were a reporter?"

"No, I'm a friend of Wendy Kemp. Gregory Tyson was killed outside her house. She asked me to do a little investigating."

"Like a private eye, eh?"

"Something like that."

"I've already told the police all I know, which isn't much." Mr. Norton shook his head sadly. "I still can't believe Greg is gone. It's a dangerous world we live in, that's for sure."

"I understand he was in Florida on business."

"That's right. I sent Greg down to go over a contract with one of my clients. Fairly standard stuff, and since I was busy, I asked him to take care of it for me." Mr. Norton sounded pained. "In a way, I feel responsible for his death."

"You had no way of knowing."

"No, but he'd still be alive if I hadn't sent him . . ." He grimaced. "Since you're here, I take it the police haven't found the person who killed him."

"Not yet. Do you know of anyone who had a problem with Tyson? A belligerent client or disgruntled customer? Perhaps an antagonistic coworker—anybody who might have a grudge against him?"

"I told the police about one man, Sam McGregor. He didn't like Greg. Not one bit. To put it mildly, he thought Greg was an opinionated know-it-all, but it wasn't serious. They just rubbed each other the wrong way. They would argue about anything and everything from global warming to the Tennessee Titans, but Sam never would have harmed Greg."

"Could I speak to Sam?"

"He doesn't work here anymore. Quit about four months ago and moved to Minnesota, I believe. I can have my secretary get his contact information if you want. She already gave it to the police detective. Other than Sam, Greg was liked by just about everyone." He paused. "Well, maybe not so much by some of the younger fellows. You see, Greg could talk a lot—"

"Did he now?" Erica said, encouraging him to go on.

"Once Greg got wound up, he could talk for hours. Still, the worst you could say about him is he could talk your ear off. He was a good guy, always upbeat, always on the lookout for a break—sure something good was just around the corner. He was friendly too—liked to know all about you and what you were doing. Greg also had a great memory—could remember the names, ages, and occupations of your kids, all that kind of stuff. He was very punctual too; I liked that."

"Did anybody ever take offense at the interest Gregory took in their personal lives?"

Mr. Norton looked surprised. "Not that I know of. Greg was just very sociable—he liked to talk to others and ask questions. He wasn't superficial like a lot of people. He really cared."

"I heard he had a temper and could hold a grudge." Erica was fishing, but Mr. Norton didn't have to know that.

His brow furrowed. "I never saw that. Greg was quite easygoing—you know, mellow."

Mellow? "Did you know Gregory was carrying a switchblade the night he was killed?"

"A switchblade? Greg?" Mr. Norton was clearly startled. "No, I didn't."

Erica went on to other things. "Was Gregory paid on salary or commission? I heard he was a bit anxious lately. Could he have been worried about money?"

Running a finger around his collar, Mr. Norton said, "Greg had a base salary but was paid on commission. He used to earn a decent living, but sales have been falling off during the past few years. Sometimes I gave him extra things to do, like the Orlando job, so I could pay him extra." He frowned. "I don't like saying anything against him, but Greg just wasn't all that successful in sales. What with the bad economy, a lot of our old, reliable customers have gone out of business or cut back, which meant Greg had to deal with new people, and well, he just didn't look the part, you know? He tried hard, but in this line of work, a good appearance means a lot."

Erica remembered the thin face, sparse hair, and melancholy eyes.

Mr. Norton went on. "The crazy thing is Greg loved his job; I didn't have the heart to let him go. I never have to fire people in sales," he said frankly, spreading out his hands. "If a person can't sell enough to make a living, they quit, but not Greg. He was always optimistic, sure things would be better tomorrow. All Greg wanted was an opportunity. And since he seemed satisfied with his paychecks, who was I to say he ought to quit and do something else?"

"So, he was just getting by."

"His wife, Vauna, worked too, so they were usually able to make ends meet."

Erica was quick to pick up on that. "Usually, but not always?"

A shadow fell across Phil Norton's face. "Sometimes Greg got behind on his bills."

"And—then what?"

A pause. "I helped him out a few times." Mr. Norton shrugged as if it was nothing. "Greg was a friend."

"I see."

"And he always paid me back." Mr. Norton wanted to make sure she knew this.

"Did he ever ask anyone else for money?"

"If he did, I didn't know about it."

Erica dropped that line of questioning. "The police don't think it was a robbery attempt."

"It was probably some kid on drugs. Punks nowadays will kill you for pocket change."

"It happens," Erica acknowledged. "Can you think of anything that might have a bearing on this case, no matter how slight?"

He thought hard. "Well, there is one thing, but it's probably not important."

"What is it?"

"When you asked if he'd asked anyone else for money, I remembered something. Before Greg left for Florida, he said he was going to see an old friend—someone who was going to be rich. I remember that because it sounded so odd."

"Did he mention a name?"

"He did. Now what was it?" Mr. Norton thought hard a few seconds. "Let me think. Stuart? Simon? No, but I think the name started with an *S*."

Not wanting to lead him, Erica thought of names that started with the same letter. "Scott? Shawn? Shane? Samuel? Stanley? Stephen?"

Smiling brightly, he pointed at her. "Stephen—that's it!"

"Did he say anything else, like how Stephen was going to become rich?"

"No. I remember being curious, but I didn't pursue it."

Erica thanked him for his time and gave him her cell number in case he remembered anything else.

She had a lot to think about as she stopped at a fast food place for a grilled chicken sandwich to silence her rumbling stomach. She went to the restroom and pulled one of the zippered bags of soap out of her purse. The second bar was for friends. She lathered up with the bar of Lava. So Stephen was going to be rich? He already appeared well off—fancy car, expensive clothes, and upscale apartment, but he hadn't mentioned anything about coming into money. And how did a person suddenly *become* rich anyway? By winning the lottery? Perhaps some savvy investments were paying off. It couldn't be due to his job—he or Reed surely would have mentioned that.

But if Tyson was right, why hadn't Stephen mentioned anything when she asked about his finances? Maybe Stephen thought such a disclosure would point another finger at Wendy since she was his beneficiary. Then again, maybe Tyson had gotten it wrong. If he was struggling to get by, it's possible he thought that since Stephen had a good job and was earning a good salary, he was going to become rich as he worked his way up the ladder. Regardless, it seemed possible Stephen's impending wealth could be the reason Tyson had planned to see Stephen while he was in Florida.

* * *

After eating, Erica drove west until she reached the suburbs, then she let the GPS guide her to a quiet street where she parked in front of a small, dilapidated white house with leaf-green shutters. The front porch steps had been painted green, and a white, older-model Grand Am was in the carport. Erica's eyes went to the middle house number, which was tilted. It resisted her efforts to straighten it, so Erica dug through her purse for the Leatherman tool that she kept for just such emergencies. Loosening the screw, straightening the number, and retightening the screw took only a few moments. She then rang the doorbell and happily watched two fluttering sparrows dip and splash in a cement birdbath next to the house until she heard a slight noise from inside.

The pleasant-looking woman who answered the door was in her sixties and had short gray hair that was tightly curled. With a smile that was friendly, if a bit trembly, Mrs. Vauna Tyson held the door open and stood aside so Erica could enter.

"Just go into the front room; it's on your left," she directed.

The walls were covered with faded pink rosebud wallpaper, and the bookshelves and tabletops were crowded with books, pictures, and knickknacks. Erica and Mrs. Tyson sat on opposite ends of a well-used couch, and though the blinds were tilted against the sun, golden dust motes were visible, dancing in the slanting afternoon light. When Erica offered her condolences, Mrs. Tyson's eyes welled up, and Erica saw that her eyes were red and puffy as if she had been crying.

"You'll have to forgive me, dear. Sometimes I do so well, and other days I can't turn off the waterworks. Today's the latter."

"I'm very sorry about your husband, Mrs. Tyson," Erica said gently as the older woman pulled tissues from a box on the coffee table. "It's a very difficult time for you, I'm sure. I hope it won't be too upsetting if I ask you a few questions."

"Please, call me Vauna. You've caught me on a bad day, but go ahead. You've come so far; I wouldn't turn you away now. And you look just as nice as you sounded on the phone. It's just that—thinking about it brings everything back. But I'll do anything if it will help you find out who did it." She dabbed at her eyes.

"I'll do my best. Now, did your husband know a man named Stephen Watkins?"

"Oh yes! They both worked at Cicero. Anthony Bronson owned the company—he was fabulously wealthy, you know." Vauna leaned forward and confided, "Stephen was Mr. Bronson's personal assistant. He had a very cushy job, I must say. Greg and Stephen were great friends."

"So Stephen was a personal assistant to the owner? I imagine that could have been quite stressful. I ought to ask Stephen about it sometime."

"Oh, you know Stephen?"

"I met him through a friend of mine, Wendy Kemp."

Vauna's face softened. "I bet Stephen could tell you some great stories! He and Mr. Bronson were very close. Greg told me they did everything together: fancy parties, weekends in Paris or Madrid, exotic vacations in Zanzibar, Nepal, Bhutan. They were like father and son. And Stephen doted on Mr. Bronson's daughter, Linda."

At Erica's look of interest, Vauna went on. "Oh, it wasn't romantic—Linda was like his little sister or niece. You see, Stephen and his wife weren't able to have children—she had a bad heart. She had an operation for it but died during surgery." A look of sadness crossed her face. "Anyway, Stephen and Linda stayed close even after Mr. Bronson died. Neither of them had much family. Linda's mother had died years ago."

Vauna stopped and smiled apologetically. "I'm sorry, I'm rambling, aren't I? Greg always told me I was a great talker. Of course, I couldn't hold a candle to him!" Her eyes suddenly overflowed again, and she pulled another tissue. "Anyway, that was a long way to answer your question. But yes, Greg and Stephen were good friends."

"Did they keep in touch after Stephen moved to Florida?"

Vauna frowned. "Things changed after Richard died. He was Stephen's twin brother, you know. Stephen quit his job very suddenly and moved away. Didn't even tell Greg he was leaving. Greg called and left messages, but Stephen never returned them." The lines in the older woman's face deepened. "Wait a minute—I take that back. He did call and talk with Greg once."

"I heard that your husband planned to see Stephen in Florida."

"Greg was so excited when his boss asked him to go to Orlando. He thought it was a great opportunity—you see, he'd recently found out that Stephen had moved to Kissimmee." Mrs. Tyson went on sadly, "Greg was really looking forward to seeing Stephen again. But he never got the chance."

"I suppose he called to let Stephen know he was coming?" Erica asked, double-checking Stephen's story.

"No, Greg wanted to just show up and surprise him. That was Greg—always positive, hopeful, looking on the bright side. I told him he should call first. What if Stephen happened to be out of town? But he wouldn't listen. To tell the truth, I think Greg was a little worried Stephen might not want to see him. You know—because he hadn't been very good about returning Greg's calls."

"This morning, Phil Norton said your husband told him Stephen was going to be rich soon. Do you know anything about that?"

Vauna tilted her head, deep in thought. "Greg must have been talking about Stephen's inheritance. But Stephen won't be getting that for a long time, if ever."

"What inheritance?"

"From Mr. Bronson, of course. Well, actually it's not coming straight from Anthony—he died a long time ago—it's coming from his daughter, Linda."

"I'm not sure I understand."

"When Mr. Bronson died, he left most of his fortune to his daughter although I'm sure he left Stephen *something*. Linda's the one who's leaving most of her money to Stephen."

"Do you happen to know where Linda lives?"

"She's still in Chicago, I should think. Moved back home after her last divorce, right before her father got sick. Mr. Bronson had a big place just outside the city."

The phone rang, and Mrs. Tyson bustled to answer it. When she came back, she settled on the couch again. "That was my daughter. She's going to take me shopping when we're done."

"I've only got a few more questions. Why is Linda Bronson leaving her fortune to Stephen? I know you said Linda didn't have much family, but doesn't she have anyone?"

"Linda was divorced twice and never had children. There was a brother, but I don't think they ever had much to do with each other. From what I understood, he was the black sheep of the family. So, really, Stephen is the only family Linda has, even if they aren't related by blood."

"I see."

"Of course, Stephen isn't likely to inherit anything since Linda is a lot younger than he is."

Erica nodded, switching topics. "When did you and your husband move away from Chicago?"

"Oh, it's been about a year and a half. The company changed so much after Stephen left." Vauna's voice hardened. "Suddenly, there was no such thing as loyalty to old employees, and Greg was laid off. Our daughter lives here in Memphis, so we came here and Greg was able to find a job."

"One last question. Do you know why your husband was carrying a switchblade?"

A tinge of pink colored Vauna Tyson's face. "The police told me about that, but Greg never carried a knife. At first, I thought somebody must have left it on him. Then later, I wondered if Greg had bought it for protection."

"Protection?"

"He was mugged once, a year ago, when he was traveling. The robber took his wallet then beat him up. He spent two days in a hospital. After that, Greg was always nervous in strange cities. He must have bought the knife after he arrived in Florida."

Erica picked up her purse. "Thank you for letting me come and talk with you. You've been very helpful. Again, I'm very sorry for your loss. I hope you're getting along all right."

Vauna took a gulp of air and although her eyes filled with tears, her voice was firm. "I'm blessed to be near my daughter. She checks in on me nearly every day. And I have a job at the hospital. It helps pay the bills."

"Are you able to make ends meet?" Erica asked gently.

The woman dabbed at her eyes. "My goodness, that's sweet of you to ask. To tell the truth, lately Greg and I have been a little worried. We've had some medical bills, and then our car broke down. But Greg had a life insurance policy, so I'm using that to pay off the bills, and my son-in-law is going to help me get a more reliable car. The rest is going in the bank for a rainy day."

On impulse, Erica gave the older woman a hug. "Thanks for letting me come see you. You take care of yourself now."

"Well, aren't you a dear! Good luck with your investigating. I'm counting on you to find out who did it!"

"I'll keep in touch," Erica promised.

The rest of the afternoon was spent visiting Vauna's neighbors. Most of them knew Gregory, and she gained a fuller picture of a man who was friendly, excitable, and loved to talk. They were horrified at his death and solicitous of his widow.

The sun had set by the time she boarded her plane. Erica leaned her head back and thought about her visit with Mr. Norton. According to him, Tyson was ever the optimist. Perhaps Tyson had seen an opportunity with Stephen—an opportunity to get a loan. Hadn't Mr. Norton said that Tyson was always on the lookout for a break?

Unbidden, a quote came to mind. "Something will turn up." Benjamin Disraeli. Something *had* turned up for Tyson—Stephen coming into money. It could very well be that Tyson had gone to Florida intent on capitalizing on that opportunity. Instead, he had ended up dead.

Closing her eyes, Erica went over her conversation with Vauna Tyson. So, Mrs. Tyson thought her husband had bought the switchblade for protection. Was she right, or did he buy it with the intention of assaulting someone? Someone like Stephen?

* * *

When the plane touched down in Orlando, Erica called Wendy then dialed home.

Her son, Ryan, answered. "Did you find out who killed that man?" His voice was eager.

"Not yet. I'm waiting for him to step forward and confess."

"Oh, he'd never do that." Ryan was very sure.

"Then I'll just have to keep looking. Hey, what are you doing up so late?"

"I had homework."

"Your homework is supposed to be done *before* dinner. Unless I'm helping you online."

"Dad lets me do it after."

"He does? I think your father and I need to have a little talk."

"Oh, Mom!" Ryan cried. "Chill out."

"Never mind. How's basketball going?"

"Great! I scored six points in my last game!"

"Kobe Bryant, you better watch your back!"

After talking for a while, he said, "Dad's here. He wants to talk with you."

They chatted for a while then Erica said, "Ryan told me that since I left, he's been doing his homework *after* dinner."

"Yep. Doing a good job too."

"But he *wasn't* doing it when I was home. That's why I told the kids they had to do their homework *before* dinner. To make sure it got done."

David was flexible. "He's been doing okay, but I can change it if you want."

"Well—" Erica was a believer in the old adage. "If it ain't broke, don't fix it. I guess if he's doing it, it's okay, but if it doesn't work out, have him do it before dinner. Is Aby doing the same thing?"

"Yeah, with a slight twist." David chuckled. "Every night she tells me she has too much homework to help clean up after dinner."

"Sounds familiar."

"I told her that everyone in the family helps. That didn't have much of an effect, but telling her that the TV doesn't go on until her homework is done has made quite a difference. Somehow, she always manages to get done before her favorite show comes on. So, how was your trip?"

She told him about meeting with Phil Norton and Vauna Tyson.

David whistled softly. "So Stephen is next in line to inherit a fortune—I can see someone wanting to bump him off if he'd already inherited, but it doesn't make sense for someone to kill him *before* he gets the money."

"True." Erica sighed. "At first I thought I'd finally found a motive, but unfortunately it looks like a dead end. When I go to Chicago next week, I'll check out Cicero, where Stephen and Gregory worked. While I'm there, I'd like to talk with Linda Bronson. I'll get her number from Stephen."

"Good luck. Just be aware that the ultrarich don't usually give interviews. Say, what does Stephen think about his inheritance? Is he drooling?"

"Apparently not. He didn't even tell me about it when I asked about his finances."

David was quiet a moment. "That's strange. Then again, he might be thinking the same thing as Mrs. Tyson—that he's never going to inherit anyway so why mention it?"

"Wendy's never mentioned it either."

"She probably doesn't know. Maybe Stephen wants to make sure she loves him for him—and not his money."

"You know, I wish I knew what was going on with Wendy because *something* is. I get the feeling like something inside is about to bubble over, but whenever I ask about it, Wendy claims she's fine. Personally, I think whatever it is has been bothering her for so long she doesn't even realize it's affecting her."

"Maybe its Megan," David suggested.

"I don't think so. Personally, I'm starting to wonder if she's having second thoughts about marrying another man who wants nothing to do with religion."

"Could be. If you have a strong testimony of the gospel, it would be hard not to be able to share that with your spouse."

"I'm not sure about this whole marriage thing," Erica said.

"Really? I thought we were doing pretty good," David teased.

Erica laughed. "Sorry! That came out wrong! No, I meant Wendy and Stephen. *Our* marriage is heavenly."

"That's because I'm married to an angel. But as for Wendy and Stephen, you're always saying what a great guy he is."

"He is." Erica sounded glum. "But there just aren't any sparks."

"Sparks?"

"You know—excitement, rapture, the whole head-over-heels-in-love thing."

"Wendy and Stephen aren't teenagers anymore."

"There should *always* be sparks," she insisted, "no matter how old you are."

"Come home and I'll show you some sparks."

She giggled. "It just seems that their relationship is built on convenience. Wendy's like Cher in that old movie *Moonstruck*. Remember? Cher was going to marry Danny Aiello, and there weren't any sparks. Cher acted more like his mother than his sweetheart—putting a napkin in his lap when he ate, making travel arrangements for him—"

"Then along came Nicolas Cage."

"Yeah, and sparks. *Major* sparks."

This time David was the one laughing. "Okay. So, other than a serious shortage of sparks, how is Wendy holding up?"

"She's scared the police consider her a suspect, and she's worried about Stephen. He came so close to dying."

"Yeah, I can understand her worrying. It can be tough getting a corpse to propose."

"David!" Erica gasped. "That wasn't funny!"

"Then why are you laughing?"

"I'm not," she lied. "But you make it sound like she's only worried about Stephen because she wants to marry him. She cares about him as a person."

"A person who might marry her."

"Stop that!"

"Okay, okay." He went on. "Hey, you never told me if Wendy was grateful for you bailing her out with Detective Lund. I still can't believe you did that. Wendy should have gone in."

"I know," Erica admitted, "but it actually turned out pretty good. We had a good talk, and he's starting to trust me more. Besides, I think Wendy might have fallen apart."

"You protect her too much. I think you have a blind spot where she's concerned."

"I understand her. No one else does."

David groaned. "Hey, did you ever go back to that motel and talk with the employees?"

"Yeah, but they didn't have anything helpful. I'm still waiting for that one guy, Matt Watters, to come back from vacation." She changed the topic. "Were you able to call poison control and find out anything about Dalmane?"

"Let me grab my notes. Okay, here they are. Dalmane has a high toxicity level and is very lethal. It's a muscle relaxant and is most often prescribed to relieve anxiety. It's similar to Valium and affects the central nervous system. Dalmane is sometimes prescribed as an anticonvulsant. With an overdose, victims experience impaired breathing, drowsiness, and usually become unconscious."

"How long does it take to work?"

"Ten to twenty minutes."

"Which fits right in with Stephen having been poisoned at the party."

"Since Dalmane can be prescribed for anxiety as well as an anticonvulsant, it wouldn't be too hard for someone to get ahold of it."

"I asked Stephen about his prescriptions just in case he took Dalmane for epilepsy or some similar condition. But the only prescriptions he takes are for high cholesterol and heartburn."

"You've probably already asked Wendy about her prescriptions—" David knew she was prone to depression and anxiety.

"Yeah. No Dalmane. I asked Wendy if she'd ever used it and she had, years ago."

"A lot of people hang onto old prescriptions."

"I asked about that too, but Wendy said she hadn't kept any. To be sure, I searched the house when she was at work. I felt like a traitor."

"As an investigator, you can't take anybody's word," David said. "At least she's not on it now. The police will check on Wendy's medications, though, especially since she helped make the coffee." Then he said, "By the way, there will be a surprise for you when you get to Wendy's house."

"Really? What is it? And don't say, 'It won't be a surprise if I tell you.'"

"You took the words right out of my mouth." From his voice, Erica knew he was grinning. He added, "Save your breath, 'cause I'm not telling. In any case, you'll know soon enough."

That was true. After she hung up, Erica went out to the pick-up zone at the airport and, while watching cars pull up, thought about what

David had said. And what he hadn't said. They both knew the police were bound to consider Wendy their number-one suspect. And she was going to continue to be their prime suspect until Erica could prove her innocence.

A key part of Erica's job was remaining dispassionate enough to be objective, but that was nearly impossible in this case, especially when it meant considering the possibility Wendy might actually have poisoned Stephen. Just thinking about it made Erica feel shaken. The bad part was that although Erica was convinced of Wendy's innocence, she still had to investigate all possibilities even when it entailed double-checking on her friend. Erica bit her lip. She hated thinking of Wendy as a suspect. Just hated it.

CHAPTER 9

WHEN HER PHONE RANG SUNDAY morning, Erica ran for it. It was David, just as she thought. "Happy Mother's Day, sweetheart!" he said.

"Thanks," Erica said, slipping into a chair at the kitchen table and looking at the dozen mauve roses arranged in a clear vase. White waxflower was tucked in and around the roses. She had already pulled off the few petals that had been slightly bruised and made sure none of the leaves were below water level. Erica touched the soft petals. "Thank you again for the roses. Wendy had hidden them. When we got home last night, she had me close my eyes then brought them out. They're gorgeous! And you even remembered I like waxflower instead of baby's breath!"

"I'm glad they look okay." David sounded relieved. "I hate ordering things like that long distance. I made sure he knew I was a policeman though."

Erica giggled. "Why? Do you think he's afraid of you flying out and arresting him if I got wilted flowers?"

"Nah, I just like throwing my weight around. Hey, I was going to mail you a present to go along with the flowers, but the kids wouldn't let me."

"They wouldn't?"

"Aby came up with a great idea, and Ryan and Kenzie liked it too. They want to celebrate Mother's Day when you get back, so they created a new holiday just for this year. They're calling it 'Parents' Day.' We're going to hold it on Father's Day."

"Hey, that sounds great! Not every mother gets to celebrate Mother's Day twice."

Erica was still talking to her children when Megan and Brandon came in and began making a special breakfast for Wendy and Erica. Erica laughed when she saw the square pancakes and square omelet. As they ate, the children presented Erica and Wendy with cards. Brandon had made his, and on the front of each card, he'd drawn a picture of a dog. Megan gave her mother a new blouse, and Brandon surprised her with an LDS novel.

Then, Wendy gave Erica a framed picture of David and the children. "I know you miss them, so I had David e-mail me a picture and I had it enlarged and framed."

Erica held the picture next to her heart a moment. Her eyes began to sting. Then she gave Wendy a greeting card that had a gift card inside.

"Unimaginative but useful." She grinned. "Also, nearly square."

Wendy laughed. "So it's nearly perfect."

The kids insisted on clearing up and after Wendy left for work, Erica went to church with Megan and Brandon. Afterwards, Erica called her mother, mother-in-law, and grandmother.

It was early evening when Wendy returned, flinging herself into a chair in the front room. "I hate working Sundays," she said, running her fingers through her hair. "Especially on Mother's Day, but I got time and a half, plus great tips. It'll help pay a few bills." She looked around. "Where are the kids?"

"Brandon's around someplace. Megan went to see Kimberly after we got back from church."

"Megan went with you? What did you use? Duct tape or chloroform?"

"Both," Erica grinned. "Now, close your eyes."

"What? We did presents this morning."

"Close your eyes," Erica said more firmly.

"All right, but I'm warning you; I'll be asleep in five seconds. Or less."

Erica hurried into the bedroom then, coming back, said, "Okay, open your eyes." She held out a vase filled with purple and white daisies. "Happy Mother's Day!"

"But you already—"

"They're not from me. Read the card."

As Wendy read, her face softened and a tender smile appeared. "They're from Lee! Wasn't that nice of him!" She fingered the stem of a purple daisy. "How did he know daisies are my favorite?" She smiled then set the flowers on the coffee table. "It was sure busy at work today! My feet are killing me. And I haven't even thought about what to have for dinner. Boy, my next house isn't going to have a kitchen—just vending machines. Does anything sound good to you?"

"I have a great recipe for Crock-Pot Chicken."[6]

"Oh, we'd have had to start that—" She stopped when Erica smiled broadly. "You didn't." Wendy jumped up and, going into the kitchen, took the lid off the Crock-Pot and sniffed. "Hmmm, that smells wonderful. I don't know if I'll ever let you go home!" She replaced the lid. "Looks like it's just about ready."

They went back into the front room, and Wendy settled on the couch this time. Taking off her shoes and socks, she reached for the bottle of lotion she kept on the corner table and began massaging her feet. "Boy, it sure was a long day. I feel wiped out."

Not a good time for a serious discussion, Erica thought, but on the other hand, the kids weren't around, so they could talk privately. She decided to jump straight in. "Wendy, what's bothering you?"

Wendy looked up, surprised. "Besides my feet?"

"Yes, besides your feet. I just feel like something's bothering you."

"Gee, does having someone killed in my driveway and having my boyfriend poisoned count?"

"You know what I mean. You were acting different long before Stephen was poisoned—before I even came out. At first I thought it might be problems with Megan, but there doesn't seem to be anything new there. Then I wondered if you were having more financial problems."

"Do you always play the investigator with your friends?" Wendy asked as she rubbed her foot with unusual vigor.

"Only the ones I care about."

"You asked me about this before, remember? And I told you I'm fine."

"Would it have anything to do with Stephen's feelings about the Church?" Erica persisted.

The question seemed to hover in the air as they stared at one another. In the silence, the words expanded, taking on a life of their own. Finally, Wendy broke eye contact and bent over to pick up her shoes.

She stood, giving Erica an oblique look. "What time did you tell Megan to be back for dinner?"

"At six."

"I've just got time to shower, then." And without waiting for a reply, Wendy walked out.

* * *

---

6   See appendix at the end of the book for this recipe.

Bright and early Monday morning, Erica called Stephen, arranging to meet him later at his office after she took Wendy to work. However, when she arrived, a sharp-faced Diana Evans said Stephen wasn't back yet from an appointment. He'd called, though, Diana sniffed, and was on his way back. Stephen wanted Erica to wait in his office. Third door on the left.

When Erica pushed open the door, a startled Reed Devoe whipped around from an open file cabinet. "Oh, I'm sorry," Erica apologized, backing out. "I was looking for Stephen's office."

"This is his office," Reed muttered, his lips thin. "I was just looking for a file Stephen forgot to give me." Erica wondered about the apprehension she thought was in his eyes.

"I was supposed to wait for Stephen."

Closing the drawer, Reed asked, "So, how is your investigation going?"

How had he managed to make an innocent question sound so sarcastic? She ignored the tone and replied, "Very well, thank you."

"I'm curious," Reed said, sauntering around the side of the desk. "Exactly why did you get involved in this?"

"Wendy wanted my help. She was worried about Stephen."

He made a small sound of derision. "Wendy worries if Stephen sneezes."

"He *was* poisoned," Erica responded in a faintly indignant voice.

"And you and Jaime could easily have been yet weren't." Reed looked at her. "Isn't it interesting that neither you nor Jaime drank your coffee. That was quite . . . *lucky*, wasn't it?" His emphasis on *lucky* rankled. Reed didn't seem to expect an answer and went on. "I'm not sure why you're determined to believe that the would-be killer only meant to harm Stephen. The poison could have easily been meant for Jaime. She's quite taken with Stephen, and Wendy seems very jealous of her, or hadn't you noticed?"

If this unpleasant man was aware of that, others would be too, Erica thought with some alarm. Reed went to another line of attack. "Although it's gallant of you to try your hand at finding the aspiring killer, it's my understanding that a good portion of our taxes go to policemen to handle matters like this. It is their job, after all—"

Erica interrupted deftly. "It's my job too, and like I said, Wendy is concerned about Stephen."

"Ah yes, she believes wedding bells will soon be ringing. However, I'm not sure her feelings are reciprocated."

The arrogance of the man! "Isn't that between Stephen and Wendy?"

"Certainly," he replied calmly. "Still, I can't help but wonder if there might be some other reason for your investigating."

Erica took a seat. "What do you mean?"

"Could it be that you want to pin the blame on someone else because otherwise your friend might go to jail? Wendy *is* the main suspect, now, isn't she?"

Erica would not give him the satisfaction of saying so. "What makes you think that?"

"Come now," Reed said, giving her a look of mock astonishment. "One man is killed at her house, and another one is poisoned. Wendy's a regular black widow."

Incensed, Erica flashed, "Wendy had nothing to do with Tyson's murder."

"Oh no? Then why did she leave the house just before Tyson was shot, after neatly getting rid of you?"

"I went out for ice," Erica told him stiffly.

"The police might not look at it that way. They might think Wendy asked you to go buy ice so she could be alone and slip outside without anyone knowing. And the night Stephen was poisoned, she was in the kitchen, wasn't she? Helping Jaime with the coffee?"

"You're forgetting a couple of important things," Erica said coldly. "The first is that Wendy loves Stephen. She wouldn't do anything to hurt him. And second, all three cups were still on the coffee table when the police came to collect samples the next day. Only an imbecile would poison the coffee and then leave the cups out until the police came."

"Enough said, then."

Erica gasped as Reed walked out. It was a good thing he left quickly, or else she might have decked him. As it was, Erica was so angry she stood, balled up her fists, and took a few swings at the spot where Reed had been standing. An uppercut to the jaw and a hard right hook made her feel a great deal better. When she heard something, Erica dropped her arms. Jaime peered in the open doorway, looking sleek and sophisticated in a pale gray dress that fit her curves.

"Hello there," she said, looking at Erica curiously. "What are you doing here?"

"I came to see Stephen."

Just then, there was the sound of footsteps, and Jaime looked down the hallway. "Speak of the devil!" she said with a smile. "Hey, Stephen, you've got a pretty lady waiting in your office." Then, in a mischievous voice, she added, "You just have a fatal attraction to women, I guess." She waved and was gone.

"Hello, Erica. Sorry about that," Stephen said, waving a hand toward the door. His cheeks were faintly flushed. "Jaime likes to tease." Taking his chair behind the desk, Stephen invited Erica to sit then asked, "Any news on who poisoned the coffee?"

"Not yet."

He frowned. "I suppose these things take time. How did your trip to Memphis go?"

"Very well. I was able to talk to Gregory's boss, Mrs. Tyson, and a few of their neighbors, and I found out a little more about Gregory. He seemed to be a nice guy. Very friendly. Maybe a little too talkative but likable."

"That's Greg," Stephen smiled affectionately. "He did love to talk. Some people thought he was a little nosy—prying even—but he just liked people." His look turned to one of concern. "How is Vauna? I must call her. She and Greg were very close."

"She's grieving, naturally, but trying to move forward. I'm sure she'd appreciate hearing from you." Erica kept her eyes on Stephen's face. "While I was there, I learned something interesting—you're going to inherit a fortune from Linda Bronson."

He jerked slightly. "I'm in her will, yes," he replied, looking ill at ease.

"As the primary beneficiary." Erica looked at him reproachfully. "Why didn't you tell me?"

"I didn't think it had any bearing on the case."

Very slowly, Erica counted to ten. "I *asked* you about your finances because it was important," she corrected him, her voice crisp. "*Anything* you can tell me is important. Do I have to remind you that someone tried to kill you?"

"The poison might have been intended for you or Jaime."

"We've been over this. You're the likeliest candidate."

"But it's not like I have any of that money now," Stephen protested. "If someone was trying to kill me for my inheritance, wouldn't they wait until *after* I got the money?"

"On the surface, it would seem so," Erica replied enigmatically.

Stephen looked at her. "You have some idea in your head, don't you?"

"Maybe money isn't the motive. It could be something else. Tell me more about Anthony and Linda Bronson. Mrs. Tyson said you used to be Anthony Bronson's personal assistant."

"Yes, but we didn't just work together, we were good friends— actually more than friends. We spent a lot of time together, especially after his wife died."

"When was that?" Erica reached out and idly straightened a pile of papers on the desk.

"About twelve years ago. We were together so much I became part of the family. Linda and I were close too. She was a great kid—used to call me her 'Unkie Steve.' She was pretty young when she married a fortune hunter. He showed his true colors soon enough, and they divorced. She remarried, but that didn't work out either. She never did have kids. When Anthony died about eight years ago, he left most of his money to Linda."

"Mrs. Tyson thought Linda and her brother were estranged."

"That's right. Charles is her older brother, but they were never close. Charles didn't have much to do with anyone in his family. He and his wife, Areli, had one son, James."

"Did you know Charles?" Inching her chair closer to the desk, Erica straightened another pile as Stephen watched her with one eyebrow raised.

"I never met him." Stephen sounded regretful. "Linda told me her brother was very rebellious as a teenager and argued constantly with his parents. He left home when he was nineteen. She had very little contact with him after he left."

"So Charles never made up with his parents or sister?"

Stephen shook his head sadly. "Anthony and I talked about Charles from time to time, but Anthony was dead set that his son was never going to get his hands on the family fortune. Charles had a gambling problem, you see. He'd call every once in a while, Anthony said, asking for money and saying he had medical expenses. Anthony bailed him out a few times then found out Charles was using the money to pay off gambling debts. When Anthony stopped the handouts, Charles was furious and stopped calling."

"Did he ever ask Linda for money?"

"I only know of one time." Stephen smiled wryly. "Linda's not one to mince words. She told Charles he was a spoiled brat and had treated their parents disgracefully. She said he needed to stand on his own two feet and she wasn't about to give him a dime. Later, when Charles found out that their father had left everything to Linda, he called and started shouting at her. He accused Linda of conniving to cut him out of the will. He was pretty bitter about it."

"And the years haven't changed his feelings?"

Stephen rubbed his face wearily. "No, and it's too late to mend fences now. Charles died about a year and a half ago in a car accident. He lived in Puerto Rico. I hear they drive like maniacs down there. It wasn't until after my own brother died that Linda told me she'd named me as one of the beneficiaries of her will."

"So there are others?" When Erica leaned over to reach a pile of folders, Stephen put his hand on them.

"It's okay. I'll put them away after you go." When Erica sat back with a small sigh, Stephen went on. "Anthony was a great philanthropist, and Linda's following his lead, giving quite a bit to a number of charities. She's also leaving something to Areli and her nephew."

"Have you ever met Areli or her son?"

"No, and neither has Linda." Stephen's face hardened. "Charles bore a grudge to the bitter end—refusing to let his wife or son have anything to do with Anthony, his wife, or Linda. Even after Charles died, there was no contact. I guess Charles's bitterness rubbed off on Areli and James."

Erica was taken aback. "Wow. That really is sad."

"I never knew him, but from what Linda has said, Charles was a very hard man. I can't understand people like that. To me, family is every-thing." Stephen's face looked sad. Possibly he was thinking of his brother. Then he said softly, "It's going to be hard to lose Linda."

"Lose Linda—what do you mean?"

"About five years ago, Linda got breast cancer. The doctors gave her chemo and radiation, and it went into remission. Linda was doing pretty good until about two and a half years ago when the cancer came back." Stephen spoke in careful, measured tones, but Erica was aware of bewildered grief. "There's nothing the doctors can do. She's going through chemo again, but it won't change the outcome—it'll only give her a little more time."

It took Erica a moment to absorb this. "How long does she have? Months? Years?"

"It's been a while. She's down to just a few months now."

"I'm so sorry," Erica said regretfully. It had obviously been difficult for Stephen to lose his only sibling, and now he was going to lose Linda, whom he thought of as family. Her heart went out to him. "Mrs. Tyson said that you and Linda were very close. This must be very hard."

"Yes . . . yes, it is," he said flatly. She noticed how his shoulders drooped.

"While I'm in Chicago tomorrow, I'll be stopping by your old company and talking with people there. Then, I'll go talk with some of your old neighbors—see if I can come up with a reason why someone would want to bump you off. While I'm there, I'd like to visit Linda. If you'll give me her phone number, I'll call today and set it up."

Stephen looked dismayed. "I'm not sure that's a good idea. Linda's immune system is very low because of the chemo. She can't take a chance of catching anything—even the smallest illness could have devastating consequences. Plus, talking about this would only upset her."

"I'm perfectly healthy," Erica reassured him. "And she might be able to provide information that would help me find out who poisoned you."

"I don't care about that," Stephen declared. "The last thing I want to do is add to her worries. Linda has more than enough to deal with right now." His eyes were anxious.

"If Linda cares about you as much as you care about her, she'd want to help."

"Of course she would—that's the kind of person Linda is. I'll give you her number if you insist, but I wish you wouldn't bother her."

"I'll keep it upbeat, Stephen," Erica assured him. "I'm really sorry about her prognosis, but right now, I have to worry about saving *your* life."

* * *

When Megan offered to pick up her mother, Erica decided to take a break and read for thirty minutes. She was reclining on the sofa in the front room when the back door opened. Suddenly, Wendy's purse went sailing across the room like a missile, landing in the corner. Erica raised up in alarm.

"Oh my goodness!" Wendy exclaimed, hand over her heart. "I didn't know you were in here! I almost nailed you, didn't I?" She threw herself into a chair. "Too bad you weren't Jaime."

Ah, so that was the problem. "What's going on?"

"I asked Megan to stop at Stephen's office on our way home so I could see him for a minute. I was in his office when Jaime came in." Color surged into her face, and she flung an arm out for dramatic emphasis. "The door was *shut*, and she didn't even *knock*, just barged right in."

"So . . . were you and Stephen, ah, doing anything?"

"No!" Wendy snapped. "You have a dirty mind."

"I just wondered if you were kissing," Erica said defensively.

"Oh, well—" Wendy was slightly mollified. "No, we weren't. Anyway, she showed some papers to Stephen, asking if she'd done the report right. She was cooing like a lovebird, saying she'd taken extra care because she knew this report was important to him, and all the time she's standing so close I could hardly put a hand between them."

"You're kidding."

"It was sickening." There were two bright spots of red on Wendy's cheeks as she got up and began pacing. "But you want to know what was worse? Stephen! He acted as if it was perfectly normal! I mean, does this kind of thing happen all the time?" Wendy moved around the room with nervous energy, turning the cyclamen toward the sun, adjusting the curtains, straightening a book on the table—empty gestures meant to keep her hands busy. Suddenly she turned to Erica. "Do you think Jaime is the reason Stephen hasn't proposed?"

"I don't think so. Stephen can't possibly want her over you."

"Of course not," Wendy said sarcastically. "Any man would prefer a middle-aged woman who's put on a few pounds and has battleship hips to a hot young babe with legs a mile long and eye-popping cleavage." She reached the wall and did an about face, complaining, "Just when I start getting my head together, my body starts falling apart."

Fighting the urge to smile, Erica said, "I know Stephen cares about you!"

"I thought he did." Wendy's hands began to twist as she blurted, "He *can't* dump me now. He just *can't*! I've worked too hard. We've been together for so long—and now, Stephen has this gorgeous girl fawning all over him. I'd like to wring her scrawny neck!" There was something new in Wendy's eyes, a kind of edge—a thin hardness like lacquer.

Her outburst was so impassioned, it made Erica uneasy. Wendy seemed determined to marry Stephen. How far was she willing to go to achieve that aim? Erica had the uncomfortable feeling that maybe she didn't know Wendy as well as she thought. Had years of hardship changed her?

Suddenly, Wendy's pent-up energy evaporated and, dispirited, she sank onto the couch beside Erica. "You don't know how hard it's been, being alone for years—raising Megan and Brandon on my own after Dennis married that bimbo and moved to Virginia. I don't mean to sound mercenary, but I'd been looking forward to marrying Stephen and having some financial security. I'm tired of panicking every time one of the kids gets sick or has to go to the dentist. Whenever the car makes an odd sound, I'm scared to death it's going to break down. Last year, it was terrible telling Brandon that Santa wasn't going to bring the skateboard he wanted."

"It's been tough, I know." Through e-mails, calls, and texts, Erica knew a little about her friend's loneliness, financial worries, and insidious fear that life might never improve. It was natural to want to be financially secure, but Erica hoped it wasn't the main reason Wendy wanted to marry Stephen. In fact, Wendy's faith seemed so strong that Erica was surprised she would marry someone who wasn't a member of the Church— especially after the experience she'd had with Dennis. Even though her last attempt hadn't gone well, Erica decided to broach the subject again. Still, it was a delicate subject . . . even between close friends.

"Can I ask you something?" Erica began slowly. "I'm not quite how to say it though . . ."

Wendy's brows came together in curiosity. "What is it?"

"I know you really care for Stephen and of course he cares for you, but I also know how important the Church is in your life. I suppose you and Stephen have talked about that—"

"You know we have," Wendy said with a heavy sigh. "Like I said, he doesn't have any strong feelings one way or another. Stephen has come to church with me a few times on Sundays, but he didn't like it. He doesn't believe in organized religion but said he doesn't mind if I go."

"Are you're okay with that?" Erica asked softly.

There was a long silence as Wendy stared at her lap. Then she looked up, and her eyes were filled with tears. "It's not the way I hoped it would be. Now that Stephen's close to proposing, I find myself doing a lot of thinking." Her voice cracked. "I don't want to go to church alone! I want to marry in the temple and have my husband hold the priesthood!"

Erica slid over and put an arm around her friend. Wendy sniffed. "I asked him if he'd take the missionary discussions—just to learn about the Church, but he didn't want to. So I guess I'll just have to keep praying that someday Stephen will feel a need to have God in his life."

"You know how I've been asking if something is bothering you? Well, I think this is it. Ever since you and Stephen started getting serious, I've sensed that you've been struggling inside. Are you having second thoughts? Are you sure you want to marry Stephen?"

Wendy stiffened. "Of *course* I'm sure! Yes, I'd like him to be an active member of the Church, but he loves me and we get along great. So he's not perfect—who is? And in case you haven't heard any of the hundred times I've mentioned it, I *want* to marry Stephen."

"You do, huh?" Erica looked at her.

"Yeah, I do. No pun intended. How many times do I have to tell you?"

"You don't have to convince me. I think the person you have to convince is yourself." In the ensuing silence, Erica could hear the faint tick, tick, tick, of the clock on the wall. Finally she said, "Look, I just want what's best for you. I just don't want you to settle for anything less than you deserve."

"Oh, Erica! You mean well, but you have no idea how hard it is to find a good man when you're my age. Look at my crow's feet! Look at my hips! Unfortunately, it's not my jeans that make my butt look fat." Wendy bowed her head. "Sure I wish Stephen believed in God, but he could in time. I'm praying for him. And I'm so afraid of growing old alone."

Her friend seemed so conflicted that it wrung Erica's heart. "Wendy, you can't make a decision about marriage based on fear!"

"I'm not! I want to marry Stephen because he's a wonderful person and he loves me."

There was no mention of Wendy loving him, Erica noticed. Feeling her way carefully, she said, "It's not easy living alone, but when the Church is the center of your life, it seems like it would be hard to live with someone who doesn't believe the way you believe. And what if you have children? How does Stephen feel about that?"

"I think he wants children. He and his wife weren't able to have any—because of her heart condition."

"That's why she died, isn't it?"

"Yes. They'd thought about adopting, but her health was too bad. But the important thing is that Stephen is a good, kind man. Once he sees what a wonderful thing the gospel is, he could change his mind."

Erica looked at her steadily. "Are you willing to take that chance?"

There was a pause, then Wendy said, "He hasn't asked me to marry him yet."

* * *

Tapping away on the keys of her laptop while sitting on her bed, Erica didn't even hear Megan come down the stairs. She jumped when Megan said hello.

"Whoa, didn't mean to scare you," Megan said, trying not to smile. "Although it would have been funny to see what would have happened if I'd snuck up and then jumped at you." She giggled just thinking about it.

Erica still had a hand over her heart. "You would have needed to use CPR to get my heart going again if you had."

Megan sat beside her and gave her a searching look. "I really scared you, didn't I? Sorry."

"That's okay. It's just that . . . oh, never mind."

"What?"

Erica hated to admit it. "I don't do so well in the dark—at least not when I'm alone."

Megan's look softened—a distinct change from her usual abrasive expression and attitude. It struck Erica that if she confided in the girl, she might create a bond between them.

"It's embarrassing, but I'm afraid of the dark."

A skeptical look crossed Megan's face. "Oh, come on—" Then she looked closer at Erica. "You're serious, aren't you?"

"I've tried to get over it and am a lot better than I used to be, but I still have a hard time."

"Wow, you're not as perfect as I thought you were."

Erica laughed at the incredulity in the girl's voice. Then she turned serious. "It's a phobia I developed when I was six." When Megan tilted her head, looking curious and waiting, Erica reluctantly went on.

"I had an older cousin who was always teasing me. He was constantly taking my things and hiding them. So one day, I tried to get back at him by hiding his bicycle behind the garage. I didn't know it would make him so angry. When I confessed I'd taken his bike, he said he'd get even. A few days later, I couldn't find my favorite stuffed dog. He told me he'd hidden it in a closet in the basement. We went downstairs to get it, and when I opened the door and looked inside, he pushed me in then put something against the door so I couldn't get out."

"Oh, Erica." Megan's voice was full of compassion.

Erica tried but was unable to keep the bitterness out of her voice. "He left me there. No one else was home. I screamed until my throat was raw. Five hours later, my parents came home."

Reaching over, Megan took hold of Erica's hand.

"I had nightmares for a long time," Erica confided. "Still do, once in a while."

"How do you stand being down here then?" Megan glanced around the basement.

"I rely on night-lights." Erica nodded toward one by the stairs, another on the far wall, and one by her bed. "I'm just a big baby."

Unexpectedly, Megan threw her arms around Erica. "You can have my room if you want. I'll sleep down here."

Erica's heart melted. It was so nice to see Megan's warm, caring side. "That's sweet of you, but as long as the electricity holds out, so can I."

They talked a while longer, and there was none of the harshness or rebellion Megan usually displayed but a warmth instead. When they said good night, Megan gave Erica another long hug and even turned before going up the stairs to give Erica a little wave.

David was never going to believe this, Erica thought.

* * *

The following afternoon, the door slammed and Brandon came sliding into the kitchen. "Can we go now?"

"Don't you want a snack first?" Erica asked. Shaking his head, Brandon flung his backpack in a corner. Erica got an apple from the fridge anyway and handed it to him. "Here, this will tide you over until dinner." Then she called over her shoulder, "We're going to the pet store now, Megan! Bye!"

When they arrived, Erica slipped on a pair of gloves. Just inside the door was a pen that held rabbits, and Brandon knelt to watch them twitch their ears and wiggle their noses. Next, they went to a pen where Brandon put his fingers through the wire for a dachshund puppy to chew.

"He's just like yours!" Brandon exclaimed, glancing up at Erica. They visited a sleeping cocker spaniel and a playful beagle and then looked into a window-lined room that held more puppies. A fluffy Pomeranian chewed on a blue squeaky toy while a brown and white rat terrier lapped at his water dish. Brandon was able to pet the kittens and guinea pigs but was especially taken with the hamsters. Several of them were going round and round on a wheel.

"I like that one," Brandon said, pointing to a tan hamster with a white underbelly.

"He's cute all right," Erica agreed. After the rats and mice, they visited the birds—flighty finches, green-masked lovebirds, an African gray who eyed them intently, and then the aviary, which was filled with parakeets in colorful hues of yellow, blue, and green.

"Why, Brandon! What are you doing here?" A tall man with a thatch of thick white hair stopped and beamed at Brandon. His face seemed familiar, and Erica tried to place him.

"I'm looking at the animals," Brandon replied helpfully.

"And I'm here to buy some parrot food," the man explained, extending a hand to Erica.

Suddenly she had it. "Oh yes, you're the bishop, aren't you?"

"Yes, Byron Heaps. And you're Wendy's friend, Erica, right? How is she doing?"

"Pretty good, considering."

His face turned solemn. "She's been through a lot." He turned back to Brandon. "Well, I'd better find my wife before she thinks I got lost. You have a good time now."

"I will," Brandon said then headed back to the hamsters. When an employee asked if Brandon wanted to hold one, he quickly pointed out one with a white underbelly.

The employee told Erica, "Our cages and supplies are on sale today."

Brandon looked at her hopefully, "Do you think Mom would let me have one?"

"I don't think so." After the employee put the hamster back, they went to see the fish, but Brandon lost interest quickly and returned to the hamsters. When he put his face next to the cage, the tan hamster came over, stood on his hind legs, and stared at Brandon with beady black eyes.

"See, he likes me!"

It *was* cute. She'd always had pets—couldn't imagine life without them. Erica looked closer at Brandon, who was making faces at the little rodent. Hamsters were easy to take care of, she thought. Aby and Ryan each had one.

"Brandon, I'll be right back. You stay here." Going to a nearby aisle that had bird supplies, one where Erica could still see Brandon, she dialed her cell phone. As she talked, she straightened the bird toys, arranging them by size with large ones for parrots on the left. When she came back, Brandon was still watching the hamsters, most of which were now sleeping.

"So, you think you'd like a hamster?"

Something in Erica's tone made him look up quickly. "Can I? Can I get one?"

"I just called your mom and asked her if it was all right if I bought you a present." As his eyes widened in delight, she continued, "But there *is* a problem. You see, hamsters have to be fed and watered every day and have their cage cleaned regularly."

"I can do that!"

"You promise? Your mom is too busy to do it for you," she warned. When he crossed his heart and hoped to die, Erica inclined her head toward the rodents. "So, which one would you like?"

In no time at all, they were walking out the door, with Brandon carefully cradling a little cardboard box with holes.

When Wendy got home, Brandon grabbed her hand and took her to his bedroom to show her his hamster, which he'd named Buster. She turned to Erica with a frown.

"I told you Brandon could have *a* hamster. I never said he could have two!"

Erica stepped over to the second cage. "This one's mine." She slipped on a pair of gloves and picked it up with a smile. "I couldn't resist."

Shaking her head, Wendy said, "You're as bad as a kid. Just remember, when you leave, it leaves."

"It'll make a great surprise for the kids."

"Not to mention David," Wendy reminded her. "What are you going to tell him?"

"I've got that all worked out. I'm going to tell him its big black eyes reminded me of him and I missed him so much I had to get it."

"Think that will work, eh?"

Erica sighed. "Probably not. But he's used to me coming home with animals."

Brandon then gave his mother a minute-by-minute breakdown of their trip to the pet store, including seeing Bishop Heaps.

"When did Bishop Griggs get released?" Erica asked as Brandon stroked his hamster.

"Not soon enough" was Wendy's cryptic response.

Erica glanced at her in surprise. Just then Brandon asked, "Can I show Buster to Ryan and Kenzie?" Brandon had started talking online with Erica's children after seeing Erica helping them with homework. He now borrowed Erica's laptop frequently to talk to Erica's two youngest children.

"It's bedtime," Wendy said. "You can talk with them tomorrow." He grumbled a bit then asked if they could do family scripture reading and prayer in his room so Buster could listen. Wendy gave in although Megan was greatly annoyed. After hugs, Wendy and Erica headed for the front room while Megan got a snack and went to her bedroom.

"What would you like to do?" Wendy asked. "Play a game? Watch TV? Read?"

"Actually, I'd rather talk. I was curious about what you said about Bishop Griggs."

"Sorry. That wasn't very nice." Wendy reached for the remote. "Let's watch a movie."

Erica looked at her. "A few days ago, when we talked about the time you stopped going to church, you said Bishop Griggs was helping you and Dennis—and then you got kind of upset."

Looking sheepish, Wendy said, "Sorry about that. I know I kinda freaked out. I don't know why. I think I was just overtired."

Choosing her words carefully, Erica said, "I know you were seeing the bishop right around the time you decided to get a divorce. I also know something happened then, though you've never told me what it was. But from what you said the other day, it must have been something huge—" She paused. "If you still don't want to talk about it, that's okay."

Bringing her legs up under her, Wendy grabbed a throw pillow and hugged it for comfort. "Oh, I'm okay talking about it now. Actually, you'll be the first one I've told. I haven't even told my mother. Megan is the only one who knows, and that's because she was there."

"You know I'm always here for you," Erica said sincerely.

"You always have been. Honestly, I don't know what I would have done without you." Wendy stared at the floor. A car went by—the boom, boom, boom of its speakers echoing through the night. The house creaked slightly, and a dog barked in the distance. Finally, Wendy began to speak, and it was soon apparent that what had happened had lost none of its clarity or force.

"I told you that when Dennis and I first separated, he still wanted to work things out. Well, I had been talking to Bishop Griggs for quite a while. He'd been giving me a lot of advice and told me that Dennis and I ought to see a marriage counselor. So we started going. Then I told Dennis that I wanted him to go with me each week when I met with the bishop."

"And things got a little better, right?"

Wendy nodded. "Yeah, things were actually going pretty good. Then Dennis started talking about coming back home. He said that he had changed. I have to admit he *was* acting better. I talked privately to Bishop Griggs, and he said that if Dennis was still drinking, I ought to say no. I agreed. A few weeks later, Dennis told the bishop he'd stopped drinking."

There was a strange tone in Wendy's voice that made Erica ask, "Had he?"

"I don't know." Wendy's voice was mournful. "I believed him at the time, and so did Bishop Griggs. Anyway, Dennis kept saying how lonely he was and how much he missed me and the kids and that he wanted to come home. A week later, the bishop told me that I ought to let him come back home. I said I didn't think I was ready, but he felt I ought to give Dennis another chance."

As Wendy hugged her pillow fiercely, Erica had a sinking feeling in the pit of her stomach.

"I didn't *want* Dennis to come home, but Bishop Griggs felt I ought to. He seemed so sure that I didn't know what to do! He'd been so patient and spent so much time with me. I trusted him completely. Plus, since he was the bishop, I knew he was entitled to inspiration concerning me." Wendy's hazel eyes clouded over. "So I told Dennis he could come back. For about two weeks, everything was fine. Then one night, Dennis came home and he'd been drinking." Wendy's voice turned brittle.

"Oh no."

Looking as if she'd swallowed something bitter, Wendy went on. "Megan went straight to her room, and I sent Brandon over to the neighbors. Dennis and I started arguing. I'd been reading self-help books the past few months, and I stood up for myself. That was something new, and it made Dennis angry." She grimaced. "He was yelling and carrying on. Even though we were in the kitchen and Megan had her door closed, I'm sure she could hear everything."

Wendy's mouth began trembling, and for a moment she could not speak. The silence in the room had the quality of deafening sound.

"It happened so quickly." Wendy's voice was low and strained. "Dennis grabbed my arm, and I started hitting him until he let go. Then he grabbed both my arms and shook me. I screamed, and he backed me against the wall next to the basement door and held his hand over my mouth and nose." Wendy's eyes were swimming like liquid amber as tears fell. "I was having a hard time breathing and kept trying to get free. Then Megan came out and started screaming at Dennis. She tried to pull him away and kept yelling that she hated him—that we all hated him."

"You never told me . . ." Erica whispered.

"No," Wendy said simply. After a few moments, she went on. "Then I bit his hand, and he shoved me away. The door to the basement was open and—and I fell down the stairs."

Erica gasped.

"I remember looking up. I was dazed, but I still recall Dennis looking down at me. Then he turned and left." Wendy's voice trembled with remembered pain. "He didn't ask if I was all right. He didn't come down and help me up. He just left me in a heap at the bottom of the stairs." There was a thin silence that came from a woman on the far side of grief.

Anger such as Erica had never known flashed though her. There did not seem to be enough air in her lungs to speak aloud. All she could do was go to her friend and hold her close. Wendy's tears scalded through her hair. The pain was so engulfing it seeped into Erica's very core.

After a time, Wendy pulled back. "Megan called my neighbor, Suzanne, and she took me to the hospital." In a raw voice, she added, "That night I had a miscarriage."

Erica had to remember to breathe—it seemed her heart was stopping the breath in her throat. She whispered, "I didn't know you were pregnant."

"Nobody knew. Not even Dennis." As Wendy's self-control crumbled, a sob broke out then another. Her sobs became gut-wrenching as she covered her face with her hands. Erica was bereft of anything to offer besides the arms she wrapped around her friend. She held on, thinking she had never seen such grief. It was as if someone had grasped, beaten, and wrung out Wendy's heart. For a time there was silence because there could not have been any words.

Eventually the tears slowed. When Erica pressed tissues into her hand, Wendy wiped her eyes and looked around blindly as if wondering where she was. Her face was so ravaged that Erica didn't think she would have known her if she had come upon her unexpectedly.

Finally, Erica asked, "Did you contact the police?"

"No. I should have, but right then I couldn't handle it. I filed for divorce two days later," Wendy said jerkily. "Then I called Dennis and told him that he'd killed our baby. I also called Bishop Griggs and told him that I wouldn't be back to church—that none of this would have happened if he hadn't told me that it was all right to have Dennis come back."

Erica felt stricken to stone.

"I thought a bishop was supposed to be called of God—to have inspiration—yet he told me to let Dennis move back home!" There was rage and tearing grief in Wendy's voice. "God knew what would happen if Dennis moved back. If Bishop Griggs had really been called of God, he never would have told me to let Dennis come home. God never would have wanted me to lose my baby. *He couldn't want that,*" Wendy gulped. "It's because of the bishop that I lost my baby . . . My poor, sweet baby."

CHAPTER 10

THE FOLLOWING MORNING WAS HECTIC, with everyone trying to get into the bathroom at the same time. Erica couldn't help thinking about last night's revelation and was able to catch Wendy as she came out of the bathroom and Megan slipped in. Noticing some puffiness around Wendy's eyes, Erica asked how she was feeling.

"I'm fine," Wendy replied, giving a little smile. "I'm sorry I lost it. Usually I'm fine, but once in a while, it still hits me hard, you know?"

"I can understand that," Erica said, giving her a hug. "If there's ever anything I can do, let me know. "

Wendy glanced at her watch. "I know you wanted the car today; could we leave in about twenty-five minutes?"

It was tight, but they made it. After dropping Wendy off at work, Erica followed the directions Patrick Lund had given her to the Green Cat, a nearby coffeehouse. Patrick had snagged a small table and stood up when he saw Erica.

"I ordered you a hot chocolate," he said as Erica took a seat. "Tell me about your Memphis trip." The waitress brought their order, and Patrick sipped his cappuccino and listened to Erica's findings.

"So, Tyson was in trouble financially." Patrick set his cup down. "He must have been quite a character. Imagine having the chutzpah to borrow money from your boss!"

"Since Mrs. Tyson also mentioned they were having money troubles, I think it's very possible Tyson meant to borrow money from Stephen."

"Probably, but since Stephen hadn't inherited yet, Tyson couldn't have been looking for a huge handout. And from what you said about Linda being younger, Stephen may not inherit at all."

"Actually, there's a new development there," Erica said. "I talked with Stephen yesterday and found out Linda has breast cancer. Apparently she's been battling it for years, but now she only has a few months to live."

Patrick raised his shaggy brows. "Ah ha! That puts a new light on the picture. Maybe Tyson found out about the cancer and decided that if Stephen knew he was going to inherit in a few months, he might be willing to part with a substantial amount now. Still, whether or not Tyson was going to ask to borrow money doesn't explain why someone killed him."

The detective went on. "However, if *Stephen* was the intended victim, there is one person we know who might have tried to kill him for financial gain." When Erica sighed, Patrick said, "Apparently you know about Stephen's will and that Wendy is his beneficiary."

"Stephen told me just before I went to Memphis," Erica said glumly.

"Did he also tell you he'd made his will just a couple of months ago?"

"Yes, but Wendy would have to be an idiot to try to kill Stephen right after he put her as his beneficiary in a new will."

"It happens, and we'd be crazy not to look into it a little closer, especially when Wendy nagged him relentlessly to write it."

Erica was startled. "Come again?"

"Stephen didn't tell you about that? One of my men interviewed Stephen, who said Wendy pressured him into making a will."

"That's quite different from how he explained it to me," Erica protested. "Stephen said he'd been planning to make a will and that Wendy simply encouraged him to go ahead."

"It could be a matter of semantics, but what it boils down to is Wendy being very eager for Stephen to make a will. He also listed her as the beneficiary on his life insurance policy."

This was not good—not good at all. Erica took a moment to think as she drained her mug. "Oh, I almost forgot—I asked Mrs. Tyson about the switchblade. She didn't know anything about it but thought her husband probably bought it for protection. He'd gotten mugged once and felt uneasy in strange cities."

"We're trying to find out where it was purchased," Patrick said. "Still, it's a bit odd that he'd buy something like that for protection. Switchblades are the preferred weapon for young punks, not old men."

Erica knew this was true, and his statement confirmed her opinion that Detective Lund was a good man to work with. Besides being knowledgeable, he had a lot of common sense.

"Have you come up with anyone who might have wanted to kill Jaime?" Erica asked.

"I talked with her, and while there don't seem to be any recently spurned lovers, Jaime did mention that Wendy is very jealous of her."

"I thought she might. But Wendy would never try to poison Jaime and Stephen."

"I don't know about that; love triangles can be deadly." Patrick looked at her shrewdly then moved his cup away so he could put his arms on the table. "Also, I haven't ruled you out as the intended victim. I'm sure you're aware that killers don't care for investigators. Someone could be trying to silence you. By the way, when are you going to Chicago?"

"This afternoon. I was able to make an appointment with Linda Bronson too. I'll meet with her tonight and then talk to some of Stephen's old neighbors tomorrow."

"Let me know if anything turns up."

* * *

Erica went to Tom Addison's Gun Shop and, feeling a little rankled, paid the fee to pick up her own pistol that David had mailed along with her holster. After making a quick stop at the Winn-Dixie supermarket, Erica picked up Megan, who had another early-out day from school. They arrived home the same time as Brandon, who'd ridden home on the bus. He helped carry a sack of groceries inside and was excited to see a gallon of chocolate milk.

"Can I have some?" he asked eagerly.

"With lunch. Thanks for helping bring in the groceries. You too, Megan." Then she asked, "And for lunch, how about grilled cheese sandwiches?"

"Isn't it kind of early for lunch?" Megan remarked.

"It is, but I have to be at the airport by one." After washing her hands thoroughly with her bar of Lava at the kitchen sink, she turned on the griddle and began slicing cheese. Brandon washed up too and came back to watch. He reached out and snatched a piece.

"Hey! You're lucky you didn't lose a finger," Erica scolded.

Brandon was unconcerned. "I'm going to be in a school play next week. It's about spring, and I'm going to be a rabbit. I've got big ears and everything. Can you come?"

"Sure, sounds great."

Megan spread out a tablecloth, and Brandon got the chocolate milk, carrying it as if it were a special treasure. Megan insisted on pouring.

A big girl who had not yet outgrown her teen years of awkwardness, Megan spilled a little, causing Brandon to groan. Erica brought over the sandwiches she'd cut into perfect squares, causing Megan to roll her eyes.

"Try one, and you'll see they taste better this way," Erica said.

"On your planet, maybe," Megan replied.

Brandon volunteered to say the prayer and grabbed a sandwich before the *amen* had died away. "How is Mom getting home? Her car's here."

"As soon as we're done eating, you and I will pick her up at work and go to the airport."

"Mom said she's going to buy me new shoes today. Look at this." Brandon lifted his foot and, putting his shoe on the table, demonstrated how he could pull the top of the shoe apart from the sole.

"Get your stinkin' foot off the table, moron," Megan hissed.

Erica admonished him as well. "Brandon, you know better than that."

"I hope Mom remembers. She was going to take me to get shoes last week but didn't."

"Your mother's got a lot on her mind right now," Erica commented.

Brandon looked worried. "Is something wrong with Mom?"

There was a snort from Megan. "What *isn't* wrong with her?"

"That was uncalled for," Erica said, turning icy green eyes on the girl. Then she said to Brandon, "Your mom's been very worried lately."

"Why?"

Megan groaned. "You are so obtuse, Brandon."

"Am not," Brandon countered. Then he asked Erica. "What's *obtuse?*"

"You are!" Megan said.

Fortunately, Brandon was more concerned about his mother than arguing. "Is it because that man got killed? Are the police going to arrest Mom?"

Megan turned on her brother, her great dark eyes burning with fury. "You are such an idiot! You don't know anything."

"Do so!" Brandon was stung. "I know a lot." He paused then added triumphantly, "I know you snuck out of the house last night!"

Megan put her hands on the table, looking like she was about to catapult across the table and reach for his throat. Brandon scooted his chair closer to Erica. Megan took her dishes to the sink but on the way to the hall glowered at Brandon and kicked the step stool, which ricocheted into the philodendron, breaking the pot. Rich black earth tumbled onto the linoleum. Erica remembered what Jaime had said about Megan being mentally unstable. Was she right?

"Was that necessary?" Erica asked crisply.

"It was in my way."

"Let me know if I ever get in your way. I'd hate to end up like that plant."

"You're just as stupid as Mom," Megan said then stomped off.

Erica looked over at Brandon, who was sitting as still as a mouse that has seen a shadow overhead. Reaching over, she patted his arm. "Don't worry about Megan. Some people have a hard time controlling their emotions, but it gets easier with practice."

Brandon looked thoughtful. "I don't think Megan practices much."

It was impossible to stop the laughter that bubbled up. Erica ruffled his hair. "Just make sure that *you* keep practicing, all right?"

He grinned, a chocolate-milk mustache on his upper lip. "All right."

* * *

The Orlando airport was becoming more familiar to Erica. While waiting to board the plane, she saw a young family—a tall, young husband, slender wife, and their baby who looked to be around six months, with its chubby cheeks and dandelion-tufted hair. The mother looked a bit like Wendy, with tousled fair hair and hazel eyes. As she watched the mother take the baby from the stroller and cuddle it, Erica remembered that Wendy would have had a third child if it hadn't been for that miscarriage. Poor Wendy. Yet she was not the only one affected by that tragedy. As they had talked on into the night, Wendy had said that after the miscarriage, she began noticing a change in Megan. Gradually, Megan took to wearing black and became increasingly rebellious. She refused to have anything to do with her father and, after the divorce was final, was hostile toward anyone Wendy dated. Stephen had been Wendy's first serious boyfriend, and Megan's antipathy knew no bounds.

Knowing the full story helped explain why Megan harbored such ill feelings toward Stephen. Clearly, the incident with Dennis had made her distrustful toward men. Brandon had also been affected but not to the same degree. Now, Erica was able to comprehend more fully the depression that had fallen upon Wendy at the time of her divorce. It was a time when painful, shifting emotions had spiraled her life out of control, not because she hadn't tried, but because there had been nothing there for Wendy to take ahold of. Wendy's own mother had said she could get over her depression if she would just pull herself up by her own bootstraps. As Erica knew, medication and counseling were vital to the healing process, and in time Wendy had returned to her old self.

Still, even though she understood some of Wendy's sorrow, Erica was disturbed by her bitterness toward Bishop Griggs. Bishops were entitled to inspiration, but they were not mind readers and could not foretell the future. Surely he had done what he thought was best. There was no way of knowing his advice would have such horrifying consequences. He must have felt terrible.

Once she'd landed at Chicago's O'Hare Airport, Erica studied a map then wiped down the inside of her rental car with her packaged wipes. With the help of the car's GPS, Erica made her way to Linda Bronson's residence. The mansion and grounds were gated, and she used a call box to ring the house. When the iron gates swung open, she drove up a red cobbled driveway lined with cypress trees. Erica drove slowly, awed by the massive three-story brick house with its huge pillars, numerous chimneys, and mullioned windows that reflected the sunlight. There was a wraparound porch that ran the full length of the house; white wicker furniture and hanging plants made it inviting and cozy. North of the five-car garage was a white-fenced pasture where a number of sleek-coated horses grazed.

A maid led Erica into an elegant room that was papered in heavy silk in shades of mauve and tan. Glancing around the room, Erica almost purred in satisfaction. Every picture was straight, every rug lined up, and all sofa pillows were plumped and in place. The neatness of the bright room made it a place a person could really relax in. Erica stepped over to look out the tall windows, which offered a magnificent view of spacious, sloping lawns and manicured gardens. The light from the sun as it slanted in the western sky was richly golden and brought out darker shades of green in the trees, creating a deep, glowing effect.

The door opened, and Erica turned. Linda Bronson was fairly tall but frighteningly thin and walked with the aid of a bright pink cane. Although she was only in her thirties, Linda's halting walk aged her. Well-cut trousers of mocha tweed were topped by a loose brown silk blouse. The women shook hands and sat in matching black leather chairs near the windows.

"You're looking at my scarf," Linda observed with a gentle hint of amusement in her voice.

"Oh yes, it's lovely," Erica said, somewhat discomfited.

"Don't be embarrassed," Linda said, patting the brightly printed head scarf that framed an attractive face with lively blue-gray eyes. "It's easy nowadays for men who are having chemo to be bald but not women. Still, chemo gives me an excuse to put off my accountant or whoever else wants to meet with me. If I don't feel up to it, I can just say, 'Not today. I'm having a no-hair day!'"

Erica chuckled. "You have a wonderful sense of humor."

"It's either that or sit and cry all day, and I've never been much of a crier. Besides, if I ever get tired of fighting for my life, I can always get on my Harley-Davidson and leave the helmet at home." She looked at Erica. "You've got gorgeous hair. I used to have hair like that, thick and shiny." She shrugged lightly. "Oh well. I will again soon."

Feeling a little awkward, Erica said, "Thank you for letting me come and talk with you."

Suddenly, a quiver of pain shot across Linda's face. She adjusted the small pillow behind her back and then rearranged her expression. She then replied spiritedly, "Nonsense. I should thank *you* for coming to see *me*!" There was an air of breeding about Linda Bronson that bespoke her privileged status in life, yet her smile was warm and genuine. "I only wish you could have brought Stephen with you. I haven't seen him for ages— his work keeps him so busy. However, he keeps in touch regularly. He's always sending me lovely bouquets of flowers or boxes of chocolates!"

"Amazing. And without a wife to do it for him."

Linda's laughter was vibrant. "It's extraordinary, I agree! But then, Stephen was always thoughtful."

"How long did he work for your father?"

Linda thought back. "It must have been about fifteen years. Stephen and my father really hit it off, and after a year or so, Dad made him his assistant. It was an ideal position for Stephen—he was so good with people."

"I hear he became part of the family."

"Oh yes!" Linda's smile softened the sharp lines of her thin face. "It wasn't long before I thought of Stephen as an uncle or brother. We did everything together. He often asked if his brother, Richard, could come with us for weekends, parties, and vacations."

"Richard worked at Cicero too, didn't he?"

"Yes, but in another department, so I didn't see too much of him. Richard was nice enough but quite different from his brother." Linda looked thoughtful. "It sounds terrible now that he's gone, but Richard was a trifle dull compared to Stephen, who was always making me laugh."

A maid knocked and, after entering, stood quietly by the door. Linda asked Erica, "Would you like anything to drink? Coffee, tea, soda? Perhaps one of those vitamin waters?"

"I'd like a lemonade, please."

"Bring two lemonades, please," Linda told the maid. After the door closed, Linda turned her intelligent gaze on Erica. "Now, you had some questions for me?"

"Yes, I did. Now, I understand Stephen has already told you he was poisoned."

"I couldn't believe it!" Linda face reddened. "It's shocking. Who would want to hurt such a dear man?"

"That's what I'm trying to find out."

Linda eyed her. "You look very capable. I bet you *will* find out."

"I imagine Stephen also told you about Gregory Tyson, the man who was killed outside Wendy Kemp's home?"

"He did. Wendy is Stephen's fiancée, isn't she? I hope she's good enough for him."

"She is," Erica assured her. "But they aren't engaged yet. Now, I'd like to talk with people who worked with Stephen. Would it be possible to get a list of names and numbers from you?"

"Certainly." Linda pulled out her cell phone. "I'll call my secretary right now. He has an office on the second floor." She gave him a few names and told him who to call to get others. As she tucked her phone into her pocket, Linda said, "He'll compile the information and have the list ready before you go."

The maid brought in glasses that had slices of sugar-dipped lemons on the rim. Erica took a sip. "Wow, this is great! It's been a long time since I've had fresh lemonade." Then she sat back. "Do you mind if I ask a few questions about your family?"

"Not at all."

Questions about her parents, Anthony and Kathleen, were answered readily. Linda's manner was easy and matter-of-fact until she was asked about her brother. Suddenly, a ferocious frown appeared. "Folklore has it that the youngest child is always the spoiled one of the family. Not so. Charles was eight years older than me, and he was a spoiled brat if there ever was one. I didn't mind telling him so either," Linda admitted frankly. "Charles thought of no one but himself, and I hated how he treated Mom and Dad. They gave him everything, but all he could do is complain about this or that and whine about how they really didn't love him. What a bunch of garbage! Charles never appreciated anything they did for him. All he could do is gripe and argue. He rejected every bit of advice they gave him. Why, he even refused to go to college just because Dad expected him to. How stupid was that? And all because Charles couldn't stand having anyone tell him what to do."

Erica wasn't sure how to respond. Fortunately, her surprised expression kept Linda going.

"There was one thing, however, that Charles *would* accept from my parents. Money. I think they used it as a way of keeping him close, but Charles blew it all gambling. Sad-sack psychiatrists call gambling an addiction, but I say it's a lack of self-control. When my parents wouldn't pay his gambling debts, Charles started coming up with various stories as to why he needed money. His car had broken down, his wife was sick, his house needed a new roof. They gave him money every time."

Linda set her empty glass on the end table. "The end came when Charles ran up a really big debt. This time, my father insisted on the truth. When Charles broke down and told Dad he'd been gambling, there was a huge fight. I won't bore you with details, but in the end, Dad gave him the money but told Charles he wasn't going to get one more penny. Charles took the money, and all was quiet for a while. Then a year or so later, he asked for more, and when Dad wouldn't give him any, Charles got angry— said Dad valued money before relationships. Hogwash! Then Charles swore he'd never speak to Dad again. What an idiot," Linda said wearily. "It's like that old adage: he was willing to cut off his nose to spite his face."

"Did you two stay in touch?"

Linda gave a short, bitter laugh. "Charles thought I was just as bad as my father. You see, I always sided with my father."

"Stephen told me Charles left home when he was nineteen. Where did he go?"

"To Puerto Rico, of all places."

"He got married there, didn't he? Did he invite any of you to the wedding?"

"Charles didn't even tell us. I guess that upset his bride, Areli, because she wrote afterwards telling us they were married. Areli said Charles didn't know she was writing, but she felt we ought to know. Mom had to get someone to translate the letter because Areli wrote in Spanish."

Erica looked across the room to where three portraits hung in ornate frames. Linda followed the direction of her eyes and said, "The large family picture in the middle was taken about two years before Charles left. The picture to the left is of Charles, and that's me on the right.

Erica got up to take a closer look at the family portrait. Anthony Bronson was handsome with strong features: penetrating eyes, a large nose, and thick eyebrows. Wearing a blue chiffon dress and pearls, Kathleen Bronson was slender and pretty with classic, well-chiseled features. Linda stood beside her—a younger version of her mother. Charles was a handsome, if somewhat arrogant-looking, young man with black hair and the same aristocratic nose as his father. He was turned slightly, making his nose, which was rather large, look like the beak of some bird of prey. Something about him seemed familiar. The individual pictures were of a much younger version of Linda, with her keen, intelligent look, on the right and Charles on the left, with his dark mop of hair and patrician features.

"Did Charles make peace with your parents before they died?" Erica asked, sitting down.

"No, he remained bitter to the end." Linda had the haggard look of a person who had suffered much.

"Stephen said you had a nephew."

"That's right. We wouldn't have known about him either if it hadn't been for Areli. She called one day and talked to Mom. It was very hard for Mom to understand; Areli could barely speak English, but she wanted Mom to know she was a grandmother. Areli said they'd named the baby James."

"That was kind of her to call."

"Yes it was. Unfortunately, Charles found out. He wrote a blistering letter to my parents. Going clear back to when he was a child, he blamed them for everything that had gone wrong in his life. Charles said my parents had forfeited their right to be a part of his baby's life and that since they had never acted like parents he didn't expect them to act like grandparents."

"How terrible!"

"I was so furious, I couldn't see straight." Linda's eyes were flashing. "Dad was too, but Mom was devastated. Shortly afterward, my father changed his will and left everything to me. Then, he wrote and told Charles what he'd done."

"Oh dear."

Linda sighed heavily. "I wish that had been the end of it, but of course Charles wouldn't let it go. He wrote me one of his poison pen letters, asking me if I was satisfied now that I had managed to persuade Dad to cut him out of his rightful inheritance. It was the same old, same old.

Everything bad that happened to Charles was always due to someone else. Nothing was ever his fault or due to the way he was acting."

"I'm so sorry."

"So am I," Linda stated matter-of-factly. "Even though we'd never been close, I always hoped to have a relationship one day, but his final letter closed the door on that. Thank goodness I had Stephen in my life. I could always count on him. When my mother passed away, I wrote and told Charles but there was no response. Then, after Dad had a stroke and became an invalid, I tried calling, but he hung up on me. It was only after Dad had died and the will had gone through probate that Charles started phoning. His calls always followed a pattern. First he'd ask how I was and then he'd tell me about some fantastic scheme that was guaranteed to make money."

"Let me guess," Erica said. "He needed capital to get started."

"Bingo." Linda smiled sadly. "I hadn't realized how hard it must have been for Dad to keep turning Charles down. He could be charming when he wanted something badly."

"Did he keep calling?"

"Of course." Linda grimaced. "I'm sure he wanted the money for gambling, though he never admitted to it. Then, after I got breast cancer about five years ago, I drew up my own will. The next time he called, I told Charles I was leaving half of my money to Stephen, one fourth to him, and one fourth to various charities. Charles was angry, but I told him Stephen had been ten times the brother that he had been. That shut him up."

In a hesitant voice, Erica asked gently, "Stephen told me your cancer flared up again about two and a half years ago. Have you talked to Charles since then?"

Linda's face went still. "When I first found out I had cancer, I wanted to mend fences and called Charles. I told him about my cancer, and he sounded sympathetic. Later, I told him about the will. I suppose he was angry about the will because afterwards he never called—not even once—to see how I was doing, how the chemo was going, how the radiation was, nothing. I was hurt at first then angry. I never called again. Then, I got a call from Areli about a year and a half ago." Linda's voice became rough. "She told me Charles had died in a car accident."

Erica was sympathetic. "I'm so sorry."

"It was quite a shock." Linda took a moment to regain her poise. "It was quite hard to understand Areli. Evidently, she'd learned some English, but her accent was thick and she kept lapsing into Spanish. I understood she was talking about Charles, of course. She was crying and saying *murió, accidente*, and *de coche*. I knew *murio* was *dead* and *coche* was a *car*. *Accidente* was clear enough. When I asked about the funeral, she said *ayer*. Yesterday."

"Have you ever talked with your nephew?"

"No. I gather he left home when he was a teenager. After Charles died, I changed my will so that his portion would go to James. I also included something for Areli. I figure she deserves something for putting up with Charles and trying to keep us informed. It can't have been an easy life with someone like that. I sent a certified letter, with copies in English and Spanish, explaining it all to Areli. I also invited them to come and visit, saying I would pay their airfare, but they didn't take me up on the offer."

"Neither one of them wrote or called?"

"There was nothing from James. It's highly likely Charles poisoned his mind against me. However, Areli wrote a very nice note saying that she appreciated it all very much. I got the feeling she didn't completely understand the documents, but that's all right—she and James will get the money, and that's the important thing."

"You're being very generous to James when you haven't even met him."

Linda sighed. "My lawyers think I'm crazy. But he *is* my nephew and the only family I have, besides Stephen of course. A lot of it is guilt. I feel bad that I let a feud with my only brother go on for so long. It's too late to tell Charles I'm sorry, but I'll try to make it up to his son."

"That's very kind of you."

"I meant to try and find him this past year, but I just haven't had the time or energy—with all the doctor appointments, chemo, and everything." Linda's blue-gray eyes darkened.

Erica was not one to offer false platitudes. "It must be terrible. I had a friend with cancer and know a little about what it's like. I wish you didn't have to go through this."

"That's not on the list of options," Linda said wryly. "Thank you for not telling me to look on the bright side and to be glad it's not worse." She added, "I asked Stephen to try and locate Areli and James, but unfortunately, they moved. I thought about hiring a private investigator, but if I don't get around to that, the executor will just have to find them when the time comes."

"I know your estate is considerable, but if you don't mind me asking, just how much are we looking at?"

"Most of it is tied up in company holdings, assets, and property, as well as in stocks and bonds, which fluctuate daily. Considering everything, the entire estate is worth about two billion."

Erica tried not to let the shock show on her face. In anyone's book, this was seriously big money. There were a lot of people who would do just about anything for a chunk of that kind of money.

CHAPTER 11

AFTER LEAVING LINDA BRONSON, ERICA drove to Buffalo Grove and checked into a local motel. She opened her suitcase, got a fresh bar of Lava, and washed. Digging into her bag again, she pulled out a box of triple chocolate M&M's, settled into a chair, and began calling people on the list Linda's secretary had provided. After an hour, she had left three messages and talked to four people, none of whom had provided any useful information. However, the chocolate was great consolation as she checked the TV guide and found that *Singin' in the Rain* would be on later. Erica persevered in calling and got lucky when she reached Blaine Henderson.

After introducing herself, she explained, "Linda Bronson gave me your phone number. I'm investigating a case concerning Stephen Watkins and Gregory Tyson. Linda said you knew them."

"I sure did," Blaine said in a deep, hearty voice. "We all worked at Cicero."

"Could you tell me a little about Gregory? What kind of a person was he?" Blaine went on at length, confirming the picture Erica already had of Gregory Tyson as friendly and rather inquisitive.

"Were he and Stephen friends?"

"I should say so. Even though Greg was older, he looked up to Stephen, but then a lot of people did, with him being Anthony Bronson's assistant and all."

"I heard Stephen quit his job rather suddenly."

"Yeah, after his brother died. Everyone felt pretty bad for Stephen— he took Richard's death really hard. The next thing I knew, he'd moved away."

"So you didn't have a chance to say good-bye?"

"Nah, but Stephen had a lot on his mind. I remember Greg felt kind of bad about Stephen leaving without saying anything."

"Would you say Greg was angry about it?"

"More like hurt." Blaine seemed to be scratching his head mentally. "Still, I'm sure he understood Stephen was broken up about his brother."

"He must have been to quit his job, sell his house, and move to Florida."

"Stephen was like that—once he made a decision, he acted. He wouldn't have lasted in the position he had unless he could be decisive and act promptly," Blaine asserted. "I figure the house had too many memories and he wanted to get out as soon as possible."

"Did Stephen or Gregory have any enemies—people who disliked them, anything like that?"

"They were both well liked." Blaine sounded definite. "Although I would say people liked Stephen more. Greg could be a know-it-all at times and was a bit nosy. Stephen was friendly but never pried into your personal life. He was outgoing and had a great sense of humor. He was a busy guy but always had time to talk to you."

"I see. Well, I certainly appreciate talking with you. If you think of anything you'd like to add, please give me a call."

"I'll do that. Good luck with your investigation, and take good care of Stephen."

* * *

The next morning, Erica drove to Arlington Heights and found the house where Stephen and his brother used to live. It was a large, well-built brick rambler with a detached three-car garage in an exclusive neighborhood.

Erica drove to the house next door, which was a similarly built, cream-brick home with white shutters. The name on the mailbox said *Kincaid*. When Erica rang the doorbell, a dog began barking inside. A small, wiry woman with short salt-and-pepper hair opened the door and looked at her expectantly. Myrna Kincaid was a vigorous-looking woman of sixty-odd years with a determined chin.

Erica introduced herself, explaining that she was a private investigator and wanted to know more about Stephen Watkins. As she talked, Myrna tried ineffectively to get Buckles, a fluffy sheltie, to stop sniffing about Erica's ankles. Her husband, Coby, came to the door. He was small and round and had wispy white hair that was thicker over his ears.

After his wife explained why Erica was there, he invited her inside and led the way into the front room. Erica sat, fished out a pair of disposable gloves, and pulled them on with the Kincaids staring at her.

"Just a precaution," she said placidly. "You understand." She snapped her fingers for Buckles, who came over at once to be scratched around the base of his ears. He showed his appreciation by wagging his plumed tail gracefully.

"What's this all about?" Coby asked genially. His mouth appeared to be set in a permanent smile. "Why are you investigating Stephen? He hasn't done anything wrong, has he?"

"Not at all, but someone tried to kill him."

Myrna gasped. "No!"

"He was poisoned."

"Poisoned!" Myrna shrieked. "But you just said someone *tried* to kill him! I didn't know he was dead! And just two years after his brother!"

Erica rushed to reassure her. "He's not dead. Stephen *was* poisoned, but he got to a hospital very quickly and he's fine now."

"He can't be too fine if someone's trying to murder him," Coby said pragmatically.

"I'm trying to find out who did it before they can try again."

This intrigued Myrna, who leaned forward. "So you're tracking down the killer, are you?"

"I'm hoping to find out who did it, yes."

"Oh my!" Seeming unable to contain herself, Myrna jumped up. "Let me get you a cup of coffee. Or maybe you'd prefer iced tea."

"Juice would be fine if you have it or even a glass of water."

Mr. Kincaid stood. "I'll see if I can hurry her along, or else we'll be all day." He returned shortly, carrying a small yellow plate with cookies. Offering her one, he waited while she took off her gloves, then he confessed, "Myrna always has cookies on hand, but she hides them—says that if she didn't, we'd never have any left for company." Sitting down, he patted his round belly. "I suppose she's right, but I do enjoy something sweet now and then."

"Now's your chance," Erica whispered, sliding the plate toward him.

Glancing toward the kitchen to make sure the coast was clear, Coby Kincaid grinned like a little boy. "I'll stow these away for later," he said, stashing several in his pocket. "I've always believed in a balanced diet—a cookie in each hand!"

Erica giggled but stopped abruptly when Myrna came back with drinks. "This is so nice of you—I hope I'm not imposing."

"Posh, it's no bother at all." The timbre of Myrna's voice was attractive—deep and resonant. She picked up her cup. "Now, you wanted to know about Stephen and Richard."

"They were real nice people," Coby began. "They weren't home a lot, but sometimes we'd talk over the fence. Stephen was a real likeable fellow. Always asked about my arthritis."

"And he just loved our little dog," Myrna added, bending to stroke the sheltie's head and give him a morsel of a cookie. "He used to carry little doggy biscuits in his pockets to give to Buckles. He made quite a fuss over him."

Coby continued. "Richard was the quiet one. He'd wave and nod, but he usually wouldn't come over to the fence to talk."

"It was such a shock when he died!" Myrna broke in. "Richard was so young—well, young compared to us! But then, the obituaries are full of people who die too young. We felt so sorry for Stephen. The two of them were devoted to each other."

Coby shook his head ruefully. "Stephen took it real hard—even had a private funeral."

A hint of a scowl appeared on Myrna's face. "If you ask me, it's only right to let friends and neighbors pay their last respects."

Obviously, this was still a sore spot. Passing over it, Erica asked, "What did Richard die of?"

"Heart attack," Myrna said. "Got him in the middle of the night." She reached for a cookie. "When it's my time, that's how I want to go. In my sleep—quick like."

"Still, it's a shock for those left behind," Coby commented.

"It's better than a lot of ways," Myrna argued. "Now, take my brother; he got pancreatic cancer. That's an awful way to go. At the end, he was in terrible pain."

"Now Myrna, this nice young lady doesn't want to hear about all of that," her husband remonstrated gently. "She wants to know about Stephen."

Myrna went back agreeably to the topic at hand. "Oh, he was just the nicest man."

"Sometimes Stephen would come over and help me wheel out my trash can if he saw me taking it out," Coby said, taking a sip of his coffee.

"They have such big cans nowadays," he added with a frown. It was easy to picture the small, rotund Mr. Kincaid wrestling with an oversize garbage can. "We had Stephen and Richard over for dinner once in a while, didn't we, dear?"

"Oh yes. They'd bring flowers every time. And they always offered to help me wash up afterwards." She winked. "Sometimes I even let them! Lovely boys."

Erica smiled to hear Stephen referred to as a "boy." "How did they get along with your other neighbors? Did any of them have any bad feelings or quarrels with Stephen?"

Myrna and Coby looked flabbergasted that Erica could think such a thing was possible. "Heavens no," Myrna burst out.

"Is there anybody else nearby that knew him well? I wanted to talk with as many neighbors as I could."

This time Coby spoke up. "The house just north of Stephen's sold a couple of years ago—the new people wouldn't know him, but I can give you a couple of others places you could stop. The best person to see, though, would be Timothy Peterson."

"That's right," Myrna agreed. "Timothy was real good friends with Stephen and Richard."

"Great. Do you have his phone number?"

"I can get it but it won't do you any good," Myrna said. "Timothy's off visiting his daughter in Montana, and he doesn't have a cell phone." She shook her head. "Now who in their right mind would want to live in Montana?"

"Montana can be nice," her husband remarked, but there was a lot of doubt in his voice.

"With all those bears?" Myrna scoffed. "I want to die in bed, not ate up by some grizzly."

"He'd hardly be likely to bother you with me around," Coby told his wife dryly, giving his protruding stomach a pat. "Not if he had an ounce of sense, anyways." He stood. "I'll go get those numbers for you."

When he came back, Erica put the list in her purse. "You've both been very helpful. Thank you so much."

"Call us if you need anything else," Coby said earnestly. "I put our number on that list."

"Tell Stephen we're glad he's not dead." Myrna paused then said doubtfully, "Wait, that didn't sound very good, did it?"

"I'll tell Stephen you spoke very highly of him."

"Hold on just a minute." Myrna rushed off.

While she waited, Erica reached out and straightened a family picture. When she saw Coby eyeing her, she said, "It was tilted."

"Well, there's a reason for that." He pointed to where he stood at the end of a row. "This sides heavier because that's where I am."

When Myrna returned with a small plastic bag, she scooped the rest of cookies off the yellow plate and into the bag and handed it to Erica. "Here you go. You need to put some meat on those bones, and Coby and I certainly don't need cookies around here tempting us."

Patting his pocket surreptitiously, Coby winked at Erica.

* * *

Dropping the names "Coby and Myrna Kincaid" worked like magic in getting the neighbors to open up about Stephen. She heard many interesting slices of life, but none of the neighbors knew Stephen as well as the older couple. Before leaving, Erica called Timothy Peterson's number and left a message on his answering machine.

She was at the O'Hare airport, waiting in line to go through security, when Stephen called. He had planned on picking her up since Wendy was working, but a problem had come up at work and he was sending Jaime instead.

The plane landed on schedule. At curbside, Erica put her carry-on in the trunk of Jaime's white Saturn. Jaime closed it then climbed in gracefully, watching with a half smile as Erica pulled out her wipes and went over her seat and what she could reach of the dashboard.

"Are you sure you don't want to do my side and the steering wheel?" Jaime asked.

"I'd love to. Thanks." Erica slid over and wiped away as Jaime leaned back against her seat to give Erica room. When she was done, Erica sealed the used towelettes in a zippered bag in her purse. "There. That's better, isn't it?"

"I guess so, but it was certainly odd," Jaime said then merged deftly into traffic. "Would you like to stop for a late lunch?" she asked. "Unless you had something to eat at the airport—"

The invitation was a surprise, but Erica accepted. "That would be great."

"Good. Stephen was going to go with me for lunch, but he had a problem with a client." When Jaime glanced at her, Erica saw a brightness in the young woman's eyes that suggested nervous anticipation. Jaime Russell had invited her to lunch for a reason. Erica would be patient. It was just a matter of time until she knew what it was.

Travel on the interstate went smoothly until they exited at Kissimmee, where orange cones divided the roadway. Erica's eyes widened when Jaime blew past a stop sign.

She was relieved when they crossed the intersection without meeting another car but felt compelled to speak up. "Ah, Jaime, did you see that stop sign back there?"

Jaime shrugged. "They make them so hard to see."

"Yeah, they're pretty good at hiding them by putting them on top of tall posts and painting them red," Erica said dryly.

Suddenly Jaime yelped, "Hold on! I've got to pull in here!" Erica swayed against the door, unable to catch herself as Jaime braked and turned sharply into the parking lot of a small grocery store. "I'll be right back," she said, half way out of the car before Erica could say anything.

She was back in a few minutes, looking like a contented cat as she buckled her seat belt.

"I buy a lottery ticket here every Friday. It's my lucky day."

When Erica smiled, Jaime responded, "You think I'm being silly, but one day I'm going to strike it rich. My only problem now is what to have for lunch. I only have two bucks left."

"You bought a lottery ticket when you didn't have enough money for lunch?" Erica was amazed. "Isn't eating more important than a lottery ticket?"

Jaime laughed—a light sound like wind chimes. "Not for me. Better to buy a ticket and be hungry than miss your big chance."

"Have you ever seen the odds? The chances of winning are microscopic."

"But the payoff is gigantic!" Jaime's eyes were sparkling. She pulled up to a Mexican fast food place. "Hope you don't mind. I'd planned on something classier, but—"

"This is fine," Erica assured her. Inside they ordered then went to the restroom.

Erica went in first, and Jaime asked, "Why didn't you open and close the door twice like you usually do?"

"You're very young, aren't you? There's no need to do that with swinging doors." Then she got out her zippered bag of soap and looked toward Jaime. "I've got another bar of Lava if you want to use it. It's the original heavy-duty hand cleaner that's been used since 1893 by coal miners and oil rig workers. And it has moisturizers."

Jaime's mouth was hanging open. "You sound like a television commercial. Do they pay you for advertising?" Then she used the wall-mount soap dispenser.

Erica shook her head as they exited the restroom. "You don't know what you're doing."

They picked up their food and went to a booth. "Hold my tray, will you?" Erica asked, digging into her purse and pulling out a small white square. She ripped it open and pulled out a plastic tablecloth, which she spread on the table.

"What are you doing?" Jaime hissed, glancing around at the other customers, who were watching with expressions of amazement.

"You can't be too careful. Tables at places like this are a hotbed of germs." Erica took her tray and sat down before asking comfortably, "So, how long have you been in Kissimmee?"

Jaime's cheeks were faintly flushed as she sat and took another look around. "Remind me never to eat with you again," she muttered then took a sip of her soda to steady herself. "About six months. When I got here I was so broke that I started working at a place like this." Jaime's nose wrinkled as she glanced around the place. "I hated it but couldn't get a decent job. Everyone wanted experience." She frowned. "How are you going to get experience if people won't hire you?"

Erica looked at her curiously then asked, "How's it going at Stephen's office?"

"Reed's office actually, but it's going great."

"Even with Diana?"

Jaime laughed out loud. "I don't let Diana get to me, and that drives her wild. I get along fine with everyone except Reed. He gives me the heebie-jeebies." She gave a mock shiver. "So, how's the investigation going?" Jaime's words were casual, but her eyes were glued to Erica's face. This, then, might be why she had invited Erica to a late lunch.

"It's coming along." Erica's answer was deliberately brief—a test. Would Jaime drop it or pump for more information?

"Have the police come up with any suspects?" Jaime asked.

Pump time.

When she had called Detective Lund that morning, he had let it drop that Wendy was at the top of their pitifully short list of suspects. It would be interesting to see Jaime's reaction to that.

"Actually, Wendy is their best suspect."

Jaime began coughing. She took a sip of water then asked, "What makes them think that?"

Not wanting to mention the will or life insurance, Erica said blithely, "Opportunity. The murder and the poisoning both took place at her house."

Jaime nodded as if in perfect agreement. "That does seem very suspicious. I worry sometimes about Stephen. That is one jealous lady."

Counting to ten helped Erica bite back a bitter reply.

Once they were back on the road, Erica asked, "Does anyone at the office have bad feelings toward Stephen?"

"I've thought about that, but there really isn't anyone except for Reed. I swear—that man's a psycho."

"What is up with him? He seems so bitter and angry."

"Who knows? He probably got dropped on his head as a baby." Then Jaime answered seriously. "Actually, I guess he has got a couple of reasons for always being in a bad mood. I know that in the past year the president of the company has been on his back about the business even though things are slowing down everywhere. But for Reed, that means Armageddon is here. His whole life revolves around his job."

"Is Reed married?"

"For now. From what I hear, his marriage is on the rocks."

"Do you think he might have a grudge against Stephen?"

"Reed has a grudge against *everyone*." Jaime glanced at her. "Wait a minute. You're serious, aren't you? Do you think he might have been the one who tried to poison Stephen?"

"In a lot of ways, Reed fits the profile of the killer I'm looking for, but looking at it from a purely psychological angle, I'd say it was a woman that poisoned Stephen." A sudden spurt of gas caused the car to jump ahead as the light turned green.

"Sorry," Jaime said. "It's these high heels."

Erica went on. "So although Reed seems to be about the only person that doesn't like Stephen, he's also a man."

"And an ugly one." Jaime giggled. "Sorry, couldn't help myself. Actually, I'm not sure what you're getting at with all this psychological stuff."

"The method of killing often says a lot about the murderer. Some methods are more commonly used by men, others by women," Erica explained. "Research has shown that a woman is much more likely to poison someone, and a man is more likely to stab someone." Before Jaime could jump in, Erica added, "And no, I don't believe Wendy poisoned Stephen. But there *were* other women there that night."

"I hope you're not thinking of me," Jaime said tightly, flinging a glance her way.

"Everyone is a suspect at this point."

"I didn't poison Stephen."

Little was said after that, but Erica had the feeling Jaime was leaving something unsaid. Her real feelings and thoughts seemed to slip through Erica's fingers like fine sand. Was that because Jaime was a private person or because she had something to hide? Tension was visible in the way Jaime drove, and Erica was glad when they pulled up at Wendy's house.

* * *

It was always fun when Erica called home and David and the children got online so they could see and talk with each other. They did this frequently, and David confided that the children often "saved" their homework so they could do it online with their mother rather than with him.

"It's the novelty of it," Erica assured her husband. "Soon I'll be back, and they'll be wishing they were doing homework with you and my mother again!"

After Aby sang the song she had performed for choir tryouts, Ryan showed his mother how he could tie different knots. Not to be outdone, Kenzie sang a Primary song and showed off a new bracelet Grandma had bought her. David then took over.

When Erica finally shut down her laptop, she stretched and went into the backyard. It was a lovely May day, and her eye caught a neighbor's towering tulip tree with its showy flowers. Floating on the breeze were a few bright songs of unidentified birds. Erica had seen orioles, yellow-throated warblers, and blue jays, although her personal favorite was the brightly colored cardinal. She inhaled deeply, enjoying the scent from the magnolia tree. When she heard a car pulling into the driveway, Erica went past the fence line of scarlet-flowered coral bean shrubs to where Wendy was climbing out of the car.

"Isn't it a beautiful day!" Erica said, throwing out her arms and enjoying the warmth of the sun on her skin. Wendy looked around as if noticing it for the first time, and Erica went on. "I know it's always nice in Florida, but I'm from Utah, the land of the frozen chosen, and the weather here has given me spring fever. Let's go for a walk!"

"I promised Brandon I'd help him with Cub Scouts when I got home. He wants to work on his Bobcat badge."

"You can do that later—the requirements are easy. Besides, he's off playing with friends. Come on, let's go on a walk." Perhaps a little relaxation would help Wendy. She still had a strange edginess that Erica was beginning to fear was due to her relationship with Stephen.

"I can hardly refuse a direct command," Wendy teased. "Let me change, though."

They headed south, past homes with peeling paint, overgrown yards, and broken-down fences. "I hope you brought your mace," Erica quipped. "It's mandatory for walking around this neighborhood, right?"

"You're the one who wanted to go for a walk," Wendy reminded her. "Besides, it's not that bad."

Erica sidestepped an old tire that was partially blocking the cracked sidewalk. "Your nose is growing."

"How did things go in Chicago?"

"There wasn't anything groundbreaking, but I was able to pick up a few tidbits here and there." Two children on bikes approached, and Wendy and Erica moved smoothly out of their way. "I talked with several of Stephen's neighbors. Everybody liked him and felt bad when his brother died. It sounded like Stephen was really broken up when Richard died."

"Stephen doesn't like to talk about it, even now," Wendy admitted. "It must have been devastating to wake up one morning and find your brother unconscious in bed." As they turned the corner, Wendy changed the subject. "While you were gone, a detective came by to talk to me."

"Detective Lund? I called him today, but he didn't mention seeing you."

"It was another detective. I think his name was Perez. He had some questions about the night Stephen was poisoned, and he also asked about Stephen's will. The police really think I'm the one who poisoned Stephen." Wendy sounded discouraged. "This guy acted like I was some kind of grasping gold digger who bullied Stephen into writing a will so I could bump him off. Jerk."

"The police are just grasping at straws." Erica tried to soothe her.

"I'm so glad you're here, Erica. You'll be able to make them see I had nothing to do with it. I told Detective Perez that Stephen had been planning to write his will for a long time but just hadn't gotten around to it until recently."

"Stephen told me it was hard to make his will because it brought back memories of his brother."

"Yeah, he told me that too, but he talked about it so much that, frankly, I was getting tired of it. He kept going on and on until I was nearly comatose. Finally, I told him to just go and do it."

"And he did. Naming you as his beneficiary."

Wendy's face bloomed toward her in surprise. "I had no idea about that until the police told me."

"I suppose you realize that Stephen's putting you as his beneficiary is the main reason the police suspect you of poisoning him?"

"But we're nearly engaged! I wouldn't try to kill my fiancé!"

"I know that, but the police don't." Remembering Reed Devoe's comment, Erica added, "There are a lot of women—and men—who get involved with someone because of money." When Wendy looked stricken, Erica added quickly, "All I meant is that in murder cases, the police always take a good, hard look at people who stand to benefit financially from the victim's death."

"But I'd never want to kill Stephen! Oh, there was that one night when he wouldn't give me the remote, but—"

Erica's laughter broke the tension. Wendy smiled and went on, "I've tried to think of who could have done it, but I don't know anyone who doesn't like Stephen. He doesn't have any enemies!"

"Au contraire," Erica declared. "He's got at least one."

They waited for a car to pass then crossed the road. A butterfly joined them, floating delicately on the air in front of them, then lagging behind, and finally coming alongside, as if listening to their conversation. Erica watched, fascinated, until the butterfly was distracted by a flowering verbena.

"I'm a little surprised Stephen hasn't proposed yet." Erica took care to speak lightly.

Wendy looked pensive. "Yes, well . . . Stephen's very disciplined and orderly. He likes to plan things out far in advance, which is good, but sometimes—" Suddenly she blurted, "Sometimes I wish he was impulsive and romantic—like David! You guys are so amazing. It's like Brad and Angelina. Sometimes I hate you because you're both so perfect!"

"You know we're not. We have our problems, the same as anyone else."

"Oh, right. Like he sprinkles red rose petals on your bed when you've told him a hundred times you prefer pink." Erica burst into laughter, and an elderly woman who was sitting on her front porch, knitting, stared at them. Wendy went on. "You two are like little magnets that can't do anything except cling to one another. And David's so thoughtful. He calls you every day, helps you make dinner, buys you flowers . . ."

"Leaves his socks on the floor, hasn't a clue where I keep the frying pans, and refuses to ask for directions when we get lost," Erica added. "On the other hand, he has so many good qualities I can't name them all." She linked her arm through Wendy's. "I was pretty lucky to meet my two best friends at college."

"It must have been pretty romantic to meet your future husband in a law enforcement class on how to subdue criminals and properly use stun guns!"

Erica smiled. "Actually it *was* romantic. David can make anything romantic."

"Oh please—you're making me gag. I don't think Stephen even knows the meaning of romance."

"Sure he does. Stephen's got a lot of great qualities—you've got to focus on them. Think about all the nice things he does. And he *does* care about you."

"I guess so. And we do have a lot in common. We both like to read. We like the same TV shows. Neither of us likes rock music, we like to go for walks, we love old movies—" It was if Wendy were reciting her grocery list. Then she brightened. "And we both hate opera!"

"Now there's something you can base a long-term relationship on!"

They walked on in silence for a while. Then Wendy said, "I hate to admit it, but sometimes I think our relationship is about as romantic as a pair of old house slippers."

Just like Cher in Moonstruck, *but you had to look for the positive.* "House slippers can be good, though. Let's see—comfortable, always available, reliable."

"I guess so." Wendy sounded dubious. "But once in a while, I'd like high heels."

There it was again—this *had* to be the inner conflict Wendy was struggling with, one that she seemed to be more aware of as time went on.

Erica spoke cautiously. "Have you ever thought about leaving the slippers behind and looking for some high heels?"

There was a long silence. Then she muttered, "But I've been waiting so long. Stephen's the first decent guy I've dated. If we married, I'd be able to spend more time with the kids. And it'll be nice having something other than hot dogs for dinner and having to buy gas five dollars at a time."

It was true Wendy would be gaining security, but at what cost? However, she had to make her own decision. They passed an old, weathered house that had a rusted old Ford in the middle of its half-dead lawn surrounded by knee-high weeds. The side yard was piled with rubbish. Inclining her head toward the mess, Erica said, "The only downside to marrying Stephen will be leaving this great neighborhood."

Wendy had to smile. "You probably think I'm very materialistic."

"Hey, I've been poor too, you know. Living on beans and swiping hot sauce from Taco Bell isn't as much fun as it's cracked up to be." In a more serious tone, she added, "If you love Stephen, that's what matters—as long as you're sure about marrying someone who doesn't believe the same way you do." Erica let that hang in the air.

"Stephen is so unselfish and so generous. He had new brakes put on my car last year then made my mortgage payment in August so I could buy school clothes for the kids." She sighed. "I try to take things one day at a time, but then several days attack me all at once."

Erica got the giggles. Wendy smiled then picked up a small stick and, as they walked along, systematically broke it into tiny pieces. "Every year, Brandon asks to play soccer, and every year I have to say no. Megan wanted dance lessons, but there was no way. I get panicky sometimes, lying awake at night wondering how I'm going to pay my car insurance. I'd do just about anything to get out of this hole I've been living in."

There was such passion in her voice that Erica felt a little apprehensive. Watching her friend from the corner of her eye, Erica remarked, "I was surprised to find out Stephen is going to inherit a fortune."

Wendy's expression remained the same. "I couldn't believe it. Stephen told me about it while you were in Chicago. I was surprised he hadn't told me before. I didn't think we had any secrets from each other."

"Pretty big secret."

"It is exciting, though, isn't it?" Wendy looked at her as if seeking confirmation. Then she smiled. "Life is really going to change once we're married."

Erica had been wondering if Wendy would marry a pair of house slippers just to be financially secure. For the moment, it seemed the answer was yes.

* * *

"Look at the time," Wendy said as they went into the kitchen. "I'd better start the spaghetti. I just wish I knew if Megan was going to be home for dinner. I ought to call her, I guess, but she gets so annoyed whenever I do."

"I don't mind leftovers, but if you do, you'd better call."

Wendy was heading for the telephone when it rang. "Hello? Kimberly, is that you? Have you got a cold?" A long pause. "*What? Where is she?* Lakeview Hospital? I'll be right there." Wendy hung up and put both hands on the table as if to hold herself up.

"What happened?"

Wendy took a deep breath. "Megan tried to commit suicide."

CHAPTER 12

IT WAS DÉJÀ VU, BEING in the waiting room again at the hospital—with everything eerily similar to the night Stephen had been poisoned. Once again, Wendy was tearful and anxious; there were whispered conversations, phone calls, and hours spent shifting in uncomfortable chairs while pretending to watch the flickering scenes on the overhead TV. Megan's friend Kimberly was also there. She was a gangly, pale girl who could only talk, it seemed, while twisting her long, blonde hair that had been streaked with black and purple.

When Erica and Wendy first arrived, Kimberly explained that Megan had taken a mixture of prescription drugs, which she'd gotten from Wendy's medicine cabinet. Kimberly swore she didn't know about the pills until they'd gone to her house and Megan had started behaving strangely, like she was sleepy or drunk. Alarmed, Kimberly had demanded to know what was going on. When Megan admitted taking the pills, Kimberly had alerted her mother, who had called 911.

After a nurse took Wendy back, Kimberly went to a corner of the waiting room, head down as she busily texted friends, who soon began arriving, congregating in a corner. Erica was nervous, which worsened her compulsions, and it took a lot of effort for her to straighten the magazines on various tables, with an even number on each one, and make sure all chairs were lined up precisely, then do it all again as people came and left with no regard for precision and order.

At one point, a hefty woman, who had been there the entire time watching Erica, came over. With a hint of steel in her voice, she told Erica, "If you don't stop rearranging the chairs and magazines, I'm going to use my scarf and tie you to a chair." Erica relented and restricted her impulses to simple pacing until Stephen arrived. Shortly after, Lee came with Brandon.

There was profound relief when Wendy came back with the news that Megan was going to be all right. Wendy hugged them all, weeping great tears of relief as she threw her arms around Erica, Stephen, and Lee, then Kimberly and her friends.

"The doctors want to keep Megan for a while," Wendy explained. "Stephen, could you give Brandon and Erica a ride home? I'll bring Megan home when they release her."

"Don't worry about coming in to work tomorrow," Lee said. "You're going to be exhausted."

"I have to work," Wendy smiled grimly. "I'll need every dime to pay the hospital bills."

Brandon had been listening. "I've got some money in my piggy bank you can have." Wendy's eyes teared up again, and she hugged him wordlessly.

Stepping closer to Wendy, Stephen spoke in a low, urgent voice. "I'll help—you know that. You're working too hard."

"Thank you, Stephen. I'll keep that in mind, but first I'll try to handle it myself."

Kimberly came over again. Tears welled up in her big brown eyes. "Mrs. Kemp, I just wanted to tell you how sorry I am." She gulped. "I didn't even know Megan had taken the pills at first. She told me she wasn't trying to—to—" She stopped, unable to get the rest out.

Wendy hugged Kimberly fiercely. "It's all right. I'm just glad you were with her and got help. And Megan told me the same thing; she wasn't trying to kill herself. She was just—experimenting."

There was another round of hugs as good-byes were said. "Are you going to be okay?" Erica asked Wendy as they hugged.

Wendy pulled back. Her eyes were bright with tears, but her voice was resolute. "I have to be." She went back to the doors that led to the emergency treatment rooms and gave a small wave before nodding to a nurse who unlocked the door for her.

* * *

"You look pretty happy," Erica said, setting a plate of scrambled eggs and her signature square toast on the table as Brandon, wearing a big smile, plopped into a dining room chair.

"I went in Megan's room to see if she was all right."

"Oh no! Did you wake her up?"

"Yeah," he said, sounding unconcerned. "She told me I was acting like a moron and to go away." He smiled then took a large bite of toast. Evidently, that was all Brandon needed to know that his sister was fine.

Wendy dragged herself into the kitchen a short time later. At the table, she held her head in her hands. "Days like today make me wish I was a coffee drinker."

Erica set a plate in front of her. "Eat—you'll feel better."

After breakfast, Wendy changed into her uniform and checked on Megan again. "I'll call on my break to see how Megan's doing."

"I'll keep a close watch on her. Don't worry about a thing."

It was early afternoon before Megan woke. Her wan face with its woebegone expression would have made anyone's heart twist. Erica went to the window and opened the blinds to let the sunlight in. She then went to the bed and, bending over, put her cheek against Megan's.

"I'm *so* glad you're all right." The girl's eyes showed faint surprise as Erica pulled a chair close to the bed and sat down. "Everyone's been so worried about you, Megan, especially your mom. She's called twice already." She heard a scratching sound and looked at the dresser. Brandon's hamster cage was there. Buster was on his hind legs, stretching and sniffing as if he knew he was in new territory. "What's that doing in here?"

"Brandon brought it in. He said he didn't want me to be alone." Megan stared at the cage, her eyes suspiciously bright. Erica pretended not to notice and chatted about other things, deliberately keeping the conversation light. However, during a pause in the conversation, Erica felt a distinct impression that she needed to talk seriously to Megan. She questioned it, feeling it was not her place to talk to Megan about taking drugs. The impression came again, clearer this time.

Not about the pills. Talk about the night Wendy had the miscarriage.

"Why are you frowning?" Megan asked, looking at her curiously.

"Was I? Sorry. My mind was wandering." Saying a quick prayer in her heart, Erica jumped in. "Actually, I was thinking about something your mother told me a few days ago."

"I suppose she was talking about me." Suspicion was heavy in Megan's voice.

"It was more about your mom, but you were part of it. She told me about something that happened three years ago." Erica could see the wheels churning in Megan's mind and added softly, "About the night your mother fell down the stairs."

"She had no business telling you that!" Megan started to rise up angrily.

"Your mother and I are best friends. She confides in me, just like you confide in Kimberly."

There was nothing Megan could say. Looking slightly mollified, she laid her head back against the pillow.

"I can't imagine how terrible that must have been for you." Their eyes met and held. As Erica looked into Megan's dark, wounded eyes, she realized—in a split-second crack of clarity—that Megan had been injured right down to the marrow. The girl swallowed hard, as if in remembered pain, and turned her head. Reaching out, Erica took hold of Megan's nearest hand, clasping it firmly.

"Now that I know what you've been through, I think I understand your feelings better."

Megan rejected that outright. "No, you can't."

"I can try. Have you told anyone about it?"

"Just Kimberly."

"I'm glad you told someone because talking can help you feel better. Sometimes, bad experiences can act like poison inside your body. If you don't get that poison out, it'll keep making you sick and feeling bad." Megan gave her a searching look.

"I know what I'm talking about," Erica murmured. "I had some bad things happen to me when I was growing up. It wasn't until I was an adult that I was able to talk about them. My psychiatrist said talking was like lancing an old boil and getting rid of the pus and infection that had been causing me pain for years and years. After that, I began to heal."

"*You* saw a psychiatrist?" There was great wonder in Megan's voice. "But—but you seem so normal. Except for your OCD, I mean."

"Everyone says I'm OCD, but I like to think of it as striving for a higher order of precision. Ah well, true greatness is often misunderstood by others." Erica grinned.

"What did you see a psychiatrist for? Because you're afraid of the dark?"

Inwardly, Erica shrunk. Being afraid of the dark was not the only disturbing thing that lay in her past. The other one was not something Erica liked to talk about, yet how could she ask Megan to confide in her when she was unwilling to do the same?

"I got counseling because when I was a child I was sexually abused."

Megan's eyes opened wide, and her face showed her shock. "I'm sorry, Erica. I didn't mean to be so nosy."

"It's all right. I thought I'd gotten over it, but after I'd been married about twelve years, I started having problems. Maybe you've heard the old saying, 'Feelings buried alive never die'? Well, I can tell you that's true. But I started seeing a good counselor and was able to move on." Erica put on a slight smile, hoping to relieve the girl's distressed look. "Anyway, because of that, I can tell you from experience that you need to talk about what's bothering you so you can get it out of your system. Then you can start to feel better. You don't want to dwell endlessly on it, but you do have to get it out."

Erica waited a minute then said, "Tell me what happened that night. Your mother said you were very brave."

Megan was still for so long that Erica wondered if she was going to respond. Then, possibly influenced by Erica confiding in her, Megan began speaking—slowly at first then faster and faster until her words were falling all over themselves in a near frantic tumble.

All of it came out—the fear, confusion, and anger, starting with when her father had come home drunk. As they'd started arguing, Megan had paced her bedroom and when her parents began yelling at one another, she'd covered her ears to block out the sound—until the shouting had increased and fear caused her to venture out. Tears began falling as she told how crazy and out of control her father was—and how helpless her mother was when he pinned her against the wall.

When it appeared her father was trying to smother her mom, Megan began flailing at him with her fists, screaming at him to stop. Megan jerkily related how she'd watched in horror as he'd pushed her mother away. It was an image that had been seared into her brain, and Megan said that even now she could see her mother tumbling down the stairs as if in slow motion.

Intense emotion seemed to change the very color of the air as Megan described rushing down the stairs and seeing blood running down her mother's face. The groans had been awful. Megan had run to the phone and called her mother's friend, Suzanne, who had taken Wendy to the hospital.

When the telling was done, Megan covered her face with her big hands, her body jerking with sobs. Erica put her arms around the girl and tenderly smoothed the hair away from her face.

Finally the sobs stopped and then, in a twist of emotions, the pain and fear morphed into hot rage. "Why did Mom have to let him come back?" Megan cried angrily. "Why? It was so stupid!"

She didn't expect an answer, and Erica gave none. Now was not the time. Erica thought of what Louise J. Kaplan had once said: "Children, even infants, are capable of sympathy, but only after adolescence are we capable of compassion." Was Megan old enough to be capable of getting past her hurt and anger and feel compassion toward her mother? Could she understand that Wendy had been doing her best even though it had turned out so tragically? When the tears slowed, Erica went for a cool washcloth. After Megan blew her nose, Erica had her hold the washcloth against her eyes.

"Sorry for being a big baby," Megan said in a raspy voice.

"You are definitely not that," Erica assured her. "It was a terrible thing to have happened." Again, Erica felt a smoking curl of anger toward Dennis Kemp. Did he understand the emotional trauma he had inflicted, not only on Wendy but on his daughter?

"I'm so sorry you had to go through that," Erica murmured, reaching out to stroke Megan's hair.

Megan lowered the washcloth. Looking at Erica out of bleary, reddened eyes, she said, "I really *wasn't* trying to kill myself. No one believes me, but it's the truth. I just wanted to feel—I don't know—good for a change, I guess."

"That's understandable, but pills aren't a good way to do that. Mixing drugs can be very dangerous. You took a real risk by taking your mom's meds."

"The doctor already talked to me about it."

"Good." Erica paused. "Um, is this the first time you've done this?"

"What? You think I do this all the time?" The teen's reddened eyes were wide with fresh outrage. "Maybe you think I'm a drug addict—" The old sensitive Megan was back.

"No, I don't think that—you're much too careful about what you eat to mistreat your body with drugs. But you *did* take your mom's meds, and even occasional use can lead to addictions. I'd hate to see you go down that road. I know that when a person is hurting inside it's natural to want to do something to deaden the pain."

After thinking about it, Megan said, "You can relax. I'm not into drugs."

It was good to hear that, but after listening to Megan's outpourings, Erica was sure the girl needed support. "If you ever want to talk, I'll be glad to listen. Even when I go home, you can call or e-mail me. But it would be good if you had someone to talk with here. I know you have your friends, but sometimes it's good to talk with someone older. What about your mom?"

Megan rolled her eyes. "She'd never understand."

"She might understand more than you think, but that's up to you. Is there anyone else?"

"Well, my advisor in Young Women is pretty cool."

"Talk to her, then. And also talk to Heavenly Father. He loves you and can help. Just ask and He'll be there."

"I don't think He'd want to help someone like me," Megan muttered. "After all, the Spirit withdraws if you do bad things, doesn't it? And aren't there some things He just can't forgive?"

"God is *always* there for us," Erica said firmly. "Even if we think we're unworthy, He'll never turn His back on us."

"Even if a person does terrible things?"

"Even then."

"What about murderers? The Bible says they don't deserve to live."

"If you're thinking about your father, he did a terrible thing, but it's up to God to judge him. Besides, not all men are like him."

"No, not all. Just ninety-nine percent." Megan's voice was cold, as if coming up through fathomless black water.

"I'm sure you don't mean that," Erica said, a little frisson of alarm sounding in her mind.

"I bet you think I poisoned Stephen," Megan said accusingly.

"Well, did you?"

Megan's eyes opened wide. Clearly she had expected a denial. "No, I didn't."

"Good. Now that that's settled, you must be hungry. What can I get you to eat?"

"I don't want anything." Megan began plucking at the bedspread listlessly.

"You already skipped breakfast. How about a nice green salad? Or I could make Whole Wheat Pancakes.[7] What about a tofu steak? Anything you want, but I'm not leaving until I get your order, ma'am."

The dark eyes that had been filled with so much sorrow now held a small gleam. "Sorry I've acted like such a brat since you've been here."

"That's okay. I was once a brat myself. Sometimes I still am!"

Megan smiled. "Thanks for being so understanding."

"You caught me on a good day. Now, what'll you have?"

"I think pancakes. I still can't believe you make them square."

---

7   See appendix at the end of the book for this recipe.

"They taste better that way. I'm sure you've noticed. All right, pancakes coming up; I'll be back in a flash."

She was nearly to the door when Megan called out, "Erica?"

"Yes?"

"Thanks."

* * *

While the house was quiet, Erica called Doug, her boss at Pinnacle. Ever since her visit to Linda Bronson, she had been itching to get on her laptop and start searching for Areli and James. Although Erica considered herself an expert at locating people, such searches required the right databases—ones that were only available to private investigators who shelled out large yearly fees. After hearing her story, Doug agreed to let her access Pinnacle's databases. She'd just gotten off the phone when Wendy walked in.

"I thought you had to work until four," Erica said.

"Lee insisted I come home early. With pay. I tell you, that man is a saint. How's Megan?"

"She's doing great. Just finished off a pile of pancakes."

"Wonderful!" Wendy smiled, and it was like the coming of a new day. "I'll go see her."

When Brandon came home from school, he asked, "How's Megan and Buster?" When she replied that they were both doing fine, he took off down the hall.

Half an hour later, the doorbell rang, and Wendy opened the door to find Kimberly. Today, she had her long hair twisted up and pinned in back. Her eyes were still anxious. "Is it all right if I see Megan?"

"Sure. Come on in. You know the way."

It wasn't long before Brandon bounded into the kitchen, followed by Wendy. "I thought I'd let the girls visit," she said.

"What can I have to eat?" Brandon asked, burrowing into the fridge.

"How about a peanut butter sandwich?"

After he took it outside, Wendy sat down. She put her elbows on the table and clasped her hands together. "I talked with the doctor last night. She doesn't believe Megan's story about 'experimenting' with pills. She thinks Megan's trying to cover up an attempted suicide and that I ought to have her see a counselor."

"Megan told me she wasn't trying to kill herself, but I still think it's a good idea to have her see a therapist. Do you think Megan will agree to it?"

"Since I want her to see one, Megan will refuse of course. But she's going to go," Wendy said determinedly. "One way or another."

Erica was pleased to see Wendy standing firm. Although Wendy could be emotional at times, she had a certain toughness when the chips were down. Once her mind was made up and a direction chosen, Wendy could be utterly focused and determined.

"Megan and I had a long talk today," Erica said. "She was really traumatized the night Dennis pushed you down the stairs. I don't think she's gotten over it."

Wendy sighed. "I've tried and tried to talk to her about it, but she refuses."

Erica noticed the tired lines on Wendy's face. "You look exhausted," Erica said. "Why don't you take a nap? You had a long night last night." When Wendy glanced in the direction of her daughter's room, Erica added, "Megan's fine. Kimberly's with her, and I'll look in."

"All right," Wendy said, giving in. "I think I will lie down."

While her friend napped, Erica went out to the porch and, pulling a chair into the shade, called Detective Lund. He had given her his cell number, and she knew he'd want to know about Megan. Erica quickly filled Patrick in, including Megan's denial that it had been a suicide attempt.

"I'm not sure we can take her word for that," Patrick said somberly. "Denial is common for suicide survivors. Megan seems like a troubled girl, and some of her comments are disturbing. It's possible Megan tried to kill herself because she had a guilty conscience," the detective speculated. "She hated Stephen, poisoned him, then felt guilty about her actions and downed a bunch of pills."

Erica didn't like to think Megan was capable of that. "I suppose it's possible, but she's so young. It could be she's just struggling with the old trauma she went through with her parents."

"There's no set age for killers. I've heard of elementary school children killing in cold blood. Besides, young people are impulsive; they don't think about the consequences. Is she a habitual drug user?"

"I don't think so. I asked Megan about that, and she said no."

"Again, we can't assume she's telling the truth. You've gotten to know Megan a little. Tell me about her. What's she like?"

Erica did her best.

"Unhappy, moody, and angry," Patrick said thoughtfully. "A bad combination. And what's this old trauma you mentioned?" After Erica explained, he said, "I'll look up the police report."

"Wendy didn't call the police."

Growling in frustration, Patrick said, "Typical. Do you know how many battered women cover it up and say it was an accident? At least she's not with him anymore. A lot of women stay in abusive situations. Now, going back to Megan. She's the only person we've found that hates Stephen." The implication was clear, and Erica fought it.

"I don't think she tried to kill him."

"You also don't think Wendy, who is the only one who stands to gain financially from Stephen's death, poisoned him. You have a kind heart, Erica Coleman, and always believe the best of everyone, but that's not helping us here."

"And believing the worst *would* help?"

"Certainly. I'm trying to find the worst—someone who killed a man then tried to kill another. Let's look at the facts. Wendy had a motive and the opportunity. Megan also had a motive—she hates Stephen Watkins and doesn't want him to become her stepfather. She also had the opportunity. Let's say she got ahold of Dalmane somehow. Then, on the night of the dinner party, Megan goes into the kitchen and sees Jaime making coffee. She sees her chance." Erica listened uneasily as Patrick went on. "Megan gets the poison from her room and, when Jaime's back is turned, puts poison in the cups. Stephen miraculously survives, but Megan, because of her religious upbringing, becomes overwhelmed with guilt and tries to kill herself."

"It's possible, I suppose." Heavy doubt tinged Erica's voice.

"There's another scenario. Instead of guilt, Megan becomes depressed when she sees that by poisoning Stephen she's only brought him and her mother closer, so she tries to commit suicide."

"But Megan says she wasn't trying to kill herself."

"The girl took a prescription-drug cocktail. Is that the action of someone who wants to live?"

* * *

Later that evening, the doorbell rang. A big smile lit up Wendy's face. "I bet that's Lee. He said he was going to stop by after work and see Megan." She ran to the door.

It was hard to see Lee, hidden as he was behind a huge stuffed bear. He was also carrying flowers and a package of licorice. He grinned when he saw Erica looking at the candy.

"I didn't think Megan would want chocolate—she said something negative about it once."

"Yeah, she's the tenth person." When Lee looked puzzled, Erica explained, "Someone did a survey and found that nine out of ten people like chocolate, and the tenth person was lying."

Wendy and Lee laughed. It was amazing to see how, when Lee smiled, his face bloomed into something extraordinary. He handed the flowers to Wendy. "These are for you," he said, appearing suddenly shy. Then he looked around. "Where's Megan?"

"Cloistered with a girlfriend in her room, but you can go in," Wendy said.

He hesitated. "I don't want to disturb them."

"Nonsense," Wendy said smiling. "She'll be happy to see you. Hold on a minute, though. I was just getting Megan a drink, and I want to see her face when she sees the bear."

Erica followed her into the kitchen and watched as Wendy put the flowers in water. Keeping her voice casual, Erica said, "Lee's rather good-looking, don't you think?"

"I'd say that's a big yes," Wendy replied as she poured some juice.

"Has he ever asked you out?"

"Lee?" Wendy chuckled then glanced toward the front room. "He's not interested in me that way," she said in a low voice. "I'm just an employee and Brandon's mom."

"Oh, that explains the flowers, then."

"Oh, come on," Wendy said. "You're kidding, right? Why would he be interested in me?"

"Because you're pretty, smart, and fun to be around."

"Says my beautiful best friend."

"So I'd be the person to know, wouldn't you say?"

Looking amused, Wendy merely shook her head and headed for the front room. They were nearly to Megan's room when Lee stopped and put a finger to his lips. Reaching out, he pushed the door open with his foot while remaining out of sight.

Extending his arm, Lee held the bear in the doorway and, doing his best to sound like a bear, said in a rough baritone, "I heard there was someone in here who needed a 'bear' hug!"

When the girls giggled, they all went in. Since it was standing room only, Erica only stayed a few minutes. In the front room, she picked up the *Ensign* and tried to read while periodic bursts of laughter came from the bedroom. Once, everyone cheered. Lee's visit certainly seemed to be doing Megan a lot of good.

After a while, Lee came out and took a seat on the sofa. "Wendy will be out in a minute," he said. "Megan looks good, I thought. It was quite a shock when Wendy called last night."

"The doctor is advising her to get Megan into counseling."

"Good. I wish Wendy would go too—she's so stressed out lately. At work, she's tense and anxious—like a walking time bomb that could go off any minute."

"She's gone through a lot lately."

"Agreed. Plus, she's working such long hours. If any of the other waitresses needs someone to pick up their shift, Wendy's the first person they call."

"She's having a hard time financially."

"And now she'll have hospital bills on top of everything else. I've offered to help, but Wendy always refuses. Yet she seems so desperate. I worry that one day she'll just snap."

Erica could feel the intensity of Lee's concern. This was not the mild interest of a manager who was worried about an employee. His eyes went down the hall. "I thought Megan and Wendy needed a diversion, so I told them I was taking everyone boating this Saturday. You too."

"So that's what all the cheering was about!"

* * *

After saying good night to everyone, Erica went to the basement, opened her laptop, and connected to the Internet. First, she talked with the children. Aby showed her a test where she'd gotten an A-. Ryan moved the computer so she could watch him play a piece on the piano. Then Kenzie, not to be outdone, showed how she could do cartwheels and front rolls. She and David talked about their days, then Erica told him about Detective Lund's theories regarding Megan.

Patrick was not the only one harboring suspicions about the girl. "I didn't want to mention anything, seeing how you've gotten close to her," David admitted, "but it's crossed my mind that Megan could have poisoned Stephen. I know it's hard when you're living right there, but you've got to keep an open mind."

Anxious to change the subject, Erica said, "Guess what? I get to go boating. Lee's taking everyone out on Saturday."

"Is the husband of the beautiful private eye invited?"

"Sure! Come on out!" She laughed. Then she told him how worried Lee was about Wendy.

"That doesn't sound good," David said thoughtfully. "It's almost as though he's trying to plant some doubt in your mind about Wendy's mental stability."

"I didn't take it that way, although it did worry me."

"Just an idea. Lee's a suspect, and guilty people often try to redirect attention to someone else. I just wondered if Lee was deliberately trying to instill misgivings in your mind about Wendy."

Erica was tempted to reject the idea out of hand, but she rarely dismissed ideas simply because they didn't fit her own way of thinking. *Could* Lee have been trying to plant doubts about Wendy? He had seemed innocent and sincere at the time, but now that she was away from Lee and his charm, Erica began to wonder.

David went on to other matters. "By the way, is Jaime still making a play for Stephen?"

"When she picked me up at the airport, Jaime said she'd invited Stephen to lunch."

"And she didn't mind telling this to Wendy's best friend?"

"I don't think Jaime cares," Erica replied. "I wish I knew why she's so interested in him. I mean, Stephen's a great guy, but Jaime is young, gorgeous, and—other than believing she actually has a chance at winning the lottery—fairly intelligent. She could have any guy she wanted. Why a paunchy, middle-aged man?"

"My guess is that she foresees a life of luxury."

"If Stephen never told Wendy that he's going to inherit a fortune, I doubt he'd tell Jaime."

"From what you've said, Jaime sounds pretty sharp. Since she works at Stephen's office, she could have looked through his letters or overheard a conversation, but I bet she knows about the money." David was very sure. "Why else do gorgeous young babes hook up with old men? No one, except the rich old man himself, believes that girls find flabby abs and receding hairlines sexy."

"I do. Why do you think I married you?"

In mock outrage, David said, "I'll have you know I have 15 percent body fat—not bad for my age—*and* I was in the top 10 percent of all the officers in Davis County at our yearly physical. *My* abs are in great shape, and my hairline is holding steady."

"Thanks to Rogaine."

"Ha! I don't need that stuff. I'm better than the day you married me."

"I know, I know, buff boy. I was only kidding. But please, no more talk about your hot bod, or I'm going to have to jump on the next plane home."

CHAPTER 13

WEDNESDAY MORNING, ERICA DROVE TO Stephen's office in downtown Kissimmee. Diana Evans was at the front desk, wearing an oversized blue sweater that hung on her thin frame. Her bright eyes were watchful.

"Can I help you?" she asked coolly, as though she'd never seen Erica before.

"I'd like to see Stephen, please."

Deciding to assert her authority, Diana sniffed and said, "I'm not sure he's available. Let me check." As she picked up the phone, Jaime walked in, her silky hair combed back in a ponytail. Her distinctive nose gave her face a unique look, and she appeared very chic today in an emerald green suit. It was obvious from her look of amusement that she'd overheard Diana.

"Of course Stephen's available! Reed's with him, but you can go on back. Do you remember where his office is?" Jaime paid no attention to Diana who had compressed her lips and was looking daggers at her for having usurped her authority.

"I do."

"Good. See you around." Jaime picked up a folder and left. Erica remained prudently silent (who knew how many times in the future she might have to face Diana?) and hurried down the hall. Stephen's door was open.

"Come in, Erica," Stephen said when he saw her. Reed was in a chair facing Stephen, and when he turned, his thin face looked impatient.

"Hope I'm not interrupting anything," Erica began.

"Not at all," Stephen said, coming around to pull a chair over for Erica to sit. Just then the phone buzzed.

"What is it, Diana? Yes, Erica's here. Yes, she found my office all right, thank you." Stephen winked mischievously at Erica. Evidently, he was familiar with Diana's ways. Stephen listened further. "Chad's here now? Tell him to hold on; I need to ask him something. I'll be right there." He hung up.

"I'm sorry, Erica, but someone came to drop off some papers, and I need to ask him a couple of questions before he leaves. I'll be back in a minute."

As he hurried off, Reed looked after him, his lip curled in a strange expression. "Makes a great show of staying busy and looking important, doesn't he?" It wasn't really a question.

Erica didn't understand. "Stephen said he needed to ask the guy something."

"Reading the papers would have answered his questions," Reed drawled, "but Stephen likes to act as if he were crucial to everything that goes on here." Seeing the look on Erica's face, he added, "I suppose you think it bad taste to speak ill of coworkers, but I'm not one to mince words. Stephen spends far too much time talking and doing stuff that doesn't matter. If he managed his time better, he'd be able to finish his projects without me having to bail him out."

"I'd have thought talking with people and building good relationships would be beneficial to the company."

Reed's dark eyes looked at her thoughtfully. "In today's economy, it's important to get the job done *quickly*. People who hire us expect prompt results. When Stephen takes too long on a project, it creates a bottleneck and a lot of ill will. But I don't want to bore you with office politics. It can get rather nasty."

It already has—with you talking about Stephen behind his back.

Reed stood. "When Stephen gets back, tell him I had work to do and that I'll go over the Swenson account with him later." His voice was edgy.

When Stephen returned, she delivered the message, noticing Stephen still had a haggard, worried look—an air of not having had much sleep of late.

"I won't keep you long; I know you're busy," Erica began. "But I had a couple of things I needed to ask you about. One was when you told the police that Wendy had pushed you to make a will. I wanted to make sure that was an accurate statement."

"What? I never said Wendy pushed me! One of the policemen kept asking over and over why I suddenly decided to make a will, and I made the mistake of telling them Wendy had encouraged me." Stephen shook his head in disgust. "He jumped on that like a dog on a bone and made a big deal out of it even though I told him I'd been meaning to make a will for a long time."

"After talking with you, the police have placed Wendy at the top of their list of suspects."

Stephen's face was red and angry. "Just because the police can't find the person who tried to kill me, they try and pin the blame on the first person they come across—so it looks like they're doing their job. They must be pretty desperate if they think Wendy had anything to do with it. It's absurd!" He snorted. "Why, when Wendy found a mouse in her kitchen, she couldn't even stand to put mouse poison out. Megan had to do it."

Erica was doing her best to listen, but a small part of her mind was distracted by the container of paper clips. Her eye kept returning to it and finally, she picked it up, dumped the clips out, and began separating the colored ones from the ordinary silver ones as Stephen talked. When he stopped, she glanced up to see him watching her, his head tilted to one side.

"They're all mixed up, you see," Erica said as if that explained everything. Deftly she moved silver clips away from the colored pile. "You'll thank me when I'm done. Anyway, getting back to Wendy. Right now, she's the only one that could benefit from your death since you don't seem to have any enemies." She said the last sentence casually, hoping it would lead to some disclosure. Erica was rewarded by a flicker that came over his face. "*Do* you have enemies?" she prodded.

Stephen looked at her with that quiet calmness he always wore. "I would prefer not to say."

"So you'd rather be polite and keep quiet. Is that it?" Erica was annoyed. She shoved the colored clips into the container and set it down with a bang. "And what would it take to make you change your mind? Wendy being arrested? Having someone tamper with your brakes? You ending up in the morgue? The only thing is that, by then, it will be too late to talk about enemies."

Stephen was taken aback at her vehemence. "I don't think it will go as far as that."

She wanted to shake him. "Someone tried to poison you!" Erica ground out.

"Maybe it wasn't intended for me. There was poison in your cup too, and Jaime's."

"The police are looking into that, but right now, you're the likelier candidate. And while hesitating to tell me about possible enemies may show that you're a nice guy, it isn't helping the investigation at all."

For a few moments, Stephen sat quietly. Then he got up and shut the door. "I feel like a jerk for saying anything," he said softly as he sat down. "But ever since I started working here, Reed Devoe has seemed to have some sort of personal grudge against me. I've never understood why." He shifted uncomfortably. "Of course, I may be taking it too personally since he seems to act that way toward everyone."

"He does seem to have a permanent chip on his shoulder. Do you know why?"

"I've been here for two years, and I've tried to be friends, but Reed is still cold and often rude. He takes everything I say negatively. I keep trying to be nice, to build a relationship, but nothing seems to work." Stephen wore a look of troubled perplexity. "I know he's worried about the company. Possibly he sees me as a threat. Still, just because someone dislikes me doesn't mean they would try to kill me."

"You'd be surprised at how little it takes." Reed Devoe was indeed someone to consider. He seemed strangely bitter and intolerant. Had he always been that way, or was there something deeper behind his surliness?

The door opened, and Jaime glanced at Erica in surprise. "Oh! You're still here! I was just going to ask Stephen if he wanted to go out for lunch."

"No thanks," Stephen said. "I brought mine today."

Jaime's face fell, and at that moment, there was something familiar about that disgruntled look. Erica thought hard, but whatever was nudging her would not come clear.

"Another time, then." Jaime's high heels clicked as she went down the hall.

"Thanks for leveling with me, Stephen. Now, is there anyone else that is unhappy with you in any way?"

"There's no one else," Stephen replied quietly. "I've given it a lot of thought."

"All right. I'll let you get back to work." She stopped at the door then walked back. "Oh, I forgot to give you these." She opened her hand and gave him the silver paper clips. "Put them in your desk," she admonished. "Whatever you do, don't mix them up with the others."

In her car, Erica pulled down the mirror and reapplied her lipstick. She stopped to check traffic before pulling onto the road, and as she waited, she glanced back at the office. One of the curtains was pulled slightly to the side. A woman was standing there, half hidden, looking out at her. A woman in a green suit.

* * *

After picking up Wendy from work, the women went to Highlands Elementary School to see Brandon's play. Wiggling his nose, Brandon energetically hopped about the stage like a good bunny. Toward the end, he really got into character. Turning, he twitched his little cotton tail at the audience, which hooted with laughter. There was mad applause at the end then punch and cookies.

When they got home, Erica checked her cell phone for messages. One was from Timothy Peterson.

She hit the button to return his call, and after a couple rings a strong, firm voice said, "Hello, this is Timothy."

"This is Erica Coleman. Sorry I couldn't take your call earlier. Coby and Myrna Kincaid gave me your number. They said you were good friends with Stephen Watkins."

"Yes, I lived just a couple of houses down from Stephen and Richard."

"I met Stephen through a mutual friend, Wendy Kemp, who lives here in Kissimmee. Not long ago, a man was murdered outside her home. Then a week later, Stephen was poisoned at her house."

"Poisoned?" Timothy cried out. "I can't believe it! How did—"

"Stephen's all right," Erica cut in. "I'm sorry. That's the second time I've scared someone to death. Stephen was taken to the hospital, but he's fine now."

"Praise the Lord," Tim declared fervently. "How was he poisoned?"

"Someone put poison in his coffee."

A pause. "You mean it was deliberate?"

"Yes."

Timothy's voice was bewildered. "It's hard to believe that someone would poison Stephen. Are you sure it wasn't an accident?"

"Very sure. I'm a private investigator and a personal friend of Wendy Kemp, who's asked me to look into this. I wanted to ask if you knew anyone that might have a grudge or bad feelings toward Stephen."

Timothy took time to think. "No, can't say that I do." Erica believed him. Although he was a bit shocked, he sounded intelligent and level-headed. Timothy added, "Stephen was just one of those people that everybody liked."

"How long have you known Stephen?"

"Ever since he and his brother moved to Chicago. Let's see, Richard's been gone a couple of years, so I guess I've known them about seventeen years. I knew Stephen better than Richard—Stephen was the outgoing, sociable one. Had quite a sense of humor too. They were good neighbors—helped me out several times. When my daughter got married and moved to Montana, Stephen and Richard helped us load the truck. And when I was remodeling, they came and gave me a hand. Stephen, especially, spent a lot of weekends helping—when he could get away from his job, that is."

"That was nice of him."

"It sure was. I always told people Stephen was a fantastic guy—and that he had the scars to prove it!" Timothy laughed heartily.

"Sounds like there's a story behind that."

"Oh, there is. My wife and I were remodeling our bathroom, you see, and Stephen came over to help me tear out the tile shower. He was having a good old time, just swinging away with that sledge hammer but got a little too eager and cut his arm on a jagged piece. I had to take him over to the emergency room and get him stitched up."

"I hope it wasn't serious."

"He bled like a stuck pig, but I got a towel and had him put pressure on it until we got to the hospital. They took care of it okay. Stephen told the nurse in the emergency room that I'd been working him too hard and this was the only way he could think of to take a break." Timothy chuckled at the memory. Then he said, "I sure hope you find the guy who poisoned him."

"If you happen to think of anything that might help, don't hesitate to call back."

"Sure thing. You tell Stephen hello for me. I don't believe we've had a good chat since he left."

"I'll do that."

* * *

That evening, she and Wendy prepared dinner together. Erica slid the carrots she'd sliced into a pan and said, "I'm not going to be able to go shopping with you and Megan like we'd planned. I need to take another trip, and Chris told me the only time that looks good for flying standby is late Thursday night. I'll be back Friday."

"Where are you going this time?" Wendy asked.

"I can't say."

"You're going to be all mysterious, are you?"

"Yep."

Megan walked in and got a glass of water. "When is dinner going to be ready?"

"In about ten minutes," Wendy said, putting the hamburger patties in the frying pan. "And yes, I remembered to fry your tofu in a separate pan. I won't be eating with you tonight because I'm going out with Stephen. Oh, and honey, we're going to have to put off our shopping trip with Erica."

"I knew it," Megan flashed, setting her glass down so hard it was a miracle it didn't shatter. "I knew you were lying when you said we'd go shopping."

Erica was annoyed. "Your mother did *not* lie! I have to go out of town unexpectedly. I'm the one who changed the plans, not your Mom."

"You and I can still go shopping if you want," Wendy said, trying to placate her daughter.

"No! I want to go with Erica."

"Okay. When Erica gets back, we'll set another day." She turned to Erica. "I've got to go, but dinner's nearly ready. I'll see you later." Wendy went to give her daughter a hug, but it was like trying to hug a post as Megan remained stiff and unbending.

After the door closed, Erica glared at Megan. The girl tried to ignore the look then blurted out sullenly, "What are you looking at?"

"A child who was very rude to her mother."

"I'm not a child, and I wasn't rude. I was telling the truth. Unlike Mom. I know you won't believe me, but Mom lies—all the time."

It was hard to know what was going on inside this young woman. Since coming home from the hospital, Megan had been fairly pleasant, but tonight she was back to being petulant and sullen.

"Megan, I want to ask you something, and I hope you'll be honest with me. I'm not sure exactly what's going on between you and your mother, but I'd like to know why you treat her the way you do." Erica thought Megan would deny treating her mother poorly, but the girl remained silent. Then Erica remembered the talk they'd had after Megan came home from the hospital.

Something propelled her to ask, "I know you were upset that she'd let your father come back, but it's more than that, isn't it?"

Megan jerked slightly then turned away.

Bingo.

"I guess things were bad for a lot of years, especially when your dad drank."

Megan threw her a look of disbelief. "You're kidding me, right? I thought Mom kept you up-to-date on everything, but obviously she didn't tell you all of it."

"Why don't *you* tell me?" Erica turned the burners to low before sitting at the table.

With her back to Erica, Megan said in a hard voice, "I'm sure you know they fought all the time, but I bet you didn't know my dad treated me like garbage and Mom didn't care. Once he made me walk to school just because I looked at him the wrong way. Mom didn't say anything to him. I thought she might come and pick me up, but she didn't."

Megan turned then, her eyes narrow as she held on to the back of a chair. Standing ramrod straight, her mouth twisted as though the words were bitter. "My dad would go through my room and take things of mine, and Mom never stopped him. He was always yelling at me and Brandon, but Mom never stood up for us—not once. I was so glad when he left. I couldn't believe it when Mom told us he was coming back home." Her voice buzzed with outrage as she cried, "After all he'd done, and she *still* let him come back!"

"Your mom thought he had changed," Erica said softly. "Even the bishop thought so."

"Well, he *hadn't.*" There was a ring of steel in Megan's voice. "Anyone in their right mind could see he wasn't ever going to change—that he wasn't going to stop drinking!"

"Your mother thought she was doing the right thing."

"And look what happened because of it. I'd have a baby brother or sister right now if it wasn't for him," Megan hissed. She was gripping the back of a chair so tightly, her knuckles turned white. Erica's skin prickled as she looked into Megan's dark eyes. Thank goodness she was going to see a counselor was all Erica could think.

Then those same fathomless eyes welled up with tears, and words began rushing out. "How could Mom let him come back after how he had treated us? He was always telling us how stupid and clumsy we were. We practically lived in our rooms, he grounded us so much. He hated being around us." Megan shook her head as if trying to rid herself of the memories. "How could Mom let him come back after the way he'd treated us? Why? It was so stupid! Mom didn't care about us at all." Megan wept with more intensity than ever, scrubbing away her tears with her hands.

Sadness lay like a glacier around Erica's heart, and it took an effort to keep her voice even. "I didn't know it was that bad. It must have been horrible for you. And for your mother too."

"At least *she* had a choice!" Megan flashed, her eyes burning. "I didn't! She could have protected us, she could have stuck up for us, but she didn't. *She didn't!*" With that, Megan turned abruptly, hitting a chair, which fell over as she ran awkwardly out of the room.

* * *

Wendy got home from her date in good time, but Megan had already left with friends, so she, Brandon, and Erica had scripture reading together. After putting her son to bed, Wendy went to the front room. Switching on the lamp beside the couch, she started to repair a tear in a pair of Brandon's pants. "I thought I'd fix these before I go to work. It's the late shift for me tonight," Wendy said with a sigh.

"Fixing those would be a lot easier with a sewing machine," Erica observed.

Digging deep into her pocket, Wendy feigned surprise then dug into the other pocket. "Nope, no money in that one either. Guess it's back to needle and thread."

"Ha, ha," Erica said dryly. "I forgot you didn't have one." She peered at the tear. "I'm pretty good at sewing. How about I fix that for you and you do something for me?"

"Oh boy, here it comes." Wendy brushed her hazel hair out of her eyes. "What do you want?"

"I need you to have another dinner party."

"*You have got to be kidding!*" Wendy said, emphasizing the words heavily. "Stephen nearly died after my last one!"

"I hardly think that's going to happen again."

"You bet it's not. And you know why? Because I'm never inviting anyone over for dinner again. Ever!"

"Come on, you have to! There's something very important I need to find out."

"You can do it without me."

"Are you always this snippy when you have the late shift?"

"It has nothing to do with work, as you well know. My boyfriend almost died the last time I had a party. That gives me a right to be snippy. It's in the Bill of Rights."

"I really need you to do this," Erica begged.

Wendy laid the pants in her lap. "What part of *no* don't you understand? Besides, nobody would come—they wouldn't dare. People are terrified of the place. I see people walking by, pointing at the house. At Halloween, kids are going to dare each other to ring my doorbell."

"Be serious."

"I *am* serious—that's the sad thing! So just forget it. I'm done with dinner parties and *anything* that involves people coming to my house. But you can still do the pants . . ."

"Oh, give me those," Erica grumbled, taking them. "You're doing it all wrong anyway."

Wendy grinned. "Thanks. I usually don't have to work the late shift, but a friend at work had a minor car accident and asked me to take her place."

"You work too hard. Why didn't you say you couldn't? I mean, you're so good at telling people no."

Wendy cut her eyes at Erica, but she refused to engage and said simply, "I didn't have any choice. I have bills to pay."

"You always have a choice," Erica remarked. Suddenly, she had an impression to take the conversation in a certain direction and she added, "There *is* such a thing as agency."

"You're not serious are you? My friend desperately needs time off to recover from whiplash, and I desperately need money. Not much agency there!"

"Everyone has their agency," Erica repeated, keeping her tone casual. "Even people like Dennis have the right to choose what they're going to do."

"*People like Dennis?*" Wendy's eyes narrowed. "You're classifying Dennis as a human being, which he most definitely is not. So what's your point? I'm assuming you have one."

"All I'm saying is that people have the freedom to make their own decisions."

"So Dennis had the freedom to be a jerk-face or not be a jerk-face?"

"Basically, yes."

Wendy frowned. "Well, we both know what he chose. Why are you bringing him up anyway? Thought I was feeling a little too happy about having to work tonight?"

"No, I was just thinking about what you said about Bishop Griggs," Erica confessed. Wendy's face hardened, and Erica knew that one misstep could be like throwing a lit match on a bonfire. Proceeding carefully, Erica said, "It's kind of involved, but it's about when you said Bishop Griggs couldn't have been called of God because he made the wrong decision when he told you to let Dennis come back home."

It was a wonder she didn't melt from Wendy's laser stare. Erica went on. "First, I just have to say that I believe every bishop is called of God. I've known a lot of bishops, and they were all good men who sincerely cared about members of their ward. I'm sure Bishop Griggs cared about you and did what he thought was best for you and Dennis."

Her friend made a gesture of impatience. "It was hardly best to say Dennis should come back home and hurt me."

"But that's where agency comes in," Erica said. "Bishop Griggs didn't *know* Dennis was going to do what he did. All he could go by is what Dennis told him, and Dennis *said* he had changed."

"*But he hadn't!*" Wendy's fingers were beginning to twine and untwine.

"Bishop Griggs didn't know that," Erica said flatly. "A bishop is many things, but he is *not* a mind reader. Now, at the time, everyone, even you, thought Dennis had stopped drinking. Right?"

"Right," Wendy said reluctantly.

"So everything *could* have been fine except Dennis—using his agency—decided to start drinking again. It's not Bishop Griggs's fault that Dennis made a bad choice. If you're going to point fingers, point them at Dennis Kemp, not at your bishop."

"Am I supposed to be understanding this?" Wendy's voice was cold.

"Let me try again," Erica pleaded. "Look, Bishop Griggs thought Dennis was sincere, that he had changed, and that he ought to be given another chance. Dennis had his agency and, after he moved back, made a series of very bad choices."

"That's an understatement." Wendy's voice was bitter.

"But think about it. When Dennis moved back, it *could* have worked out and been for the best *if* he hadn't decided to drink. He could have chosen *not* to, you know."

"Bishop Griggs should have known something terrible would happen if Dennis came back. He's supposed to be inspired."

"*He should have known?* Wendy, listen to yourself! Bishops *are* inspired, but they can't read people's minds—and they can't foretell the future. They're only human!" Erica had the uncanny feeling someone was whispering in her mind. There was no need to stop and search for words as she went on.

"Do you remember on Sunday when the teacher talked about how the Israelites freaked out when Moses went to get the Ten Commandments? Someone mentioned that Moses didn't know the Israelites would make an idol when he left them to go up the mountain. What do you think?"

"Well, I don't see how he could have known the Israelites would talk Aaron, of all people, into making a golden calf."

"But wasn't Moses called of God? Wasn't he inspired? Shouldn't he have known what would happen when he went up Mount Sinai?"

Wendy had no answer.

"Although Moses was a prophet, I don't think he knew. Remember when he came down? Moses was so mad he broke the tablets. Likewise, I don't think Bishop Griggs had any idea Dennis was going to get drunk and hurt you." Erica paused to let Wendy consider that. "None of our Church leaders, including Moses or Bishop Griggs, can *force* a person to do what's right. Bishop Griggs thought it would be all right for Dennis to come back home, and it could have been *if* Dennis hadn't used his agency to make some very bad choices. But everyone has their agency, including the Israelites, Dennis, you, and me."

Wendy was sitting so still that she might have been part of the couch.

"All I'm saying is that the consequences of Dennis's actions should not be laid on the bishop's shoulders. Bishops *are* called of God, and besides our support and respect, they need people to cut them some slack and allow them to be human. If you have to be angry at someone, be angry at Dennis—or at Satan, who tempted him in the first place."

They sat in silence for a time; the only sound was an occasional passing car.

Wendy's voice was very small when she finally spoke. "I know I shouldn't have stopped going to church because of Bishop Griggs, but I was so angry."

"You felt confused and betrayed," Erica said. "And that makes it easy to be offended. Nearly everyone struggles with being offended at a Church leader at some time—and some pull away from the Church because of it. But we need to base our testimonies not on a person, but on Jesus Christ. He is the one and only sure foundation. If we base our testimony on someone else, we're going to be disappointed. Look at Joseph Smith—he's done more for mankind than anyone else except for Jesus Christ, yet when he was alive he had lots of people angry and upset with him. They expected him to be perfect and to be inspired about everything."

Wendy was listening intently, so Erica went on. "Joseph Smith and other Church leaders started a bank. A lot of the Saints deposited money in it, but the bank failed. It was natural for the Saints to be upset, but then they blamed Joseph for not foreseeing that the bank would fail. They felt Joseph should have been inspired to know what was going to happen."

"I didn't know that."

"Prophets are divinely inspired in regards to leading the Church, but they may not always be inspired in secular areas. If they were, wouldn't they all have made millions in the stock market?" Erica smiled slightly. "We need to avoid judging and let our leaders be human." She paused. "I hope I haven't offended you. You know how much I care about you."

Wendy's face had softened. "I know. And really, I *have* been working on forgiving."

"I'm sure you have. I'm surprised at how strong you are even after everything you've been through. You're an amazing person."

Her friend refused to accept the compliment. "That's kind of you to say, but I feel like a failure. If I were a good person, I wouldn't have gotten so upset at Bishop Griggs. I wouldn't have stopped going to church. That was a huge mistake"

"You're being too hard on yourself," Erica said. "It's easy to get sidetracked by hardships and challenges, and you've had so many. But, 'A failure is not always a mistake; it may simply be the best one can do under the circumstances. The real mistake is to stop trying.' B.F. Skinner said that, and he's *never* wrong." Erica smiled. "Satan threw everything he could at you, but you came back! You never stopped trying—that's the important thing! It shows you have a real testimony. That's what we all need: a testimony that is based on a personal relationship with Jesus and Heavenly Father. Now, before I get off my soapbox, there's one more thing I need to say. I can see how very important religion is to you—it's part of your life; it's who you are. Now, I know Stephen is a good guy and he's got a lot of great qualities, but I wonder if you've really thought about how life will be if you marry someone who doesn't believe in ideas and principles that are vitally important to you."

"I know, I know. I've always wanted to marry someone who was strong in the Church, but there aren't a lot of LDS men breaking down my door. You live in Utah; it's different there. But here, there are very few men my age who are LDS and single."

"I know, but I don't want you to settle for less, not when so much is at stake." When Erica saw Wendy's face flush, she ended by saying, "Enough said. All I'm asking is that you pray about it. Pray very hard and listen to the Spirit."

* * *

After Wendy left for work, Erica checked on Brandon, who was asleep huddled under his covers while Buster went around busily on his wheel. Erica decided to treat herself and, after dishing up a bowl of chocolate ice cream, clicked through the channels until she found an old movie—*The Philadelphia Story*—that had two of her favorite movie stars, Katherine Hepburn and Cary Grant. Erica settled in happily and was enjoying the witticisms of the sparring couple when the phone rang.

A voice that had been deliberately lowered to a hoarsened level whispered, "Don't ask so many questions, Erica. It's bad for your health." The caller then hung up.

Erica replaced the phone slowly. Try as she might, she couldn't place the voice. It had been disguised so well it was impossible to even tell if it was a man or a woman. Although her heart was beating faster, part of her was pleased, for the phone call made one thing clear—she was on the right track.

However, the call also made it so Erica was unable to sleep even after her ice cream. She went through her nightly rituals: exercise—an even thirty minutes—washing and moisturizing her face, brushing her teeth exactly two minutes with thirty seconds each section, and changing into pajamas. Yet she still felt wide awake. Finally, Erica curled up on the end of the couch in the front room to read. Strange that Megan wasn't home yet. Then again, knowing her mother was at work, she probably figured it was safe to stay out later than normal.

Engrossed in her favorite genre, an LDS mystery, Erica jumped slightly when the front door opened. Megan was also startled.

"I didn't see you there at first," Megan said. "What are you doing?"

"Just reading. You know the old saying, 'Outside of a dog, a book is man's best friend. Inside of a dog, it's too dark to read.'"

Megan groaned. "Oh, that's bad. Who said that?"

"Groucho Marx."

"Who's that?"

"Never mind. So, did you have a good night?"

There was a look on Megan's face that Erica couldn't interpret. "Yeah, sure."

"Where did you go?"

"Kimberly's," Megan said in a strangely defiant tone.

"What did you do?" Suddenly, Erica realized what she sounded like—an interrogator. "I didn't mean to give you the third degree. I was just making conversation."

Megan seemed to relax. "Oh. Well, we just hung out." She turned to go. "Guess I'll go to bed."

"Wait a minute," Erica said quickly. "I've been thinking about what you said this afternoon, about your mom not protecting you. I still think you ought to talk with her and tell her how you feel. Don't you think it would help?"

"No!" Megan said scathingly, as if the answer was obvious to anyone with half a brain.

"But your issues aren't going to resolve themselves until you do talk about them. I'm not saying you'll be able to understand everything your mom did or didn't do, or that you'll resolve everything, but I think it's something you have to face."

"Mom would freak out," Megan said shortly. "I wouldn't know how to tell her."

"Gee, how to communicate . . . that *is* a problem. If only humans could make sounds. If only the larynx was capable of—"

"Okay, okay, I get it," Megan broke in.

"You've got to talk to her sometime. She needs to know how you feel."

"Then you tell her." Megan made another move to leave.

"Me? This is between you and your mother."

"You're her best friend," Megan countered. "Besides, you told me how you guys talk all the time about everything."

Clearly, it had been a mistake to share that particular piece of information. Then again, perhaps she could help smooth the way. "Well, maybe I *could* prep her by explaining a little and telling her to talk with you."

"Just let me know when you've talked to her," Megan said. "I'm going to bed now. Good night."

It was strange, wasn't it, how anxious Megan was to go to bed? How Megan would have slunk by with hardly a word except for Erica's attempts to engage her in conversation? Erica looked down the hall after the girl; then her eyes went to the kitchen, toward the telephone. Was it possible that *Megan* had made that anonymous call?

CHAPTER 14

AN UNEASY PRICKLING STARTED AT the back of Erica's neck when the phone began ringing just as she was coming up the stairs the next morning. No one was in the kitchen, although she could hear the shower running in the bathroom. After the call last night, one thought had plagued her. The caller had clearly expected Erica to answer the phone. Was that luck? Or had the caller known Wendy and Megan were gone and that Brandon was usually in bed at that time of night?

This time, there was no shadowy, hoarse voice on the phone but a bright and eager one. It was Matt Watters from the Starlight Motel. He apologized for not calling sooner then explained he had been on vacation and then had misplaced the note Daisha had given him, just finding it again yesterday.

"I'm so glad you called," Erica cried. "I'd about given up. Are you at work today? Could I come and see you?"

"Tomorrow would be better."

"Rats. I'm going to be out of town. How about Friday?"

"That's my day off, but I could meet with you Saturday if it was early, like at eight."

"That should work. I'm going boating, but we're not leaving until ten. See you then."

* * *

After breakfast, Erica called David and told him about Matt's call. He sounded hopeful. "Maybe he'll have something so you can crack this case."

"I hope so. I've been able to piece a few things together, but I still need answers to a couple of questions. I should be able to get them next week. Now, how are things on the home front? How are the kids?"

"They're doing great." There were sounds of scuffling in the background, then David started talking aside. "Hey, stop it! Come on . . . because I'm not done yet, that's why. Hold on!"

"David, what's going on?"

"Kenzie's attacking me, and Ryan keeps trying to take the phone away. Aby is here too; they all want to talk to you."

She smiled. "Okay, put them on, and you and I can finish our conversation after."

When David got back on, he said, "I took the car in for an oil change while I was waiting." When Erica laughed, he said, "Where were we? Oh yeah, you were talking about wrapping up this case."

"It should be soon, honey. First, I need someone to have a dinner party, and unfortunately Wendy turned me down flat."

"Why do you need to have a dinner party?"

"So I can wash dishes."

"I know you like doing that, but hey, if that's all you want, come on home—we have plenty."

"Sorry, it has to be here. There's something specific I need to check out."

"Do you have any plans to tell me what washing dishes has to do with the case?"

"Of course not, darling. You know I never spill the beans until I'm sure. But if my hunch is right, I'll have a big piece of the puzzle." Erica sounded faraway and dreamy. "You see, there were a few things that didn't quite add up when I was in Chicago. Then, something Timothy said reminded me of something Linda Bronson said. When Timothy was talking about remodeling his house, I got the idea for the dinner party. Of course, even if I'm right, there will still be a few holes I'll need to fill in, but at least I'll be going in the right direction."

"Okay, you've officially lost me."

Paying no attention, Erica went on wistfully, "The only problem is getting someone else to host a dinner party since Wendy won't." Her voice was full of disappointment.

"You can hardly blame her. Having one of your guests carted off in an ambulance would make anyone leery about inviting people over."

She sighed. "Maybe I could talk Lee or Stephen into it. I bet even Jaime would be willing to have a party if I told her it was for Stephen."

"You're playing with fire there . . . Wendy might end up poisoning the hostess."

"And you thought nothing good could come from this—" David laughed, and Erica continued. "Another thing—I need to go on one last trip. I called and asked Linda Bronson a few more questions yesterday and although I'm sure I'm on the right track, I need more information."

"I know you're not going to tell me anything definite, but you *can* tell me where you're going, right?"

"Absolutely, sweetheart. Remember how I told you I've been searching for Areli Bronson? Linda's sister-in-law? I was finally able to find them— though I never could have done it without using Pinnacle's databases. So I'm going to Puerto Rico. I'll tell Detective Lund but no one else. I want to keep this trip under wraps."

"Just be careful," David implored. "If someone is trying to knock Stephen off and you get in the way, they just might try to get rid of you too."

That reminded Erica of the phone call. Although she didn't want to worry David, they never hid things from one another. She quickly filled him in.

"See! That's just the kind of thing I've been worrying about!" He took a deep breath. "The only thing that makes me feel better is that you've got your Glock. Have you told Detective Lund about the call?"

"I'm going to, but don't worry. Calls like this are just part of the job. We've talked about this, right?"

"I know," he admitted grudgingly, "but I don't like having someone frightened enough to try to scare you off. You'll have to be extra careful." His voice was urgent. "Promise me you won't take any chances."

Erica hated knowing David's handsome face was full of anxiety. "I'll be very careful. Don't worry. Everything will be fine."

* * *

As she walked into Friendly's, wonderful smells of homemade rolls and roast beef wafted through the air. Erica had arranged to meet Wendy during her break, figuring the restaurant would be a good place to talk about Megan. The hostess showed her to a booth near the kitchen. Business was slow before the lunchtime rush, and Erica was alone in that part of the restaurant. While she waited, Erica straightened the packets of sugar at her table.

Wendy went by, carrying a load of plates on a large round tray. "Hi there!" She smiled brightly. "I'll be with you in a few minutes." She went to a distant table and set steaming plates in front of two middle-aged couples. Both women nodded and thanked Wendy, as did the man in the navy blazer, but the big man with the small, piggy eyes spoke up sharply.

"I asked for double sour cream on my potato! And you forgot the lemon for my wife's tea."

"I'm sorry, sir. I'll go get it."

"Maybe you ought to write it down this time."

"I'll be right back."

"Just don't take all day."

Wendy was back in a few minutes, but it wasn't soon enough for the big man, who grumbled, "You sure took your time."

"I'm sorry, sir. Someone asked me for a drink refill."

"And you took care of them before us?" His voice was loud and disbelieving.

"I was right next to the drink machine. It didn't take long."

"And of course it's all right to make *us* wait even though you got our order wrong." Erica was appalled as the man went on. "Look at this!" he bellowed, stabbing his meat with a knife. "I asked for rare. Does this look rare to you?"

Wendy bent closer. "No, sir. I'll take it back to the kitchen and get another one."

"By the time it's ready, my wife and friends will have finished eating!"

Lee stepped over to the table. "I'm Lee Grover, the manager. Is there a problem?"

"There certainly is. This waitress is incompetent. We asked for lemon and sour cream, and she forgot both of them. Then she brought me this dried up piece of steak when I specifically asked for rare."

"I'm sorry, sir." Lee handed the plate to Wendy. "Take this to the kitchen and get a rare one. Tell the cook I'll talk with him later." He turned back to the big man. "Is there anything else I can do for you?"

"All I want is decent service," he grunted.

"I'll serve you personally. And today dessert is on the house. For all of you."

Raising an eyebrow, the man looked smugly at the others. "That's more like it."

Wendy was waiting by the doors as Lee strode toward the kitchen. A low wall with a lattice top separated Erica's booth from the kitchen doors. It was difficult for them to see her, but Erica could hear them plainly.

"I'm sorry about that," Wendy began. "I can take care of him."

"Don't worry about it. The man's an oaf, and I won't have you around him. I wanted to tell him to put that dried up steak on his head because it'd look better than that hairpiece he was wearing."

By turning a little, Erica could see the two. Wendy giggled then leaned forward and kissed Lee on the cheek. "Thanks for taking care of him. You're so sweet—I don't know what I'd do without you." Erica turned away.

"Will you stop that?" Lee's voice was cross.

There was a moment of dumbfounded silence before Wendy asked in a confused voice, "What do you mean?"

"If I didn't know better," Lee said in a tone that was low and rough, "I'd think you liked making things hard for me."

"I—I don't understand."

"That's right, you don't. You don't understand anything. For an intelligent woman, sometimes you're not very smart." Lee lowered his voice further, but it still reached Erica faintly. "You really don't get it, do you? Why do you think I keep hanging around?"

"Well . . . I . . . we're friends, aren't we?" Wendy said in a small voice.

"*Friends!*" Lee scoffed. "Is that all I am? Is that all you see? Can't you see how I feel about you? You tell me I'm sweet and pat me on the head like I'm a good little dog, then you go running off to Stephen."

Erica squirmed. Somehow, she had to let them know she could hear. But then again, maybe it would be a kindness if she didn't. Surely this conversation couldn't continue much longer. It was surprising no other waitresses had come in or out of the kitchen.

Wendy spoke hesitantly. "I didn't know that you thought of me . . . like that."

"Obviously. You can't see what's right in front of you." Lee's words came out like a whip. It was so unlike Lee that Erica had to turn briefly to make sure it really *was* him. "You're so focused on Stephen you can't see anything else. I would never keep stringing you along like he does. You've been dating him forever. What's he waiting for? What are *you* waiting for?"

Wendy was speechless.

"Stephen doesn't deserve you. He lets you wait and wait, and what's worse *you let him.* That's what drives me crazy."

There was no help for it; Erica had to peek again. Lee was running his fingers through his hair when Wendy timidly put a hand on his arm. He jerked as if her touch burned.

Her voice was soft. "I thought Stephen needed a little more time to, you know—"

"But he *hasn't* proposed, has he?" Lee whispered gruffly. Then his look softened. "You're so blindly loyal you can't see anybody else, but you're the only one in the world I *can* see."

Turning back, Erica put her hand over her heart. She was going to cry; she just knew it . . .

"Look, I'm sorry," Lee murmured, sounding defeated. "Forget what I said. I don't know what came over me. It's been a rough day, and I just lost it. Shauna and Val are looking at us. They need to go into the kitchen and backed off when they saw us. Let's get back to work."

"I don't think I can forget what you said."

There was a groan. "I've really messed things up now, haven't I?"

"No, you didn't," Wendy whispered. "You know, sometimes I wondered if you liked me, but I just kept telling myself I was imagining things. I couldn't believe someone like you could care for someone like me."

For the life of her, Erica could not stop from turning around.

Lee had shifted so his back was to the restaurant, and he reached out and stroked Wendy's cheek tenderly. Tilting her chin up, he murmured, "If only you could see what I see—"

If this were a movie, Lee would have given her a long, lingering kiss. Instead, Wendy reached up and touched his hand as it gently stroked her face. It was a moment frozen in time.

"I should have spoken up sooner," Lee said in a muffled voice. "How were you to know when I never said anything? It's not fair to expect you to know what I'm thinking. I just kept hoping that one day you'd see how much I cared for you."

"Today's the day, I guess." Wendy smiled at him tremulously.

One of the other waitresses approached tentatively. "Ah, Lee? Sorry, but there's a man over at that table who wants to talk to you."

"Okay. I'm coming."

It wasn't until a passing waitress looked at her strangely that Erica realized she was smiling. But then her smile vanished. All along, she'd been trying to come up with a reason why someone would want to kill Stephen. Now she had one. It was a classic love triangle—Lee loved Wendy, but there was one person that stood in his way.

Stephen.

* * *

The ceiling fan gently stirred the papers on Detective Patrick Lund's desk as he looked at Erica with contemplative eyes. It was midmorning, and Erica had stopped by the police station to tell him about her planned trip.

"How did you locate them?"

"It wasn't easy because Linda hadn't kept Areli and Charles's former address." Erica grimaced. "The thing that made it hard is that Spanish names are different than English names. Not only do they have a first name, a middle name, and a last name taken from the father, but they also have a second last name which is taken from the mother's maiden name. Some of Pinnacle's databases don't accommodate the Spanish name structure and gave poor search results. I wasn't able to locate James but finally found Areli."

"Does anyone know where you're going?"

"Just my husband. I thought about telling Wendy but haven't yet."

"I wouldn't."

"She's not guilty."

Shrugging his heavy shoulders, Patrick grunted. "I wouldn't rule her out. What exactly are you going to do in Puerto Rico?"

"First, I want to find out where Areli and James were the night Tyson was shot and the night Stephen was poisoned. Then, I want to find out how they feel about Linda's will."

He nodded. "Let me know what they say." It was a sign of how much Patrick trusted her that he didn't ask her to hold off until he had sent a detective to Puerto Rico.

"Also, Matt Watters called me. He's the kid that works at the Starlight Motel. Matt was working when Gregory Tyson was there, but he went on vacation the next day. I've arranged to see him Saturday morning."

Patrick looked interested. "I'll let my people know."

"Oh, I almost forgot to tell you. I got an interesting phone call the other night."

After she told him, Patrick frowned, looking ferocious. "This is exactly why I don't like civilians getting involved. You're stepping on someone's toes, and they don't like it."

"At least we know we're on the right track."

"Yes, and we also know that someone out there wants you to back off bad enough to call and take the chance of having you identify his or her voice. My advice is to stop now. Go home. We can take it from here." He paused, looking defeated. "I don't know why I'm wasting my breath. It's obvious from the look on your face that you have no intention of stopping."

"See that?" Erica pointed at him. "*That's* why you're such a good detective—because you're so good at reading faces." She added, "You don't have to worry; I can take care of myself."

"Do you have a gun?"

"After much trial and tribulation, I picked my Glock up at Tom Addison's on Monday. My husband mailed it priority. And I have a concealed weapons permit. Fortunately, Florida honors Utah permits. I'm a great shot, and I already told you about my black belt."

The frown lines relaxed but only a little. "Back to the phone call. Did the voice sound familiar at all?"

"No. It was hoarse and raspy. Whoever was calling did a good job disguising it."

"Male or female?"

"I couldn't tell, but if I had to guess, I'd say it was a woman's voice."

"Was Wendy home at the time?"

Erica sighed. "No, she was at work."

"What about Megan?"

"She wasn't home either."

"I see." Erica didn't like the look on his face, but Patrick went on to other matters. "What do you know about Lee Grover?"

"Not a whole lot, but personally I like him. Lee's quiet but very nice. Actually, it's funny that you should mention him. I always thought he liked Wendy and found out for sure that he does."

Patrick's bushy eyebrows went up. "Ah—that's interesting. Lee's interested in Wendy, but she's seeing Stephen. There could be something there. When I met Lee, I got the impression he was very mild mannered. Would you agree?"

"Yes, I would. Why?"

"Because that's the type of person who would use poison to kill some-one. Placid people who are bullied as they grow up can act out when they're older."

"I remember that from my criminology classes," Erica said. "But I'm not sure that applies to Lee. While he *is* easygoing, he's not excessively so. Besides, Lee seems pretty levelheaded."

"Adults learn to hide their weaknesses, which can make them treacherous because no one suspects them of being violent," Patrick argued.

"How many times have you read about a man opening fire on someone and when his neighbors are interviewed, all they can say is they can't believe it because the guy always seemed so *nice*."

Such scenarios were commonplace, Erica knew.

Patrick added, "Since Lee has feelings for Wendy, it's possible he poisoned Stephen in order to get rid of a rival. We'll dig a little deeper into his background."

As she left Patrick's office, Erica thought about Lee Grover. From what she knew of him, Lee didn't seem the sort of person to directly challenge anyone. It was possible he could have chosen poison as a quiet, nonconfrontational way of removing Stephen from the scene. Plus, Erica had to admit that jealousy was quite often a motive for murder.

One other thing was clear; Lee was very good at hiding his feelings. Look at how well he'd managed to hide his affection for Wendy and how conciliatory he had been with that oaf at the restaurant. He'd only revealed his anger later, when talking to Wendy. Of course, managing louts was part of his job description, but still . . .

On the surface, Lee Grover seemed the most pleasant and amiable of men, but was that likable face only a facade? Erica was filled with forebodings she could not put aside.

* * *

On an impulse, Erica stopped at Stephen's office on her way home. After a brief sparring match with Diana over why she had opened the door, shut it, and opened it again, Erica slipped down the hall to Stephen's office. He smiled at her with delight and motioned her into a chair. Feeling only slightly guilty, Erica put on a troubled expression and explained how worried she was about Wendy.

"What Wendy really needs is a relaxing evening with a few friends," Erica added plaintively. "But she doesn't feel she can invite anyone over. You can understand that of course." Playing shamelessly on Stephen's emotions, Erica said Jaime had told her the pool and clubhouse at Stephen's apartment complex, Lake Tivoli Gardens, was first-rate. It was just the sort of place Wendy needed to relax.

As expected, Stephen was eager to help Wendy and jumped at the bait. And just like that, the dinner was on. Stephen's only objection was having it so soon, on Friday night, but his fears were allayed when Erica said if he'd bring something from the deli, she'd take care of the rest of the food. Privately, Erica thought a relaxing evening might do Stephen some good as well. Today he was looking especially haggard and drawn, showing the strain he had been living under lately.

That night, Erica and Wendy went to a combined Relief Society night, which involved the entire stake. The special guest speaker was Mattie Orton, mayor of Kissimmee. An intelligent and knowledgeable woman, Mattie encouraged her audience to become politically active and make a difference in government, whether it was on a city, state, or federal level. Mattie held the audience spellbound with her enthusiasm, and while driving home afterwards, Wendy asked about Erica's stint on the city council in Farmington.

They were discussing local parks when they pulled into the driveway. Wendy was starting to open her door when Erica said, "Before we go in, I'd like to talk to you about something." When her friend looked at her expectantly, Erica added, "It's about Megan."

Instantly, Wendy's expression changed. "What's she done now?"

"She hasn't done anything. I was going to talk to you at Friendly's, but—" Her voice trailed off. It had been more than a little awkward that afternoon when Erica had to confess she'd overheard Wendy and Lee's conversation. It wasn't a good time to talk about Megan.

Erica decided to be short and succinct. "Megan needs to talk to you."

"Oh really?" Wendy replied flatly. "I've been trying to talk to her for years, and it's like talking to a weasel."

"I think I know why she's been acting that way."

"She's a teenager," Wendy shrugged. "They say it's all those hormones, but I *never* talked to my mother the way Megan talks to me."

"It's a little more than hormones."

Wendy looked frightened. "What is it?"

Taking a breath, Erica plunged in. "You're not the only one Dennis hurt. Apparently, he treated Megan very badly. She told me a little about it when she came home from the hospital. I told Megan she needed to talk with you, and she asked if I'd mention it—just to prepare you."

"Great. So you're prepping me—for what?"

"So you don't freak out."

Wendy briefly closed her eyes. "This is sounding better all the time," she said caustically. "Exactly what is it that Megan thinks I can't handle?"

This was not easy. Erica swallowed hard. "Megan has some very strong, deep feelings about how her father treated her and Brandon. She feels you didn't protect her and Brandon from Dennis when he was drunk, which seemed to be a good part of the time."

All the air came out of Wendy's lungs in a whoosh, and she looked as if a balloon inside her had deflated. "You're kidding." Wendy glanced toward the house. A vertical slice of light showed through the curtains at the front room window. Then she straightened her shoulders. In a grim, determined voice, she said, "I think I'll talk with her right now."

This was not what Megan or Erica had in mind. "I told Megan I'd tell her when I'd had a chance to talk with you," Erica blurted.

"Let's go in then, and you can tell her right now," Wendy said levelly, gesturing toward the house. When Erica hesitated, Wendy glanced at her watch. "It's all right. You said you were already packed, and we've got plenty of time before I need to take you to the airport."

Feeling fatalistic, Erica trailed after Wendy, who strode up the sidewalk. Brandon was sprawled on the floor watching TV, and Megan was on the couch with a book in her lap.

"Hi!" Wendy said, putting her purse on an end table. "You should have come with us tonight, Megan. I think you would have liked it."

Megan scowled. "Yeah, right. I just love spending time with a bunch of old ladies."

"Brandon, did you get your homework done? You had a page of math problems and were supposed to practice your cursive."

"I'll do it after this show. It's almost over."

Wendy went to the TV and turned it off. "Would you look at that—it just got over."

"Mom!" he wailed. "Can't I watch the end?"

"No. It's nearly bedtime, and your homework's not done. I want you to do it now—in your bedroom." She fixed him with a piercing look, and Brandon left, grumbling all the way.

Looking uneasy, Megan looked at Erica, who nodded slightly, causing Megan to wince. Wendy sat next to her daughter and looked at Erica.

That was Erica's cue. "Megan, I, ah, talked with your mom tonight and told her that you two needed to talk."

"I'm kind of busy right now," Megan said, glancing at her book then at her mother. "I've got a big test tomorrow, and you're always telling me to study more."

"Interesting way to study—with the TV on," Wendy stated frankly.

Erica started backing away. "I'll let the two of you alone so you can talk."

"Oh no, you don't," Wendy countered.

"It was *your* idea," Megan told her mutinously. "You've got to stay."

Erica was still hesitating when Wendy pointed to a chair. "You can sit there and referee." Suppressing a groan, Erica sat as directed.

Megan still had doubts about talking to her mother. "You're not going to understand," she complained.

"I might if you'd just tell me," Wendy said impatiently. She cleared her throat. "I think we would both agree our relationship has been, how shall I say it—rotten?—the last couple of years. Apparently you have some feelings about how badly I handled things when your dad was here. Imagine my surprise to find out you've been upset about this for years even though you've never said one word about it to me."

Definitely not the best of beginnings, Erica thought dismally. Megan flashed Erica a furious look that clearly said, *Thanks for making it worse!*

It was time for the referee to speak up. "Wendy, Megan didn't want to hurt your feelings—that's why she never said anything. But she *was* deeply affected by the way her dad treated her."

"I'd like to know exactly why *I'm* to blame for what *he* did," Wendy said with acid in her voice. "Why am I the bad parent? Was I the one who stayed out late drinking? Was I the one who either screamed at or ignored my kids 24/7? Am I the one who lost my job because I was unreliable?"

Glancing at Erica, Megan ground out, "I *told* you she'd freak out."

"Wendy, listen," Erica pleaded. "No one is saying you're not a good parent, but Megan *was* badly mistreated by her father and . . ." She stopped and shook her head. "Wait a minute. This is no good—having *me* explain what Megan felt. This conversation has to be between you two. Wendy, your daughter wants to talk to you, but she needs you to listen with an open mind and heart. Can you do that?"

Taken aback at first, Wendy acquiesced. "I'll try."

"Okay, Megan, just explain how you felt—and remember, no blaming or accusations."

In a voice that trembled at times, Megan talked about how she'd been punished, often in cruel ways, for minor offenses, such as when her father threw her dinner out the window—plate and all—when she said she didn't like green beans, or when she was sent to bed without dinner for not holding her fork correctly, or when he yelled at her for missing the bus when it had come early. Each time, Megan hoped her mother would see how unfair her father had been and stand up for her, but it never happened. Erica's throat tightened and her body tensed as Megan haltingly recalled how he had bullied her, called her stupid and clumsy, and how afraid she'd been of him when he'd been drinking.

When she stopped, the silence was thunderous in its intensity. Tears were running down Wendy's face, which was twisted in pain. "I know it was awful for you when he drank." Wendy spoke simply, but there was so much anguish in her voice that Erica cringed. Although she didn't speak of it, Erica knew Dennis had been just as cruel, if not more so, to Wendy.

But Megan was not thinking of that. "Then why didn't you do something, Mom? He treated me and Brandon like crap, and you never said anything to him. Ever!" Wendy winced as Megan went on. "All those times he yelled at me or grounded me because I didn't hang up my coat right or because I walked across the floor too noisily; you never stood up for me. Why did you let him treat us so horrible? You didn't care how bad he treated us!"

A horrified look flashed across Wendy's face. "*I did care!* It tore me up inside. And I *did* talk to Dennis. *I did!* I told him to leave you alone over and over! Surely you remember . . ." There was a pause, then she admitted, "Most of the time, though, I talked with Dennis when we were alone because if I tried to defend you in front of him, it only made him angrier and he would be much harder on you."

"After he left, things were a million times better. Then you let him come home." Megan was shouting now, and her words were like a lash, causing Wendy to recoil. "Why did you do that? Why?"

Wendy struggled to collect herself. "You seem to forget that I was the one who told him to leave. Did you ever wonder *why* I kicked him out? It was for you and Brandon. I couldn't bear how he was treating you. Then, after a couple of months, Dennis said being on his own had made him wake up and realize what a jerk he'd been. He told me over and over how sorry he was and that he was scared of losing us. Then he begged me for a chance to prove that he could be a good husband and father."

"It was all an act, Mom!" Megan wailed. "How could you believe him? When he was home, how many times did he get drunk, say he was sorry, then go out and do it again?"

"I know, but—but this time was different. I told Dennis he couldn't come back unless he went for counseling, and even though he'd always refused before, this time he agreed. He even went with me to see Bishop Griggs. Dennis said he'd given up drinking for good and was attending AA." Wendy looked at Megan earnestly. "I—I really thought things would be different. Even Bishop Griggs thought he'd changed. So did our marriage counselor. Besides, I was scared I couldn't support us on my own. I never graduated from college, and I had no skills." She paused. "Maybe that's why I believed Dennis—I guess I *wanted* to believe."

"I gave up believing a long time ago." Megan's voice was threaded with misery.

Wendy wiped her face. "I was wrong, Megan. I was wrong in not standing up for you. I shouldn't have let things go on as long as they did. That's all I can say other than I'm sorry. I failed you and Brandon, and I'm sorry. I really am." With tears glistening on her cheeks, Wendy put her arms around her daughter. When Megan's arms came up and enfolded her mother, Erica rose quietly and slipped out.

CHAPTER 15

THE INTERIOR OF THE CAR was sporadically illuminated by the tall lights lining the interstate. Going well over the speed limit, Erica watched Wendy concentrate on driving as the car's headlights cleaved through the darkness. Pulling up to the curb at the airport, she stopped with a jerk.

"I'm sorry to make you late," Wendy apologized again.

"That's all right. I started it by telling you about Megan. I'm just glad it turned out all right."

"Me too. We got a lot of things cleared up."

Erica got her bag out then glanced at her watch. "And I'm okay on time, especially since I don't have to check a bag." She gave her friend a hug. "See you tomorrow night."

The security line was short, and Erica was waiting at the gate when her cell phone rang. It was David. "I couldn't sleep, so I thought I'd call."

"You timed it perfectly," Erica said. "The regular passengers are just starting to board, so I've got a couple of minutes. How come you couldn't sleep?"

"Worried about you. I'll be glad when you're back home with me."

"I will be soon. Thanks for calling Areli and arranging for me to see her." David had gone to Chile on his mission and spoke Spanish fluently.

"I bet you told Wendy where you were going."

"Au contraire. I held firm like I told you I would. The only ones who know are you, Detective Lund, and of course Chris."

"I'm surprised Wendy didn't beat it out of you," David said. "How's she doing?"

"She had a rough night—but a productive one since she had a talk with Megan that was long overdue." Erica had told David about Megan. "It might take a while for Megan to get rid of all the anger she's been carrying, but this will certainly help. Oh, there's some major news on Wendy's love life."

"Stephen finally proposed?"

"No, and you'll never guess, so I'll just tell you. Lee is in love with Wendy."

"Yeah, right," David chuckled.

"I'm not kidding. I was right there when Lee told Wendy."

"Whoa! That'll certainly make things interesting at the dinner party tomorrow. How does Stephen, who's been skating around the *M* word, feel about that?"

"He doesn't know. Wendy didn't even know."

"*She didn't?* So much for women's intuition," David said in a rather snide tone of voice, Erica thought. Then he asked, "Why did Lee declare himself with you there?"

"Well, that's the embarrassing part." Erica explained.

David was astounded. "You mean you just sat there and listened to them?"

"What else was I supposed to do? I was trapped!"

"So you just eavesdropped on a very private conversation—"

"And it was *wonderful*," Erica gushed. "Just like in the movies!"

"You ought to be ashamed."

"Yeah, I know. But I'm not." She giggled.

"You're incorrigible. Guess that's why I love you."

"Ah, that's sweet."

"Now, get some sleep on the plane and call me when you get to Puerto Rico."

"I will. I've been able to piece a lot of things together, but *something* is still wrong. I can't quite put my finger on it, but there's got to be more. That's why I'm hoping to get some answers from Areli Bronson."

"If anyone can find out, you can. Good luck, sweetheart."

* * *

Once she landed in Puerto Rico and rented a car—wiping the seats and steering wheel carefully—Erica found herself in the land of one-handed drivers. An astonishing number of drivers used one hand to hold the wheel and with the window down used the other to beckon other drivers forward or, more often, signal them to stop so they could proceed themselves. Traffic lights were nothing more than colorful decorations.

Her innate sense of direction served her well, but the streets were confusing. She did take one wrong turn, but her rental car's GPS guided her back. Finally, Erica pulled up in front of Areli Bronson's compact, bright blue home with its colorful, red-tiled roof. The house was small but well-kept with carefully tended flower beds in the tiny front yard and a banana tree in the corner. Walking up the gravel path, Erica admired a prickly tropical shrub with brilliant reddish blossoms. Coconut trees lined the edge of the property.

A small, thin woman with black hair heavily streaked with gray opened the door.

"Erica?" Areli Bronson asked in a heavy accent. When Erica nodded, Areli smiled widely, reaching out and hugging her as if she were a long-lost relative. She then looked toward the car as if expecting to see someone else. Areli looked much older than her years. Her eyelids, drawn down over her eyes, were bruised looking, and her skin was as fine as crumbled tissue. She invited her guest inside, sitting close beside her on a floral couch. Erica found her broken English enchanting.

"Happy you here!" Areli exclaimed, her expression kindly. "Your husband call," she said, nodding her head rapidly. Then she asked expectantly, "Where Linda? Come later?"

Apparently Areli had misunderstood David. "Linda isn't coming," Erica explained. "She's sick and can't travel."

"Ah!" Areli nodded. "She have cancer, very bad, I know." Her expressive face was downcast. "I sorry. Linda always nice for me. Kathleen *tambien.*"

"You never met Kathleen, Anthony, or Linda, did you?"

"No." Areli shook her head regretfully. "Charles very angry with them. Not like me talk to them. I tell him, 'We family,' but no. Charles no like."

"That's very sad."

A mischievous expression appeared on Areli's lined face. "He no call, but I do. I call when baby born. Charles, he angry at me. Oh, so angry! I ask, why? Why like this?" Areli Bronson spread out her hands, palms up, her face showing the naive perplexity of a child. "I tell him grandmama and grandpapa should know. So I call. Tell about baby."

Erica eyes strayed to the wall where there was a picture of Charles and Areli. Noticing, Areli rose, beckoning Erica. "Come! Come see!" Areli pointed at her husband, a man with an aristocratic nose, dark hair, and mesmerizing eyes.

"This Charles," she said proudly. The good-looking man pictured here was older but still recognizable as the man in the portrait Linda Bronson had shown her. Looking at it gave Erica an unsettled feeling even after she straightened the picture slightly. In some vague way, his face seemed familiar. She assumed it was because that nose and those heavy brows were so like the picture she had seen of his father, Anthony Bronson.

Areli seemed pleased that Erica was studying Charles's picture intently. She looked at the picture lovingly. "Handsome, yes?"

"Oh, yes," Erica agreed, trying to figure out what it was about his expression that was slightly unnerving. There was something untamed in those dark eyes—defiant even. This was a picture of a man who was used to getting his own way.

"I have other pictures. You want see?" Areli face was alight with childish animation.

"*Por favor*, I'd love to." Now she was doing it—speaking in both languages.

Going to a small chest of drawers, Areli pulled out an album. Sitting close to Erica, she turned the pages eagerly. The first pictures were of their courtship and marriage. Then Areli pointed at a picture of herself holding an infant swaddled in white.

"*Mi bebe*, see?"

"Oh, how sweet," Erica replied. As they progressed, Areli occasionally lapsed into Spanish, delightedly explaining the particulars of this picture or that. She was pleased at Erica's genuine interest as they pored over photos showing the baby growing into a child then a young adult.

Areli begged her to stay for lunch, and Erica accepted. It was a traditional meal of *arroz blanco con habichuelas*, or white rice with beans, accompanied by a small bowl of *Pollo Guisado*,[8] which turned out to be a tasty chicken stew. Areli spooned her stew over her rice, and Erica did the same. Areli had also made some *tostones*, or fried green banana chips. They talked and laughed until it was time to go. Feeling that she had made a new friend, Erica hugged Areli and bid her good-bye.

There was still work to do, and Erica went to see Areli's neighbors. By the time she finally headed for the airport, Erica was tired but boarded the plane with a sense of accomplishment.

* * *

---

8   See appendix at the end of the book for this recipe.

Wendy picked her up curbside, waiting impatiently as Erica pulled out her trusted towelettes and wiped down her side of the car and dashboard. "No, I will not get out so you can wipe my side. We need to get to the party." She pulled onto the road, checking over her left shoulder, then looked at her friend. "You're disgusting, Erica. How can you look so good when you took the red-eye last night, worked all day, and just got off another flight?"

"If I look half as tired as I feel, I'd frighten dogs."

"Well, you can just relax tonight at Stephen's."

"Thanks for taking care of the food for me. I told Stephen I'd handle it."

"And you did, mostly. Those wonderful Orange Rolls[9] you made before you left look yummy. Good thing I froze them or there wouldn't have been any left."

When Erica reclined her seat, Wendy asked, "Hey, before you start snoring, did you find out any juicy secrets?"

Shutting her eyes, Erica wore a slight smile. "I sure did. And it's about the biggest, juiciest one you can imagine."

* * *

Wendy drove straight to Stephen's apartment at Lake Tivoli Gardens. "I brought the food over earlier when I dropped off Megan, Kimberly, and Brandon."

"*Megan came?*"

"She did." Wendy's smirk made Erica suspect blackmail. Going through the clubhouse, they saw Stephen standing beside the pool talking to someone in the water. He turned slightly as they approached, and Wendy went to him—not into his arms as a woman might when seeing the man that she loved—but simply to stand quietly beside him. Of course, such a low-key greeting could have been due to the fact that Stephen had been talking to Jaime, who was wearing a black and white bikini. Erica tried to conceal her surprise—Jaime's name had not come up when she and Stephen had talked about who to invite.

"Erica! You must be exhausted," Stephen said.

"Hi Wendy, Erica!" Jaime said, smiling brilliantly up at them. "I was getting a few laps in, but Stephen distracted me. I'll finish up now." She pushed off and headed for the far edge of the pool, avoiding Brandon,

---

9   See appendix at the end of the book for this recipe.

who had just slid down a small slide and splashed into the water. Kimberly and Megan were on inflatable rafts, trailing their fingers in the water. Kimberly's black and purple streaks were barely visible in the blonde hair she'd pulled back into a sleek ponytail. Wendy was eying Jaime surreptitiously when Brandon climbed out and started running to the ladder.

"Don't run!" Wendy shouted. Brandon slowed to a fast walk then climbed up.

"Mom! Watch me!" Lying on his stomach, Brandon went down the slide head first, making a large splash as he hit the water.

Wendy and Stephen went into the clubhouse, and Erica walked to the other side of the pool to take a chair under a shady magnolia tree. She dialed Detective Lund and, while waiting, looked around appreciatively. The apartments were nestled in a beautiful setting. To the south was a small lake that had a fountain in the middle, and to the east was a small stand of woods. Palm trees, thick shrubbery, and barrels of bright red and white geraniums surrounded the pool. After hearing about her trip, Detective Lund reminded Erica to call if she found out anything from Matt Watters the next day. Jaime left the pool, and Erica was watching Brandon's antics when Reed came through the far gate, from the direction of the lake.

"Hello, Reed. Did you go for a walk?" Erica asked pleasantly as he took a chair beside her.

"I needed to stretch my legs after sitting at the office all day."

"You should have brought your swimming suit," she said then winced as Brandon did a belly flop. "Ouch! That had to hurt."

Reed looked at her out of hooded eyes, his expression coldly reptilian. "I heard you went out of town again. How is the investigation going?"

"Very well. I have a few new leads." It was interesting to see Reed's reaction as he started ever so slightly.

"And what have you found out?"

"Sorry, I can't divulge that." Even talking with Reed could not dispel the sense of contentment Erica felt from relaxing in such an idyllic setting: sparkling blue water, colorful flowers, shade from tall trees. "This is a lovely place. It was certainly nice of Stephen to invite us."

"It's easy to have a party when you don't have to do any work," Reed sneered. "It's not like he had to mow the grass or clip the hedge. Plus, he had you organize it, although I understood you had to leave part of that in Wendy's capable hands." His dark eyes were intent. "Why were you so anxious for Stephen to host this little party? So you could observe the suspects up close? Or were you hoping someone else would get poisoned?" He laughed shortly, but there was nothing cheery in it.

Was it possible for anyone to be as disagreeable as Reed? "Having someone poisoned is the last thing I would want," Erica said coolly. "But yes, I was hoping to get a little more information."

He looked at her speculatively. "I'm not sure what else you can find out since you've already talked to everyone, but I wish you luck." He started to rise. "I'm going to see if anyone wants a game of pool." He paused and with a slight smirk added, "Oh, you'd better watch what you eat tonight. You never know."

Erica frowned as he walked away. Was that a veiled threat or just Reed's macabre sense of humor? What an odd man he was!

Stephen had come out and called out encouragingly as Brandon swam across the pool. "Great job, Brandon! Try to keep your knees straight. That will help." He strolled over to Erica. "This was a great idea. Wendy was a little stressed when she first got here, but she seems more relaxed already."

Erica looked at him. Was it possible he didn't have a clue that what had Wendy stressed was the unexpected presence of Jaime in a skin-baring bikini?

When Brandon called out for them to watch, Erica kept her eyes on him, even as she commented to Stephen, "It's beautiful here. Do you do a lot of swimming?"

"Not as much as I should, but I use the pool now and again to exercise. I try to come when there isn't a crowd—I don't want to distress any more people than necessary," he joked, patting his ample stomach. Then he asked, "Any luck finding out who shot Greg?"

"Not yet."

"I don't suppose the police know who poisoned the coffee?"

She shook her head. "All I know is that they're still focusing on Wendy."

Looking disturbed, Stephen said, "I find it very frustrating that the police are wasting time investigating an innocent woman when they ought to be trying to find the real killer."

"They have to consider Wendy their prime suspect since she's your beneficiary."

He scoffed at that. "That's crazy—Wendy would never try to kill me. Even though the police don't know Wendy like I do, surely they realize that if she wanted to kill me, she'd wait until after I'd inherited from Linda Bronson."

Erica paused to think about his words. "That does put a kink in their assumption. But there are a number of people who might have tried to kill you, including Areli and James Bronson."

Stephen looked astounded. "But I've never even met them."

"People don't always know their killer. I've started to wonder if my premise about you being the target was wrong and that the person who shot Tyson meant to do just that—kill Gregory Tyson."

Stephen drew his brows together, looking puzzled. "But why? The man barely had two nickels to rub together."

"I don't know what the motive is, but I don't think it was a botched robbery."

"Personally, I've always thought a drug addict shot Gregory."

There was a slight sound behind them, and he and Erica both turned. Behind the thick bushes, a woman stood. It was impossible to see who it was, but when they looked that direction, a woman stepped around the hedge. Jaime. How long had she been standing there listening? At least she'd put on some clothes.

Stephen didn't seem to find her behavior odd. "There you are," he said with a smile. "I wondered where you'd gone to."

"I had to go and get dressed."

Just then, Wendy and Lee appeared at the door of the clubhouse. Erica was glad they'd had some time together and wondered if they'd talked about what had happened at the restaurant.

"Stephen," Wendy called, "could you come here a minute?" Her voice sounded a bit flustered, Erica thought. Stephen hurried off, and Lee, who was wearing bathing trunks, went to the pool and dove in by the girls, deliberately splashing them and causing them to squeal.

"The master calls, and the slave must obey," Jaime drawled. It was an irritating remark, and Erica looked at her sharply. Jaime merely stared back at her obliquely out of large, dark eyes. "I overheard what you said to Stephen—that Tyson might have been the intended victim after all. You're kind of flip-flopping, aren't you? And how do you explain Stephen being poisoned? Or do you think the poison was meant for me or you?"

"I don't think the killer was after me. He was after either you or Stephen."

"Even though there was poison in your cup?" There was exasperation in Jaime's voice.

"The psychology doesn't fit."

Jaime looked puzzled. "What do you mean? What psychology?"

"The psychology of the killer. You see, I think the killer is intelligent, careful, and precise. If someone meant to kill me by poisoning my coffee, I'd be looking for someone who is either lazy or stupid. You see, a killer with any intelligence would never have put poison in a cup of coffee that I would never drink—they would have taken the time to learn about the type of drinks I like." Erica left the subject. There was something she wanted to know, although she had her doubts about whether Jaime would be straightforward.

"How are you and Stephen getting along?"

Jaime gave her a long look under dark lashes. "I suppose Wendy wanted you to ask me."

"No, I was wondering. That's all." She smiled at Brandon, who was splashing water at Lee.

"We're doing fine." Jaime looked faintly amused. Then, in an abrupt shift, she said, "I hear you have a husband and children back in Utah." Just as Erica was wondering where Jaime was going with that, Jaime added, "Aren't you worried your husband might get lonely and start looking for some companionship?"

Erica was thunderstruck at Jaime's impudence. "My husband and I are faithful to each other and our wedding vows. He approves of my staying here to help a friend."

"Still, if I were in your shoes, I wouldn't stay too long. It could end up very badly for you."

Was that a warning? If so, Erica wasn't about to let it pass. "Just what are you saying?"

"Oh, nothing really," Jaime backtracked quickly then in another shift asked, "Are you going boating Saturday?" As always, Jaime continued to be an enigma.

"Why yes, I am," Erica replied, startled and wondering how Jaime knew.

"I'm going too," Jaime said smugly, her face smooth and beautiful. "When Stephen mentioned that he was going boating tomorrow, I was so envious that he invited me." She added, "And yes, he called Lee, who said it was fine for me to tag along."

Rats. Jaime tagging along was hardly going to be fine with Wendy. What could Stephen have been thinking? Erica wondered grimly. Was it possible he was unaware Jaime had him in her sights? For all his years, there was a curious air of innocence about Stephen, so such a thing was possible, and yet—

Feeling vaguely disturbed, Erica said, "I think I'll go and give Wendy and Stephen a hand with the food." When she got to the clubhouse, most of the food had already been set out. She slipped into the kitchen and, after washing with Lava, began to rearrange the dishes. First, she put the largest dish on the far left and arranged the rest to the right in descending size, making sure each dish was exactly two inches from the front edge of the table. She could tell just by looking if it was even a quarter of an inch off.

Wendy brought in two pitchers of punch and smiled when she noticed the rearranged table. "You just couldn't help yourself, could you?" she said wryly.

"What?" Then Erica understood. "Oh, the table. I knew you'd want the dishes organized. Say, who brought the Swedish meatballs and wild rice?"

"Stephen did, along with the cheese tray. I made the fresh fruit platters, and the ambrosia salad is Jaime's. Deli, of course. I don't think she'd know how to peel an orange. And here are your orange rolls. They look delicious—can't wait to try one."

After getting everyone out of the pool and into the clubhouse, Wendy asked Lee to say a blessing on the food. Everyone filled their plates and went outside to sit in a loose circle in the shade of a large red oak. Lee was at the end of the line, having gone to change after the blessing. He started toward Wendy, but when Brandon took the chair by her, he sat by Reed.

As they all chatted, Erica noticed Jaime eyeing her furtively. There was something about the young woman that was hard to define. Jaime seemed very aware of everyone and was listening with great interest—as if she wanted to draw the most she could out of everyone. Jaime was acting like a person who was trying to find out a secret. Or was it that she had a secret to hide?

Of course, Jaime wasn't the only person acting differently. Although Stephen thought Wendy was relaxed, to Erica, her friend seemed on edge. And she was aware of the many darting looks Wendy directed toward Lee. Whenever a comment or question was directed her way, it seemed to take a moment for Wendy to pull herself back to the present. For his part, Lee was friendly and talkative with everyone, but his eyes also kept turning to Wendy. Then there was Megan, who appeared to be watching Stephen. Although she laughed at other people's jokes and comments, her face was blank when Stephen was the one making the joke. After Wendy finished eating and her hands were free, her fingers twined together, the many rings she wore glinting in the dusky light. After Erica got up to refill her plate, she went to sit beside Megan.

"Where's Kimberly?"

"She went to the bathroom." This simple answer seemed full of gloom.

"What's the matter? You don't seem very happy tonight."

"How can I be, with that?" Megan nodded to where Stephen and Wendy were sitting together.

"Stephen is always very nice to you."

"Yeah, and it makes me want to puke."

Feeling a little impatient, Erica asked, "Why did you come tonight if you dislike him so much?"

"You mean Mom didn't tell you? That's hard to believe." Then Megan grinned. "She said she'd buy me a ticket to Pink if I came tonight and went boating tomorrow."

Ah, so there *had* been a bribe.

"I *really* want to go to that concert," Megan said, stating the obvious. "I know Mom's trying to get me to like Stephen, but I *don't* and I never will." She was getting worked up now. Her face was flushed as she hissed, "He just can't marry Mom. *He can't!*"

There was no sense in pursuing it, so Erica changed the subject. When the cleanup began, Erica made a suggestion to Wendy. "Since the kitchen is so small, why don't Stephen and I wash up, while you and the others clear up out here?"

"I can take the dishes back to my apartment and wash them later," Stephen protested.

"We can have them done in no time; there aren't many." Going to the sink, Erica pulled out her gloves, turned on the water, and stopped up the sink. Somewhat reluctantly, Stephen unbuttoned his cuffs, rolled up his sleeves, and set to work.

Kimberly and Megan began picking up while Wendy consolidated the leftovers and packed up supplies. There was splashing and laughter from Brandon, who'd jumped back in the pool, while Reed watched idly from a chair. Lee rearranged chairs while Jaime swept, then Erica helped Stephen carry supplies to his apartment. When they returned, Wendy had managed to get Brandon out of the pool and wrapped in a towel.

Stephen smiled at Brandon. "Did you have a good time?"

"Yeah! Can I come again?"

"Absolutely!" Stephen said. "I'm counting on it."

"Thanks so much for a lovely evening," Wendy said then cut her eyes at Megan and Kimberly.

Kimberly spoke first. "Yeah, thanks. It was great."

Wendy leaned slightly into Megan, who then said mechanically, "Thanks."

"You're very welcome," Stephen said graciously. "I'm glad you came."

Megan and Kimberly started toward the car as Lee approached. "Thanks, Stephen, I had a great time."

"We'll have to do it again," Stephen replied. But Erica wasn't even sure Lee heard—or Wendy, for that matter. They were looking at each other's faces as if searching for answers.

Finally, Wendy lowered her gaze. "We'd better be going. Good night, everyone."

At home, Wendy herded Brandon to bed, telling him, "We're going to have a big day tomorrow. You need your rest." As Kimberly and Megan padded down the hall, Wendy called, "Don't stay up late, girls. You need to get some sleep too." She turned to Erica. "Since Kimberly's going with us tomorrow, I thought it would be easier if she just stayed over." Then Wendy asked, "Did you get what you wanted tonight?"

Erica was taken aback. Sometimes Wendy surprised her. Her pleasant nature sometimes fooled people into thinking she was a bit slow, but Wendy was actually quite sharp and observant.

"I got one of my hunches confirmed, so it was a very productive evening."

Wendy sighed. "And you're not going to tell me what you found out, are you?"

"Nope."

"I didn't want to know anyway," Wendy said with a light shrug.

Erica smiled. While it was true that the night had been very illuminating—with a large piece of the puzzle falling into place—it had actually stirred up more questions than it answered. And how exactly did this new puzzle piece figure into Tyson's murder? Was it integral to the case, or might it be one of those meandering tangents that seemed so promising at first but useless in the end? But since her gut told Erica it was the former, there was more work to be done, much of it cerebral. Erica needed to take time to ponder the evidence and examine it from all angles, twisting this and tweaking that to discover how all the parts fit together.

CHAPTER 16

With a slight shake of his head, Matt Watters shook his longish, fair hair out of his eyes as he took a seat beside Erica Coleman in the foyer of the Starlight Motel. Curtains had been drawn against the early morning sun, and there was the smell of coffee percolating. The uneven sound of a vacuum came from a nearby room. Matt was in his midtwenties, and as they shook hands, Erica noticed how rough and calloused his were.

"I did a lot of rock climbing when I was on vacation," he explained.

"What exactly do you do here?" Erica began.

"I'm a maintenance engineer, which is a fancy way of saying if something breaks, I fix it. Or at least I try to." He grinned. "I do a lot of different things, from fixing broken blinds to stocking supply closets." Apparently, Matt was a man of many talents. Although slight in build, he appeared capable and energetic.

"So, you move around the motel quite a bit."

He nodded, replying cheerily, "They keep me jumping from one thing to another."

Erica showed him a picture of Gregory Tyson. "Do you remember seeing this man? It's been a few weeks since he was here."

"It's been a while since I was here too," Matt smiled, "but yeah, I remember him. I saw him the night before I left."

"Did you talk with him?"

"Not really. I had some cases of soap and shampoo on a dolly, and he and this other dude were in my way, standing in front of the supply closet, talking. I asked them to move, and they walked off."

"Did you know the other man? Does he work here?"

"Nah, I know everyone here. I figured he was another guest."

"If I showed you a picture, do you think you might recognize him?"

Matt shrugged, a faint nervousness in his manner. Thankful she had come prepared, Erica pulled out a file with pictures of Reed Devoe, Stephen Watkins, Lee Grover, and a number of other men—off-duty policemen at the police station. Matt looked the pictures over carefully. Finally, he touched one.

"I think that's the guy."

"Look at them again—take your time."

He leaned over, squinting at each one. Finally, he picked up the one he'd pointed at before. "That's the dude, all right."

It was Stephen Watkins.

"Do you remember what time of day it was when you saw them?"

Matt scrunched his face, trying to think. "I think it was late afternoon, but I'm not sure."

"Can you show me where you saw them?"

They went down a narrow hallway and near the end, Matt pointed out a door marked *Housekeeping*. "They were standing there."

"After you asked them to move, where did they go?"

Frowning, he thought hard, looking down the hall as if that would refresh his memory. "I think they went down there, by the ice machine, and kept talking."

"Could you hear what they were saying?"

Matt shook his head. "Nah, I wasn't paying any attention."

"Did either of them seem happy, angry, sad, or anything like that?"

Matt grimaced. Apparently, he could only think when contorting his face. "I don't think so. I probably would have remembered if they were laughing or yelling." Then he added, "Actually, now that I think about it, they were talking kind of serious-like. Intense, you know?"

"Okay. Is there anything else that you remember about Tyson and this other man? Were they wearing anything different, carrying anything, or doing anything out of the ordinary?"

"Not that I can remember."

"I guess that does it." Erica held out her hand. "Thank you, Matt. You've been very helpful."

Matt shifted and looked at her closely. "Hey, are you really a private eye?"

"Yes, I am. Why do you ask?"

His fair skin colored slightly. "I just thought you might be a model or something."

* * *

Looking at her watch, Erica decided she had time to stop and see Detective Lund. She filled him in on her conversation with Matt Watters then gave him a small piece of blank white paper in a sealed baggie.

"Would you have your people test this and see if it's the same as the paper that was found on Wendy's front room floor?"

"Mind telling me where this came from?"

She wore an inscrutable smile. "I'll tell you when you get the results back."

Pulling up at Wendy's house, Erica dialed her husband.

"Hi, sweetie. I thought I'd call and say hi before we went boating. We probably won't get back from the lake until it's too late to call. How are the kids?"

"Great." David went on to talk about the latest.

Then Erica asked, "How are the dogs?"

"They miss you."

"I suppose they told you that?"

"Yep—in doggy language."

"As in; 'Bowwow, arf, arf?'"

"Not *verbal* doggy language—*body* doggy language. I haven't wanted to tell you before because then you'd start worrying about them, but whenever I come home, Biscuit follows me around like she's afraid I'm going to disappear. Snickers, on the other hand, has developed a psychosis. No, actually it's more of an anxiety disorder. Every night, she sneaks into our closet, grabs one of your shoes, and puts it in her bed."

"You're kidding."

"Every morning when I wake up, she's got a new shoe. At first, I'd put it back every morning, but the next night she'd sneak back and grab another one. She doesn't chew them or anything, so I finally decided to let the neurotic little beast just keep them. But one isn't enough for her, and each night she gets another one. Now her bed looks like the floor of a shoe store on Black Friday."

"Oh, the poor little thing."

"She sleeps right in the middle of them, burrowing in so that all you can see is this little black snout poking out of this huge pile of shoes. Can't be comfortable." Erica laughed, and David changed the subject. "Hey, weren't you supposed to talk to that guy at the motel this morning?"

"Been there, done that. Matt wasn't too sure about me—asked if I was really a private eye."

"What did he think you were? A reporter?"

"No, a model."

"And I thought I was the only one who got that line." Then David turned serious. "Hey, was he trying to hit on you?"

"No, nothing like that. Matt's just a kid. He even blushed when he asked me."

"All right then. Guess I don't have to come out there and punch his lights out. So, did he have any useful information?"

When she told him Matt had identified Stephen, David was genuinely surprised. "Hey, this is *major!* Hasn't Stephen been saying all along that he *hadn't* talked to Tyson?"

"That's right," Erica said, sounding troubled. "So either Stephen or Matt is lying, and there's really no reason for Matt to lie."

"Maybe he was trying to look good in front of the pretty investigator," David theorized. When Erica snorted, he insisted, "Hey, it's possible. It's not uncommon for witnesses to make stuff up so they can feel important. Besides, you said it took Matt a while to pick out Stephen's picture. Plus, he only remembered that Stephen and Tyson were talking seriously *after* you asked if they were mad or laughing."

Erica had her doubts, but David went on. "Wait a minute! Matt said he saw Tyson and Stephen in the late afternoon, but Stephen was at Brandon's baptism. What time was that?"

"At three. Stephen picked us up around 2:30."

"So, unless Stephen has a double, he couldn't have been at the motel that afternoon."

"Interesting that you'd mention that," Erica said.

"Mention what?"

"I'll explain later."

"I hate it when you do that," David complained.

"Sorry. Anyway, moving on. It's possible Matt got the time wrong. I mean, it *was* a few weeks ago, and he didn't sound certain by any means," Erica said.

"You need to find out what Stephen was doing before he came over to pick you guys up."

"I'll ask him today. Still, even if Stephen *did* meet Tyson, it doesn't mean he killed him."

"Try telling that to the police."

* * *

Megan and Wendy were packing food in a cooler when Erica walked in. Megan was moping a bit because Kimberly couldn't go after all. Her friend had woken with a migraine, and Kimberly's mother had already come and taken her home. Also, Stephen had called to say Jaime was running half an hour late and they should go ahead. He'd pick Jaime up when she was done and meet them at the lake. When Lee arrived, he said that would work fine since he needed time to gas up the boat at the marina.

Erica wiped down the car, front and back, while the others loaded the food in the trunk of Lee's Camry. Wendy sat up front while Erica, Brandon, and Megan squeezed together in the back seat. Surprisingly, Megan didn't complain—probably because her only other option was to come later with Stephen and Jaime.

"Where are we going?" Erica asked as Lee turned onto Highway 92.

"Lake Tohopekaliga, or Toho for short," Lee replied. "It's very close. Kissimmee, or Allendale, as the city was first called, was built on the north end of the lake. When the Civil War ended, the whole area was in pretty bad shape, but that changed when a man by the name of Hamilton Disston paid twenty-five cents an acre and bought four million acres."

"It cost twenty-five cents?" Brandon said.

"For each acre. Even at that price, it added up to about one million dollars. The story goes that he saved Florida from financial disaster by buying the land." Lee passed a car. "Disston also helped Kissimmee by draining the marshes and deepening the river so goods could be shipped to the Gulf of Mexico."

"Then disaster struck," Megan added with a kind of gloomy satisfaction. "There was a big freeze, and a lot of people left and moved south."

Lee glanced at Megan in the rearview mirror. "You know your history, don't you? Anyway, after that, Disston's company stopped payment on his bonds, and so he returned to Philadelphia. But he really helped out Florida while he was here."

They pulled into the parking lot and, carrying bags and coolers, walked by docks extending from the shore like long, gray fingers. Sloops and catboats were bobbing at the docks, their canvasses lapped tight and buttoned around their masts.

Erica looked around at the picturesque houses hugging the shoreline. What would it be like to live by the lake with the sound of water being the last thing you heard at night and having the stipple of water reflecting on your ceiling when you first woke up?

Lee noticed Erica looking at the old houses. "Do you know much about Kissimmee's history?"

"Megan told me a little about Chief Osceola, but that's all. Who originally settled Florida?"

"The Spanish were the first in the 1700s. Later, the British gained control. During the Revolutionary War, Florida remained loyal to the British, but eventually the Americans took control." Lee stopped to let Brandon, who had lagged behind—goggle-eyed over the boats—catch up.

They filed down a weathered dock, past a line of dinghies and boats, then Lee called out, "There she is!" Proudly pointing at *Wide Horizons,* a neat white cuddy cab with red trim, he said, "It belongs to my parents, but my brothers and I are the only ones who use it regularly."

After passing out life jackets, Lee made sure everyone had them on correctly before going for gas. They returned to the dock a few minutes later to pick up Stephen and Jaime and then glided out where the sun reflected off the water, creating a great, glittering brightness on the fractured diamond surface of the lake. The air was crisp and fresh, and in the distance a number of white sails flitted against the green horizon.

They were all voyagers on a small, snug craft with the entire day before them. As Lee drove, he explained various boating terms such as *port* for the left side of the boat, *starboard* for the right, *bow* for the front, and *stern* for the back.

Erica shook her head. "I'm just going to call them by the terms they use on planet Earth—*left, right, front,* and *back.*"

"Don't listen to her," Lee said in a stage whisper to Brandon. "She's just a landlubber."

He then went on to explain the rudiments of longitude and latitude while Erica watched in fascination as they passed little islands that seemed to float on air instead of water. Many of the small islands were sown thick with rocks and brilliant green moss, but some of the larger ones had low dunes that topped the beach and were crowned with undulating green sea grass.

Once they were far out in the lake, Lee pulled back on the throttle and the boat slowed. "This is great," Erica said as she looked over the shimmering lake. "Remember going boating on Bear Lake, Wendy?" They'd gone several times with Erica's older brother, Konner, and her younger brother, Chris.

"That was so much fun," Wendy said. "Except for the time I didn't use any sunblock and got fried to a crisp! That's not going to happen again!" She, Megan, and Erica coated themselves liberally, and Wendy slathered sunblock on a complaining Brandon.

After he was released, the boy asked Lee, "Can we go out on a tube now?"

"Sure thing."

Jaime held the wheel while Lee went to a storage compartment and pulled out a towable. Megan and Brandon unfolded it, and Lee connected an air pump to the boat's battery. In no time, the raft-like tube was inflated.

Dancing in anticipation, Brandon shouted, "I want to go first!"

"This is a two-person tube," Lee said. "Who wants to ride with Brandon?"

"I'll go," Megan offered.

Wendy looked worried. "I think I'd like to go with him the first time."

"Oh, Mom," Megan complained. "Nothing's going to happen."

Wendy refused to budge, so Lee hooked the rope to the boat, then she and Brandon clambered onto the tube. Handing Megan a red flag, Lee instructed her to hold it high when someone fell into the water.

Megan and Erica took a turn next, followed by Jaime and Stephen. Brandon had trouble with the concept of taking turns. Whenever anyone got off, he'd cry, "It's my turn now!"

"Shut up!" Megan told him more than once. "You're already getting more turns than anybody else." It was true, but Brandon was young and eager, and Erica enjoyed seeing him have so much fun. The adults took turns holding the wheel so Lee could go out once in a while. When he wasn't riding the tube, Brandon loved the responsibility of holding the red flag.

Midmorning, Wendy went into the cab and when she returned, Jaime had moved close to Stephen. She stood there, laughing up at him, then gave him an affectionate hug. Erica, who was sitting in the shade, caught the small, clear flare of triumph in Jaime's dark eyes as she peered at Wendy over his shoulder. Stephen pulled away abruptly, then seeing Jaime's eyes, he looked around at Wendy, who turned away stiffly. She went to the starboard side of the boat and gripped the rail as though needing it for balance. Stephen hurried over while Jaime stood there, one corner of her mouth turned up.

At that moment, Erica disliked Jaime heartily. At the same time, she realized it would take some effort not to allow her personal feelings to influence her investigation. But then, Erica didn't need to like or trust this woman to find the truth.

The boat stopped to allow a switch in riders. As it started up again, Erica went over to Megan, who was holding the flag trying not to stare at Stephen and her mother who were talking so earnestly. When Stephen put his arms around Wendy, Megan's face twisted with annoyance.

"You'd better keep an eye on Brandon," Erica said to distract her. Megan frowned but turned to watch her brother.

When Jaime went into the cuddy, Erica followed. Jaime was taking a bottle of water out of a cooler when she saw Erica. Hoisting the bottle aloft, she asked casually, "Want one?"

"Sure."

After handing Erica a bottle, Jaime opened her own and took a long drink. Erica remembered how Jaime had watched her from the office window. Could she have been the one who had called the other night and warned her that she was asking too many questions? There was no way of knowing for sure, but right now Erica wanted to talk about the little scene between her and Stephen.

"You do know that Wendy and Stephen are seeing each other?" Erica asked evenly.

Thick lashes veiled Jaime's eyes. "So?" Although her face gave nothing away, her one-word answer was swathed in defensive overtones.

"That display you put on a few minutes ago seemed to be for Wendy's benefit."

As Jaime tossed her head back, black hair swept over her shoulders. "I only gave Stephen a hug—there's nothing wrong with that."

"You did it to make Wendy jealous."

"Wendy is not married to him," Jaime cried. "She doesn't own Stephen—and it might be that he likes me better." Erica watched the strong, confident line of the young woman's chin. Jaime was someone who would always be sure of herself.

"Stephen and Wendy have been dating for several years."

"That's a long time without a ring." Jaime flashed a brittle smile. It was paper thin—artificial. "Maybe Stephen doesn't like her as much as you think. Why don't we let him decide who he likes best?" She drained the last of the water and climbed up the stairs.

After a few minutes, Erica followed and saw that Jaime was at the wheel and Stephen and Brandon were climbing onto the tube. She went over to Wendy, who was holding the flag high as Lee and Megan climbed up the ladder and onto the boat.

"It's finally out in the open," Wendy whispered. "Jaime is after Stephen. She has been for a long time."

"But you saw how Stephen pulled back. He's not interested in her."

"I've talked to Stephen about Jaime several times, and each time he's assured me nothing is going on, but—" Wendy bit her lip slightly. "But how can he not be interested when a gorgeous young girl throws herself at him? Why else did he invite her to come today?"

"Because he's a nice guy! You know that. Maybe you're making this a bigger deal than it is. Yes, Jaime is making a play for him, but he likes *you!*"

"I thought he did," Wendy said hesitantly. Her eyes shifted to Jaime, who had given up the wheel to Lee and was now leaning against the rail, watching Stephen and laughing. "But to me, this is a very big deal. If you don't mind, I'd like a few minutes alone. I just need to pull myself together."

"All right." Erica patted Wendy's hand before wandering over to Lee, who looked at home on the deck in his T-shirt and knee-length shorts. He looked back once in a while to make sure the riders were still on the tube and smiled as Erica approached, friendly as always. Lee had straight features, steady brown eyes, and a firm mouth.

Erica said the first thing that popped into her mind. "You're handsome as can be!"

"It's the light. Your eyes are playing tricks."

"Ah no. It's the truth."

Lee went scarlet. His very eyebrows blushed, and he tried to mask his embarrassment by joking, "I was going to ask if you wanted me to show you how to steer the boat, but now I'm not sure I trust you alone with me."

She laughed. "I'm sorry. That sounded like I was flirting, didn't it? I really wasn't. I'm married to a handsome hunk of my own back in Utah."

"Well, in that case—" He moved to the side and motioned Erica to take hold of the wheel.

After a quick wipe with her towelettes, Erica grabbed the wheel. "This is great!" she exclaimed looking out at the vast expanse of water. "I like that there's nothing I can run into."

"That's the beauty of a really big lake."

Just then, Wendy shouted that there were riders in the lake. Lee took the wheel and, cutting the motor, circled back to pick up Brandon and Stephen. When they came aboard, Lee pronounced it time for lunch.

"We'd better wash first," Erica said, opening a sack filled with new bars of Lava. "I brought enough for everyone." Stephen and Lee were unfamiliar with this particular compulsion and looked at Wendy for clues on what to do.

"That is so nice of you," Wendy said. "Why don't you leave the sack in the bathroom. There's also a bottle of hand soap in there if anyone wants to use that."

Erica smiled. "Sometimes you are so cute, Wendy. As if anyone would want to use that when they have this." She held up a red-packaged bar and pointed. "It says right on the box, 'Lava has clean written all over it.'"

Coolers were brought up, and Wendy began handing out sandwiches.

"Try the Egg Salad Sandwiches,"[10] she advised. "They're delicious—Erica made them. We also have ham and turkey." Veggies and chips were also distributed.

Megan opened the cooler with the drinks and smiled. In the manner of someone making a public announcement, she said, "Erica has been at it again. You'll notice the drinks are organized by color, with water on the left, then Sprite and Fresca, lemonade in the middle, and colas on the right."

"Very convenient, don't you think?" Erica asked, looking satisfied.

"Very," Lee said, trying to hide his smile.

"Absolutely," Wendy added. "Why, I might have died of thirst in the extra ten seconds it would have taken to find a Sprite."

It was a time to enjoy the bright day, and earlier tensions were put aside. As they ate, there were jokes, laughter, and an easy, if somewhat forced, camaraderie. They topped off the lunch with brownies Jaime had brought.

With full stomachs, everyone's energy level dropped. Even Brandon did not immediately beg to go back on the tube but asked Lee if he could steer the boat. Lee pulled a box over for him to stand on while Wendy got her camera. The others meandered over.

"Watch out for icebergs, now," Lee warned Brandon, who peered out at the lake all squinty-eyed. Brandon studied Lee's face, not sure if the man was joking.

---

10   See appendix at the end of the book for this recipe.

In a serious voice, Jaime asked Brandon, "Didn't you notice the name of our boat? It's the *Titanic*." When the others smiled, Brandon's worries disappeared.

"Hey, I've got a joke," Lee announced. "A Coast Guard cutter got a distress signal from an inexperienced skipper of a yacht that was in trouble. Panicking, the skipper told them to hurry because his yacht was sinking. When the Coast Guard asked him what his position was, the man replied, 'I'm the executive vice president of First Global Bank—will you please hurry?'"

They all roared.

Wendy spoke up, "I heard a good one at Friendly's the other day. What do you call three men and a baby? Four men coming back from a fishing trip where only three of them caught fish."

They convulsed again. Megan's laugh started out thin but ended up a loud belly laugh.

"I don't understand why we're laughing," Erica said. "It wasn't *that* funny." For some reason, that broke everyone up again.

"It's the spray," Megan chortled as the feathery spray came up the side of the boat and settled on them mistily. "It's done something to our brains."

Brandon was tired of jokes. "I want to go faster!"

"Aye, aye, captain." Lee obliged, his tanned face alight, and he helped the boy push the throttle.

They all planted their feet, except for Megan, who went portside, her face bright and alive as they planed over the lake. Enthralled with the feel of the mist on her face, Megan was like a child of the water and the wild as she threw out her arms wide to catch the spray. Watching her, Erica remembered how it was to be a teenager. Much of the time, it was like living on a seismograph, unexpectedly careening, plummeting, and soaring from the spasms that made up life. She was glad Megan had come today— it was wonderful to see honest pleasure and excitement on the girl's face as her hair blew wildly in the breeze.

Lee had begun to slow down when Stephen went to take the drink cooler down into the cuddy to get it out of the sun. Jaime followed. When Stephen came up, his eyes darted one way, then another, then he made his way to the closest person, Erica. His face was flushed, and there was perspiration at his hairline.

"It's warmed up, hasn't it?" Erica commented.

"It certainly has." Stephen took off his cap to wipe his forehead.

Just then, Jaime came up, her eyes searching the boat. Abruptly, Stephen turned toward the lake. Erica smiled and did likewise. There were a few boats like theirs on the lake, along with an occasional small sailboat that crossed and recrossed the soft breeze. Ski jets with their loud motors skimmed along the water's surface.

"This is great," Erica said. "David and I go with my family to Bear Lake once in a while, but the water is still freezing this time of the year."

"You ought to move to Florida," Stephen told her. "Get out of the cold. I'm glad Lee asked us to come; I'm afraid you haven't had much fun during your stay."

"Oh, but I have. Wendy, Brandon, and I went to SeaWorld when I first got here. Of course I'm anxious to get home. The sooner the case gets solved, the sooner I can get back to my family. That's great motivation."

"I bet it is."

"Lately, I've been double-checking the facts, which takes a lot of time. Yesterday, I was going over the day Tyson was killed, and I couldn't quite recall when Brandon's baptism started. I guess I'll have to ask Wendy." She actually remembered the time perfectly, but did Stephen?

"It started at three."

"That's right," Erica acknowledged. "And you picked us up about 2:30?"

"Right around then."

"Whew, that was a busy morning!" Erica recalled. "Wendy had to work, and I was rushing around trying to get everything ready. Then she called from work and wanted me to go pick up some rolls." She laughed lightly. "Wendy was so stressed she'd forgotten *she* had the car! She said she'd called you to see if you could get them, but you didn't answer." Erica watched him carefully.

Stephen's brow furrowed slightly. "She did? I was home and could have done it. I was just paying bills and cleaning the place. Maybe she called when I took out the garbage."

No mention was made of going to see an old friend. Erica would have to go to plan B.

"This morning I went to the Starlight Motel and talked to Matt, an employee," Erica said. "He remembers seeing Tyson talking with another man." Stephen startled slightly, glancing at her then looking away. "Matt didn't know who the other man was, so I showed him some pictures. I had one of Lee, Reed, Patrick, other cops in plain clothes—and you."

Stephen swallowed heavily before looking at her despairingly. There it was—the admission.

"Why didn't you tell anyone you'd talked to Gregory Tyson?" Erica asked.

"It was stupid of me," Stephen admitted, shaking his head. "But I was the only one that knew Greg. If I had admitted that I'd gone to see him that morning, the police would have thought I had something to do with his murder."

"All right. So you went to see Tyson. What did you talk about? How did he act?"

"He seemed kind of nervous and a little jumpy, which was unusual for him. We started catching up, but when I told Greg I didn't have a lot of time, he told me the real reason he wanted to see me was to ask for money. I guess that's why he was on edge."

"Why would he ask you?"

"I'd loaned him money before, back in Chicago, which was a big mistake. I don't like lending money, and after three or four times, I told Greg I wasn't going to do it anymore. But he kept asking." Stephen looked upset. "So I started avoiding him. I know it hurt Greg's feelings, but I didn't know what else to do."

"Mrs. Tyson told me Greg knew you'd be inheriting from Linda Bronson."

"Yeah, that was another mistake. I never should have mentioned it. I'd told him about that when we were both working at Cicero. After I quit, Greg still called me occasionally, and one time we got talking about the Bronsons. That's when I told him Linda had cancer and that it was terminal. At the time, Greg didn't say much about it, but when he got into financial trouble, he must have remembered. That's why he came here to see me. I guess he thought that since I'd be inheriting soon, I'd change my mind and give him a loan, but I told him no."

"How did he take it?"

"I've never seen him so upset. Greg said it was a matter of life and death and that he'd borrowed money and needed to pay it back. But he's told me so many stories that I figured this was just one more." Stephen made a gesture of despair. "I'd give anything to relive that day so I could give him the money. Greg was such a talker I just assumed he was making a mountain out of a molehill."

"Did Greg mention who he owed money to or if he was being followed?"

"No. I only spent a few minutes with him. To tell the truth, I was kind of irritated he was asking me for money again. Greg was a good guy, but he could be annoying."

"I assume Greg came to Wendy's house to see you. How did he know where she lived?"

"I told him where I was going that night and mentioned Wendy's name. I didn't give Greg her address, but obviously he found out."

"I see. Is there anything else Greg said that might help us find out who shot him?"

"Believe me, I've racked my brain trying to remember everything he said. If Greg had said anything I thought might help, I would have told you."

An arm slipped around Stephen's shoulder, and he jumped. Wendy looked at him in surprise. "Sorry. I didn't mean to scare you."

They talked about other things, and after a while Erica went over to Megan, who was holding the red flag and watching Brandon and Jaime.

When Lee looked back toward the riders, he called, "Hey Erica, you haven't been out for a while. Want to be next?"

"Yeah, come and go with me!" Megan urged her.

"Yeah, sure!"

As they waited, Erica thought again how nice it had been to see Megan looking so relaxed and carefree. Impulsively, Erica put an arm around Megan's waist and pulled her close.

"I'm so glad you came with us today!"

Megan's face glowed with pleasure. Erica counted it as a major step forward that Megan had not been outwardly rude to Stephen once during the entire trip. Yes, there had been dark looks, but that was a marked improvement.

"It's been fun today, hasn't it?" Erica said, looking out over the crystal lake.

"Yeah, it has." Megan sounded somewhat surprised. "I love being out on the water."

Lee turned the boat, causing Brandon and Jaime to cross the wake and bounce high. Erica asked, "So, how's it going with the counseling?"

"It's *so* stupid," Megan grumbled, rolling her eyes and brushing back her black hair, which was blown about by the breeze.

"Why is that?"

"The counselor is *such* a moron! She keeps asking me stupid questions. And she still thinks I tried to kill myself and keeps trying to get me to admit it. She also wants me to talk about, well, you know—about what happened that night with my dad."

"That's because our past can affect our present lives. I found that out. Sometimes, things that happened in the past injure us so much emotionally we can't move on until we work them out." Sensing Megan was pulling back into herself, Erica reached over and patted the girl's hand. "Just remember, if you ever want to talk, I'm here. I know you might feel hopeless and think certain things are out of your control, but they're not. You're strong. You can take care of yourself."

"You're right about that," Megan declared forcefully. "There are a *lot* of things I can do." Erica looked at her thoughtfully. It was not the words as much as the girl's tone that set Erica back.

Lee curled the boat back toward the tube and stopped to let Erica and Megan get on and take a turn. After they had ridden, Lee asked Stephen to steer so he could go on the tube with Wendy.

When she hesitated, Stephen grinned. "You don't think I can drive this boat, do you? Well, you don't have to worry. I won't steer you wrong!"

Groaning at the pun, Wendy climbed down into the water.

It was so peaceful whenever the boat stopped and the engine became quiet. The sun was high and honey gold and the light clear and radiant—shimmering like diamonds on the water. Later in the year, the heat would be overwhelming, but for now the May warmth was immensely enjoyable. It had been a peaceful, lazy day, and Erica had thoroughly enjoyed it all, from the call of the gulls to the slap of the water against the boat's hull. For a time, no one spoke in that great expanse of fresh air, high sun, and blue lake. Then, the engine roared, and they were propelled forward once again.

When Lee reclaimed the wheel, Stephen took Wendy's hand and led her to the starboard side of the boat. Lee had been talking and smiling with Erica, but when he saw Wendy and Stephen holding hands, his smile died. Looking hurt, he faced forward, seeming intent on driving.

It was early evening when Lee finally pulled in the tube and they started back. Coming to stand beside Erica, Megan handed her a bottle of water. "It's still cool."

"Thanks."

Megan had gotten most of her color back since leaving the hospital, and it helped that she had stopped putting on white face powder. Brandon walked by, his light brown hair lifting in the wind, his tan a smooth golden glow. Just then, the boat hit a wave, causing Brandon to bobble on the deck like a drunken sailor. Laughter bubbled up from under Megan's ribs, making Erica and Brandon laugh as well.

On the drive home, Megan leaned into a corner and closed her eyes while Brandon kept watch out the window. Lee reminisced about past boating trips with his family. His dry wit kept Wendy and Erica laughing, but the closer they got to home, the further Erica's thoughts drifted from the conversation. The pieces were coming together. It wouldn't be long now.

CHAPTER 17

THE SMELL OF FRYING BACON Sunday morning wafted down to where Erica slept, and after waking her, it pulled her up the stairs.

"Thought I'd give you a reason to get out of bed," Wendy said, putting some strips on a paper-towel-lined plate. She put it on the table by Brandon, who was nearly done eating.

"Say, where's Megan?" Erica asked.

"She's gone," Brandon said helpfully, crunching his toast.

Wendy elucidated a bit further. "Megan has a friend who's going on a mission, and she went to hear him speak. I'm surprised she made it. I thought she'd be dead tired from yesterday." She dished up scrambled eggs for herself and Erica. "Brandon, when you're finished, rinse off your plate and go take your bath. And don't use all the hot water." Erica was pouring juice when Brandon shoved the last of his bacon in his mouth and ran off.

Looking at his plate, which he'd left on the table, Wendy said ruefully, "I swear, he's got the memory span of a goldfish. Did you know they can't remember anything past three seconds?"

"Who can't remember anything past three seconds?"

"Very funny." Wendy sat down. "Megan seems to be better lately, don't you think?"

"I was thinking that yesterday. She *has* been a lot more pleasant."

"I guess it was a good thing we talked." Wendy looked thoughtful. "I never knew Megan felt I didn't protect her. I still can't believe she doesn't remember all the times I stood up for her!"

"Children have selective memories. A lot of what happens goes right past them. A few months ago, Aby asked me why I wouldn't let her play soccer when she was in elementary school. I was dumbfounded. I'd asked her over and over if she wanted to play, and each time she said no. Now, she doesn't remember me asking and to this day believes I wouldn't let her play."

"Kids are so positive they're the only ones that can remember what *really* happened—"

"That's because they think Mom is so old that half her brain cells are dead." Erica shook her head. Youth was so sure of itself—so certain that it alone knew the right way. She was glad to have reached another, slightly wiser, age.

"I've done a lot of thinking since you and I talked. You know, about Bishop Griggs." Wendy paused to take a sip of orange juice. "I think I came across as more angry and unforgiving than I actually am. I was really bitter toward him for a long time, but about a year ago, I began praying that God would help me forgive."

She frowned. "Problem was nothing seemed to change. Then Elder Boyd K. Packer gave a talk during conference that really hit me. He told the story of a little girl who was upset when her brother built a trap to catch sparrows. She didn't want him to hurt the birds, so she knelt down and prayed. Afterward, she told her mother that her brother wasn't going to catch any sparrows because she had prayed about it. In fact, she said she was *positive* he wouldn't catch any birds. Her mother asked why she was so sure, and the little girl replied that after she'd prayed she'd gone outside and kicked the trap all to pieces."

Erica laughed. "Faith in action! Now there's a good example of that old saying: pray as though everything depended upon God and work as if everything depended upon you."

"Right. That story woke me up, and I realized I had been expecting God to do all the work," Wendy said ruefully. "So I decided I had better put some effort into it. I started reading articles about forgiveness and pondering on it. It helped when I started going back to church."

"Going to church helps me feel the Spirit more."

"At the risk of giving you a big head," Wendy said, "I have to tell you that after you lectured me, I did a lot more thinking and praying. It took a while, but I think I understand now what you were talking about."

It was tempting to shout *yes!* but Erica resisted.

Wendy continued. "Another thing that helped was when I read an old conference talk by President Gordon B. Hinckley. In it, President Hinckley said he'd agreed to be interviewed about the Church by Mike Wallace, a tough reporter, for the TV program *60 Minutes*. President Hinckley said that since Mike would also be interviewing critics of the

Church, it was unlikely the show would be entirely positive. However, President Hinckley felt the interview offered him an opportunity to present some good information about LDS people to millions of viewers and decided to go ahead with it." Wendy smiled slightly. "I was surprised when President Hinckley said he didn't know what the outcome would be. He said that if the interview turned out favorable, he'd be grateful, and if it didn't, he'd never get his foot caught in that kind of trap again."

"I remember that!" Erica said. "I laughed when he said that; he's so funny."

"That was the same thing you were telling me about Moses—Church leaders *are* inspired, and the prophet will *never* lead the people astray, but prophets don't always know how some things are going to turn out. Even President Hinckley wasn't sure how the interview was going to pan out, and I'm sure he prayed before agreeing to it."

Wendy sighed. "And I'm also sure Bishop Griggs prayed about me and jerk-face, er, Dennis. I guess I really *was* expecting him to be a mind reader and know ahead of time that Dennis was going to start drinking again. Looking back now, it was just easier to blame my problems on the bishop rather than myself. I was so depressed at how rotten my life was. Sometimes it felt my life was spinning so fast that I was thrown off from everything I knew."

"You were just overwhelmed," Erica said quietly. "You'd lost your baby, and now your marriage was over."

"I know, and deep inside I think I always knew Bishop Griggs was just trying to do what he thought was best. And he did so much for me! I called him so many times at crazy hours, and he was always loving and patient." Wendy paused. "After the miscarriage, Bishop Griggs called me two or three times, but I wouldn't talk with him. I had to have someone to blame. But blaming him didn't do any good. It didn't bring my baby back, and it took me away from church. It took a long time before I realized I was basing my testimony on a man and not on Christ."

Wendy's eyes were focused on the far wall as if concentrating hard on something there. "I kept thinking about what you said—that everything *could* have been all right if Dennis hadn't decided to start drinking again. That was so true. So, a week ago, I decided to call Bishop Griggs."

"*You did?* How did it go?"

"Better than I expected. I was kind of nervous, but Bishop Griggs was great. So sweet and kind—like always. He didn't try to make me feel bad or lecture me—like you did!" Wendy flashed Erica a lopsided grin.

"He just listened and apologized and told me how terrible he felt over what had happened. Talking with him made me feel so much better— like a twenty-ton weight had been taken off my shoulders. I know that's cliché, but that's how I felt. Now, I can think of what happened without all that bitter pulling and tearing."

"I'm so glad." Erica paused then said hesitantly, "I thought of a good quote."

"You and your quotes," Wendy said teasingly. "All right. Let's have it."

"'Forgiveness does not change the past, but it does enlarge the future.' Paul Boese."

Wendy thought on it deeply. "You're right—that's a good one, and that's just what happened now that I've forgiven him: I feel like my future *has* expanded. I just wish I hadn't gotten so upset with him in the first place, but I think I've grown from it. Looking back, I realize I wanted him to be perfect, but even bishops have human frailties. But now I know that even when everything else in life falls apart, God is always there for me."

Erica agreed. "People may fail us, but Jesus Christ never will."

"Oh, I've got to show you something!" Wendy jumped up, rummaged around in her purse, and extracted a small square of paper. "I was reading the scriptures one night when you were gone, and this verse jumped out at me. So I wrote it down. Read it."

Taking the paper, Erica read out loud: "And now, my sons, remember, remember that it is upon the rock of our Redeemer, who is Christ, the Son of God, that ye must build your foundation; that when the devil shall send forth his mighty winds, yea, his shafts in the whirlwind, yea, when all his hail and his mighty storm shall beat upon you, it shall have no power over you to drag you down to the gulf of misery and endless wo, because of the rock upon which ye are built, which is a sure foundation, a foundation whereon if men build they cannot fall. Helaman 5:12."

Still holding the paper, Erica said, "That's one of my favorites too. And you're not the only one who's been doing some thinking lately. I don't know if you've thought about it, but there's a similarity between what happened between you and Bishop Griggs and what happened between you and Megan."

Wendy rolled her eyes. "This isn't going to be another lecture, is it?" Then she added, "I'm just kidding."

"Okay," Erica said. "I just wanted to say that for years Megan blamed you for not protecting her, just like you blamed the bishop for not protecting you. You say that now you see that Bishop Griggs was a good man who was just trying to do what he thought was best. In the same way, Megan will realize someday that you're a good mother and that you were doing the best you could at a difficult time. Everyone is human and makes mistakes."

"But I made so many—and my children suffered because of it." Wendy's face clouded over. "And even now, there are some terrible things I've done."

"Everyone makes mistakes," Erica repeated. Then she glanced up at the clock. "Oh no! Look at the time!" They both jumped to their feet.

It was only by frenzied efforts that Erica, Wendy, and Brandon arrived at church not only on time, but a few minutes early. They took their places with a sigh of relief, but every few seconds Wendy turned to look at the open doors where the ushers stood.

"You're not expecting anyone are you?" Erica asked.

"Well, I wondered if Lee might come," Wendy said self-consciously, glancing at the doors again. Her eyes, a lovely amber with flecks of gold, were hopeful.

"You think?" Erica teased. Then she added, "Don't worry. He'll be here."

It was amusing to think that, although Lee had been sitting with them for weeks, Wendy was still uncertain whether he would today. But that was Wendy, always afraid of overbidding her hand. For as long as Erica had known her, Wendy had been lacking in self-confidence. That was probably why she had never seen Lee Grover's admiring looks and why she didn't know he was smitten until that day at Friendly's.

It was as Erica had said. No more than three minutes had passed before Lee sidestepped down the pew, squeezing past Brandon to sit by Wendy. He was cleanly shaven, had splashed on a piney aftershave, and was handsome as could be. When he sat down, Lee reached for Wendy's hand, and she gave it. A current as ancient as time seemed to spring between them.

Leaning over, Erica whispered in Wendy's ear, "Told you so."

* * *

That afternoon, Erica made three phone calls. The first was to Patrick Lund. She hated to call on a Sunday, but it was important to bring him in on what she was planning. As expected, Patrick confirmed that the paper she'd given him was the same as the paper that had been found on Wendy's floor the morning after Stephen was poisoned. They talked for nearly an hour.

Next, she called her brother Chris to make more flight arrangements. Chris asked few questions, knowing it had to do with the investigation.

Erica then made her third call and had to provide lots of reassurance. "Of *course* it's legal! My brother Chris works for United Airlines, and he's arranged everything. You'll be flying standby on what is called a companion pass. The only costs are taxes and fees, and I'll pay those." Erica listened then said, "I appreciate your willingness to come, and I apologize for the short notice." She relayed the flight information then said, "You're all set. I'll pick you up tomorrow." Then, so that she'd made an even number of phone calls, she called her mother.

Afterwards, Erica walked to a nearby park. It was a warm day, and she'd tied her long hair back with a scarf. A delightful fragrance of resin scented the air as she passed a stand of sweet gum trees. She headed for a bench in the west end of the park, where oak and maple trees edged a small copse. There was a whispering of branches overhead, and as the sun shone brightly through the trees, it outlined each leaf, tracing it in silver.

Erica was sure everything would work out, but there were still enough variables to cause concern. She had stashed a bar of milk chocolate with hazelnuts in her pocket earlier and pulled it out now, thinking of David and how he had surprised her by sending a box of candy bars and chocolates from Mrs. Cavanaugh's Candies a few days ago. Erica smiled. When she'd opened the box, there had been a note from David. "Love both gives and receives, and in giving it receives." Thomas Merton. Clearly, David was hinting that he'd like some chocolate when she returned home! He'd also included two issues of Dilbert comic books, knowing how much she enjoyed them. She unwrapped the bar, licking her fingers where the chocolate had melted slightly. Years ago, when she'd started working at Pinnacle, Erica had jokingly told David chocolate cleared her mind and helped her think. From then on, whenever she was working on a difficult case, he'd bring her home a couple of chocolate bars. Remembering her delight at receiving the box from David, Erica's heart swelled with love and longing to be with him. But soon—very soon—she would be home.

A squirrel chattered in a nearby tree but remained invisible. Shadows lengthened as Erica ran through everything in her mind, looking at the case from all angles until she was sure she could explain things smoothly and succinctly. The only unknown was how people would react; what Erica had to say was sure to surprise many and anger some.

* * *

Megan was reading in the front room when Erica opened the door slightly, closed it, then opened it, and walked in. Megan was used to it by now and only grimaced slightly.

Erica peered at the title of the book Megan was holding. "Ah, *Les Misérables*. I remember reading that when I was in high school."

"You couldn't have. They didn't publish it until 1862," Megan explained mischievously.

"Watch it," Erica growled. "You're being mighty disrespectful of your elders. Besides, I hate to break it to you, but the years are marching by for you too!"

Megan grinned. She appeared relaxed and content, a far cry from the taut, humorless girl she'd been when Erica arrived. Although most of her clothes were still black, as were her fingernails, she'd cut back on the makeup.

"Is school going okay?"

"Yeah, pretty much. Can't wait to graduate. Just two weeks left."

A car honked out front, and Megan marked her spot and put the book aside. "That'll be Kimberly. We're going to a fireside."

"Hey, are you going to be around tomorrow night?"

"Yeah, I think so. Why?"

"I'm inviting a few people over. I wanted to talk to everyone."

Megan gave Erica a guarded look. "Is Stephen going to be here?"

"Yes."

"Then I won't be." She started toward the door.

Erica called after her. "I'd really appreciate it if you were here, Megan. It's important."

The girl hesitated by the door, a large, awkward figure. "Oh, all right," she said ungraciously then turned and slipped outside.

* * *

Megan and Brandon had already left for school the next morning when Erica came into the kitchen. Wendy was rinsing the last of the dishes. "I certainly slept in, didn't I?" Erica said, feeling somewhat groggy. "I had a long talk with David last night and had a hard time going to sleep afterwards."

"That's too bad," Wendy commiserated. "What would you like for breakfast? The kids had cereal, and I had toast and juice."

"Toast and juice would be great."

"Could you take me to work this morning and pick up Brandon later this afternoon?" Wendy asked, putting bread in the toaster. "He wanted to ride home with a friend after school."

"Yeah, I can do that. I was going to ask if I could borrow your car today. I need to pick someone up at the airport."

"Ouch, hot." Wendy dropped the toast on a saucer and began buttering. "Is David coming out?"

"No, it's someone else."

Wendy glanced up. "Someone else? Does this *someone* have a name?"

"Yes."

"*Yes?* Is that all you're going to say? Listen, this toast is officially being held hostage until you tell me." She spread raspberry jam on it. "Ooooh—and look how yummy it is!"

"Give me that," Erica said, reaching out and snatching the toast. "I can't tell you right now, but I will tonight. You have the night off, and I'm planning a get together here."

"Not another one! Don't you ever stop?"

"This will be the last one, I promise."

It took a moment for that to sink in. "*The last one?*" There was a note of alarm in Wendy's voice. "So you know who poisoned Stephen and shot that man? Who was it?" Her hands began to twist and turn.

"Tonight," Erica said firmly.

* * *

It was almost comical to see Diana Evans's head jerk up as the door opened. She gave Erica her usual glacial glare and parried her request to see Stephen until Erica tired of playing the game and said she'd just go to his office and see if he was free. Defeated, Diana reached for the phone.

Stephen welcomed her cordially. "Always nice to see you, Erica. What can I do for you?"

"I wanted to invite you to come over to Wendy's house tonight."

"Special occasion?" he asked, smiling genially.

"Very special."

His eyebrows raised. "A break in the case?"

"Yes."

Stephen looked interested but didn't pursue it. After chatting a few minutes, Erica said, "I'd better let you get back to work. Oh, is Jaime here?"

"She went out. Not sure when she'll be back."

"What about Reed?"

"He's here. Are you inviting him too?"

"I am."

She was in Reed's office only a few minutes, adroitly sidestepping all of his questions. When she went down the hall, Diana looked at her a bit curiously.

"Did you get everything taken care of?" Diana asked.

"I did. Thank you." Erica made a quick exit, aware of Diana's eyes burning into her back.

* * *

At Friendly's Restaurant, Erica explained to the hostess that she needed to talk to Lee.

His face lit up when he saw her. "Did you stop by to get a good meal?"

"I wanted to see if you could come over to Wendy's house tonight."

"I don't get off until six."

Erica didn't tell him that she already knew that. "Why don't you come by at seven?"

"What's going on?"

"I'd like to talk to everyone about Gregory Tyson's murder and Stephen's poisoning."

"But you've already talked to everybody, several times."

"This time I'll be doing most of the talking."

A look of apprehension came into his eyes. "Oh . . . so you know who did it?"

"See you at seven."

* * *

Back at the house, Erica called Jaime, braving Diana Evans to do so. When Erica explained she was inviting people over, Jaime drawled, "Well, aren't you the party animal."

"It's not really a party."

"What is it, then?" There was immediate suspicion in Jaime's voice.

"Just some friends getting together."

"In that case, I'll pass. You see, I *am* a party animal, and this sounds a little boring."

"Stephen's coming."

"And you're inviting me? To Wendy's house? You must be a sadist. And here I thought you liked Wendy."

"I'd really like you to come."

A short laugh. "Is that supposed to make me come running?"

"You can walk."

This time Jaime laughed for real. "Okay, I'm curious now. If Stephen will give me a ride, I'll come."

* * *

Late that afternoon, Erica called Detective Lund. "Hello, Patrick? This is Erica Coleman. I wanted to make sure we were still on for tonight."

"As long as you're bringing the steaks."

It would be good to have Patrick there. His calm, matter-of-fact manner was reassuring. Patrick trusted her completely now, as she did him.

"Is Wendy all right with you pulling a Sherlock Holmes at her house?" he asked.

"A Sherlock Holmes?"

"You know, when the great detective gathers all the suspects and points out the guilty one."

"Oh, I suppose so."

"You don't sound too sure. How *does* Wendy feel about it?"

"She's a little nervous." Erica remembered the anxious eyes and twisting hands.

"Did your friend get into town yet?"

"I picked him up this afternoon. He's at a local motel."

"Is there anything you want me to provide tonight, besides intimidation?" Patrick chuckled in a self-satisfied way.

"You're a master at that. Actually, there are a few things I'd like you to be prepared to talk about." She quickly explained.

"Are you expecting any trouble?"

"Not with you there."

"All right, I'll see you later—just watch your back until then. I don't want any nasty surprises."

"Neither do I," Erica asserted fervently.

* * *

The strain Wendy was under showed in her darting glances, the way she jumped when the phone rang, and her hands that clutched and twisted.

By quarter to seven, whatever self-control she had was hanging by a thread.

"Erica," Wendy pleaded, "why can't you just tell me? Do you really know who killed that man and who poisoned Stephen?"

"I do. It was just a matter of getting all the information and putting everything in order."

Wendy turned even paler. Just then, the doorbell rang, causing her to jerk. She put on a lopsided grin and said self-depreciatingly, "Look at me, all jittery."

Detective Lund was the first to arrive. He walked in, big and broad shouldered, and after formally shaking hands with them, he eased himself into one of the chairs that Erica had arranged in a neat square around the room. When Wendy left, Patrick opened his jacket slightly, allowing Erica to see his holstered Glock 19.

"You never know," he muttered. "I thought it best to be prepared." Erica nodded solemnly, glad she had asked Wendy to send Brandon to a friend's house.

Megan came in, walking so slowly Erica wondered if she'd make it to the couch before next week. Then Lee arrived, followed shortly by Stephen and Jaime. Jaime looked beautiful as always but appeared watchful and wary.

When Reed arrived, he was his usual sour self. "Guess I'm the last one," he grunted, glancing around the packed room. He sat on one of the kitchen chairs, which had been brought in.

"At least I get a comfortable seat," he said sarcastically. Looking at Erica, he added, "I guess you can start your little show now."

Erica took the last chair, and when Patrick nodded, she began in her calm, clear voice. "As you all know, Wendy asked me to investigate Gregory Tyson's murder and Stephen's poisoning. The police also worked hard on these cases. Detective Lund?"

Patrick's big, booming voice took over. "I won't go into details, but there was little to go on when Gregory Tyson was murdered. However, when Stephen was poisoned, we had a number of suspects. We discovered he had a significant insurance policy and a will, which he'd written fairly recently and which left everything to Wendy Kemp." Everyone's eyes went to Wendy, who looked frightened.

"It's not easy being a single mother," Erica commented in a commiserating tone. "Wendy has struggled financially for years. It's been a hard life, one that Wendy hoped one day to escape. Part of her was attracted to Stephen because of his affluence."

Detective Lund added, "Poverty is an ugly thing and can make usually honorable people desperate, causing them to do things they normally wouldn't."

Wendy closed her eyes briefly as a current surged through the room. Erica could feel it rippling like water does when you toss something heavy into it.

"Now wait a minute," Stephen spoke up. "This is ridiculous. Wendy and I love each other. She can't have been the one who tried to kill me."

Erica looked at him. "Did you know that this is the first time I've ever heard you say the word *love*? I've always wondered what kept you and Wendy together. Although you seem close and are compatible, neither one of you seems to be *in* love. Didn't you ever wonder why Wendy kept prodding you to make a will?"

"She knew about that fortune you're going to inherit," Reed remarked slyly.

"*I didn't know about that!*" Wendy's retort was sharp and shrill. "And I didn't know I was the beneficiary of his will!"

"I can vouch for that," Stephen said earnestly. "I already told the police I didn't tell Wendy!"

"So you said, but was it the truth?" Detective Lund replied in his calm way. "It's unusual to keep such a big secret from someone you're so close to. Was it because you sensed something about Wendy—something that told you she was not to be trusted? Or *did* you tell Wendy, and both of you are lying now?"

"Erica, I didn't know," Wendy cried out plaintively as her hands twisted. "You believe me, don't you?"

"Initially, I did. But shortly after Stephen was poisoned, he said something very curious. Stephen told me that if he *had* been killed, you wouldn't have had to worry about money anymore and *you knew that.* I didn't pick up on it at the time, but when I found out about the will and the life insurance, it was clear you knew you were the beneficiary."

"One of the questions we asked ourselves," Detective Lund said, "was why Wendy would want to kill Stephen *before* he received his inheritance."

"That didn't make sense," Erica admitted. "Then, I talked with Linda about her will. It's a very unusual one." The room was very quiet. "You see, Linda believed Stephen was going to marry soon, so she added a stipulation to her will, stating that if Stephen should pass away before she did, the beneficiary of *his* will would receive $500,000."

Erica turned to Stephen. "This shows how devoted Linda is to you. She wanted to provide for the woman you loved. I realized that if you'd told Wendy she was your beneficiary, you would have also told her about the inheritance and the specifics of the will. That was a big mistake on your part."

"It was such a small amount compared to what I'd be getting from Linda that I didn't think it mattered if I told—" Stephen broke off suddenly, realizing he had revealed himself. He began to backpedal, "No, what I meant was—"

"We know exactly what you meant," Detective Lund broke in. "Stop trying to protect Wendy. It might be a small amount compared to what you'll be getting, but to someone like Wendy, it's a fortune. However, I doubt money alone would be enough of a reason for Wendy to kill you. There was another motive that drove her—jealousy."

Patrick nodded slightly to Erica, who said, "Jaime Russell is young, beautiful, and made no secret about the fact that she was attracted to Stephen. Wendy admitted several times that she was jealous and was afraid Jaime might take Stephen away from her."

Wendy's hand went to her throat, and Megan hissed at Erica, "Why are you being so horrible? I thought you were our friend." The anger and hurt in her eyes was painful to see.

"I *am* your friend, and I'm sorry to hurt you both, but I had to find the truth," Erica said. "That's what Wendy asked me to do." She went on. "Over time, Wendy assumed the worst and became convinced it was only a matter of time before Jaime succeeded in taking Stephen away. She decided to act—in fact, she didn't dare wait—because she feared that at any time, Stephen might change his will and list Jaime as his beneficiary. Wendy had to decide whether to settle for what he had now or the possibility of getting nothing if Stephen broke up with her."

Patrick picked up. "Like poverty, jealousy is a powerful emotion and can cause people to do terrible things. If you'll recall, there was poison in three cups. That's because Wendy wanted to kill Jaime as well. Poisoning them was an ideal solution—for Stephen it was a just reward for a fickle man, and for Jaime it was punishment for openly seducing the man Wendy hoped to marry."

When Stephen spoke to Erica, his voice was sorrowful. "But the poison was in your cup too. Why would she try to poison you?"

"I was always safe. Wendy knows I don't drink coffee. The only two people that were ever in danger were you and Jaime."

Wendy stared at Erica. "I didn't poison Stephen, I swear. Why would I ask you to investigate if I had tried to kill him?"

"That's exactly what I asked myself over and over." Erica replied. "It was hard to continue when things started pointing to you. We've been friends for so many years that I found it nearly impossible to believe you could have tried to murder someone. Still, you had asked me to investigate, and when the police started zeroing in on you as their prime suspect, I thought I could clear you. Then, they began to suspect you of murdering Tyson too."

"I had nothing to do with that!" There was a tremor in Wendy's voice.

"While we didn't have any hard proof, there was a lot of circumstantial evidence," Patrick said. "Tyson was shot just outside your house, and you had left the house right about the time he was shot. Plus, you lied about your whereabouts."

"There were a lot of things that kept pointing to you," Erica said to Wendy. "But as I continued to investigate and learned more, I came to believe that your leaving to get that serving plate at the exact time Tyson was shot was just spectacularly bad timing. And that although you had both the motive and the opportunity, you were *not* the one who poisoned Stephen and you did *not* kill Gregory Tyson."

CHAPTER 18

FOR A FEW MOMENTS, WENDY had her mouth half open, staring numbly. Erica said, "Except for the circumstantial evidence Detective Lund mentioned, I never found anything connecting you and Gregory Tyson. Since I'd felt all along that Tyson's murder and Stephen's poisoning were linked, I had to look for someone else who had a motive for wanting Stephen dead and who was connected to Tyson." Erica glanced at Megan, who was perched awkwardly on a chair by the window. The girl's cheeks were flushed, as if she had a high fever.

"After I got home from Chicago, I started to wonder if Areli Bronson, Charles's wife, might have a motive," Erica continued. "So I called Linda and asked what would happen if Stephen should die before she did. In that case, James would inherit Stephen's portion minus the $500,000. Linda had told me previously that Areli knew James would inherit half of a fortune since everything was spelled out in a certified letter she'd sent."

"Ever since marrying Charles, Areli had known about his family's fantastic wealth but, because of her husband's cantankerous ways, had been denied it herself. It was possible Areli could have flown to Florida and somehow discovered that Stephen was going to be at Wendy's house that night. She could easily have hidden across the street, waiting for him to arrive. Then, when a man walked up to the house, fitting Stephen's height, weight, and general description, Areli pulled out her gun and mistakenly killed Gregory Tyson instead of Stephen Watkins."

Everyone in the room was listening breathlessly except for Jaime, who scoffed contemptuously. "This is crazy!" There was real fire in her eyes and ice in her voice. "You don't even know Areli Bronson, and yet you're accusing her of murder?" Jaime's indignation was plain, evidenced by the brightness of her fixed stare and her white-knuckled hands which clenched the chair's armrests. Megan and Wendy stared at her in surprise.

"I thought it was a possibility," Erica stated calmly. "So I flew to Puerto Rico to see Areli." Jaime jerked and started to rise, but conscious of the curious eyes that turned to her, she sank back down. "After visiting Areli, I knew she wasn't the type to murder someone for money. Although she is not well-off, Areli is cheerful, pleasant, and satisfied with life. The psychology of a murderer was not there. Talking with her neighbors not only confirmed my impressions, it also provided Areli with an alibi. She had been seen by several people the same night Gregory Tyson was killed."

"So you went all that way for nothing," Reed interjected derisively.

"I wouldn't say that," Erica said coolly. "While there, I discovered something *very* interesting."

Everyone was looking at Erica curiously—everyone except Jaime, whose face was full of unaccountable fury.

"Once I realized Areli had nothing to do with Tyson's murder, it occurred to me that her son, James, was a more likely suspect, especially since he'd be inheriting directly from Linda. There was only one problem. *Areli and Charles did not have a son.*"

For a moment, the air was tense, electric. Then Stephen sputtered, "But, but Anthony and Kathleen and Linda, they all talked about Charles and Areli's son—"

"Areli and Charles had a child, but it was a girl. There never was any James. They named their daughter Jaime."

All eyes turned to the dark-haired beauty who was staring at Erica with slitted eyes.

Erica went on. "You see, when Areli called to announce the birth of her child, Kathleen thought Areli had said *James* when actually she had said *Jaime*. It was an understandable mistake—Areli was just learning English and had a very pronounced accent. When I visited Linda, the picture of her brother, Charles, caught my attention, but I didn't know why. Then, in Puerto Rico, I saw more pictures of Charles and finally caught the resemblance between him and his daughter: the aristocratic nose, the eyebrows, the dark, penetrating eyes. The clincher was when Areli showed me her photo album, which contained pictures of her beautiful *daughter* from when she was born to now—an adult."

Reed was skeptical. "Surely at some point, Anthony and Kathleen Bronson would have found out that their grandson was actually a granddaughter—"

"That never happened because Charles had no contact with his parents. Linda never knew either since Charles had very few conversations with her, and all of those revolved around money."

Stephen turned to Jaime and plied her with questions. "Is this true? Why is your last name Russell? Why didn't you tell me you were Charles and Areli's daughter?"

Patrick Lund answered for her. "Jaime took the name Russell to hide her identity."

"I've done nothing wrong," Jaime cried out, but there was a tremor in the voice that was usually so confident and strong. When she looked at Erica, her eyes were so full of hatred Erica felt certain that if Jaime could have, she would have torn her into pieces.

"Let's take a look at the things we *do* know," Erica said. "For one thing, Jaime, I know your father brought you up to be just like him, full of resentment and bitterness. Areli told me you didn't want anything to do with your grandparents because they had treated your father poorly. You never contacted your Aunt Linda either, holding the same grudge against her as your father had—believing she had poisoned your grandparents' minds against Charles and had convinced them to cut him out of their will. Without ever meeting her, you hated Linda for taking money you felt rightfully belonged to your father."

Erica looked around the room. "When Charles found out Linda had cancer, he knew he would inherit a portion of the Bronson estate, which was still a vast fortune. In fact, Charles bragged to one of his neighbors that he was going to be a rich man. He told Jaime that one day, she'd have all the money she deserved. His expectations were never realized because Linda's cancer went into remission, and then Charles was killed in a car accident."

Jaime's face was as smooth and hard as marble when Erica spoke directly to her. "Your father instilled more than bitterness in you, didn't he? You also inherited Charles's love of gambling. Even though you left Puerto Rico many years ago, the neighbors still remember how much you liked to gamble and—just like your father—didn't know when to stop."

Detective Lund was looking at Erica fondly, like a teacher would a prize pupil. She went on. "My guess is that you suffered some heavy losses and started thinking about how unfair it was for Linda to give such a huge chunk of money to Stephen, who wasn't even a blood relative. So you found out where Stephen lived, flew to Florida, and moved into his apartment complex. You found out everything you could about Stephen—waiting for just the right opportunity."

Jaime's face was deadly pale even as her mouth curved in scorn. Throwing her head back in defiance, she said savagely, "You're crazy if you think I poisoned Stephen."

"You slipped badly when you picked me up from the airport," Erica continued. "Do you remember? You mentioned how hard it was to get a job in Kissimmee because no one wanted to hire someone without experience. Yet weeks ago you'd told me you had experience as an administrative assistant."

Speaking to the group, Erica said, "All along, I was puzzled by Jaime's interest in Stephen. He's years older with a less than striking physique and personality. Why would a beautiful young girl, who could have anyone she wanted, pursue a man like him so relentlessly?"

Everyone waited for her answer. "It was for the simplest of reasons. Jaime knew that if Stephen were to die before Linda, she would get half of a very large fortune." Erica turned to Jaime. "But inheriting half of Linda Bronson's fortune wasn't enough, was it? You wanted it all."

"She wanted to marry Stephen to get her hands on his inheritance!" Wendy blurted.

"As far as motives go, money is one of the most powerful," Erica said. "At first, Jaime thought of killing Stephen, but why take the chance of being convicted of murder when she had a very good chance of marrying him and getting the entire fortune?" She paused. "Perhaps Jaime planned for Stephen to have a fatal accident at some point after they married, but that's something we'll never really know. Regardless, Jaime was worried enough about my investigating to call me anonymously one night and tell me to stop asking so many questions."

Reed was impatient. "Okay, so if Jaime didn't try to kill Stephen, who did? And you still haven't told us who killed Tyson."

"I'm coming to that. Still, I had the same problem with Jaime as I had with Wendy—I couldn't find anything connecting Jaime with Gregory Tyson. Then, as I continued investigating, I became aware of something rather odd. When talking with people who knew Stephen, I noticed their descriptions of him didn't seem to fit, but their descriptions of his brother *Richard* did."

Patrick Lund stopped her. "Everyone's looking a little puzzled, Erica. Why don't you give them a few examples?"

"All right. The Kincaids, one of Stephen's neighbors, said he often gave her dog a little treat, but Wendy said Stephen didn't like dogs. Several people talked about Stephen's keen sense of humor, but I thought it was below average. Others mentioned how sociable and outgoing Stephen was, but I certainly wouldn't describe him that way. On the other hand, they said his brother, Richard, was very nice person but rather quiet and unassuming." She paused. "Then, I talked to Timothy Peterson, who lived near Stephen and Richard and knew them both very well."

Erica spoke to Stephen. "Timothy and I had an interesting conversation. During it, he mentioned how, when you first moved in, some of the neighbors got you and your brother mixed up."

"Oh, yes," Stephen replied, looking faintly startled.

"That was a great clue and gave me an idea. To check out my idea, I needed someone to hold a little party. Wendy refused," Erica glanced at her reproachfully. "But Stephen agreed to have it. While we were washing dishes, I got my question answered."

"What question?" Lee asked.

Erica paused. "Sorry, I'm getting ahead of myself. Let me go back. When I was talking to Timothy, he told me Stephen was always helping others and that he had the scars to prove it. When I asked him what he meant by that, Timothy said Stephen cut his right arm very badly when he was helping demolish a tile shower."

"And bad cuts always leave a scar," Detective Lund interjected. When everyone looked at him, Patrick looked abashed and cleared his throat. "Um, sorry. Go on, Erica."

"So, after the party, I asked Stephen to help me wash the dishes. Naturally, he had to roll up his sleeves." She turned to Stephen. "Why don't you roll up your right sleeve and show everyone the scar you got helping Timothy take out that shower?"

"No one's interested in that," Stephen objected.

"I think they'd be very interested in seeing it. I certainly was."

"There's no need."

"You're perfectly right," Erica agreed. "Because there's really nothing to see, is there? You don't have any scar."

There were murmurs from around the room.

"I don't understand," Wendy said.

"There isn't any scar because this man is not Stephen Watkins. He's *Richard* Watkins."

Silence lay heavy in the room until Wendy gasped. For a moment, it looked as though she might faint. In a gesture that spoke of deeper feelings, Lee reached out to take Wendy's hand.

"I can't believe you're even suggesting such a thing," Stephen said adamantly. "Why, the whole idea is absurd."

"Is it, now?" Detective Lund replied. "Erica and I think you switched places with your brother for the simplest of reasons—to inherit a fortune. Now, do you still deny that you are Richard Watkins?"

"Of course I deny it!"

"I had a feeling you wouldn't admit the truth," Erica said, "so I invited someone to join us tonight. He's been waiting in the basement. I'll get him." Erica left and returned with a tall, intelligent-looking man with shrewd brown eyes who looked to be around sixty-five years old. He walked into the room looking poised and self-assured.

"This is Timothy Peterson," Erica explained. "He lived a couple of houses away from Stephen and Richard for many years."

Timothy went to stand in front of Stephen, whose face went slack. The twisted smile on Timothy's face was not pleasant. "Surprised to see me?" he asked. "When Erica called and told me she thought you had traded places with your brother, I thought it was crazy—impossible! Then, when Erica phoned later and told me you didn't have a scar, I agreed to come. Now, I find out she was right. Why did you do it, Richard?"

There was a moment when indecision was plain on his face. Then he seemed to visibly shrink. "It was all so unfair," Richard said in a resigned voice. "Stephen and I had looked forward to that inheritance. We were going to travel the world, go to first-class resorts, eat at fine restaurants, live the good life."

Then his voice changed—became more forceful. "That money *belonged* to us! Stephen worked his tail off for the great Anthony Bronson." A bit of a sneer came into his voice. "He had no life of his own and was on call 24/7. I worked at Cicero too—Stephen got me hired—but to Mr. Bronson I was a zero, a nothing. Stephen told me to wait and be patient and that in time, we'd be rewarded and have everything we could ever want." Richard grimaced. "So for years, I stayed in the background, waiting."

"The newspaper said Richard had a heart attack," Timothy said. "Is that what happened to the real Stephen?"

"Yes." Richard's voice was oddly flat, and his eyes were pained. "One morning he didn't come down to breakfast. I went upstairs and found him in bed. He was unconscious but still breathing, so I called 911.

Still, I knew it was too late. As I sat by him, waiting for the ambulance, I thought of all the plans we had for the future. It just wasn't fair that my brother should die before we got what we'd worked so hard for. The more I thought about it, the more I knew Stephen would have wanted me to go ahead with our plans, even if he couldn't be there."

"Usually, you're a careful, prudent man," Erica said quietly, "but when this opportunity came, you took it even though normally you wouldn't try anything so bold and risky."

Richard listened without visible reaction. In a strangely detached voice, he said, "Stephen and I had talked about it so much—envisioning the day we'd have plenty of time and money to take a safari in Namibia, float down the Grand Canal in Venice, see St. Peter's Basilica in Rome, walk the Great Wall of China. I knew Stephen wouldn't want me to be cheated out of that. I also knew that my brother died because of the stress and pressure of working nonstop. Anthony Bronson worked my brother into an early grave. We *deserved* that money."

Timothy looked at him reprovingly. "Did you really think you could get away with something like that?"

"I wasn't sure." Richard looked a little surprised. "When I went to the hospital, I put Stephen's wallet in my pocket and as his closest and only relative, I was able to provide all the information the hospital and mortuary required."

"But what about your friends and business associates?" Lee asked. "Weren't you afraid they would catch on?"

Erica answered for him. "That's why Richard quit his—or rather Stephen's—job and arranged for a private funeral. If the few people he did see noticed him acting differently, they put it down to grief. Since he needed to distance himself from anyone who knew him or his brother well, he moved away quickly and refused to have any contact with his old friends. Switching places with his brother also explains why he's never once flown to see Linda during the past two years even though he was supposed to be devoted to her."

"Wait a minute," Reed spoke up. "This is all very interesting, Erica, and I'm sure you're waiting for us to tell you how very clever you've been to figure it out, but does anyone except for me realize that Stephen's deception does not explain how or why he was poisoned?"

"You've spent all your time finding out that I traded places with my brother when you should have been finding out who tried to kill me," Richard said levelly.

"Once I found out about the switch, it wasn't hard to figure out who'd poisoned you," Erica replied easily.

"So who *did*?" Wendy asked.

"Richard did that himself," Erica answered.

"*What?* But why would he poison himself?" Wendy cried. "He almost died!"

"He was never in any real danger." Erica shrugged. "Taking the poison at your house ensured he'd get prompt medical attention. Richard faced a far greater risk by being the only person connected to Gregory Tyson. You see, if the police suspected him and began digging into his past, he feared they might discover the truth and everything he'd worked so hard for would have blown up in his face. Richard wouldn't have admitted he was even acquainted with Gregory Tyson except he knew that sooner or later the police would find out. So, he had to divert their attention, and what better way than to make it look like someone was trying to kill *him*."

Turning to Richard, Erica said, "When Jaime went to get the cookies and I went to the bathroom, you added poison to each cup—enough to kill me and Jaime but only a small dose in your own—just enough to make you very sick. You were careful to choose a poison that doesn't cause serious damage to internal organs."

Erica told the group, "After he drank half his coffee, but before his symptoms started, Richard added more poison to his cup, knowing the police would test the coffee. There had to be a lethal dose in his cup too. But of course, Richard never took another sip, though he pretended to."

"How did you find out he'd poisoned the coffee?" Jaime asked. "You thought I'd done it."

"That's true," Erica admitted. "But once I found out Stephen was actually Richard, everything changed and the pieces started falling into place. I'd wondered about the piece of paper that was found on the floor in Wendy's front room, which held traces of poison. There could only be two reasons for its presence. Either it had been planted to divert attention away from whoever had poisoned the coffee, or it had been accidentally dropped by the person who poisoned the coffee. On the night of Richard's dinner party, I managed to get inside his apartment. He keeps a very tidy desk," Erica said approvingly. "I took a piece of paper from the notepad he had by his telephone and asked Detective Lund to compare it with the paper the police had found. They matched exactly."

Detective Lund said to Richard, "It was a clever and gutsy move to deliberately ingest poison, and it had the exact effect you wanted—to convince us someone was trying to kill you."

"A lot of the initial misdirection in this case was my fault," Erica acknowledged. "I thought the killer might have intended to kill Stephen and had mistakenly murdered Tyson. That's exactly what Richard was hoping would happen when he wore similar clothing that night."

"Well then, who *did* kill Tyson?" Reed asked Detective Lund.

Patrick looked at Erica. "You're the one who found that lead. Go ahead and tell them."

"There was a real break in the case when Matt Watters, who works at the Starlight Motel, told me he saw Richard talking with Gregory Tyson."

"I told you about that," Richard jumped in. "Greg wanted to borrow money from me."

"Oh yes, he wanted to borrow money, but that's not why you shot him. After you switched places with your brother, everything was going according to plan. No one suspected a thing. All you had to do was wait for Linda to die so you could get your hands on the money. But Tyson threw a kink into your plans when he came to see you—he was one of the few people who knew you and your brother very well."

Something in Richard broke. "He was going to ruin everything."

"So, when Tyson showed up, poised to destroy everything you'd worked so hard for, you turned on him," Erica asserted.

"Why did you meet Tyson if he could recognize you?" Patrick asked.

"I tried to put him off," Richard said bitterly, "but Greg never could take no for an answer. He said he'd camp on my doorstep until I had time to see him."

Timothy was curious. "What did Greg say when he recognized you?"

"He didn't recognize me," Richard said in an odd, toneless voice. "I was only with him a short time—told him I was late for a baptism. I was hoping he'd be satisfied with a short chat and leave me alone, but no, he needed to borrow money. Greg was desperate and insisted on seeing me when we had more time even if he had to stay a few days." Richard's forehead was sheened with cold sweat. "I couldn't have that, so I told Greg to meet me that night. He's a very punctual man."

Erica finished the story. "You slipped out of Wendy's house and hid across the street until Tyson showed up. After you shot him, I drove up and you slipped in the front door."

Richard hung his head. It was over.

Detective Lund stood, a solid, calm tower of strength. Pulling out his radio, he called in officers that had been standing by outside.

As Richard was led out, Patrick turned to Erica. "I have to hand it to you. You did some great detective work."

"Thanks for working with me."

He grinned engagingly then clasped her hand in his huge one. "If you ever need a job—"

"You'll be the first to know."

Patrick gave her a wink, and then he was gone. Erica went over to Lee and Wendy. Erica saw something in Lee's face that had always been there: a kind of goodness. But there was something else as well: a deep aura of peace—exactly the kind of quality that had, Erica guessed, captured Wendy's heart. It was something Wendy had been searching for and not yet found, until now.

Wendy was no longer crying but still seemed dazed. "I can't believe he actually switched places with his brother."

"Richard is a very clever and devious man," Erica said. "All along, he tried to get me to suspect you. Like when he *accidentally* let slip that you knew he'd named you as his beneficiary."

"He was a liar from start to finish," Lee declared.

Wendy shuddered. "And to think he was the one that shot that poor man!"

"When his brother died, Richard saw an opportunity—and took it. The success of that stratagem must have gone to his head; otherwise, he'd never have gone through with his plan to murder Gregory Tyson. Without one, the other would not have occurred. The first was a flash of inspiration—trading places with his brother to inherit a fortune. The second came because he couldn't bear to have his dream taken away."

"And he almost got away with it," Lee said in wonder.

"Very nearly. When Richard traded places with Stephen, he was successful because of his rapid execution, but it all started to unravel when Gregory Tyson came to town."

* * *

"Hey," Erica called from where she was sitting in the backseat of Lee's car. "You two are sitting entirely too close. Once you're past thirty, sitting on top of the driver is not allowed."

"Megan won't ride with us anymore," Wendy giggled. "She says we make her puke."

Erica laughed. Megan had said something along those lines when she told Erica she preferred to say good-bye at the house. They had hugged each other tightly, and Megan made Erica promise to call and e-mail frequently.

"Speaking of that," Wendy continued, "*I* want to throw up when I think of Richard and all his lies. Did you suspect him from the beginning?"

"Nope. He seemed like such a nice guy. But one of my axioms is to believe nothing I hear and only half of what I see, and little things started adding up."

"Like when you straightened his paper clips, and the next time you were in his office he'd messed them all up again?" Wendy said slyly. "I remember you telling me about that."

"A man who will do that, will do anything," Erica said. "But actually, what I *meant* was like the time Richard said Linda had made him a beneficiary when his brother died. Linda told me she'd made him a beneficiary when she first got cancer, years before his brother died. One of them wasn't telling the truth. There was no reason for Linda to lie, so it had to be Richard. Part of Richard's trouble came from thinking the Bronsons owed him something. So, when his brother died, Richard thought it was terribly unfair that he might not get the money he had waited for so patiently."

Lee said, "I'm surprised Linda didn't catch on to him."

"Richard played his role magnificently. He had access to all of Stephen's correspondence and so had all the information he needed for his little deception. He studied Stephen's handwriting and style of communication and was able to write and e-mail Linda without revealing himself. He knew what type of chocolates and flowers Stephen had bought for her and continued sending them. Richard had plenty of excuses for not going to see her, and Linda believed them all. Since she was unable to travel, they never saw each other after Stephen died."

"It's too bad you were thrown off by that nightmare about Stephen being the victim," Wendy said.

"That actually turned out to be a good thing. The only reason I investigated Stephen's background so thoroughly was because I thought someone might be after him. Because of that, I was able to discover the switch and realize he was the one who killed Gregory Tyson."

"For a while, I suspected Reed," Lee said. "I hate to say it, but he's kind of mean. He always seemed like he had some sort of grudge against Stephen."

"Oh, he did!" Erica said. "Reed was facing a tremendous amount of pressure from the executives of the company because of falling sales. The top managers were really impressed with Stephen, and Reed discovered they were considering firing him so they could put Stephen in his place. Combine that with a failing marriage and a naturally offensive nature, and what do you get? Reed Devoe!"

"One thing I wondered about is how you were able to find Areli," Wendy said. "I thought Linda said she'd moved."

"Richard told her that, but it was just another lie. He didn't want any contact between them because if they'd started talking and became close, his inheritance might shrink. Areli was in the same house she and Charles had always lived in."

After pulling up to the curb, Lee popped the trunk and unloaded Erica's luggage. As Erica hugged Wendy, she was aware of a buoyant lightness, as though a tangled string had snapped and Wendy was now floating free. Then, she realized that something was different. Pulling back, Erica looked at her friend.

"What's going on? How come you're suddenly taller?"

Wendy pulled up her pants slightly, showing off high-heeled sandals. She winked at Erica then said meaningfully, "I think I like high heels!" Then, with an exuberant laugh, she turned and threw herself into Lee's arms.

Looking a bit puzzled, Lee smiled. "If this is what happens when you wear high heels, I guess I like them too." He shut the trunk.

Wendy looked at Erica. "How can I ever thank you?"

"Never ask me to buy ice again."

They both laughed. "And invite me to the wedding," Erica said, glancing at Lee. "It looks like you've found someone special."

With a beatific smile and looking relaxed and happy, Wendy glanced at Lee. "It's a miracle—that's all I can say. And to think I was actually hoping to marry Stephen—oops—I mean Richard. Looking back now, I always felt like something wasn't quite right, but I was so tired of being poor and alone that I ignored it."

"Just like you ignored that good-looking guy over there. It took you long enough to find out Lee was crazy about you!"

There were final hugs and good-byes, then Erica headed for the terminal. As the sliding doors opened, Erica stepped back and they closed. Then she stepped forward again, and as they glided open again, she glanced back. Lee was holding Wendy close, and as they kissed, it looked as though they had sealed a bargain.

* * *

After arriving at her gate, Erica called David. She'd already told him about last night's meeting, but he was just as elated now as he had been then.

"Congratulations on cracking the case! You work fast! My boss said he'd like to hire you."

"My second offer! I'd think about it, but one policeman in the family is enough."

"Who drove you to the airport?"

"Lee and Wendy. You can't believe how cute they are together! They are so in love that I could almost see the sparks."

"Speaking of sparks, I'm looking forward to some of our own." David's voice was husky. "And, once you get on the plane, if the man sitting next to you asks if you're a model, switch seats immediately!" Erica giggled, and he continued. "Once you get home, we'll have dinner with the kids, then I've arranged for them to spend the night at Grandma's. I wanted some time alone with my favorite girl without the kids asking you to proofread their book report, look at their ingrown toenail, or wash their soccer uniform."

"Good thinking!" Erica sighed dreamily. "We can just relax—go outside, sit on the back porch swing, and snuggle while watching the sunset." She paused. "So, do you have anything else planned for later, like rose petals on the bed?"

"Nope. Any and all roses will be in a vase," David said firmly.

"Good idea," Erica agreed. "Who wants to waste time sweeping petals off anyway?"

RECIPES

CONTENTS

Éclairs 266

Kelly's Twice-Baked Potatoes 267

Jen's Fabulous French Bread 268

Clam Chowder. 269

Pumpkin Chocolate-Chip Cookies. 270

TaLonnie's Crock-Pot Chicken. 271

Honey Wheat Pancakes 272

Pollo Guisado. 273

Orange Rolls 274

Egg Salad Sandwiches. 276

ECLAIRS

Pastry

1 cup water
½ cup butter

1 cup flour
4 eggs

Directions

1. Heat water and butter in pan until boiling. Remove from heat.
2. Add flour all at once and stir vigorously about 1 minute or until mixture forms a ball.
3. Remove from heat and stir in eggs, one at a time. Beat vigorously until smooth.
4. Drop dough in round or oblong mounds on greased cookie sheet and bake at 400 degrees for 35–40 minutes.
5. Cool. Cut off tops and pull out bits of dough from inside. Fill with pudding using a spoon or pastry bag.
6. Frost with chocolate icing.

Yield: 10–12

Pudding

1 large box (5.1 ounce) cook-and-serve or instant vanilla pudding.

Make according to directions. Cool.

Chocolate Frosting

6 Tablespoons unsweetened cocoa powder (or 1 square melted semisweet chocolate)
3 Tablespoons butter

2 ¾ cups confectioners' sugar
1 teaspoon vanilla extract
4 Tablespoons milk

Melt chocolate and butter, then stir in vanilla and sugar. Add milk, 1 tablespoon at a time, and beat until desired consistency is reached.

KELLY'S TWICE BAKED POTATOES

4 large baking potatoes
¼ cup milk
1 package (3 oz.) reduced-fat cream cheese, room temperature
½ teaspoon salt

1 Tablespoon butter
½ cup cubed ham
½ cup kernel corn
1 cup shredded cheddar cheese
Optional: 1 Tablespoon chives

Directions

1. Bake potatoes until done (either in oven at 400 degrees for 45 minutes or in microwave). Let potatoes cool slightly, then cut open lengthwise and scoop out insides.
2. Mash pulp with milk, then add cream cheese, salt, and butter.
3. Stir in ham and corn. Stuff potato shells with mixture.
4. Place potatoes on a baking sheet, and sprinkle with grated cheddar cheese.
5. Bake at 350 degrees for 10–15 minutes.

Yield: 4

JEN'S FABULOUS FRENCH BREAD

(Use a Kitchen Aid or some other mixer that can handle bread dough)

½ cup warm water
2 packages yeast
2 cups very warm water
2 Tablespoons sugar (divided)
1 Tablespoon salt
6 cups flour (divided) (If desired,
   you can use 3 cups whole wheat
   and 3 cups white flour.)

¼ cup oil
1 Tablespoon cornmeal
1 egg white, slightly beaten with
   1 Tablespoon of water
Optional: sesame seeds

Directions

1. Dissolve yeast and 1 Tablespoon sugar in ½ cup warm water.
2. Combine 2 cups water, salt, rest of sugar, oil, and 3 cups of flour. Mix well in mixer.
3. Mix in yeast mixture, then add rest of flour. After mixing well, let dough rise 15 minutes.
4. Turn on mixer for approximately 5–10 seconds to punch down dough. Let rest 15 minutes.
5. Repeat step 4 two more times.
6. Divide dough in half. Roll each portion into a 14 x 6 rectangle. Roll up, jelly-roll style, starting with the long side. Pinch edges and ends to seal. Place seam side down on a large greased baking sheet that has been sprinkled with cornmeal.
7. Brush with egg-white mixture, then cover and let rise in a warm place until doubled.
8. With a very sharp knife, make 3 or 4 diagonal cuts about ¼-inch deep across top of each loaf. Brush lightly again with egg-white mixture. Add sesame seeds if desired.
9. Bake in a preheated, 375-degree oven for 18–22 minutes.

Yield: 2 Loaves

CLAM CHOWDER

2 cups potatoes, peeled and diced
½ cup onion, diced
½ cup celery, sliced fine
2 cups milk
1 can evaporated milk
1 teaspoon salt
1 teaspoon sugar
4 Tablespoons butter

⅛ teaspoon pepper
½ teaspoon garlic powder
2 large cans (12 oz.) minced clams;
   do not drain
⅓ cup and 2 Tablespoons flour
   (for thickening)
½ cup milk (for thickening)

Directions

1. Boil potatoes, onion, and celery in small amount of water until tender. Drain.
2. Add milk, evaporated milk, salt, sugar, butter, pepper, and clams.
3. Put ⅓ cup flour in a bowl, and slowly add ½ cup milk, beating until smooth. Stir into soup, and heat until soup is thickened, stirring constantly.

Yield: 8 Servings

PUMPKIN CHOCOLATE CHIP COOKIES

1 cup canned pumpkin
1 cup brown sugar
½ cup granulated sugar
½ cup margarine or butter
1 egg
1 teaspoon vanilla extract
2 ½ cups all-purpose flour

1 teaspoon baking powder
½ teaspoon baking soda
½ teaspoon salt
1 teaspoon ground cinnamon
1 teaspoon ground nutmeg
1 cup semisweet chocolate chips
Optional: ½ cup chopped walnuts

Directions

1. Cream margarine or butter and sugars.
2. Mix in pumpkin, egg, and vanilla. Blend well.
3. Stir in flour, baking powder, soda, salt, cinnamon, and nutmeg, and mix well.
4. Stir in chocolate chips. Add nuts if desired.
5. Use teaspoon to drop cookies onto greased baking sheet. Bake at 350 degrees for 10–15 minutes.

Yield: 4 dozen

TALONNIE'S CROCK POT CHICKEN

4 skinless, boneless chicken breasts (can be cut into pieces or left whole)

1 cup water

¼ cup butter

1 package zesty Italian seasoning mix

1 can cream of chicken soup

1 package (8 oz.) cream cheese

Directions

1. Put butter, water, and chicken in Crock-Pot. Sprinkle with seasoning mix.
2. Cook on low for 6–7 hours or on high for 3–4 hours.
3. Mix cream cheese and cream of chicken soup, and add to Crock-Pot during the last half hour.
4. Serve over rice or pasta.

Yield: 4–6 Servings

HONEY WHEAT PANCAKES

½ cup all-purpose flour
⅔ cup whole wheat flour
1 teaspoon baking soda
½ teaspoon salt

1 cup buttermilk (Or add 1 Tablespoon vinegar or lemon juice to 1 cup milk and let stand 10 minutes.)
1 large egg
1 Tablespoon oil
2 Tablespoons honey

Directions

1. Mix flours, soda, and salt.
2. In separate bowl, beat egg, then whisk in oil, honey, and buttermilk.
3. Add liquid mixture to dry ingredients, stirring just until moistened (the batter will be slightly lumpy).
4. Pour ¼ cup of the batter onto a greased griddle, and cook until the bubbles on top just begin to break. Turn and cook briefly on the other side.

Yields: 4 Servings

POLLO GUISADO

1 whole chicken (or 3 chicken breasts)
1 teaspoon Adobo seasoning
2 ½ cups chicken stock
2 medium potatoes, cut into chunks
1 bell pepper, diced
3 plum tomatoes, chopped
1 medium red onion, diced
½ cup olives, sliced
3 Tablespoons olive oil
2 Tablespoons lime juice
1 teaspoon oregano
2 teaspoons minced garlic

1 teaspoon ground cumin
1 teaspoon chili powder
½ teaspoon black pepper
1 can (8 oz.) tomato sauce
1 teaspoon Adobo seasoning
½ teaspoon salt
2 bay leaves
2 packets Sazon Goya (seasoning mix)*
Optional:
1 stalk fresh cilantro (with leaves), finely diced or ½ teaspoon dried cilantro

Directions

1. Put chicken in pan with 4 cups water. Add 1 teaspoon Adobo seasoning to water (or substitute 1 teaspoon salt). Cook chicken for forty minutes. Cool, then pull chicken off the bones and into pieces.
2. In large pan, combine other ingredients. Simmer for twenty minutes. Add chicken and simmer for 1 hour. Serve in a small bowl or over rice.

* Sazon Goya can be purchased at Walmart in the Latino food section. It comes in a small orange box.

Yield: 8 Servings

Adobo Seasoning
(Can also be purchased at Mexican grocery stores)

2 Tablespoons salt
1 Tablespoon paprika
2 teaspoons black pepper
1 ½ teaspoons onion powder

1 ½ teaspoons dried oregano
1 ½ teaspoons ground cumin
1 teaspoon garlic powder
1 teaspoon chili powder

Mix together all ingredients and put in an empty salt or pepper shaker.

ORANGE ROLLS

2 packages active dry yeast (or
  5 teaspoons)
½ cup warm water
1¼ cups granulated sugar (divided)
1 ¼ cups milk
½ cup shortening

2 eggs, beaten
5 cups bread flour
1 teaspoon salt
1 stick (4 oz.) butter
3 Tablespoons orange zest (grated
  orange peel; avoid pith)

Directions

1. Dissolve yeast in warm water, then add ½ cup sugar and stir until dissolved.
2. Scald milk. Add shortening and stir until shortening has melted.
3. Cool milk to lukewarm, stir in eggs, then add yeast mixture.
4. In separate bowl, combine flour and salt, and then add to liquid mixture and mix. Can use bread mixer or turn onto floured surface and knead until smooth.
5. Cover and allow to rise, about 1 hour.
6. Punch down dough and place in a greased bowl. Cover and refrigerate for about 1 hour.
7. To prepare filling, combine butter, ¾ cup sugar, and grated orange zest. Mix until it resembles crumbs.
8. Roll chilled dough on a lightly floured surface and shape into a rectangle about ¼-inch thick. Spread filling over the dough, and roll up, jelly-roll style into a log. Cut slices about ¾-inch thick, and place in a greased muffin tin or on a baking sheet. Cover and place in warm area until dough has doubled.
9. Bake at 375 degrees for 10–15 minutes or until lightly brown.
10. Frost with orange cream cheese frosting.

Yield: 22–28

ORANGE CREAM CHEESE FROSTING

3 oz. cream cheese, softened
2 Tablespoons butter, softened
1 teaspoon orange zest

2 Tablespoons orange juice
2 cups confectioners' sugar
Optional: ¾ cup chopped walnuts

Directions

1. Beat cream cheese, butter, orange zest, and juice until creamy, then beat in sugar.
2. Spread on rolls and sprinkle with nuts if desired.

EGG SALAD SANDWICHES

8 eggs

½ cup mayonnaise

⅓ cup celery, diced

1 Tablespoon prepared yellow mustard

¼ cup chopped onion

½ teaspoon lemon juice

¼ teaspoon salt

Optional: ¼ cup diced dill pickle

Directions

1. Hard boil eggs. Cool, peel, chop, and set aside.
2. In a bowl, mix mayonnaise, celery, mustard, onion, lemon juice, and salt. Stir in chopped egg gently.

Yield: 4–6 Servings

ABOUT THE AUTHOR.

MARLENE BATEMAN WAS BORN IN Salt Lake City, Utah, and grew up in Sandy, Utah. She graduated from the University of Utah with a bachelor's degree in English. Marlene is married to Kelly R. Sullivan and lives in North Salt Lake, Utah. Her hobbies are gardening, camping, and reading. Marlene has been published extensively in various magazines and newspapers and has written a number of nonfiction books. Her first novel, a mystery romance, was the best-selling *Light on Fire Island.*